UNSTABLE

UNSTABLE

Danielle Leneah

Donnelly Bootcamp Series

Book Three

Boetttcher-Tuufuli Publishing LLC

Unstable

For permissions contact:
info@DanielleLeneah.com

Editing by: Krystlynn Muscutt
Copyedited by: Rebekkah Wilde

ISBN: 978-1-7325461-5-8
Printed in the United States of America
First Edition: November 2019
10 9 8 7 6 5 4 3 2 1

Dedication

To all those who have helped me along the way;
this book is for you.

Acknowledgments

It has been a long few months and I continue to surprise myself with what I can accomplished as one person. With that being said, this book wouldn't have been possible without the help of several people and the encouragement of many others. Just when I think things are too overwhelming, there are people sitting in the background that come along and push me to move forward.

To my cousin Kelly, thank you so much for everything you have been doing for me. You have been pushing these books and I am truly grateful for all your help. You have also introduced me to so many wonderful people, and I appreciate it more than I could ever express. I am indebted to you. Love you cousin.

To Krystlynne, girl you have been my backbone from the very start of this journey. There is no way I could ever repay you for all you have done. Your advice is sound, and I appreciate that you aren't afraid to tell me like it is. Thank you for sticking with me after all this time and continue to help me move forward.

To my fans both old and new, thank you. Some of you have been around for a long time, and some of you are new. You guys are what drive me and nothing makes me happier, than knowing you enjoy this story. Please don't hesitate to message me and tell me. Love you all!

UNSTABLE

PROLOGUE

HOW MANY PEOPLE wish they could start their lives over, or maybe just leave their lives behind and start with a clean slate?

There's so much bad in the world. Death, destruction, heartache and pain – it's a pillar of so many lives. Some people experience and are exposed to so little bad in this life, while others experience and endure it over and over with no end in sight.

How do we get past it? Some do it by burying it deep and moving on with their lives as if it didn't exist. While it may bring relief, there's always a looming darkness that sits at the back of their mind, ready to spring forward as soon as it gets the chance. Others don't get past it at all. They either check out of life early, or let it consume them until they eventually go crazy. Then there are the lucky few that find a way to make peace with it and are able to live life to the fullest. Whichever way a person deals with it, at some point most of us just wish we could leave it all behind and go somewhere where no one knows who we are, what we have done, or what has happened to us.

In the past, I was content with being one of those people who bury the bad and move on with life. Unfortunately, it wasn't working out so well for me. I tried with everything in me to forget the past, but the magnitude of it was too much to just bury down deep and forget. I went through life pretending there was nothing wrong, that I hadn't endured the unspeakable, that I could move on without repercussions. But that looming darkness manifested at the most inopportune times, always leading to trouble. Trouble that eventually landed me in a last chance bootcamp – a place that would change my life forever.

It was stupid to believe that it was only a small temporary situation for me. After spending time in Juvie, I thought it was just another short stop in my irritating life that would be of no consequence – boy, was I wrong. My life was turned upside down and inside out. My secrets were drawn out of me, right along with the heart that I thought had been buried with them. Death nearly found me, right along with more pain and heartache to pile on top of my mountain of misery. But something changed in me. No longer will I just bury things down deep. I'm working to repair my damaged soul and now I'm getting something that not everyone gets.

After enduring everything in my past, I'm able to start over again with an almost fully clean slate. There are still a few people that know the old me, but I'm okay with that. The only thing is, starting over isn't all it's cracked up to be, especially for someone like me.

CHAPTER ONE

(Monday, September 21st)

"YOU OKAY?" AERICK asks as he walks into the dorm.

I try to speak but the only thing that comes out is a heavy sigh. My eyes are glued to my hands knotting themselves in my lap as I push my emotions back down deep. The bed dips from his weight as he sits behind me, but he doesn't attempt to touch me. A sliver of guilt is still stabbing at me for pushing him away a little while ago. It wasn't my intention, but the enormity of the situation was just too overwhelming.

Saying goodbye to everyone and watching them leave was flat out painful. It's totally illogical, but I didn't want our time here to end. In kind fashion, Luther gave me a hint of insight, telling me that this often happens with his cadets. That spending so much time with people, living in such tight quarters, doing everything together, people tend to grow very close and it's hard to go back to life on the outside.

Only, I'm not really going back to my old life – I'm starting a new one. I'm leaving everything I know behind me. Starting my life over with a new job, new home, and a new boyfriend. As I watched the bus pull away, the unwanted tears began to fall. Aerick picked up on it quickly and tried to comfort me, putting his hand on my shoulder, but

I pushed him away, telling him to let me be as I quickly retreated to the dorm. It was too much and I refused to let the others see my tears.

Aerick has been witness to my tears on rare occasion, but the others hadn't, and it made me feel weak. I don't like feeling like that, even in front of him. I'm suddenly grateful Aerick has given me space. I expected him to follow me, with Jeff not there to stop him and remind him to give me some time, but he didn't. He left me to collect myself and calm down. My heart warms at the thought that he has learned that sometimes, being alone is what I truly need.

The bold numbers on the clock clue me in that it has been two hours since my dramatic exit from the front of the camp. It sure doesn't feel that long – it seems like only minutes since I threw myself down on the bed to sulk. He is still waiting silently behind me; he can be patient when he wants to be, though it is a rare thing. I breathe in a calming breath and wipe my eyes, making sure there's nothing left, before turning around to face him.

He's biting the inside of his cheek and concern is plastered across his face. Like me, he usually isn't the emotional type, and this is all kinds of new to him too. Feeling bad for making him worry, I give in and explain myself. "Yes, I'm okay. It's just really hard to be left behind. It's been a long time since Jeff, Patrick and I have been really close, and it kind of hurts to watch them go. Honestly, it's been a long time since I've had so many good friends, and now I'll probably never see most of them again."

He turns away but I don't miss the look of displeasure. "Do you regret it?" My brows pull together. *Why would I regret anything?* He takes in my silence and probably sees the confusion in my face. "Do you regret staying with me? Do you want to go back? Because the last thing I want is for you to feel forced into anything. I just want you to be happy."

His deep, barely audible tone makes my stomach fall. *How could he possibly think that is what's going through my head?* Insecure Aerick is a rarity but he's in full swing right now. My guilt amplifies, making me feel bad for moping and putting him in this situation.

Placing my hands on his cheeks, I force him to look into my eyes. "I don't regret staying with you. Not for one moment, okay?" I don't bother to give him time to respond, I kiss him hard and after a moment, his arms curl around me as he pulls me into his lap. My heart begins to race, but I pull back, needing to finish my thoughts.

"I'm just going to miss my friends, that's all. Jeff will be back for the next session, and I'll see him then. And even if he wasn't coming back, I have you, and that's all I will ever need." Seemingly satisfied, he pulls me back to his chest and I willingly relax in his embrace.

A loud noise makes me jump as Luther suddenly walks in and pauses at the sight of us. "Um, sorry to interrupt." I quickly try sliding off Aerick's lap, embarrassed that we were caught in such a private moment even though we weren't doing anything, but Aerick's grip tightens around my waist, holding me in place. At least I'm sitting up straight so I'm no longer lying on his chest.

"What's up, Luther?" he asks like our position is a natural thing, but he is completely tense under me. Aerick isn't really the PDA type of guy, or he wasn't until he met me, and we've never shown anything in front of Luther.

"Well, the cadets are gone, but that does not mean your jobs are done." *My job?*

He stops for just a moment, seeing the confounded expression on my face, before he breaks it down for me. "Aerick, you have a lot of paperwork to get done and we have lots of work to do around here. Nadi, since you are here, I might as well put you to work. You will be paid for this week, but you are expected to put in the work just like everyone else. You can start by cleaning the dorms. All the staff help with clean-up during the last week and you will be no different. Breakfast, lunch and dinner are served at the same time as they are when we are in session and everyone helps clean up afterward. Staff are expected to work from eight in the morning until six at night. I am sure Aerick can answer any questions you have and if you need me, I'm usually in my office."

I give him a tight nod and he turns to leave, but pauses as he opens the door. "Remember, you two are still at technically at work until six tonight – act accordingly." Aerick's chest rumbles behind me and my face heats up a bit.

"Got it Luther. We'll behave." My face turns five shades redder at Aerick's words, egging on Luther's insinuation. Luther's chuckles follow him as he exits the room and I proceed to slap Aerick on the chest.

"Seriously. That is embarrassing." He's attempting to hold in his grin, and I can't help but to mirror him. It's so adorable.

"There's that beautiful smile," he says and the weight from earlier has lifted. "Come. Let's get to work."

"So, what exactly do I do?" I ask as I move off his lap and glance back to him. He is sporting a faraway look on his face as he is focusing down at my neck.

"You're wearing your necklace." He rubs his thumb over it gently.

"I figured since everyone was gone, it would be okay. It's very beautiful."

He moves his hand up to my cheek as his eyes move to mine. "Beautiful necklace for my beautiful lady." He gives me a quick, soft kiss and I chuckle a little out of pure embarrassment.

"You are so freaking adorable sometimes," I tell him and he shakes his head as if he was just under a spell.

"We really should get started before Luther comes back in, or he will split us up, and I have no intentions of being away from you for the rest of the day," he says more seriously. "Let's get this room started – I'll show you how. Then before lunch we can go for a run.

"Sounds good to me."

* * * *

By lunch time, I feel good about how much I've been able to accomplish. I pulled out all of the cadet clothing from the chests in my dorm, stripped the bedding, separated it all into bags and took it all over to the laundry room in the supply cabin. When I finished taking everything to the laundry, I pulled Aerick away from the paperwork that he was doing at my desk, and we went on an hour long run on the trails.

Running in silence next to him, with nothing but nature around us, is like nothing else. The tension and apprehension that was still built up inside me, chipped away little by little as my feet pounded the ground. It was just what I needed.

Sitting down to eat back in the hall, the atmosphere feels a little lighter. Not having the other cadets here, it's so much quieter, even though the other staff seem more relaxed and chattier.

"Hey, brat!" Paulo says as he sits down next to me instead of Aerick.

"Hey," I beam back.

He looks at both our shirts. "Looks like you guys were being naughty."

I literally spit out my water on my food and everyone looks at me and starts laughing. Aerick's face is scrunched up trying not to show his amusement but he's failing miserably. "Paulo, don't be a dick," Aerick says letting out the slightest snicker.

I shove both of their shoulders. "Both of you can fuck off."

"Yep. She is going to fit in here just fine," Tia says, still laughing. "Better get used to it, Nadi. This is what they're normally like. A word of warning, these guys love to play practical jokes on each other – so watch out."

Aerick grunts next to me. "You mean Paulo and Trent play practical jokes on everyone. We just get them back occasionally."

I force out a laugh. I'm going to have to work on not being so embarrassed by sexual comments, because something tells me they aren't going to stop anytime soon. "So, what do you guys do when you don't have cadets here?"

Paulo's immediately gets an evil look in his eyes. "Oh, don't worry little sis, we have all kinds of fun." Worry quickly weighs down my stomach and I look to Aerick.

"You don't have to do anything you don't want to do," he says, looking directly at Paulo.

"Yeah, but if she wants to prove she belongs here, she does," Brayden speaks up quickly.

Aerick quickly reaches over the table, grabbing a handful of Brayden's shirt. "I said she doesn't have to do anything she doesn't want to do, and you will not pressure her, fuckface. You got it?"

Brayden throws his hands up in defense. Aerick can be a little scary sometimes. "Dude, I was just kidding, chill out!" Aerick releases him and sits back down. His protectiveness over me can be cute sometimes.

"Don't worry, Aerick, I wouldn't do anything I wouldn't want to do," I tell him, nudging his arm, and he gives me that smirk I love so much.

"Good to know asshole Aerick is still around," Brayden says quietly. but his face is bright with amusement.

"Do we have plans for tonight?" I ask no one in particular.

"Yes," Aerick answers swiftly.

"Really?" Paulo says, perking up in his seat. "What are we doing?"

Aerick glares at him. "You and I aren't doing anything. We – as in, her and I – have plans."

My curiosity is peaked. "What are we doing?"

He tilts his head toward me just slightly. "You'll see." He winks, giving me butterflies.

"Ah, little sis is going to have some fun tonight."

My face reddens again at his insinuation. "You know, Paulo, if I really was your 'little sis', that comment would be totally inappropriate." I try to say it as nonchalantly as possible and everyone laughs.

"It's inappropriate anyway," Aerick growls.

"Christ, Aerick, tell me you aren't going to be like this all damn week. The cadets are gone, lighten up," Trent speaks up.

I'm not sure I could ever picture Aerick 'lightening up' too much around other people. Even the night we spent playing poker, he never really relaxed. He always seemed a little on edge. Maybe it was because I was there or maybe it was because I was sitting on his lap. Maybe he will relax if we get drunk. I did notice he didn't seem to drink very much while I was around. In fact, the only times I've ever seen him drunk were the one night we spent together in the infirmary and the night he got into the bar fight. I am suddenly curious how Aerick normally acts when I'm not around.

Aerick brings me back out of my thoughts. "I will *lighten up* when people stop making ridiculous remarks about me and my woman." A hint of a smile pulls at my mouth at his reference to me.

"Okay, can everyone back off of us, because I'd really like to see what Aerick is like when he lightens up." He gives me an frustrated look and rolls his eyes, but I just laugh at him.

Suddenly Paulo puts his arm around my waist, shaking me side to side lightly. "Don't worry sis, we'll get him loose." He's cracking up, but I have gone completely still, and my chest starts to tighten. This is such a normal, friendly action, but I can't help it. I try to breathe through it and focus on not reacting, like I practiced with Christian. *Breathe.*

Aerick notices almost immediately and smacks Paulo's arm away. "Hands off, dickhead. What part of *mine* don't you understand?" I feel his eyes boring into me, but my body is refusing to cooperate, and I'm praying the others haven't noticed.

"Thanks for volunteering to clean up," he says to Paulo as he grabs my hand. "Come on, we have stuff to get done." I let him pull me out of my seat, wanting to get out of here as quickly as possible before the others notice.

"Like hell, I ain't cleaning up after you so you can go fool around."

We start going out the door as Aerick yells back at him, "I'll owe you one."

"Stay off my bed!" Paulo yells at the closing door.

As soon as we get outside, he pulls me to the wall and pauses a second. I finally let out a breath I wasn't aware I was holding. "You okay?" He asks cautiously, rubbing his hand along my cheek. After a few deep breaths, I nod my head. "You sure?" He doesn't believe me. My face must be showing it more than I thought. *Dammit.*

His hands go to my hips and his thumbs find their way just under my shirt to my bare skin, where he rubs gently. The contact makes me feel better almost instantly and I gulp one more heavy breath.

"It just took me by surprise, that's all. I've been a little too emotional today and overreacted." The uneasy feeling disappears completely and I plant a light kiss on his lips. "I'm okay, I promise. I won't be breaking his nose today."

A smirk grows on his face as he relaxes. "Oh, so you have jokes now, huh?"

I drop my head down a little, trying to hide my grin. "So, what are we doing tonight?"

He huffs at me. "You'll see tonight. Come on, let's go hit the bags for a bit." He releases me and turns, walking toward the gym. It's irritating to still be in the dark about tonight but punching something sounds like a good idea to me after just being so tense, so quickly I move to catch up with him. It seems any type of exercise is his outlet for emotional situations - something we have in common.

* * * *

"You ready?" Aerick asks as he comes into the dorm.

I finish my braid and tie it off. "Yep." He's looking extremely hot in dark designer jeans, a tight black tee shirt, and sneakers. "Where are we going?" I ask as he gives me a quick kiss on the cheek.

"You look beautiful," he says, ignoring my question.

I frown as I look down at myself then back at him. I'm wearing track pants and a fitted tee shirt; my hair is wet, and my makeup is non-existent. "Well, I'm not really dressed up or anything."

"Babe, you would look beautiful in anything. Although I think I'd prefer you in nothing, but then we would never make it out of this room." My face reddens and I push him back slightly. "This weekend we can go to the outlet strip mall in North Bend and get you some normal clothes on our way back to Seattle." I nod at him. Luther said he would have a paycheck for me on Friday, so that will work.

"You still haven't answered my question," I say realizing he has side-tracked me.

"I told you, it's a surprise. Here, Luther wanted me to give this to you. He came in while you were in the shower." He hands me a cell phone. I turn the sleek, top-of-the-line cell phone over and over in my hands. *Wow!*

"This is your company phone. It already has all the staff pre-entered, and Jake installed the tracking app we use for the cadets. You are supposed to keep it on you at all times while we're at camp, but we can use them as our personal phones too. They have unlimited everything." Luther sure likes his state-of-the-art gadgets.

"Thanks." I slip the phone into my pocket. "How can Luther afford all this stuff? I mean, you guys have tablets, phones, trackers, all the supplies, company cars – it's a lot of stuff." I don't want to pry, but it seems like a lot considering all the cadets that come here are from state facilities.

"He gets funding from several places. The state's funding is crap, but there is a lot of private funding from foundations that would rather see youth receive help instead of just throwing them into jail and having them fall victim to the penal system. As long as Luther keeps up his impressive success rate, he will keep getting the funding. It has been so successful that others are starting to take notice. Now they are talking about opening more of these camps, like over in Chicago. That's why you guys came here. Several private investors from Chicago are looking to do the same thing there if they can get the state's approval." I guess that makes a lot of sense.

"Grab your sweater, let's go." I raise an eyebrow but don't bother asking again where we're going. He leads me back into his dorm, which is empty.

"Where is everyone?" I ask curiously.

"They're all in the mess hall playing poker. Now that the cadets are gone, we don't have to hide out in our cabins." He grabs his sweater off the bed and a black backpack, and we head out the door.

We stop in the office and he grabs a set of keys. As we approach the car, he steps in front of me and opens the passenger door to the camp's Ford Expedition that we used to go to lunch. "Won't Luther get mad we are using the camp's vehicles?"

I slip into my seat and Aerick shakes his head 'no' before closing my door and walking around to get in the driver seat. "He prefers we use them while we are here. Besides, all of our cars are in the camp's garage about a half a mile from here, so this is more convenient anyway."

We head toward town but right as we start to enter, he turns off to some side road and we keep driving. We pass several houses but then they get scarcer, with only trees and land, as we seem to be going up the ridge. After a while, his hand moves to rest on my thigh, and he seems to relax as we listen to Linkin Park while we drive. The road turns into a dirt road and gets bumpier as we continue further off the main roads.

Finally, he slows and pulls into a little parking area that has a cliff in front of it overlooking the whole town. The sun is setting, lighting the skyline in every color imaginable. *Beautiful.*

After a minute, my eyes finally roam to land on Aerick, who has a bit of a smirk on his lips. "I thought maybe we could just have a quiet evening together."

I glance at him and he grabs his bag from behind him. Leaving the music on, he gets out of the car, so I follow and go around to his side. He removes a blanket from his bag and throws it across the top of the car. I eye him, confused.

"Come on, we are going up there." He opens his door again and rolls the window down before putting his backpack over his shoulder. He uses the seat and window jamb to climb up on top of the car before turning to help me up. I follow him up, grabbing his hand for help although I really don't need it.

From up top, even though we are only a few more feet up, it feels much higher. Maybe it's because we're parked on the edge of a cliff. It feels so much more open, almost like it did when we sat on the edge of the lookout. We've been through a lot since then. Even though it has only been a few months, it feels like years. I bite my lip. The Lookout is where I lost my virginity to him. I'm still not sure what I did to deserve him. He is amazingly handsome, smart, sweet, and a god in bed. Well, our experiences in an actual bed have been pretty limited, but it's just a saying. He's been amazing in all the places we have been.

"What are you thinking about?" he asks, looking curiously at me. Embarrassment heats my face at where my thoughts have led. "Tell me. You don't want my mind running rampant." He leans into me a bit, trying to coax my thoughts out of me.

My eyes fall to my hands that are playing with the edge of my shirt.

"I was thinking of our hike to the Lookout," I say quietly; that's where my thoughts started, anyway.

He hums and pulls my chin up. "That was a very memorable night. Without a doubt, one of the best of my life." He places a light kiss on my lips and I flush, not just out of embarrassment, but at the thought he enjoyed it that much. "So why do you look so embarrassed at your thoughts of that night?"

Sometimes I hate that he can read me so easily. "I don't know. I've just been closed off for so long that I never really became comfortable with things like that."

His eyebrow goes up. "Things like that?"

"Yeah, you know, intimate things."

He chuckles, "I've noticed that. You tend to blush a lot when people insinuate those things. Really though, you shouldn't. It is human nature and trust me, with you, there is nothing to be embarrassed about."

I blush again; I can't help it. He gives me another quick kiss, on the cheek this time, and reaches over to grab his bag. "Here, this will help you relax." He hands me a Corona and opens one for himself. I figure we need to lighten the mood a little.

"You trying to get me drunk? Because if you want to get into my pants, you only have to ask." He almost chokes on his beer and then grins at me. Well, that definitely lightened up the mood.

"Is that so? I will have to keep that in mind." Dropping his voice, he leans in close to my neck. "Though, I don't think I need alcohol to convince you to let me in your pants." His seductive voice hits me between my legs and I squirm a bit, making him laugh again and sit back. "Besides, I can only have a few since I have to drive back."

His face gets a little more serious. "I was thinking this morning. We kind of fell into this relationship quickly, and circumstances have pushed it even quicker than a normal relationship. We really haven't had a chance to get to know each other, other than physically that is, and as much as I would love to explore you even more physically, I figured we could talk instead. Maybe it will help you feel better, and up here we are less likely to get interrupted by a bunch of buffoons."

I smile sweetly at his gesture. "What do you want to talk about?"

We talked a lot when I was recovering from being stabbed, but it was mostly my hopes and dreams, or times when we had gotten into trouble in the past. We never really got in-depth and every time I tried to get him to talk about his family, he would change the subject.

He shrugs his shoulders. "Tell me about your family. I mean, I know about your brother, but what about your sisters?"

We sit and talk about all kinds of things. Well, I mostly talk, but he tells me about the condo where he lives and different things there are to do in Seattle. He admits he really hasn't been to 'downtown' in a long time other than the few times he went drinking with his buddies. He still refuses to talk about his family and keeps bringing our conversation back to my life.

After a few hours, while we are talking about my dream of going to London, a big grin works its way across his face. I stop talking at the change in his expression. "What?" I ask cautiously as the mischievous look spreads across his face.

"Look up," he tells me, tapping the underside of my chin. I do, curious what is going on. Above me is the most beautiful thing I have ever seen. Streaks of green, purple and pink dance their way through the sky in waves. The sight leaves me speechless; it's the craziest thing I've ever seen. I've heard of the northern lights, but living so close to the city, you never see them. I'm not sure how I didn't notice it when we were talking, other than being more focused on him.

"Have you ever seen it before?" he asks me after a minute and I just shake my head. "I heard we should be able to see it tonight. It usually happens a few times a year up here, but not always this bright."

I can't take my eyes off of the sky, it is so extraordinary. "It's absolutely beautiful." He pulls me back, so we are lying down with my head on the arm that's strewn behind me.

We lie there and watch the sky as we listen to the music coming from the car. As he rubs his fingers up and down my side, I wonder how in the world this man has given me so many memorable moments in just a few short months. I may be young, but I'm positive these memories will last a lifetime.

CHAPTER TWO

(Wednesday, September 23rd)

"TIME TO GET up, Princess," Aerick says softly into my ear and nuzzles my neck. I'm so warm and comfortable with him folded around me, I really don't want to get up. I just snuggle further into him. "Come on, it's almost six, I let you sleep for as long as I could."

I tighten my hold on him. "Tell me again why you all get up so early when there are no cadets here?" I feel the rumble in his chest. He starts to kiss my neck and a small moan escapes me.

"Well, I could think of something else we could do." He pushes himself against me and I feel his hardness. "You know, waking up with you in my bed has its advantages."

"You two better not! If you want to do that, go into her dorm," Trent says, turning my moans into a giggle and putting a damper on the mood. All of the guys have been teasing us since Monday, so I'm slowly learning to just laugh it off. I haven't spent a night in my bed since everyone left. We've been sleeping in Aerick's bed because it's more comfortable and slightly bigger. We both barely fit on my bed.

The only time we've even spent together in my dorm was Monday night, when we got back from our little trip. The minute we got into my dorm, Aerick was all over me. I have a feeling he had to really work not do it before we got there, since he had been eyeing me with those lustful eyes all night. At first, I had stopped him because of the cameras, but he assured me that the inside cameras are not on while cadets aren't here. They only keep the outside ones on for security reasons. He must have figured we were going to end up there, because he also explained no one would come in since he had warned them.

That night had been so amazing. Not only had we had the most wonderful date, talking and watching the northern lights, but when we came back, it felt so much more intimate. We had all night. For the first time, we were not constricted by time; we were free to take things slow and explore each other fully. Aerick had taken his time to make sure I was completely satisfied. I can still feel his warm lips all over my body, and I have several bite marks that he left behind. After several uninterrupted hours, we were exhausted, so I threw on my shorts and cami and we migrated to his bed.

It was a little weird at first, sleeping in Aerick's bed with a bunch of guys in the room, but the feeling went away quickly once I was snuggled in bed with Aerick. Morning brought a bunch of comments and innuendos from Paulo, Trent, and Brayden, but I let it roll off my shoulders. I was a little surprised to see that Brayden was sleeping in Brand's bed. Aerick explained that Brand was with Tia in her cabin, and Andi had joined Jake in his cabin, leaving Brayden out in the cold. I had to laugh at that, but secretly wished we had a room to ourselves.

I feel Aerick get out of bed and he throws my shorts at my head. "Get up, time to work out. You too, you lazy asses," Aerick speaks up to the guys. I slide my shorts on under the covers. We didn't do anything last night, but he had asked me to sleep in just my underwear and cami, so I did. I get out of bed to go change quickly. Even when the cadets aren't here, everyone still does morning and evening P.T. The difference is, the staff participate, and instead of one of the instructors leading it, Luther leads it. Aerick told me it was to keep us working together as a unit. He also said it reminds most of us that we were once cadets and that hard work got us here. I actually really like it, anyway, so I don't mind much.

I allow my joy to show as we all gather out at the stage; it is kind of funny to see all the staff lined up like they're cadets. Luther jumps up on the stage. "Hey guys, while I have you all here together, I wanted to make an announcement. Ayla and I will be leaving this evening to go to Seattle. We have an early morning meeting to attend so we will be going tonight. We should get back tomorrow afternoon. As always, no non-staff allowed on the premises and I expect you all to behave. Trent, this means you. I do not want to come back to dumbass practical jokes. Got it?"

Everyone laughs and I have a feeling there are several stories behind that comment. "Come on, Luther, you have to admit, some of those were hella funny," Trent defends himself. Aerick shakes his head when I look at him confused. I assume he will tell me another time.

"I am serious, Trent, this is your last warning, or you will be finding yourself on the worst duties I can think up." Trent rolls his eyes, but doesn't say anything further. "I know it isn't fair to ask, but I would also prefer if you all stayed in camp tonight. If something happens, I will not be around to deal with it, so I'd like to avoid it all together."

A series of murmurs roll around our small group, but no one complains. "Alright, now that I have that out of the way. Today I would like to finish clean-up so we can start inventory tomorrow. Nadi, now that you are done cleaning out both dorms, I would like you to help out Tia and Andi with laundry and meals, since Ayla needs Terrie's help today. Guys, you are all on grounds clean-up and instructors, your paperwork is due in my office by the end of the day. Everyone understand?" We all nod our heads and, seemingly satisfied, Luther begins leading our morning workout.

* * * *

"So, what are we doing tonight?" Paulo asks as we eat lunch.

"I say we play poker, and someone needs to make an alcohol run. I already called Shannon and Laura," Andi says quickly.

"Andi, you heard Luther," Aerick says glumly and Tia raises her eyebrow.

"Aerick, stop being so uptight. Laura is technically staff and Shannon is ex-staff. Besides, I don't want to listen to Beavis and Butthead complaining that their girls aren't here. Now, who's going on the alcohol run?"

"I'll go," Paulo offers. "Luther asked me to go pick up the mail today, anyway."

She smiles broadly. "Good. We need beer, rum, vodka and soda."

Paulo huffs, "I don't want that nasty ass shit, I want some whiskey or something. And who is paying for our little get together? I just sent money back home to my mom – I'm broke."

Everyone looks around dumbfounded until finally Aerick grabs his wallet out of his back pocket, pulling out his credit card. "Don't go crazy." He tosses it on the table in front of Paulo. "And since I am buying, the beer of choice tonight is Corona."

Aerick turns to me. "What do you like to drink?"

At least he doesn't have a problem with me drinking. "I'm fine with rum and coke."

He looks at me and I see something like amusement cross his face. "Paulo, since you are getting whiskey, might as well get everything for our special." Paulo's face grows into a big grin.

"And what is your special?" I question.

Paulo beams, "Don't worry, sis. Let's just say it will *suit* you just fine." He and Aerick laugh and I decide to drop it because I'm not sure

I want to know.

"It sucks I can't drink," Tia whines and Brand looks down at her stomach, putting his hand on it before giving her a kiss on her cheek. They are so freaking cute sometimes.

"Don't worry, Tia, I'll make you my special cake," Andi tells her, and that seems to cheer Tia up.

"Won't Luther get mad that we're all drinking? I mean, several of us are underage."

Trent looks at me like I'm crazy." He's our boss not our father and we are all adults. As long as he doesn't see you guys drinking, he doesn't care. He actually told me once he would rather everyone drinks here where he knows we're safe, instead of going out to one of the parties in the woods the local kids have. Especially after that kid died last year when he walked away from the party and fell asleep in the snow. Besides, it's normal for us to celebrate birthdays. Jake's was last Sunday, and Brayden's is coming up on the 27th, so I'm sure Luther is expecting us to, anyway."

"Oh, and Nadi, you will be joining the girls to get ready," Andi chimes in, and my eyebrows pull together. "Don't look at me like that." I see several of the guys holding in their amusement and Tia sighs.

"Trust me, there is no arguing with her, just go with it," Tia tells me. I look over to Aerick and he just gives me a 'don't look at me' sneer. *Great!*

* * * *

Oh, my sweet Lucifer! Andi is ridiculous, wanting to do my hair and makeup like I'm a damn doll. After two hours, Terrie and Andi have all of us girls' hair and makeup done. Terrie has brought me a cute pair of skinny jeans and a gorgeous tight blue blouse with a low back that goes beautifully with my necklace. I'm a bit nervous wearing the top because it's not my normal style, and it's meant to be worn without a bra. For the first time, I'm pleased I'm able to go braless.

Andi finally lets me stand to look at myself in a full-length mirror and I am shocked. My make-up is not heavy, very natural, and my hair is in large, loose curls that fall down my back and around my breasts. I actually look like a woman instead of my normal tomboy-looking self.

"Wow, thank you guys, I look great!"

"You have a lot of natural beauty Nadi, it really didn't take much," Andi tells me with complete honesty. "Let's go. The guys are probably wondering where we're at." We all get up and head to the mess hall.

When I walk in, my eyes go wide at the little set up. The normal tables are pushed up against the back wall. There's a table set up at the front of the hall with a bunch of alcohol and another table of snack food. Jake is setting up a stereo that's already playing loud music and the lights seem to be dimmed a bit. It feels more like a night club than our mess hall. All the other guys are sitting at one of the two round tables, playing poker and drinking.

It takes Aerick about two seconds to register that we've arrived and he looks up. His eyes lock onto mine and I'm suddenly nervous for some reason. He looks down my body and back up again before returning his gaze to my eyes. The grin that appears on his face makes me feel better, since it's obvious that he likes what he sees. Paulo nudges his arm, trying to bring his attention back to the game, but when Aerick doesn't answer right away, Paulo follows his eyes. Elation spreads across his face and he says something quietly to Aerick. I figure it's something completely inappropriate, because Aerick hits him hard in the arm before folding his hand and waving me over to sit by him.

I go over and give him a quick kiss on the cheek before sitting down next to him. He slides his arm around my waist and then freezes for just a moment. He leans back, looking at the back of my shirt, and I hear a low groan escape him. He licks his lips and begins moving his thumb up and then down my bare back as he leans in next to my ear. "Damn babe, you look amazing. Paulo is right, we may not make it out of this hall." I feel the red creep up my face. He kisses my neck before pulling back to place a hot, passionate kiss on my lips.

"Aerick, you playing this hand?" Brand asks, causing Aerick to break our kiss, and when I look at Brand, he's a little uncomfortable with Aerick's display of affection. Several of the others have also stopped and are staring at us.

"Yeah," Aerick tells him, still looking at me, so much promise in his eyes. "Paulo, I think we need a couple specials for the women." Aerick gets a little smirk on his face and then picks up the cards that were dealt to him.

"What are you guys playing?" I ask, trying to find a distraction from the ache between my legs that Aerick has caused.

"Just normal five card stud right now, but we like to play different games, so we'll switch it up occasionally. Once the other girls get here, we'll split up into two tables," Brand tells me, and I watch as they bid around twice before laying out their cards. Trent wins it with a full house.

"Here you go, little sis." Paul sets a drink down in front of me. I look to Aerick and he nods for me to drink, so I take a sip of it. It's pretty sweet but really good.

"So, what am I drinking?" I question warily.

"Well, *Princess,* this is called a 'Royal Fuck'. Enjoy!" He has the cutest grin on his face, and I can't help but to beam back at him.

"Well then, I guess it's fitting that my *Prince Charming* is drinking one as well. What's in it?"

"It's Crown Royal, Peach Schnapps and pineapple juice. The sweetness allows you to drink it pretty quickly so be careful, Paulo always make them strong. Don't drink more than two. I don't want you passing out on me tonight." He kisses me again along my jaw. *Urgh,* his demanding voice hits me right between my legs yet again, bringing back that ache, and I squirm in my chair. The door opens and I look over to see Laura and Shannon walk in.

"Good, now the party can really start," Brayden says loudly, and something tells me he's already had a few drinks. He jumps up and grabs Laura's hand before kissing her. Shannon goes over and sits down in Trent's lap before saying 'hi' to everyone.

We split up into two tables: Aerick, me, Paulo, Terrie, Brayden and Laura at one table and Brand, Tia, Trent, Shannon, Jake and Andi at the other. They didn't even discuss who would go where so I'm guessing this is their normal. When I go to sit down, Aerick slyly sets two rolls of quarters in my lap. I give him a questioning look and he leans over to my ear.

"This is a date and I am paying!" He's so adorably cute, and it's a good thing too because I don't have any money to play with tonight. I had worried about that, and I'm grateful he was so discreet about it.

We all decide to play Texas Hold'em for a while. I'm actually pretty good at this game and I start winning quite a bit. Everyone is relaxed, joking, and just having fun. As we play, Aerick keeps his arm on the back of my chair and continuously runs his thumb over my bare back, which is slowly driving me crazy.

"I've got an idea," Brayden speaks up after a while. "Why don't we play strip poker?"

Aerick gives a quick humph. "Not happening, kid." Brayden looks disappointed.

"I've got a better idea," Trent throws out excitedly from the table behind us. "Let's play 'Winner Picks'. We have to break in Nadi."

I'm not sure what the blazes they're talking about. "Um, first, Nadi doesn't need to be broken into anything," I tell him, but before I can continue, Paulo interrupts.

"Yeah, because we all know Aerick's already done that." Several of the guys snicker as my face heats up.

"Paulo, man, don't be an ass," Aerick says but I can tell he is trying to hold in his smile and he whispers in my ear. "But I sure wouldn't mind doing it again." I smack him on his thigh. He closes his eyes and groans. He clearly enjoyed that.

"Moving on. Secondly, I have no idea what that game is."

"It's simple. The person that wins the hand gets to pick someone to take a shot. We keep playing until someone gives up. It just adds a layer of fun," Trent explains.

That's not so bad. "Ok, I'm up for that." Everyone agrees and we start playing again, but I can't help wondering what that barely there grin on Aerick's face is for.

I soon find out. Each time Aerick or Paulo wins, I end up taking a shot, almost like they planned it. After the eighth shot, I can't take anymore.

"That's it, that is my last shot," I tell everyone and Aerick, Paulo and Trent all attempt to hold in their amusement. Every time I won, I would make one of them drink, but it was clear that they were ganging up on me. My head is spinning, and I do not want to black out tonight.

"Fine. If she's done, then it's time to play truth or dare."

"Come on, Brayden, we're too old to play that," Aerick groans.

"Whatever, dickhead. Let's go," Trent says.

Aerick rolls his eyes but stands up grabbing my hand and as soon as I stand, the room spins. I'm grateful that Aerick puts his hands on me to steady me. "Jump on, Princess," he tells me with a grin, knowing I'm completely plastered. I laugh as I jump on his back and we head outside.

Paulo brings out a case of Corona and passes them around as we all sit down in a circle on the grass. Aerick pulls me down so I'm sitting between his legs. I'm about to object, but I notice Trent and Shannon do the same, so I figure, why not?

"I'm starting," Brayden says as soon as we are all settled. "Aerick, Truth or Dare?"

"Truth," he says without missing a beat.

"You pansy!"

Aerick shakes his head. "Your dares are always ridiculous. Now, what is your question?"

Brayden thinks about it for a second. "When is the first time you dreamed about Nadi?" I freeze.

"Who said I had dreams about her?" He's a bit irritated. Brayden quickly looks to Paulo before his eyes drop down, and I feel Aerick reach over and punch Paulo in the arm.

"Sorry dude, it slipped," Paulo says, rubbing his arm.

"Come on - answer, Aerick!" Brayden whines. Aerick huffs as he pushes me forward a little and I feel him remove his shirt. I look back at him, confused.

"Really?" Brayden says. Aerick is clearly not pleased and I wonder if he didn't want me knowing that. Now I'm really curious to know the answer. He shakes his head and pulls me back against his bare chest. It feels so warm against my back.

Aerick quickly moves on. "Laura?"

"Sweet Jesus," I hear Brayden mumble.

"Definitely Dare." Brayden's face falls – this can't be good.

"Laura, I dare you to kiss Trent." I feel the rumble in his chest.

"Aerick!" Trent says as he looks at Shannon.

"Dude, it's just a game. Don't be a pussy," Aerick tells him, but Shannon doesn't seem to be bothered by it. If I'm not mistaken, she's amused.

"Sorry Brayden, but this is your fault," Laura says, as she goes over to Trent and kisses him.

Trent stays completely still and Shannon pokes fun at her. "Damn, girl. I didn't think you had it in you!" Shannon tells her. "But that was your one and only pass. Don't ever do that again." Trent lets out a huge breath of relief.

"Tia?" Laura asks.

"Truth."

Laura thinks for a minute. "Craziest place you've ever had sex."

Aerick huffs behind me and Tia looks completely embarrassed. "Um, in a bed."

Everyone snickers. "Man, Brand, you really need to give your woman some variety," Paulo bellows and it starts another round of laughter. *Poor Tia.*

"Trent?" Tia quietly asks, her face deep red.

"Dare!" He is way too enthusiastic. Andi quickly leans over and whispers in her ear.

"Hey! No helping, Andi!" Trent protests.

"Trent, I dare you to run a lap nude," Tia says, her face turning red again.

Trent jumps up, "Andi, you are ruthless. Shannon, you got your camera?" He beams in eagerness, stripping down to his boxers quickly before running away from us, then peeling off his boxers so we see his bare ass.

We are all laughing and Aerick's hand quickly goes over my eyes as soon as Paulo's rear is in sight. "Princess, I think you are too young to watch this." I try pulling his hands away playfully as he fights me and we both laugh our asses off. His lips find mine as I hear Trent running back to where he left his boxers. As we break apart everyone is staring at us.

"What the fuck? Have you guys never seen two people kiss?" Aerick asks irritably as he sees what I see.

"Aerick, man, I don't think I have ever seen you be playful. Like ever!" Paulo quips.

"Fuck off, man. Trent, your turn," Aerick says coldly, his mood doing a complete one-eighty.

"Yeah, okay. Andi, truth or dare?"

Her face turns mischievous. "You know me. Dare." Trent's eyes roam around the circle and land on me and Aerick.

"Andi, I dare you to kiss Nadi. Not that pansy shit Laura did either. Like really kiss her, open mouth and everything."

My mouth falls open. "Seriously, Trent?! What did I ever do to you?" My voice is way too high.

Andi comes over and kneels in front of me. "Come on, badass Nadi. Let's give these little boys a show."

Trent beams at me, but I ignore him and look back hesitantly to Aerick. Both of his eyebrows are raised, and he puts up his hands in a defensive position as he grins at me. "It's up to you, babe." I inhale a gulp of much needed air, and thankfully the alcohol is making me braver than normal.

"Fine, Andi. Just do it." In a second, her mouth is on mine and Aerick's hands move up to my thighs where he grabs tightly. Feeling his hands on me, so close to my center, makes me want him, and causing me to kiss her back. Andi's hand goes up to my cheek as she opens her mouth and I allow her to continue as I feel Aerick pull me tighter into him. All I can think about is his hands on me right now, and how much I want him as I feel him grow hard against me.

Andi finally breaks our kiss and turns to Trent. "Good enough for you?" she asks and he swallows as I see the other guys mouths all hanging open – with the exception of Brand, who is looking down at the ground. I pull a long drink of my Corona and I feel Aerick's lips on my shoulders.

"*Wow,* I missed that, can you do it again?" Brayden says, all breathy, and Laura slaps his arm.

"I don't know, judging by the expression on Aerick's face, I think he might bust a nut if he sees that again," Paulo says as he breaks out into a fit of laughter.

My face heats up and Aerick leans down next to my ear. "Sorry babe. I can't lie – that was fucking hot." *Typical male.*

"Well, I hope you enjoyed it because it's never happening again," I say quietly to him, but I can't help the smile on my face.

"Alright Nadi, truth or dare?" Andi asks me.

"Um, yeah, I think I will pick truth."

"What's the highest number of orgasms you have had during sex?" My face turns beet red immediately and my hands fly up to cover my face. I feel Aerick's hands tighten around my waist again. I don't think I can say it. I'm not too keen on talking about these things. I'm still barely used to hearing it.

"Say it, because you are not taking off a piece of clothing," Aerick says and his voice sounds somewhere between lustful and demanding. I hear a few of the others urging me, 'Come on'.

"Four times," Aerick says from behind me.

"Aerick!" I chastise him; he just tilts his head to the side as he shrugs and takes a drink of his beer. "What? It's the truth."

"And how exactly do you know that?" Shannon says, a little in disbelief.

Aerick raises his eyebrow like it's obvious. "Because I felt all of them," he says proudly. It still astounds me that he's so blunt.

"Hello, I'm sure she's had past boyfriends. You don't know if someone may have been able to please her better," she teases him, and I see him glare at her. Aerick was my first; that really isn't any of her business, but as I look at Shannon I see the realization spread across her face. "Man, don't tell me you took her virginity!"

I've had enough of this conversation. "Shannon, enough about my sex life," I say before thinking, then realize I pretty much just answered her assumption. I don't think I've ever been so embarrassed and I'm actually getting irritated.

"You never actually gave your answer," Andi says to me.

For Christ's sake. "You really want to know that bad? Yes, Monday night we came back here, Aerick and I fucked like rabbits and after four mind-shattering orgasms, I was exhausted and we went to bed. And for the record, he's the only one I've ever been with, so yes, he knows every orgasm I have ever had. Happy now?" Again, my mouth has a mind of its own. I down the rest of my beer, pissed at my uncontrollable mouth.

Everyone is quiet for a minute. "Wow, Aerick, you got yourself a feisty one here," Paulo says. I sigh and shake my head.

"Fuck off, Paulo." His lips part showing me a toothy grin. I believe all that came out of my mouth.

"Ignore them, they're just jealous," Aerick says into my ear as he kisses my neck, calming me and reawakening my sexual need for him. I run my fingers up the inside of his thigh and I hear him groan behind me. Within a second he gets to his feet, pulling me up with him. "I think we have had enough for tonight. We're going to bed." I hear a bunch of them scoff and mumble comments that I don't care to hear. Aerick puts his arm around me, still shirtless, and we start walking toward the dorm.

"Paulo, you can take my turn," I yell back and Aerick chuckles.

As soon as we get into my dorm, Aerick locks the door and pushes me back up against the wall next to it. His lips are on mine before I can say a word. His lips feel so amazing after him working me up so much tonight and I can't help the moan that escapes me. He has been driving me crazy all night ,and with all the alcohol in me, it is just pushing my need for him even higher. He pulls my shirt off as he begins to work his way kissing and biting down past my neck, then slows to appreciate each of my breasts, before moving down to my stomach.

He has my pants unbuttoned before his lips reach the top of my jeans and he peels off my pants and shoes. Quickly he throws them to the side before lifting my leg over his shoulder. I squeeze my eyes shut, leaning my head against the wall as he begins to lick and suck, sending me into a blissful state. My hands find his hair and I pull it hard in response to his ministrations. He hums loudly against me, sending shivers up my body. His fingers quickly find their way in me and my legs become weak from the pure ecstasy I'm feeling. His expert tongue makes quick work of me and with all the pent-up frustration and irritation, I quickly explode around his fingers as I shout out his name.

He kisses back up my body as he quickly undoes his pants and frees himself. He grabs me by the back of my thighs and I instinctively wrap my legs around him when he lifts me up. Within seconds he enters me fully before he stills, allowing me to adjust to his large size. I feel so wonderfully complete with him inside me.

"I have been dying to be inside you all night," he whispers to me as he kisses my neck. He begins moving, slowly at first, then picking up the pace. "You are so fucking beautiful." He whispers as he nibbles my ear. "Knowing you weren't wearing a bra under that shirt was almost enough to make me cum in my pants." He starts pounding into me harder and I hold on tightly to his neck, absorbing the almost painful but incredibly pleasurable feeling.

"And the back of that shirt – fuck, showing your beautiful back. I just wanted to take you right there." His words cause the feeling deep down in me to build again. His fingers dig into my sides, sending a hum through my entire body. My head is swimming with his touch, his words, and the alcohol. "Then you kissed Andi." He slams into me harder and I let out a loud moan of pleasure. "And admitted that you are mine... only mine... and every sweet, pleasurable, amazing orgasm belongs to me." His rougher side is showing itself as he picks up the pace even more. The feeling building up in me is so overwhelming, threatening to tear me apart.

"You... are... all... mine!" he says through gritted teeth, slamming into me between each word and it sends me over the edge as I yell his name again. "That's right baby. All mine," he says proudly and with a few more thrusts, he groans my name into my neck as he spills into me with unbelievable force.

He makes no move to let me down and after a few seconds of trying to catch his breath, he walks backwards until his legs hit the bed. He lies back on it, bringing me down with him so that I'm lying on his chest with him still inside of me. I'm spent and don't even try to move. Once our breathing finally evens out, I feel his chest rumble with laughter. I look up to him, curious as to what could possibly be so funny. His elation reaches from ear to ear. "I think you can now say you've been royally fucked."

CHAPTER THREE

(Saturday, September 26th)

"SON OF A bitch!" I shout.

Now I know just how much I hate Trent. Aerick and I have just fallen victim to one of Trent's notorious pranks. "Trent, you stupid bastard!" I yell at him as I crawl back on the bed, trying to avoid the traps on the floor.

"Wow Nadi, aren't you looking hot! Nice panties," he grins, and in an instant Aerick gets up off the edge of the bed to likely beat the daylights out of him. Trent is out the door before Aerick gets two steps; I hear another trap go off and Aerick starts swearing.

I look around and half the room is covered in small mouse traps. Paulo and Brayden are sitting on the beds doubled over laughing because Aerick and I were just woken up with a blow horn and as we jumped off the bed, our feet were attacked by a hundred small mouse traps.

"You two better shut the hell up before I come over there and knock your teeth down your throat," Aerick warns, beyond pissed, and the laughing quiets down but doesn't stop. He comes back over to the bed, pulling my feet out from under the blanket I threw over my bottom half. He looks down to look at my feet, running his finger over them lightly. He's so gentle as he picks up each foot and inspects it. They're red, and my pinky toe hurts, but I'll be fine. "You okay?"

"I'm fine, let's just go back to bed." The clock shows it's only three thirty in the morning. I groan and scoot back toward the wall so Aerick can lie on the outside of the bed. "When I fucking wake up, all those traps better be gone, or I swear you are going to pay for it. And tell Trent he better be gone before I wake up!" He slides in next to me.

"Does he always do crap like this?"

"Yeah. Usually he doesn't do it to me, but I have a feeling, with you around, this isn't the last time." He sighs and kisses me on my temple. "Let's get some sleep. Today is going to be a long day." He pulls me into his chest, and I coil myself back around him.

* * * *

"Mhmm." I wake up to hot lips kissing my neck. My hands find their way up into his hair and I move my head to the side a little to give him better access. As he moves to my collar bone, he bites lightly, and I let out a quiet moan as I tug on his hair. I feel the groan in his chest.

"Okay, we can hear you!" I hear Brayden say.

"Then plug your ears," I say lightly, and Aerick stops and laughs. I groan at the loss of his warmth against my neck.

"As much as I would love to be buried in you right now, I'm not keen on others seeing my woman while she is having a mind-blowing orgasm."

Now it's my turn to poke fun. "Confident, are we?"

"Always, Princess." He exclaims wagging his brows, then rolls his head back as lets out a sigh. He returns his lips near my ear. "I cannot wait until we are home in our bed, where I can satisfy my morning hunger for you." He pushes himself against me and I feel him hard against my thigh, but what really held my mind was him saying 'home in our bed'. Today I will get so see my new home, his home, and it still feels a little surreal that I'm really moving in with him already.

"Let's get up and get stuff ready to go. We all go to The Cottage for breakfast before we head our separate ways," Aerick tells me as I slide on the shorts he hands me. I notice all the traps are gone and I don't see Trent. I wonder if he really left already.

* * * *

I watch Aerick intently, who's paying close attention to the road. He has a bit of a shadow around his jaw because he hasn't shaved in a few days, but to be honest, he looks very hot like that. He keeps one hand on the wheel of his Dodge Charger, and the other holding my hand. I swear all morning he has been touching me in one way or another.

Breakfast at The Cottage was delicious. Aerick and I both had bacon, eggs, hash browns and toast. As we sat around talking while we ate, I learned that many people from camp actually live down near Aerick. Paulo stays with his brother when not up at camp, which is only a few miles from Aerick's condo. Brand, Trent and Brayden all share a rental house in the next town over. Aerick told me that he doesn't hang out with anyone other than Paulo and recently Terrie, but sometimes he sees them at Amar's Gym.

Terrie told me she has a condo in Snoqualmie, but has been thinking of moving closer to the coast if she and Paulo get more serious. They sat at our table and much to Aerick's displeasure, she sat next to me, so he was forced to sit across from me next to Paulo, but he kept his legs hooked around mine under the table the whole time we ate.

As we went to leave, we said our goodbyes to everyone and Aerick punched Trent hard in the arm, getting back at him for early this morning. A wave of joy went through me as Trent rubbed his arm with a pained expression. *Serves him right.* While Aerick was ordering us both lattes for the ride home, Brayden gave me an overly enthusiastic hug, making me freeze, but he quickly released it as Aerick gave him a death glare from his position at the counter. I almost thought Brayden was going to receive the same fate as Trent.

I froze again, but I think it was more out of shock because Luther also stood up and gave me a hug. It felt a little odd, but when he whispered to me that he was glad we found each other, it warmed my heart. In a way, it really seems like everyone who works at the camp is one big dysfunctional family. A family I am really glad to join.

"What are you staring at?" Aerick asks, cutting into my thoughts. I can't help feeling embarrassed that he's caught me staring at him.

"I was just thinking how hot you look when you don't shave." He gives me the most adorable smirk as he kisses my hand. He pulls into a parking spot and I've failed to notice we have gotten off the freeway. He said it was a mall, but it isn't an indoor mall, it is actually a strip mall that goes around in a triangle. There are so many name-brand stores, but I don't have a lot of money on me. I'm hoping the fact that they call it an *outlet mall* means that the prices are really low.

"Where do you want to go first?"

I have no idea. I have nothing and need everything – underwear, bras, jeans, shirts and even shoes. "Um, I don't know."

His lips turn up at the corner as he quickly takes my hand. "Come on. We can start at the Nike store. I need a few things from there." He gives me a handsome smile and I love how at ease he is holding my hand as we walk to the store.

* * * *

Four hours, six stores and countless bags later, we finally make it back to the car. Aerick puts all the bags in the trunk. I never knew that shopping could be so exhausting. I never really had money to just shop like that. Aerick opens my door. I sink down into the comfortable seat and inhale a deep breath, relieved that we're done.

I'm still irritated that Aerick wouldn't let me pay for anything. He just kept telling me that I needed to save my money. After the first store, when I realized he wasn't going to let me pay, I tried to limit the things I bought and just get the basic stuff I need. Then, with a little more coaxing from Aerick saying I would need clothes for the gym, or to go out on the water, I picked up a few other things. I wasn't fooled, I know it was his way of getting me to buy more.

I paid him back when I was trying on my undergarments at the last store we went to. I insisted on getting his opinion on several things I was trying on. I could tell he was getting rather uncomfortable in his jeans after the first few lacey bra/underwear sets. Finally, after several more requests for his opinion, he told me he needed to go look for some new socks. Busting up laughing, I felt satisfied that he got what was coming to him.

Once I had finished, I found him and asked him which one he liked better, the black set or the red one. He kissed me hard, grinding himself against me, informing me I would be getting both and he didn't want to hear another word about it. I couldn't help the mile-wide smile that crossed my face as he had to adjust his pants again. It was the most hilarious thing to see him all hot and bothered.

We decide to grab some hamburgers and then get back on the freeway. As I take a bite, he tells me that if traffic is okay, we will be there in just under an hour. An hour until I see my new home. A wave of anxiety hits me and suddenly I'm not so hungry.

"Nadi, eat." His use of my nickname catches my attention because he seems to only use it when he's irritated. I see that his attitude about my appetite has not changed much.

"Fine," I huff. I don't want to fight. We've been having such a great day. There's no need to spoil it now.

He moves his hand off the wheel, making me nervous since his other hand is holding his burger, but I see him bring his knee up to steer. He grabs his phone out of the charger and sets it in my hand. "Here. Pick some music to play," he tells me.

Music: he knows that is the way to calm me. I scroll through his play list and decide I am in the mood for *A Day to Remember.* I turn on the song 'Have Faith in Me,' since it's appropriate for the moment. Glancing over at Aerick, I see a tug at the corner of his lips.

As the song plays, I begin to relax a little and as the song ends, Aerick leans over, pulling my face toward him, and kisses me on my temple. "Don't worry babe, *I'd never let you go.*"

* * * *

We take the Des Moines exit off the freeway. Aerick rolls down his window and inhales the air. I mimic him and it smells funny to me. "What's that smell?"

His face brightens and he squeezes my hand. "That's ocean air."

I look at him, confused. "I thought you lived on The Sound or something like that."

"I do, The Puget Sound is an inlet off the Pacific Ocean."

I've never been to the ocean. It never occurred to me it would smell different. As the water comes into view, I take in the scenery – it's beautiful. After another minute we pull up to a building that says 'Park Place Condos'. Aerick punches in a code to open the chain-linked gate and we drive into the parking garage. Aerick grabs the bags out of the trunk and we go up to the second floor, down a short hallway, to the last of four doors on this floor.

He walks toward the other side of the large condo and sets the bags on a table. Almost in a daze, I walk to the back wall that is covered in floor to ceiling windows looking out at the water. The condo has a beautiful view, sitting back just behind the Marina. My eyes roam around the room. It's spacious and open, but not overwhelmingly large. It feels so light, airy and very clean, with a white and beige color scheme and minimalist style.

My eyes find their way back to Aerick and he's just standing there watching me as he tugs on his lip. He raises an eyebrow at me.

"Your home is beautiful, Aerick."

He walks over to me with an ecstatic expression, placing his hand on my cheek. "This is *our* home now. Come on, let me show you around." He grabs my hand. "This is obviously the living room, dining room and the kitchen," he says, waving his hand around at the open floor plan, then pulls me down past the kitchen, back toward the front door. We go down a hallway and he opens a door. There is a very neat room with a queen size bed, but there's not much in there. "This is the spare bedroom."

Through another door I can see a bathroom and we pause for just a moment so I can look inside. We come to the last door. Aerick seems to pause for a moment, almost unsure of himself, but he shakes it off quickly and opens the door, pulling me through it. I assume this is his bedroom. It's fairly big and is dominated by a huge black four-poster bed that is contrasted by the white color of the walls and floor. There are a few other pieces of standard bedroom furniture that match the bed, and a small black loveseat. It's all spaced out nicely and the bed sits in front of another wall-sized window looking out to the water. *Wow*, this view has to be worth a million dollars. I go and stand in front of the window. *It's so amazing.*

Arms circle around my waist and he lightly runs his lips across my neck. "Do you like it?" he asks hesitantly.

"I love it, Aerick!" I feel him let out a sigh, so I turn around to look at him. "You okay?"

I see him hesitate. "Yeah, it's just... I've never had anyone in my room before, girl or otherwise." He bites his lip and I raise an eyebrow.

"You really expect me to believe that?" There's no way - I know he's been with quite a few women.

"I'm serious. This is kind of like my sanctuary. I don't allow people in here." A sweet ache pulls at my heart.

I angle my head up and give him a kiss. He takes no time at all before deepening it, but his kiss is much rougher than it usually is. He picks me up quickly and carries me to the bed, laying me on my back as he crawls over me. I can feel his desperation, almost like he's afraid I'm going to disappear. "I have been dreaming about what it would be like to have you in my bed," he whispers to me between hungry kisses.

"Well, I'm here now. So, what are you going to do with me?" I ask, trying to be playful, but it comes out too breathy because all I want right now is him inside me. He pulls off his shirt and his lust-filled eyes mirror my feelings. He quickly removes my pants, then his own, and positions himself back over me.

"Babe, I swear I'll make love to you later, but right now I need this," he says, before pushing into me. "Always so wet for me," he growls as he instantly starts to move inside me. His kisses become feverish and he moves quicker and quicker in me and his lips move down to my neck. The deep pull in me begins to build quickly as I feel his overwhelming need for me. I try to pull him closer, running my nails down his back, and I'm delighted by the groan that leaves his mouth. I may need this just as much as he does. I lift my hips to meet his and he pushes deeper and deeper into me.

In no time, I'm teetering on the edge. His lips move across my jaw just under my ear. "I love you, Nadalynn," he says roughly and his words cause me to explode around him. "God you're amazing," he tells me as he spills himself into me after a few more thrusts. He rolls off me and we both try to catch our breath. That was quick, but oh-so-satisfying.

Once our breathing has evened out a little, he rolls on his side to face me. "Sorry babe, I couldn't help myself."

I snicker because there's no reason to apologize. "Aerick, you can feel free to do that to me anytime. There's nothing to be sorry for."

He kisses me on my nose. "I will keep that in mind. Now, how about we get your stuff put away? Then you can change into something more comfortable and we can walk around for a bit and go to dinner. I have no food in the house besides a few non-perishables in the cupboard."

I get up and he shows me into the large ensuite, which we get to by walking through a massive walk-in closet, so I can freshen up. After I pee and splash some water on my face I go back into the room. Aerick has brought in the bags and has begun pulling all the clothes out of them. "Tomorrow, I will move some stuff around so you have room to put your stuff, but for now I'm just going to fold it and leave them on the chest."

"I don't need much space, Aerick," I explain, but he just rolls his eyes at me.

He hands me a change of clothes. "Go ahead and change. I'll do this."

He appears a bit tense, as if he's a little uncomfortable, so I set the clothes down and circle my arms around him. "You okay, babe?" I ask him hesitantly.

After a moment, he relaxes into me and his arms around slide around my waist, before kissing the top of my head. "I'm fine, it's just a little weird for me. It's been just me for so long, but don't worry about it. Go on and get dressed. I want to show you around." A wave of excitement washes over me and I take the clothes to change in the bathroom.

The black skinny jeans and cute blue blouse Aerick handed me fit perfectly. There is something to be said about the way it feels to put on new clothes. It's not something I'm too used to, growing up with older sisters. I find a brush in a drawer and run it through my hair. Everything here is so neat, and in its own place. I'm starting to think Aerick has O.C.D. I do slightly, but I think his far exceeds mine. When I exit, he has all my clothes folded nicely on the chest and he's changed into a tight white shirt that goes well with his dark jeans. So simple but so sexy.

"Ready?" he asks and I nod. I quickly put on my new Skechers tennis shoes and we head out the door.

We exit the lobby and Aerick has my hand in his again. We walk down to the marina and out onto the long dock. "Those are Maury and Vashon Islands. There are lots of them up and down The Sound. Sometime in the next few weeks we can go exploring if you like. There's a lot of different things to see."

My face lights up. "I would love that."

* * * *

By the time we get back to the condo, the sun is setting. We walked all around town, Aerick showing me where everything was. Pretty much everything needed is within walking distance, though there are no fast food places in downtown Des Moines, but there are several restaurants to eat at. We went to dinner at 'Wally's Chowder House' and grabbed a few groceries for tomorrow.

I walk into the kitchen to put away the leftovers and when I open the door, there's absolutely nothing in it. It looks almost brand new. I grab out a few Coronas before shutting the door and handing him one. We go out and sit on the patio seat to watch the sunset. I sit with my legs over his lap and my head on his arm. We sit in a comfortable silence, just enjoying each other's presence.

"Are you happy?" Aerick asks me after a while.

I tear my gaze away from the star lit sky, my brows pulling together. "I couldn't be happier, Aerick." Maybe he's having second thoughts about this. "Are you happy?" I ask, but I'm not sure I want to know the answer.

After a beat, he smiles widely. He leans in and kisses me softly. "Not to sound corny, but this is literally a dream come true." I stare deep into his beautiful eyes and I'm a hundred percent sure, I'm exactly where I want to be.

He kisses me again, grabbing me around my waist and under my legs as he stands up. I grab his neck, holding on, and giggle out of shock. "I think I made a promise to you earlier, and I plan on keeping that promise." *How flipping cute can he be?!*

He moves us into the room and lays me gently on the bed. "Welcome home, babe," he says with so much affection, before making sweet love to me. Taking his time, loving, worshiping each and every part of me until we are both completely exhausted. As I lie on his chest, close to unconsciousness, I can't help but wonder how long this dream can last. Nothing good in my life ever lasts.

CHAPTER FOUR

(Saturday, October 3rd)

"HOW IN THE world did you get this number?" Aerick growls loudly as I slip on one of his tee shirts now that I'm clean from my bath. He sounds down right pissed. Please tell me that it isn't Liz. I don't want to deal with that bitch today. It's been such a wonderful day.

"I don't want to speak with him… You tell me!"

I stop brushing my hair. *Who in the world is he talking to?*

"*WHAT?* When?" His loud, cold tone sends a chill down my spine. I step out of the bathroom and look toward the bed where I left him lounging and reading a book, but he's no longer on it. He is standing next to the bed, his back to me.

He's just standing there, unnaturally still. Every muscle is flexed and it looks like he's not even breathing. *What the heck is going on?* I don't know what's wrong with him. I'm not sure if I should try to comfort him or let him be. He doesn't like showing weakness, and the few occasions he's done it, the result is him being hard on himself for letting me see him weak.

"I'm still here, and I don't want to see him." He rubs the back of his neck and his voice goes quiet. All the anger is gone and has been replaced with something else, but I can't tell if he's upset or nervous.

"He doesn't care about anyone but himself... I'll call *you* tomorrow." His voice has turned totally professional. Confusion and nervousness are buzzing through my body. He ends the call but continues to stand completely still as he looks at the floor.

Finally getting up the nerve, I move over to him. There's an overwhelming need in me to know what's going on – I've never seen him like this. I hesitate for a moment behind him before very slowly putting my hand on his shoulder. "Babe, is everything okay?" I ask softly.

I wait but he doesn't answer me. "Aerick, who was on the phone?" I give him a second and just when I think he isn't going to answer me, he turns around quickly, but doesn't look at me. My hand falls back to my side in slow motion and the tension spewing from him is almost suffocating.

It takes him another minute to answer me. "My mother," he says, completely void of emotion. His eyes are somewhere far off. It's starting to really worry me.

He moves past me and walks out of our room. *His mother*. He still hasn't told me much about his parents, other than the fact that they were cold, calculating, and he completely hated them. They expected nothing less than perfection from him growing up, causing him to be extremely competitive, to be the best. They also caused him to look at himself extremely negatively, since he never really could live up to their expectations.

A frown pastes itself on my face at the thought, and I follow him out of the room. He enters the kitchen and pulls a bottle of whiskey out of the cupboard. I stop on the other side of the room as I see him gulp down a long swig of it right out of the bottle.

"Aerick. What's wrong?"

He begins breathing heavily and I see the anger rise in his face like a rapidly heated thermometer. I don't know what to do; I feel so helpless. He won't look at me, he won't talk to me, he's lost in his own world, and I'm failing to break through to him. He gulp down another long drink and slams the bottle back on the counter. I jump slightly as the loud noise echoes in the room. He grabs the neck of the bottle with both of his hands. I see him trying to reel in his anger as he twists his fingers around the bottle as if he was trying to squeeze water out of a towel.

He isn't talking to me, so I guess the only other thing to do is to try to comfort him physically until he's ready to talk to me. I move a step forward and he suddenly picks up the bottle, making me stop.

"FUCK!" he screams and throws the bottle down on the floor with an unbelievable force. I turn quickly, trying to avoid the pieces of glass that fly out in every direction.

A tightening begins building in my chest. I don't know what to do: for the first time ever, Aerick is scaring the daylights out of me. I gaze up at him. His hands are resting on the edge of the counter and he's breathing heavily. A tear slips down my cheek as I try focusing on my breathing. I know Aerick would never hurt me, but I'm so frightened right now.

He finally looks over at me and I can only stare back. After a moment, concern replaces a bit of the anger in his eyes. He straightens up, taking a step toward me, and I move a step back purely out of reflex, making him freeze again. He quickly takes in the mess on the floor and then glances at me again before he closes his eyes and tilts his head to the ceiling. "Fucking screw up," he says to himself. Another tear escapes my eye and right now I want nothing more than to go over and hold him and explain to him that he's not a screw up, but I'm frozen in place.

When he finally opens his eyes, they fall down to the floor again and I can tell he's extremely angry, not just at whatever upset him to begin with, but he's upset with himself as well, knowing that he has frightened me. He opens his mouth as if to say something, but then closes it again. His hands fist at his side. *What the hell is going on?* Tears begin to flow freely down my cheeks as the rest of my body is frozen in place.

His gaze finally comes back to me and he has calmed himself just a little. "I'm sorry," he says, in a voice so quiet I almost didn't hear him, but what worries me more than his tone, is that his eyes are glazed over. He walks around the kitchen island, grabs his sneakers and heads for the door, yanking it open with immense force.

"Aerick?" I whisper. I only know he heard me because of the very brief pause in his stride before he slams the front door shut behind him.

He's gone.

For what seems like the hundredth time in the last few minutes, I wonder what's going on. I fall to my knees and try to calm myself before I pass out from lack of oxygen. I squeeze my eyes shut. *Push away all thoughts and focus on your breathing. Breathe in, one, two, three, four. Breathe out, one, two, three, four. Breathe in, one, two, three, four. Breathe out, one, two, three, four.* I hear Christian's voice in my head, coaching me through my panic attack. It starts to work, and my breathing finally begins to return to normal. The swimming dizziness in my head recedes.

I open my eyes to the mess laid out in front of me and I'm at a loss. I have no idea where he went, when he'll be back, or if he even wants me here. In the back of my mind, I knew this was too good to be true.

Well, shit. It isn't like I can go anywhere right now since I have no car, and no idea where to go. I could always call Paulo since he lives close, but I shake off the thought almost as quickly as it enters my mind. I know he would come, but then what? What would I say to him? Aerick likes to keep his private life private, and I really don't want to ask Paulo for help. I'm not some weak little girl that needs rescuing whenever something bad happens. Right now, I just want to crawl into bed, but I can't leave this mess. Taking another deep breath, I let out a sigh to release the last bit of anxiety from my panic attack.

I stand up and get the broom, trying to be careful not to cut myself on all the glass everywhere. Today was such a wonderful day and it has been marred by something that I have no clue about. I don't want to think about what just happened, so I try to focus my mind somewhere else.

This whole week was nothing less than a dream come true. We spent all week hanging out together. Every morning we went to the gym, which he explained was his normal morning routine. He told me I didn't have to go with him, but I really wanted to. The mile run to the gym and the workout reminded me a lot of camp and it felt oddly comforting. Having him beside me as an equal instead of my instructor was kind of different, but in a good way. Although he still acted like my instructor, occasionally correcting my form or pushing me to do more sets to improve my strength, my love for him just continued to grow.

The owner of the gym, Amar, is quite handsome for an older man. He immediately took a liking to me, much to Aerick's irritation. However, I believe the irritation was only due to the fact that another man was giving me so much attention. Aerick taught a few self-defense classes this week and Amar graciously let me sit in on them, although I did not participate. I watched Aerick closely, trying to remember how he executed each move, just like when we were at camp. He's really good at his job. I always thought his hard-core attitude was just to intimidate, but now, evaluating it from the other side, it seems that it's to just push people to the limit that he's certain they can achieve. Just like he pushed my limits and ultimately helped me.

Our morning workouts weren't the only thing we did every day. We have quickly fallen into a routine. Every morning we wake up tangled around each other and after some kind of amazing sexual activity, I make us breakfast before we go workout. He was insistent on making us lunch, since I made breakfast, and then we would go out to dinner each night. Not always fancy places, but anywhere we could just go sit and eat. We spent each night wrapped in each other's arms, fulfilling our insatiable hunger for each other. I have never been so content before in my life.

Today we spent the entire day downtown. We went and explored the famous Pike Place Market. There were so many cool booths and stores. Aerick was very patient as I stopped at many of them to explore. Occasionally I would buy something, or Aerick would buy it for me. This time around he actually let me pay for a few things, now that my check had been deposited in the bank and I had a nice new bank card that I was itching to use. I think he let me pay more for my enjoyment, since I actually told him that.

We joked and fondled each other as we watched the men throwing fish around. We took a few pictures of the different things around the pier while he told me a bunch of Seattle's history, like the great fire and how there is a tour you can take of what they call the 'Underground Seattle', a place that was built over afterward. He promised he would bring me one day, which excited me, giving me even more to look forward to. He was really knowledgeable about everything and it was interesting to hear about it all.

After the market, we went on the Seattle Great Wheel and had dinner at this awesome little place on the pier. Other than the guy that hit on me in the market, causing Aerick to get a little 'overprotective', it was such a great day. We got home late and Aerick chose to sit and read a book, while I decided I needed a relaxing bath after walking all day.

The tub in the ensuite is to die for, and I had picked up some bath salts at the market. I remember thinking how sexy he looked, barefoot in his jeans and tee shirt that hugged his perfectly chiseled upper body. It took all my will power to not ask him to join me, but I knew that my sexual needs would be satisfied once I got into bed. It's why I had chosen to wear his shirt to bed. I'd quickly found out earlier in the week that he loved it when I wore nothing but his shirt to bed. *So much for that idea.*

Standing up, I grab the bowl of soapy water I just used to clean up the floor and cupboards. The smell of whiskey still permeates the room, but I'm not sure how to clean it up any better. I've washed down the entire floor, all the way out into the dining room, and have scrubbed down all the cabinets on the lower half of the kitchen.

As I take in the condo, I realize how cold and empty if feels without him here. Come to think about it, this is the first time I've been here by myself. I miss him so much already and it's only been an hour. The smell of whiskey is really starting to irritate me, when it occurs to me that it splashed on me when he broke the bottle. I bring the shirt up to my nose and smell it. Sure enough, I'm smelling what's on my shirt. It's going to take another shower to be rid of this smell.

I go into the bathroom and turn on the shower. I start to put my hair up in a high bun and catch a glimpse of myself in the mirror, causing me to freeze. There is a small trail of blood leading from my neck down under the neckline of the shirt. As I examine it closer, it looks like a piece of glass must have cut me despite the distance that was between us. I inspect the rest of my body and there are a couple more nicks on my legs but nothing bad.

I inspect each one, making sure there isn't glass in any of them, and get into the shower to clean myself up. I stand under the stream of water, letting it wash away the last few hours. I begin to relax; my neck and shoulder muscles are noticeably sore from the tension that built up.

When I finally run out of hot water, I turn it off and wrap myself in a towel before I examine the cut on my neck again. It's so bad now, but it's very noticeable because it's red and several inches long. At least it isn't deep. I throw on another one of Aerick's shirts, along with a pair of underwear, and go into the bedroom, stopping at the foot of the bed. I can almost see him standing there again, upset on the phone with his mother.

That's another thing I don't get. He told me it had been a long time since he'd talked to his parents. *Why would his mom be calling him after all this time?* I'm assuming the person he didn't want to talk to was his dad, but I could be wrong. *What could make him so upset?* Not just upset, there were so many other emotions that had crossed his face in the few minutes it had taken him to get the phone call and leave.

Not to mention, something that hit him so deep that he had appeared to completely forget anything else in the world existed, including me. There's so much about him I don't know, and I wonder if this is the beginning of the end. I can't help but hear his words from what seems like so long ago. *'As much as I hate to say it, there is a good chance I will hurt you, because I tend to fuck up anything good in my life.'* Strangely enough, nothing good in my life ever stays, which makes our whole situation a disaster waiting to happen.

Where is he? I'm beginning to really worry about him. He left his phone on the counter and I have no idea where he would go this late, so I can't even go attempt to find him. I feel so tired and worn out. I don't feel right sleeping in here without him, so I grab the small fleece blanket out of the chest and go into the living room. Sitting myself on the couch in front of the big window, I stare out over the water. The moon is shining bright on the water and I have only left the dim light on in the kitchen, so the condo is fairly dark.

I draw in a deep breath and hope he'll come home soon. I don't care what he did or how he freaked out on me, I just want to know he's okay. I lay my head against the back of the couch and stare out of the window. Eventually exhaustion takes over and I fall into the blackness of unrestful sleep.

* * * *

I wake up to the strong smell of whiskey and I wonder if I didn't clean up well enough. Then I feel something lightly stroke my neck. My eyes fly open to see Aerick sitting next to me, staring at the cut on my neck. I immediately feel relief that he's home safely, then I really look over him. He off somehow. His eyes and face are drooping, his shoulders are slumped over uncharacteristically, and that overpowering smell makes my stomach sink. He's obviously drunk – not just drunk, but really drunk. He continues to stare at my neck. All the anger is gone, and his eyes are so sad.

"Babe?" I say cautiously, a little unsure of what to expect. His eyes move up to find mine and he swallows loudly.

"I'd that, din't I?" he slurs. Definitely really drunk.

I sigh loudly; at least he's back home. "I'm fine, Aerick. Are you okay?" I remove his hand from my neck and hold it between both of mine.

His eyes fall to my hands. "Don't," he tells me quietly.

"Don't what?" I'm not sure what the world he's talking about.

"I fuuucked up. 'ust like alwaysss." *Crap.*

I'm not in the mood for his self-pity. "Aerick, stop now."

He suddenly pulls his hand out of mine. "S'ok, I under..." His voice trails off before he finishes his thought and he certainly isn't making much sense.

"*Under* what?" I try to get out a better response.

"I huuurt you. Youuu and it, I don't serv you!" His voice is becoming harsh. I need to get him to bed so he can sleep this off.

I grab his face and make him look me in my eyes. "Stop," I say with as much authority as I can muster, then stand up.

"Sorrry Pincess, I really looove you. S'rry."

I shake my head. "Aerick, come on." I grab his hand and try to pull him up off the couch but he's too heavy. "Aerick, come on, get up," I whine; I'm already exhausted. He gazes at me, pulling his eyebrows together, and I pull him up again, this time successfully, but he's very unsteady on his feet.

"You kiiickin me outtt?" *Seriously?*

"Come on, Aerick." I pull him toward the room and he stumbles forward, only staying on his feet because I grab him with all my strength to steady him.

I somehow manage to get him to our room and he drops sideways onto the mattress hard, causing the mattress to bounce under his weight. Shaking my head, I kneel down and begin to remove his shoes.

"H'sss right." Now what is he talking about? "No one marrry my f'ckin asssss." *Marry? What?* "Our kidddds 'ill hhhate me." *OUR KIDS!*

Okay he's really out of it. I shake my head. *Just ignore it, Nadi.* I get up and try to pull him over to get him to lie properly on the bed but it's useless, he's out. *Dammit!* I glance down at him and wonder what's going through his head.

I'm obviously not going to get him to move onto the bed properly and there's no way I can lift his dead weight. I go around the other side of the bed, grab a pillow and, without being gentle, shove it under his head. Then on to my next problem. He may be warm fully-clothed, but I'm cold. I walk back out into the living room and retrieve the blanket. As I walk back into the room, I focus on Aerick. I hadn't noticed before, but his clothes are a bit dirty. I examine him closer and notice there's a slight bruise on his cheek. I pick up his hand but there are no indications that he hit anyone or anything. *Was he fighting?*

I pull up his shirt, checking for damage, and sure enough, there's a large bruise on his ribs. *Dammit.* I peek over to the clock. It's just after three in the morning. Okay, so the bars closed over an hour ago. Where has he been? He has a lot of explaining to do in the morning.

Carefully, my fingers feel around his head to make sure there are no lumps, in case he was hit in the head. Satisfied that the damage is minimal, I grab a pillow and crawl onto the bed sideways next to him.

On my back, the evening replays in my head on a constant loop. I'm so confused, irritated, upset, and at a loss of what to do. These feelings sucks and I want nothing more than to talk to Jeff. I crave his wisdom right now, but it's still way too early in Chicago.

Suddenly Aerick shifts and lays his head across my stomach, taking me by surprise. "Nadalynn," he whispers.

"Yeah, babe?" I quietly answer. His tone is so much different than it was a little bit ago. He doesn't say anything for a minute and I'm not sure if he's awake or talking in his sleep.

His arm fold around me tightly. "Don't leave me." His voice is so distant, I'm fairly certain he's asleep. I breathe in deeply, running my fingers through his hair, and even though he's heavy, I don't try to move him. "Stay, please." His pleading whispers come again.

"Aerick, you awake?" I ask quietly, trying to figure out if he really is sleeping, and within a minute he's snoring lightly.

I take another deep breath. I have no idea what tomorrow is going to bring, but right now I'm done trying to figure things out in my head. I close my eyes, continuing to stroke his hair, and try getting the thought out of my head as to why he thinks I'll leave. I feel a tear fall down the side of my face. The thought of leaving him actually hurts deep in my chest. I don't know why in the world he thinks I would leave him. I was more worried about him leaving me.

"I'm not going anywhere," I tell him softly before I succumb to an exhausted sleep.

CHAPTER FIVE

(Sunday, October 4th)

I WAKE UP uncomfortably hot, unable to breathe fully, and needing to pee badly. I open my eyes to see Aerick is curled up with his head still on my chest and his arm draped over me. There's still the stale stench of alcohol on him. *Christ.* Last night was so crazy.

He moves his arm slightly, causing my bladder to scream at me, before my thoughts can run away with my head. I very carefully slide out from under him, not wanting to wake him just yet. It's eight-thirty, later than we'd usually lie in, but five hours' sleep isn't enough after how drunk he was last night.

After using the bathroom, I search the cabinets until I find some Advil – he'll need it. I fill the glass on the bathroom counter with water and go back to the room, leaving them both on the night table. I shake my head as I stare down at him. It always shocks me how young and peaceful he looks when he sleeps.

I'm bothered by the now evident bruise on his cheek. My body is buzzing; I need to do something. I can't sit here, or my thoughts are going to start running wild. I cover him with the blanket and quickly kiss him on his temple; he stirs for a second, but stays asleep.

I go to the kitchen to make coffee. My body still feels tired but there's no way my mind is going to let me sleep, at least not for a while. Once the coffee is on, I stare in the fridge absentmindedly. Thankfully we went grocery shopping the day after we arrived. I decide to make him some breakfast, which may be more than he deserves after last night, but my good nature wins the internal conflict. I take a deep, calming breath. My nose wrinkles upward as it's filled with the faint smell of alcohol.

My OCD'ness gets the better of me and because he probably will sleep for a few more hours, I decide to wash down the floor again before cooking breakfast. Besides, cleaning gives me a weird sense of relief when I have pent up irritation and frustration. I get the bowl I used last night back out and fill it with hot soapy water and then decide to add a touch of bleach. I'm probably the weirdest person in the world, because I actually like the smell of it. To me, bleach is what *clean* smells like.

I find my iPod and turn on my music loud to drown out all my thoughts. I start washing down cabinets and the entire floor, singing each song to myself so there's no room for my mind to wander. Like last night, I go all the way out to the dining room, but I don't stop there. I end up washing the entire kitchen and dining room floors, as well as the floor in the entryway. I'm surprised that the floor really isn't very dirty. It must be his OCD. My lips turn up a little at the thought of him on his knees scrubbing the floor as I rinse out the bowl.

I wander over to the window looking out to the water. Clouds have rolled in overnight and covered up the beautiful blue sky. It's funny how the change in weather seems to match my change in mood since yesterday. Again, I don't want to think about that stuff right now. Searching through the songs on my iPod, I decide to listen to something a little heavy and turn on the *Full Devil Jacket* album that Aerick added onto it. I immediately fell in love with the entire album the first time I heard it.

Back in the kitchen, I start pulling out the stuff to make breakfast. It's already almost ten so it's more like brunch. I start in preparing some shredded potatoes, bacon and eggs. I keep my music up loud, singing along so I have to concentrate on the words instead of letting my mind run rampant.

With breakfast ready, I stop and draw in a breath. *I feel mighty accomplished for this morning,* I muse as I attempt to take a drink of my already empty coffee cup.

Coffee, I need more coffee.

I turn toward the coffee pot and I'm startled as I see Aerick leaning against the back of the couch, watching me. He appears freshly showered, wearing shorts and a tank top. *How long has he been standing there?* I pull my ear buds out, but he just continues to stare at me as he bites the inside of his cheek, something like shame written all over his face.

After a minute, I inhale a deep breath, and take the food to the table before grabbing us both a cup of coffee. As I set them on the table, I glare at Aerick who is still rooted in place and raise an eyebrow, silently asking him if he is going to join me for breakfast. His eyes drop to the ground as he pushes off the couch, coming to sit at the table.

I sit down as well but feel uneasy. I don't like the tension between us, and I really wish I knew what he was thinking, but I'm not sure if I should start questioning him or if I should wait to see if he explains himself. We sit in a deafening silence for several minutes and I can no longer hold my tongue.

"What happened last night?" I ask, trying not to sound too harsh, but the irritation in my voice is clear.

He puts his fork down and inhales a deep breath. "I'm sorry about last night."

"About which part," I scoff, before the filter to my mouth can kick in. He glances up at me with sad eyes and I feel a stab of guilt at my harshness.

"All of it. None of it was your fault and I had no right to take it out on you. Do- do you want to leave?"

I close my eyes and sigh. Right now, that's the last thing on my mind.

"I understand. I'll pay for your flight home." His voice is quiet; he sounds so defeated, but it just makes me annoyed all over again.

"Aerick, I don't want to leave, okay? This is my home. I just want to understand what happened last night. We had the most amazing day, then you get a phone call and completely freak out."

He gapes at me, confused. "You mean you–"

"Stop, Aerick. I said I don't want to leave."

He finally meets my eyes and I see that his are filled with longing. My frustration dissipates and when he clasps my hand, gently pulling me to him, I willingly get up and move around the table to him. He pulls me down onto his lap, arms wrapping tightly around me as he buries his face against my neck.

"Please forgive me, babe. I fucked up last night. I just – I just totally lost it." He pulls back a little and kisses the scratch on my neck. "And I hurt the only person left in this world that I care about."

I pull away, holding his jaw so he focuses on me. "I'm fine."

"Dammit, Nadi, you're not fine. I shattered a bottle and it cut you. Then I left you in the middle of a panic attack. I mean, I scared the shit out of you and then just took off like a fucking coward because I couldn't deal with my own messed up feelings."

He turns away, but not before I see that tears forming in the corners of his eyes. By this point I'm swarming wreck of emotions myself. It hurts me to see him in so much pain; at the same time, I'm exasperated that he thinks he would lose me over something like this. *Haven't we been through enough for him to know I'm not easily scared off?* Still, the biggest question is what set him off in the first place, and why he couldn't just open up about it.

"Aerick, I'm a big girl and I can deal with my own panic attacks. You didn't scare me, I just freaked out a little because I've never seen you act like that," I lie to him. "It would help if you would tell me what your mother told you to make you react like that."

He leans his forehead on my shoulder, and I give him a minute to answer me.

"My grandfather died," he whispers as I feel him swallow a lump in his throat. I don't remember him saying anything about a grandfather.

"Damn, Aerick, I'm sorry."

"He was the closest thing I had to a normal parent." He takes a deep breath before continuing. "My real parents only cared about what I looked like to everyone else. They wanted perfect sons and my brother and I were pushed, hard. Piano, guitar, French lessons, sports… our days were planned out from sunrise to sunset. Maybe it didn't seem that bad to most people, but they didn't see what went on behind closed doors. The way they treated us – well, me more than my brother. He's older than me, and everything always came naturally to him. He was the favorite." He pauses and the look in his eyes gets far away for a moment before he shakes out his head and continues.

"My father would be downright cruel to me. I was the 'accident' of the family. They never planned to have me, and he made sure I knew it. I tried my hardest to live up to their standards, but I couldn't, which often got me a smack with the belt. I knew better than to act out in front of him, so I just held it in. By the time I reached high school, I couldn't handle it anymore and started fighting. I didn't care about winning. It was just the only way to let go of some of the anger, and then for a while after I'd feel nothing… just numb.

"The only good thing in my life was my grandfather. My father's dad wasn't exactly a big huggable bear, but we were very close. He didn't show much emotion, but he also never put me down a day in my life. I could tell he disapproved of the way my parents treated me and he always put in his words of wisdom when he could. That man had a way with words. I swear he was the only person that kept me half sane. The best memories I have as a child all include him.

"On rare occasions, my father would agree to let him take me fishing. We'd sit there for hours, not say a word the whole time – we didn't need to. It might not appear like much, but for me it was an escape. Sitting out there, I didn't have to worry about my shitty life back home – no parents, no work or practice sessions, no one to tell me what a fuck-up I was. Just me and my grandfather, catching fish, and him sharing his occasional words of wisdom. He was the only person I truly cared about growing up and now he's gone."

My heart is crushed as I hear the sadness etched in his voice. I can't help but wrap my arms around him and he pulls me tighter to him.

"Crap, I don't know what I would do if I didn't have you right now. I can't even begin to tell you how sorry I am for last night." He pulls back, searching for something in my eyes. "But I swear to you, I will spend the rest of my life trying to make it up to you." He kisses my lips so softly and then pulls me back into a tight embrace.

"I love you, Aerick. I'll always be here for you," I whisper.

"I know. I love you too and I should have never shut you out like that. Please forgive me, babe."

I relax into him, gently push the hair back from his face. "I forgave you the moment I woke up this morning and knew you were safely back home with me."

Irritation flashes across his face. "Yeah, about that. You didn't happen to take my wallet out of my pants, did you?"

My lips press into a line. "No. Why?"

"Shit. I think I got robbed last night." He lets out a short chuckle and his face relaxes. "Honestly, I don't remember anything. After I left here, I wandered around for a bit before I ended up at the bar down the street. If the gym was open I would have gone there, but it wasn't. I took shot after shot until I blacked out. I wasn't... like, an ass or anything when I got home, was I?"

I deciding not to tell him what he had said. "It wasn't anything I couldn't handle. Although, out of everything that happened last night, what freaked me out the most was not knowing where you were." It was gut wrenching to not know where he was or if he was okay. "I will always be here for you, Aerick. Please don't shut me out like that again, okay?"

"Thanks, babe. Now, I better finish this fine breakfast you made me, because I have several irritating phone calls to make."

* * * *

"Hmm." Soft kisses cover my stomach, waking me from my late afternoon nap. "Wake up, Princess."

"But I don't want to," I whine playfully at him.

"Oh, really? I guess I will go take a cold shower then," he says, and I feel him rise off the bed. My joke seems to have backfired on me.

"I swear on my life, you have exactly two seconds to get back over here!" I hear him chuckle and feel the bed move as he crawls up over me. I finally open my eyes to see his beautiful eyes staring back at me.

"I have a confession to make."

A smile tugs at my lips. "Oh yeah? What's that?"

"I fucking love when you talk to me like that, and right now I want nothing more than to be buried in you." My Aerick is definitely back.

"Well then, by all means, proceed." He gives me his wicked grin and leans in to kiss my lips roughly.

After a moment he stops and pulls back to gaze into my eyes. "You up for trying something different?" His apprehensive look makes me a little nervous.

"Sure," I say, feeling anything but sure. He goes into the closet and quickly comes back out with something behind his back. I have to say, I'm a bit intrigued by the excited vibe I'm getting from him. He sits down next to me and I give him a questioning look. Leaning down, he kisses me passionately, making the world around me fall away. He pulls me to sit up without breaking our deepening kiss. He quickly pulls my shirt off, only breaking our kiss for the half a second it took for the shirt to clear our lips, and I am vaguely aware he has laid me back again.

He pauses for a brief moment but doesn't remove his lips from mine. "If at any time it is too much, you tell me immediately okay." My excitement keeps me from uttering a word. "Answer me or I will stop now."

"Okay, I'll tell you. I promise."

His mischievous smirk returns. "Give me your hands." I comply with his request and he grasps my hands in his. He bends down, kissing the center of each of my palms before gazing down into my eyes.

"I love you more than anything and I would never hurt you. What I am going to do will require you to give me your trust. Do you trust me?" The word 'yes' is out of my mouth without a thought and he leans back down, kissing me more roughly than before, then sits back up, staring intently into my eyes. He turns my hands so my palms are toward each other and holds both of them together in his one hand while he reaches for something behind him without breaking eye contact. As his hand comes back forward, my eyes glance to see what it is.

He's holding a black tie in his hand. I give him a questioning look, but he doesn't say anything. He holds the thicker end of the tie and wraps it around both my hands and then loops it between them before knotting it. The way he is biting at his bottom lip is so hot and my excitement makes an appearance in my panties. I have to admit, I wasn't sure what to expect, but this sure wasn't it. Now that it's happening, I'm a little excited.

We've never done anything like this, but any time we've had sex or made love, it's been nothing short of mind blowing. When he makes sure my hands are secure to his liking, he grabs my waist with both hands and pushes me up to one of the corners on the bed. I can't move my eyes off his face but out of the corner of my vision, I see him tie the other end to the bedpost.

When he's done, he has a look of satisfaction on his face. As he stares down to me, he bites his lip and then places another rough kiss on my lips before moving his mouth near my ear. "You okay, Princess?" he asks in a seductively low voice.

"Yes," I whisper back, too distracted by his warm lips kissing and sucking down my throat. *Damn, that feels amazing.* He doesn't stop, just continues to work his way down my body. No matter how many times he does this, I never get tired of how it feels.

"Now you can't get away from me," I barely hear him whisper on my stomach. When he makes it down to my leggings, He peels them off slowly, taking my underwear with them. His eyes follow his hands as the lust takes over him. He drags his fingers up and down the inside of my thighs. His fingernails run over the most sensitive spot between my pelvis and my upper thigh, causing my eyes squeeze shut and a moan to escape my mouth. He pulls me down a little, so my arms are fully extended. My eyes fly back open and I'm met with an evil but sexy smirk. He moves between my legs, pushing them apart, and begins kissing my stomach again before moving lower. He bites lightly along the front of my pelvis, extracting another moan from me.

He licks slowly all the way up my folds and then blows lightly over the area, sending chills up my body. "Holy fuck, Aerick!" I moan and I feel his lips turn up on mine.

"You like that, Princess?" I answer with a moan as he does it yet again.

"Always so wet for me. Hmmm, I will never tire of tasting you." He does it again and then circles his tongue around my bundle of nerves, eliciting a gasp out of me. I feel the tug deep in me start to build as he begins alternating between licking, sucking, and lightly biting me. I begin to squirm, causing him to fold his arms around my thighs and hold me down by my hips. The ache in me climbs higher and I pull at my wrists but they don't move. I've always resorted to pulling his hair as a way of coping with the intense feeling that builds inside me, but now I'm unable to do that. I moan even louder than normal as a result.

"That's right, Princess. Let me hear you." His sexy encouragement causes me to get even louder. Right now, it's the only reprieve I can get from his skillful tongue. Just when I don't think it can get more intense, I feel his fingers enter me, pushing me even closer to the inevitable. He doesn't let up as I whimper his name, pleading with him. It just drives him more as I feel his fingers move with expert persistence, pushing me to the edge. With a final nip at my clit, I'm sent spiraling over the edge, screaming his name as I fall over. As my orgasm nears the end, he quickly removes his fingers and begins licking hungrily while his thumb applies pressure to my oversensitive clit, sending another round of shockwaves through me.

Wow, that was intense. He doesn't let me rest long. Before I know it, he's naked and positioned between my legs and he thrusts into me hard. "Holy Fuck," he grunts. "That was for you, Princess." He moves slowly until he's fully out of me, causing me to whimper at the loss of contact. "And this is for me," he growls as he slams back into me again. He continues at an achingly slow pace, pulling out of me and slamming back into me over and over.

His roughness is a welcome feeling after the tension of the last twenty-four hours. "Faster, Aerick," I plead with him, needing more of him.

"That's right Princess, tell me what you want." He grips my hips tighter as he slams into me once more.

"Faster... please," I beg, needing to reach another release before I go crazy.

"That's my girl." He pauses and reaches over me, grabbing the pillow, folding it and sliding it under my hips, lifting me higher, and the next time he slams into me, he reaches even deeper in me.

"Ahh!" I scream.

"Let me hear you baby." He finally begins to pick up the pace, continuing to hit inside me harder and harder. His grunts and moans push me into unknown territory and I can't hold on much longer. "Fucking. Let. Go," he grunts in between thrusts as I begin to flutter around his engorged length. With one last thrust, I'm sent into another world as my body gives in, convulsing from head to toe. His hard thrusts continue for only a moment longer as he finds his own release, growling some form of my name through his gritted teeth, his spasming member pushing me back up into the clouds yet again.

By the time I become aware of the world around me again, he has untied my hands and is massaging my wrist and arms as I lie on his chest. "You back with me yet?" he says with amusement.

I tilt me head back to gaze in his eyes. "Hmmm."

He brings my hand up and kisses my palm. "Did you enjoy that, Princess?"

Like he has to ask. "Hmmm."

I feel his chuckle in his chest. "Speechless, I hear. Exactly how I like you." I shake my head because frankly, I can hardly move. I lightly graze my finger across his chest, and he leans down kissing, my forehead.

We lie in a comfortable silence and I'm close to falling back into my slumber. "I called my mom while you were asleep," he says quietly. My voice still hasn't recovered, so I move my fingers across his chest again to let him know I'm still listening. "You'll be meeting my family on Saturday."

CHAPTER SIX

(Saturday, October 10th)

AERICK POV

"AERICK, RELAX!" SHE tells me for the fifth time. The tension is probably rolling off me in waves – it's been building all week. I've tried to convince her that I'm not nervous, but in reality, I'm a mess inside. The only person I ever planned for and was excited to have Nadi meet was my grandfather. The rest of my family don't deserve the pleasure of meeting her and it would have made me content if she never had to endure what she is about to experience. There's no doubt in my mind, it's going to be unpleasant. I could really use my grandpa's advice right about now.

My brain is still trying to grasp the idea that he's gone. We spoke just the week before camp ended and decided to get together for lunch so he could meet her. Unfortunately, we never got the chance. It makes it all the harder for me. We should have done it sooner; if only I hadn't been so nervous about it. His opinion was the only one that mattered to me, and now he'll never know the woman that means so much to me. He's never going to get to see her beautiful smile, experience her smart mouth, engage her intelligence, or hear her heartfelt laugh. *Stop!* I have to stop thinking about that right now. I refuse to let my family see me weak.

Trying to prepare for today, I spent all week trying to relieve the tension at the gym. Nadi's been so great letting me deal with this in my own way. She just sat aside, watching me at the gym and, on a few occasions, joined me.

Amar has taken to her rather well. A few times, my hits to the bag were much harder, and it wasn't because of my family. Amar always is around, talking to her, and I don't like the cute giggles he gets out of her. She's *mine* and he really needs to back the fuck off. In the rational part of my mind, I know there's nothing to worry about, but it still irritates me. The one thing that's held me back is the many times I would catch her peeking at me with those beautiful green eyes, when Amar thinks he has all her attention. I've had to continue to reel in my irritation when it comes to men being around her.

I'm pulled out of my thoughts by a light touch as she pulls my hand up off the stick shift and brings it to her cheek. I glance over at her and she's watching at me with those soulful eyes. "Relax, it is going to be okay," she says again, with an overjoyed expression that could knock my socks off. Christ, this woman is the greatest. My lips tug at the corner of my mouth and she turns to kiss my palm that's resting on her cheek. "I love you, Aerick."

"I know, Princess." I slide my hand back to her neck, pulling her over to me so I can kiss her forehead. I don't tell her 'I love her' as much as I should, but she doesn't appear bothered by it. I really do love her; it just isn't a phrase I'm too familiar with, and saying it is still rather difficult. In fact, that's one thing I love about her. She is not one of those insecure women that needs to hear it all the time. Nothing about her is traditional, for that matter.

Most women would have been out the door in a minute after what

I did to her last week. She's proven again how much I don't deserve her. I completely zoned out last week, getting that phone call from my mother. The conversation in my head is a little mottled and I only remember bits of it. Mostly phrases such as, 'your dad's father died', and 'myocardial infarction'. Only my parents would refer to a heart attack that way and it bothers me even more that she said, 'my dad's father', like my grandfather had no relation to me.

After hearing her say my grandfather had died, things kind of went into autopilot, almost like I was lost, or there but not there. I didn't know what to do or what to say. My chest was tight and I felt like I was going to explode – which I did in a way. Though I didn't realize it until I was standing in front of a broken bottle and my girl was standing there staring at me, scared out of her mind. She's never seen my anger – my true anger. Only a handful have experienced it at its peak, and in that moment, I just wanted to die. *Fucking idiot.*

I could see it in her eyes, the way she was breathing, how her whole body had gone completely still, she was having a panic attack and it brought me back to reality. In that instant, I've never felt so ashamed. The icing on the cake was seeing the small trickle of blood run down her neck. I'd hurt her, the only girl I have ever cared for, ever loved.

My mind shattered in those few seconds and it made the most sense to leave, before she left me. I know now that my thoughts were stupid and irrational, but in that moment, I couldn't wait for her to walk out on me. With everything that was already crushing my brain, there was no way I would have been able to deal with her rejecting me, so I left her there, frozen in fear.

As I left, she whispered my name, and I thought that was it – that she was done. So, I continued out the door and slammed it behind me before she could say it. My eyes stung just thinking that I may never see her again.

Then I woke up in my own bed with a splitting headache and no idea what happened after I went to the bar. My sub-conscious probably picked that bar because the bartender Greg wouldn't cut me off like he would most people. He's an acquaintance. He knows I live right down the street and that I don't cause problems. I'm not sure how many glasses of whiskey he served me that night, but it must have been a whole bottle because I blacked out – a rarity for me.

At first, I didn't think there was any way she was still there until I squinted over at the clock and saw a glass of water and some Advil. My heart leapt up into my throat. I scrambled out of bed, creeping out of the room to see if she was still in the apartment. She was on her hands and knees on the floor, scrubbing it over and over again like there was an invisible layer of scum that was refusing to go away – she was still mad. It was best to give her a little more time, so I went back and sat on the bed, taking the Advil that I didn't deserve. I deserved all the pain that was pounding at my frontal cortex. I sat there and tried to rationalize why she hadn't left, but then it hit me: she couldn't, because she didn't have anywhere to go. She has no one here and no way to get back to Chicago since she had spent a good part of her check the day before.

I went into the bathroom to clean up before attempting to talk to her. It was only delaying the inevitable, but I had to give myself a minute to gather my thoughts. In the mirror, my eyes were drawn to the nice bruise on my face. For a moment I wondered if it was from her – wouldn't have been the first time, and it wasn't anything I didn't deserve. Then I removed my shirt and saw the rest of the bruises. As I went to remove the contents of my pockets, I realized my wallet was not in my pants and after checking back next to the bed, it was pretty clear where I'd gotten the bruises. Somebody jumped me and took my wallet. Most people aren't stupid enough to mess with me, even when I'm drunk. I must have been really plastered. *Fucking dumbass*!

I tried to mentally prepare myself as I showered and dressed. It was important for me to be strong for her and not let her feel bad for leaving. I didn't deserve her, and she deserved to be happy. It was the least I could do for her.

I went out to the living room. Spotting her in the kitchen, cooking, I couldn't help but stand there and stare at the woman who had turned my life upside down. Thinking back, I think I did it to memorize what I thought would be the last time I'd see her in such a normal setting. I was so sure she wouldn't stay. *I still can't believe she stayed.*

When she said she didn't want to leave and she let me hold her again, it took everything in me not to cry like a little baby. In that minute, I didn't want to be weak in front of her. It was bad enough I couldn't keep the sadness out of my voice, telling her what was going on. As always, she tried to hide her own feelings to make me feel better, but it only made me feel worse because I knew the truth.

I vowed to myself that morning that I'd never do anything to ever hurt her ever again, nor would I let anyone hurt her. I also decided that I'd let her in even more. I was afraid to show her all of me, which was the point of always avoided talking about my past. I'm not sure I can ever really show her everything, but I'm deadset on trying.

That is exactly what I did that evening. Not only did I need to see if she still trusts me for my own sanity, but I needed to show her a bit of me. Letting me tie her up was the ultimate act of trust she could give me after what she went through in the past. She was amazing and seemed to enjoy the rougher side just as much as I did. I've been a little reluctant to tell her about my colorful sexual past, not out of shame, but because I feared it wouldn't be something she's interested in. I've come to know her mind; she would think she was not enough for me if she didn't like it, and I don't ever want her to feel that.

At this point, it doesn't matter to me if she doesn't like that stuff, I would be content with just making love to her. After hearing her past, I figured she would never like to have a 'playful' sexual relationship, but after the way she responded to being tied up, I may have over-thought things. I won't push too much too quick. I have to take things slow with her and I'm perfectly content with that.

I blink back those thoughts as we pull into the parking lot for St. James Cathedral. The show is about to start, because to my father, that's all this is. All he cares about is what others think of him and how he is perceived. I clutch Nadi's hand and kiss the back of it. In a strange twist of events, her presence is calming to me, just as she always tells me my presence is calming to her. I slowly inhale a deep calming breath. *I can do this.*

"I should probably warn you that my parents are likely to be... unpleasant toward me when others aren't paying attention. I know you are going to want to say something, but please hold your tongue, just this time. For me." She gives me a look of disapproval. "I just don't want to make a scene. My grandfather would tell me right now that I need to be the bigger man and not react to their pitiful, misguided, disgusting behavior because it would make me the better person for it. Okay?" She gives me a tight nod.

We get out of the car and she comes around to join me as I check out my appearance in the reflection of my window, making sure my suit is straight and sitting properly. As I glace sideways, Nadi is staring at me with a cute little grin on her lips.

"What?"

"You look absolutely perfect, not to mention absolutely hot in that suit."

My lips turn up as she comes and leans her front to mine, and she grabs my tie as if she is straightening it. "Geez, I can't even fix your tie for you because it is already perfect. Now stop obsessing over your appearance." Always telling me like it is.

"You know, you are looking awfully hot yourself." Her black dress is conservative, covering her shoulders and going down to her knees, not too tight, only hugging her tightly where the small belt encircles her waist. The only pieces of jewelry she's wearing are the necklace I bought her and a pair of blue teardrop earrings. Her hair is pulled half back with soft curls down her back and light makeup. Simple, yet absolutely beautiful, so natural. She blushes a little at the compliment. I kiss her forehead lightly and take her hand as we head toward the church.

"Here we go," I say with a deep breath, trying to stay into good spirits.

As we approach the front, several people are standing around. There are several familiar faces, but many I have never seen before. I'm stopped by my grandfather's brother, Scott. "Aerick, good to see you."

I nod politely toward him. "Grandpa Scott." I had only got to see him on the rare occasions he would visit when I was a teenager. "May I introduce my girlfriend. This is Nadalynn. Nadalynn, this is my grandfather's brother, Scott."

She gives a genuine, gorgeous smile as she shakes his hand. "Nice to meet you, Sir."

He seems amused, "None of that 'Sir' business. You may call me Scott. Aerick, your grandfather told me you had a girlfriend." Nadi glances at me with surprise. Perhaps I failed to mention to her that I'd talked to him.

Giving her an apologetic look I answer, "Yes, I'm sure he did. You're the lucky one who gets to meet her first." I pull her a little closer and give her a quick kiss on top of her head.

"Well, you better keep this one around, she has the makings to be something special."

I chuckle slightly - he has no idea. "I'll be sure to do that. Thanks Grandpa Scott. If you'll excuse us, I must go find my parents. I'll catch up with you later." He gives us a nod and we continue into the church.

"So, you talked about me with your grandfather, huh?" she grins at me.

"I talked to him right before we left camp. We were planning on meeting up so he could meet you. We just didn't do it soon enough." M mask falters as the sadness breaks through momentarily.

"Aerick, it's okay. I'm here for you," she whispers. Her words send a wave of warmth through me and I tighten my hand that is around her waist.

We approach the front, where I spot my mother, father and brother. They are speaking to someone I've never met. I stop behind my parents, who still have their backs to me.

"Aerick. Good to see you again, brother." My brother steps around and gives me a pat on my shoulder.

"Greg, good to see you as well." My parents turn around and my mother's eyes automatically dart to the woman at my side, checking over her critically. *Great.* I step in to give her a kiss on the cheek because that's what she expects of me, to be a perfect gentleman. As always, she is dressed in an expensive, flashy dress with enough jewelry to feed a small village. Complete opposite of Nadi.

"What took you so long to get here?" she chides, as if I am ten years old again. As I pull back, she reaches over to pick off a nonexistent piece of lint from my jacket, before brushing over my shoulder as if to wipe it clean. *Never good enough.*

I ignore her and turn to my father, reaching out my hand. "Father."

He's completely composed as he reaches out to shake my hand. "Son." He gazes expectantly at Nadi and all the sudden I want to take her away far away from here. I don't want her anywhere near him, but I have to do this for my grandfather, and I will not let my father intimidate me.

"If I may introduce my girlfriend. This is Nadalynn. Nadalynn, this is my mother, Mary; my father, Carson; and my brother, Greg." She shakes my mother's and father's hands as they plaster their fake smiles on their faces.

My brother clasps her hand and kisses the back of it with a huge grin on his face. "Very nice to meet you. Brother, I have to admit, I think you've finally out done me." Elation fills me as my brothers' words sink in. Nadi gazes at me with color quickly rising in her cheeks and for just a moment all in the world is great – but only for a moment.

"Greg, you are just too kind," my mother responds sarcastically, giving Nadi a quick once over as if she was a bum off the street, before fixing her face and turning to the woman next to her. "Aerick, this is my colleague, Sandy. I was just explaining to her that Greg is working on his doctorate at Harvard University. He's even had two of his research studies published already. We couldn't be prouder of him," my mother gushes, effectively taking all the attention off me and putting it on my brother. *How typical.*

I glance over to my brother and he gives me an apology with his eyes. He really has never been mean to me per se, but he has always loved getting all the attention and is often full of himself, making him come off as a jerk. Just as my mother is about to continue exploiting her favorite son's accomplishments, the priest comes over and lets us know the service is going to start, and we take our seats in the front. My brother sits between my parents, his normal place. I make sure to sit on the end next to my mother and move Nadi on the other side of me, so I am effectively shielding her from my family.

"You should have told us you were bringing your girlfriend. I'm sure Sandy is thinking it has been a long time since we've seen you, as we are just now meeting your girlfriend," my mother hisses quietly in my ear.

I want so much to tell her, "Well, it is true," but miraculously, I hold my tongue. Next to me, Nadi squeezes my hand. Glancing down at her, she gives me a reassuring smile that I return and then slide my arm around her back. I ignore the heat of my mother's glare at my public display of affection. Maybe if she wasn't a cold, heartless bitch, she would understand the connection it can bring - but whatever, I really don't care.

The service is beautiful, other than when my father gets up and speaks. He's sure to mention the strong line of male descendants but looks only to my brother. It appears like no time at all until it is over and thankfully, we are instantly surrounded by others as we step forward to a waiting position, along with my Grandpa Scott. I stay in the background with my arm tightly around Nadi as people come forward to give their condolences.

As soon as everyone has come forward, my mother turns to me. "You will be taking the limo back with us," she demands.

Her condescending tone is close to putting me over the edge. "Mother, I drove my car here," I try to say strongly, but it comes out more as a defeated tone.

"It's bad enough you did not arrive in the limo with your father, brother and me. What do you think everyone is thinking?" Honestly, I don't give two fucks what others think, and my plan to exit this circus show as soon as possible requires me to have my car. Watching her expression, I internally roll my eyes, knowing there is no way out of this without a fight.

"Yes, mother," I say, letting my irritation seep through.

"Baby, if you like, I'll follow in your car. I know you wouldn't want to leave it here," Nadi says sweetly, plastering fake joy across her face, as she glances from my mother to me. Mother tries to keep her irritation hidden, but her expression breaks for a half a second.

"That would be wonderful, babe." I answer, trying to hide the smirk on my face. Taking her hand, we walk toward the door before my mother can object. I love that she just defied her without causing a scene. Definitely a win for our side. "I'll meet you at the car, Mother," I say over my shoulder. She lets out a huff as we continue walking away.

"Hurry, Aerick, we don't want to keep our guests waiting," she says smugly, heading for the limo. Nadi just pissed her off. *Definitely a win!*

"Give me your phone."

Nadi fishes it out of her purse, handing it to me and I pull up the Maps App to put in the address.

"So now I understand what you're talking about. I hope you didn't mind that I offered to take your car for you," she says quietly.

"Not at all. In fact, thank you for that. I don't want to leave it here, nor do I want to stay long at their house." I stare into her eyes and her understanding cheers me up a bit.

"Good, because her little comments are really starting to irritate the crap out of me."

I chuckle, knowing exactly what she means. I just grew up learning to ignore them.

"Aerick?" My mother calls, with too sweet of a tone.

"Coming, Mother," I call back, not wanting to leave my girl.

"When you get there, just pull through the gate, there will be valets to park the car and I will stay close to the door. We won't stay long, I promise." I lean in, giving her a kiss on the cheek as my hand slides her the keys, and then turn toward the waiting limo, hoping this is over quickly.

I inhale a deep breath before getting in and move to the side seat next to my brother.

"Driver, we are ready," my father says with a stuck-up authority.

My eyes roam the front of the car and notice it isn't their normal driver. "Where is Keith?" I ask out of curiosity. My father's brows rise in irritation.

"He was late picking me up a few months ago. Some B.S. about traffic. I had to fire him." *Seriously.* He has been their driver for like five years and he just fired him because he was late once. *That's my asshole father for you.* I don't bother expressing my disgust.

"So Aerick, where did you meet your girlfriend?" my brother asks and my mother sits up a little straighter.

"At Donnelly," I say, ignoring my mother's exasperated face. She never did like any attention on me.

"So, she works at that place you call a job?" My father's disgusted tone makes my irritation grow.

"Yes, father. She works there." It's technically true and there's no need to deal with the repercussions of telling them that she was a cadet. My father grunts and looks back toward the window.

"She's extremely smart. She is actually on a fast-track program to get her teaching degree in just a year." It comes out before I really think about it, but the need to defend her from his accusing tone draws it out.

"A teacher?" My mother's repulsed voice comes through as she rolls her eyes and my irritation grows even more. I need to get off this subject before it's no longer possible to hold my tongue.

"Brother, tell me about this research you had published," I say quickly, and he immediately beams and begins to go into a very animated explanation of his research.

Thankfully, we pull up to the house as he is finishing. Tight spaces don't normally bother me but I'm feeling suffocated in here.

"Aerick, I expect nothing less than your best behavior. People need to see that you were raised with the utmost respect and dignity," Mother tells me before exiting. *Just shoot me now.*

I exit the car and straighten my suit, hoping Nadi isn't too far off. It's ridiculous she had to drive by herself, but I'm grateful she didn't have to ride with us. Knowing her, she wouldn't have held her tongue.

An odd feeling washes over me as I step inside the house. It's been years since I've been here. The house is no place for kids; it's more like a museum than a home. It's big and immaculate. The entry way is open, dominated by two grand staircases on either side leading to the second level. There's wait staff everywhere serving the guests that have begun to arrive. Most make their way to the large sitting room or straight out to the elaborate patio in front of me, where I'm sure there is a huge set up. Light music is pouring in from the doors leading out to the back yard. I step in just a little, so others can come in, but not too far that I won't see Nadi when she arrives.

"Aerick, my boy. There you are," Grandpa Scott says, patting me on the back. It means a lot to me knowing he actually loved my grandfather. There's no doubt my father only put on all of this to appear that he was the good, loving son. To him, appearances are the only thing that matter, and it hasn't been lost on me that I didn't see my uncle Davy at the service. He's my father's younger brother and only sibling. I've only met him two or three times and each time it ended with my father and him arguing about how Davy was such a disappointment to the family.

"I'm really happy for you, Aerick."

"Why?" I query, confused. No one else is particularly pleased with me.

"You have found yourself a lovely lady. Don't let my nephew spit that bull that love is for the weak. Your father is a bitter man who will never understand what true love can do to a person. I've never seen you so happy son, and the way you two gaze at each other, it reminds me of when your grandma Tess was alive. Your grandpa loved her so much and it killed him when she passed away.

"It was hard on your pops, too. Losing his mother to cancer when you're only six can take its toll. Especially her – she was one of a kind, I tell you." I remember the few times my grandfather talked about her. The longing in his eyes and the sadness. I never pushed the subject but there's no doubt in my mind he loved her, even all these years later.

"You know, he never even looked at another woman after she passed. A love like that only comes by once in a lifetime. Remember that, boy. If she's the one, you keep her close and treat her right, you hear?" He stares at me with intense eyes and right now he reminds me so much of my grandfather, almost as if he was the one giving me the words of wisdom I was so used to.

"Yes, Grandpa Scott. I'll do that, I promise."

I'm actually starting to get a little anxious that she is not here yet.

"How is business?" I ask, trying to distract myself.

"It's going great. We've grown to the fourth-largest database company in Chicago." Relief fills me as I see Nadi come through the front door and nod at her to join us. She comes over and my arm automatically goes around her waist, pulling her in tightly to my side as I kiss her temple.

"Any problems getting here?"

"Nope, just traffic," she beams.

"Grandpa Scott, I don't think I've mentioned that Nadi is actually from Chicago." She gazes at me confused.

"Grandpa Scott lives in Chicago, where he has a very successful database company," I explain.

"No, you didn't mention that. Maybe you guys could stop by and have lunch if you visit. I would love to show you around the company." He focuses on Nadi.

"We would love to," she chimes in on cue, and grin. I don't know Grandpa Scott really well, but he seems to be a lot like my grandfather.

"Aerick." My brother comes up behind me. "Sorry to interrupt, Grandpa Scott, but Mother is requesting your presence, Aerick."

He huffs. "Better run along Aerick. You know how your mother is." I hear a giggle escape from Nadi at his sarcasm. At least she thinks it's amusing. "It was nice to meet you," he says to Nadi and gives her a quick kiss on the cheek before whispering something to her, at which she nods back at him. I'll have to remember to ask her what he said. I nod to him and he returns the gesture as we turn to follow my brother outside to the patio.

"Here he is. Aerick, you remember Janice?" Great, not what I feel like dealing with.

"Ms. Matthews, good to see you again. May I introduce my girlfriend, Nadalynn." They shake hands. "This is Ms. Matthews. She is the head of Heartly Research Facility, where my father is a lead research scientist, and my mother also is a researcher there." I can't help but notice my mother's expression. Any prouder and she would be bursting at the seams.

"My, my Aerick. Your mother hadn't mentioned you had a girlfriend," Janice says to me and there is a flash of anger in my mother's eyes for being called out.

"I've been away for work and just recently got back. I'm sure it would have been the topic of conversation had this unfortunate event not happened before she had the chance to inform you." I try to placate my mother as I turn the charm on for Janice.

"I'm sure you are right." She turns back to my mother and they start talking.

Suddenly I feel Nadi freeze and I turn quickly to see my brother's hand on her shoulder. "Would you like to see the rest of the grounds, Nadalynn? I'd be glad to give you a tour."

I clench my jaw, trying to keep my anger at bay, but push it aside as I realize that she needs me. It's clear I need to calm her down as her breaths begin to get shallower. She would be really upset with herself if she freaked out here. I run my thumbnail discreetly up and down her side, going a little lower than appropriate, and she glances at me. I give her the panty dropping smirk she loves, and she relaxes slightly.

"Actually, I really need to use the restroom," she says quietly, as if she is shy, but I know it is because she is starting to panic since my brother's hand still hasn't moved from her shoulder.

"I'll show you," I say, before he can. I shrug at my brother as if telling him that it was nothing and pull her back into the house to the guest bathroom.

Once we are locked in the bathroom, she throws her arms around me and rests her forehead against my shoulder. "Sorry, sorry. It's just..." Her breaths are now coming out harsh and I pull her into my arms.

"Stop! It's fine. You're fine. Just breathe through it." She takes several deep breaths as I rub my hands up and down her back. After a few minutes she pulls back. "Better?" I ask, gazing into her eyes, and there's finally some relief in them.

"Yes, much better. I am so sorry babe, it's just, I'm already on edge and..."

I roll my eyes at her. "I said stop. You did rather well. I mean, you didn't punch him." The thought of seeing my mother's face as Nadi lays out her favorite son is rather entertaining. My hidden enjoyment playing out in my mind, starts to break through and she gazes at me confused. I shake my head. "Never mind. You did great."

Someone knocks on the door, startling us both. "Aerick, man. You better get out here." Great, my damn brother, just who I don't want to see right now.

"Ready?" Her color is better, and her features have smoothed back out.

"Yes." Putting my arm back around her, we exit the restroom, and I make sure to stay in between her and my brother.

"Mother saw you two both go in there and she's mad." *Since when does he warn me?* "Also, Grandpa's lawyer is here. Mother is insisting that we go to Father's study immediately." He hesitates for a moment, glancing between Nadi and I.

"What?" I say forcefully, getting tired of this charade I'm putting on for everyone.

"She requested just you and I."

I glower at him with a raised eyebrow. "Well, Nadi is not leaving my side, so let me deal with Mother – and what lawyer?" He doesn't answer me, just turns and starts walking. I follow, pulling Nadi along, but there is a slight pull from her hesitation. My hand squeezes her side and it gives her a boost of confidence.

We go into the study and my mother and father are already in there with a man I've haven't met. "Aerick, finally. It's very rude to keep people waiting. We are all here, you may continue," she says to the gentleman.

He stands in front of us with a piece of paper. "This will not take up too much of your time." I'm at a loss for what is going on, but my expected manners keep me from interrupting. "I'm first to give the grandchildren these letters." He hands a letter to both my brother and me. "He requested that you read them in your own time. As per the matter of his estate. As you know, he had a successful auto parts store chain for many years, that he built from the ground up. What you may not know is that it had begun to go downhill during the recession, and he was barely able to hold onto it. He chose to sell it off before it completely collapsed so that he would be able to live out his retirement comfortably. After settling all debts, including the loan for his home on Lake Stevens, it left a small amount of money." *Here!* They choose to have the Will read here. *How tactless can they be?*

"The money is to be distributed as follows: Greg will receive fifty thousand. Aerick, you will receive twenty-five thousand." The shit-eating grin on my father's face only last a second, as the lawyer turns to me, "He'd like you to know that he is only leaving you less, because he put down the twenty-five thousand down on the condo for your twenty-first birthday. He wanted to be fair to you and your brother."

"He did what?" my mother and father say in unison.

"Why would you ask him for money? Do you not have any pride?" *Asshole.* I scowl down at my father's face and see the shame in his eyes.

"I didn't ask for it. He offered. I never said anything," I say quietly, trying not to lose my respectful tone, but my lips press into a straight line.

"Sir, if I may continue." My father just nods. "In addition, he is leaving fifty thousand to his brother Scott, to pay back the startup loan that got his business going, plus interest. Finally, he is leaving the home on Lake Stevens and the remaining amount of seventy thousand to his youngest son, Davy."

"And what about me?" my father almost yells.

"For you, sir, I have a message. He would like you to know that 'Greed should never replace love'."

My father's anger hits a boiling point. "What about all my expenses? Do you know how much this cost? And what kind of shitty message is that? And leaving my pathetic brother the house and money. He never did anything good with his life, besides work a lousy nine-to-five factory job all his life, because he never chose to be a better person. None of this makes any sense. My father's business was worth millions at one point. Are you really going to tell me it is all gone?" He doesn't give the lawyer time to answer. "This is not the end of it. You'll be hearing from my lawyer."

"Sir, I was warned this would happen, and I guarantee this was planned for. The facts are as stated. All information has been carefully documented and reviewed by several independent parties, in case you choose to dispute this, but if you want to continue this pointless pursuit, be my guest. Here is my card, have your lawyer contact me anytime. Boys, here is my card, if you have any questions, please feel free to contact me and someone from my office will be getting a hold of you to transfer your inheritance. Good day." He leaves and my father's scorching rage is as hot as the sun.

Great, here we go. "This is bullshit. There is no way that money is gone." Actually, it is. Grandpa told me when he offered to put the down payment on my condo, but I kept quiet per his request. "And you, boy. What on earth is this down-payment? Taking advantage of an old man to get something you don't deserve. You are a class-A screw up, while your brother has worked his tail off. How could he ever see you two as being equal?"

My anger, irritation, and hurt all rise at the same time. My fists clench and Nadi's hand goes to my chest, allowing me to momentarily gain control again. My brother's eyes fall to the floor as if he disagrees, but he stays quiet, like always.

Ignoring Nadi he continues, "You just stroll in here like you're just as perfect as he is." He continues, but suddenly he is interrupted.

"He is!" My dumbfounded face turns to Nadi, who's staring at my father. I've never seen anyone stand up to my father. As much as I hate to admit it, my skills in intimidation are one thing I learned from him. My whole family stares at her, incredulous.

"Who do you think you are, Missy?" my mother pipes in. "You have no right to say one word here. This is our family and just because you give it up to my son in a dirty bathroom doesn't mean you have any control over him. Oh, don't think I didn't see you two go in there. Aerick, this is your grandfather's service, and you have the audacity to come in here and lower yourself to the level of this two-bit whore."

Nadi's hand fists at my chest. "You dumb bitch," Nadi says and I grab her hand, placing my finger over her mouth before she does or says anything else. I'm done listening to this asshole. I will not stand by and let my family hurt the one person that means something to me.

"Aerick, did you just hear what she called me?" my mother says, astonished, thinking I stopped Nadi for her – boy, is she wrong. I'm merely trying to avoid what I am sure would become a scene, and my grandfather deserves more than my parent's petty behavior.

"Son, you will not stand here and allow that kind of disrespect in my house. Your girlfriend will apologize NOW," my father demands.

Nadi breathes in deeply as she tries to bring down her anger. I grab her wrist, pulling her behind me, making me feel like her shield. "You know what, Father, if the money means that much to you, take it. I will have Grandfather's lawyer forward the twenty-five thousand to you to cover all your expenses today. This is what Grandfather meant about greed. You are more worried about your precious money than the memory of your own father – you're despicable," I say as calmly as possible, but my voice slowly gets louder.

He completely ignores the last half of my rant. "It's about time you did something decent in your life. The least you could do is to pay for all this, since you already took money you don't deserve. Now, you will make her apologize to your mother."

She *tsks* from behind me and I agree. "I'll do no such thing," I damn near yell at him as my control breaks. I refuse to stand here and let him treat Nadi the way he treats me.

"How dare you use that tone with me? You ungrateful little prick. After everything your mother and I have done for you." His glare bores into my retinas until they slam to the floor under his threatening gaze. "You will do what I say, and you will do it *NOW*. Do not make me repeat myself," he demands again.

Dammit Aerick, stand up to him! I scream at myself as I inhale in a deep breath.

"I will not apologize for speaking the truth. Aerick, let's go," Nadi says as she steps up beside me. Always so strong, I muse for just a second, before watching my father turn red.

"Who do you think you are? This is my home and you will not disrespect my wife that way. Now, you show some respect little girl," he seethes, and she laughs at him. Like an actual belly rumbling laugh, shocking me speechless.

"Respect is given where respect is due, and from where I'm standing, the only one in this room who has my respect is Aerick." My chest expands in pride, but my attention quickly turns to my father as he moves a step toward her.

"You little..."

I quickly move between them out of pure reflex. "If you finish that sentence, I swear on grandfather's grave I'll lay you out right here." All my hatred, pain, and sorrow pour out in that one sentence.

His anger turns to genuine shock. "How dare you?"

I. Am. Done. My voice turns low and cold as all my emotions drive my words. "No, how dare you. You call yourself a father. You're nothing but a money-hungry, sad little man. That beautiful woman behind me is the best thing that has ever happened to me in this crappy, miserable life. She showed me what it means to live, to be cared for, to be loved, and she did it all wanting nothing in return. She's everything that my own father and mother never were, and I'll be damned if I ever let you hurt her. She's the only person in this world that matters to me now." My hands are shaking in anger. Nadi's hands run down my back and give me the strength needed to not deck him in the face.

"You leave here and don't ever come back," my father says quietly and for the first time in my life there is actually fear in his eyes.

"Gladly." His eyes turn back to anger as quickly as I can spit out the single word. "Babe, I think we've stayed long enough." Her hand presses firmly on my back and warmth spreads through my body. I move, grabbing her by the waist, and lead her out of the house. As soon as we get in the car, I take a deep, cleansing breath and it feels like a weight has lifted off my shoulders. I turn to Nadi with a lot lighter, but her eyes are on her clasped hands, almost looking guilty.

"Hey, don't you dare," I say softly as all my anger flees. She gazes up at me and it's in her eyes. "Don't you even think about apologizing. None of this is your fault; in fact, this would have happened sooner or later. Thanks to you, it happened sooner and saved me a lot of irritation and heartache." I clutch her face in both of my hands.

"I love you, Nadalynn. You're the only person that matters to me." I kiss her as passionately as my lips will allow, hoping she understands how much she means to me. When we break apart, we are both breathless as we rest our foreheads together.

"I love you too, Aerick. Always!"

Always…

"Always."

CHAPTER SEVEN

(Friday, October 23rd)

I'M SO PISSED right now. After several heated conversations with Aerick, it still blows my mind why he insists on giving his money-hungry father his inheritance. That money is rightfully his, and it really isn't that much. Trying to get a justifiable answer out of him is like pulling teeth. He just keeps telling me that, 'It isn't worth the fight' or, 'It's not a big deal'. To me, it isn't about the money. It's the fact that he is giving into his father's selfishness and giving the asshole something he doesn't deserve. Aerick's grandfather wanted him to have the money and after the way his father treated him, I'm just so flabbergasted that he'd give anything to that insufferable man.

Our ride home after the funeral was very quiet. Aerick was clearly pissed-off and frustrated, and he didn't want to talk. He almost completely shut down on me again. For a little while, I thought it was my behavior, despite what he said as we left. There was no denying that I'd acted quite rudely to both his parents, but I didn't have much time to let those thoughts run wild. Aerick seemed to hone in on my thoughts and out of the blue, he broke the silence, telling me again that he was in no way upset with me, or my actions, and that he was extremely proud of me for standing up to his father. That was the only thing he said the entire car ride home and most of the evening.

When we got home, he sat down on the couch to do something on his laptop and I made an early dinner in silence. The only time he said anything was during dinner, when he complimented my cooking. It was starting to irritate the crap out of me as we both cleaned up after dinner, until he suggested that we sit and read. We curled up on the couch together reading our books and all of my irritation melted away as he held me tightly to his side. Reading is one of his distractions when things are bothering him. I have to admit, it is very comforting to me as well, since I get lost in the stories, forgetting all of the things grinding on my nerves.

As night fell, he relaxed and was in a much better mood, so I chanced trying to get him to talk, but again it didn't work. The expression he gave me when I questioned him was nothing short of disarming. It took him about ten seconds to totally make me forget about what I'd asked him, as he began kissing me. It started out very soft and sweet, but it quickly turned into something much more demanding and lust-filled. I have no doubt that he worked out his 'frustration' that night as he fucked me very roughly, in several different positions, until we both literally fell asleep from exhaustion. Not that I'm complaining, as it was completely mind-blowing and was just as much to my benefit, but it also didn't make me forget that I still hadn't gotten an answer out of him.

After that, I didn't it up again, and we went back to our normal everyday routine, almost as if the funeral never happened. My online classes started, and I was scheduled to do some of the tests I've been studying for, but other than that things have been the same. During the week we spend quite a bit of time at Amar's gym, and eat out most nights. Sometimes we talk about various things, usually revolving around my life, and sometimes we just enjoy each other's company in a comfortable silence.

I have taken a liking to walking down to the marina and the adjacent park at sunset when the weather is nice. Aerick always joins me for my evening walks, saying that he doesn't want me to walk around alone when it is dark – which I'm grateful for, only because I love walking hand in hand with him, not because I can't take care of myself.

One evening he insisted it was time for a break from studying and we needed a date night. We went to the Southcenter Mall to watch *Crimson Peak* at the cinema there, then ate at this cute restaurant in the mall. It was a great time, and for a few hours we were able to break our normal routine.

Sometimes it's like we've been a couple for years. Everything we do seems so routine already. Every once in a while, Aerick will suggest we go somewhere we've never gone, but for the most part it is mostly the same – with the exception of our sex life. That has been in no way repetitive, as he continues to surprise me with his substantial knowledge of sexual positions. He jokingly told me once that he knew a different position for every day of the year; it's apparent to me now that he was telling the truth.

It's still hard for me to talk about anything sexual, but he's more than capable of getting enough information out of me to find out what things I like more than others. Sometimes it feels like he's holding back something when we get on that subject, but I'm probably just being paranoid. He's admitted that his sex life in the past was 'very diverse,' but he has hardly expanded on what that actually means. I don't dwell on it too much, because I'm sure I'll find out in time.

Everything was nearly perfect until Aerick received a phone call from his grandfather's lawyer's office yesterday, requesting he come in to sign off on the papers. The call brought back his irritation, along with his silence. Since the subject was back in the open, I again attempted to get some kind of reasoning out of him, but it's useless. Aerick can be so hard-headed. I wish he would just talk to me about it.

I stare out of the window in the conference room we're sitting in as the lawyer explains things to Aerick. We are on the fiftieth story of the Safeco Plaza in downtown Seattle and the view is amazing. Aerick squeezes my hand, bringing my attention back to the lawyer but honestly, I haven't been listening much.

"Aerick, are you sure about this? Your grandpa was adamant that this money goes to you and not your father. I need to know that this is of your own free will and that you are not being pressured into this," the lawyer says skeptically.

Now I understand why he brought my attention back. It's the same question I've been asking him.

"I'm not being pressured into this. I want to do this for my grandfather and for myself. This is the one thing I could do for him," Aerick says confidently. The lawyer shakes his head and has him sign the last paper and then sign the check over to his father, which the lawyer will have sent over to him.

"Do you mind if I write a short note to be delivered with the check?" Aerick asks the lawyer, who nods, pulling out a nice piece of paper with a fancy letterhead. Aerick leans forward and writes something quickly in his perfect penmanship, but he does it before I can get a chance to read what it says. He probably doesn't want me to know, so I don't question him – maybe when we are in private. He folds it once and hands it back to the lawyer.

"Alright, Sir, I think that will just about cover it. If you have any questions or concerns, please feel free to contact me anytime." He hands Aerick his card and then escorts us back to the elevator. We all shake hands and say our goodbyes.

As we get into the elevator Aerick visibly relaxes. "Feel better?" I question and he gazes down at me.

"Surprisingly, yes." He winds his arms around me. "You feel up to going out tonight? Nothing special, just drinks with Paulo and his cousin."

He must be feeling better. I haven't seen him this relaxed since before he got that dreaded call from his mother. "Sure, I would love to." I pause for a moment as a thought occurs to me. "Exactly how are you getting me into a bar?"

Aerick's lips turn up. "It isn't just a bar. We are going to The Swiss restaurant and pub. It's all ages and at night they have live bands."

* * * *

Aerick pulls along the curb and parks the car but there is no sign of a restaurant. We get out and Aerick joins me on the sidewalk, taking my hand. We walk around the corner and go down a very steep hill. I gaze at him curiously, but he just tugs on my hand and keeps walking. As we get to the bottom of the block, I see a large purple 'W' statue across the street. I glance to Aerick again and then gawk at the statue with a question in my eyes.

"That's the University of Washington Tacoma campus," he explains with a little humor.

"So, you're taking me to a college to drink?" I say with a amusement, playing along. He said we were going to a pub, not a college party. With his lips turned up, he turns me around to the right showing me a doorway half hidden by the hill we just walked down.

"No, we're going in here."

The building is old and looks like one of those hole-in-the-wall type places – which I suppose it sort of is, being it's half-buried in the hill. He gives me his cute little half-smirk and we go in. Once we're in, I am surprised at how big it is. The second floor has been knocked out, creating high ceilings. There's a spacious room with a bunch of tables that sit in front of the bar, with muffled music playing elsewhere.

Paulo isn't anywhere in sight but he just texted Aerick as we got out of the car, saying him and Terrie were already here. Aerick puts his hand on the small of my back and leads me toward the back corner of the bar, where the music gets louder. We go through a narrow doorway and it opens up into another large room with a live band playing on a stage, and a bunch more tables. We continue to walk and go through an archway to yet another large room where there are a bunch of pool tables. This place is crazy big. You would never have guessed it from the outside. I finally spot Terrie and Paulo at the pool table furthest away, with a few people I don't recognize.

"Hey Nadi, good to see you!" Terrie says as she gives me a quick hug and a kiss on the cheek. I turn to Paulo and he engulfs me in a bear hug, which is over before I really have time to react, but my body still stiffens for a moment at the sudden contact. Aerick's hand shoots out and hits Paulo hard in the arm. I see two men over by the pool table immediately jump up and come over to us. Wow, we've been here two minutes and we're already going to have trouble.

"I told you before, keep your hands off my woman."

Paulo laughs bellow loudly over the music and he claps Aerick on the shoulder with just as much force as his two companions slow their descent on us. "Relax Aerick, we're here to have fun." He turns to me. "Good to see you, sis. How's life on the outside treating you?"

"It's good," I tell him. His two companions join us, and he introduces his cousins Kalo and Poe. Although they're brothers, they are quite a bit different. Both are tall, but Kalo is skinny and Poe is very husky, almost overly muscular looking. We all go back over to the pool table where they were playing. Paulo excuses himself, saying he will be back.

"So Nadi, how have you been? How are things with Aerick?" Terrie asks, speaking loudly next to my ear so I can hear her over the music.

"I'm good, happy... and Aerick is Aerick, but I wouldn't want him any other way."

She smiles and shakes her head. "Honestly, I never thought someone would be able to tame that wild boy, but I'm sure glad you did. He's a lot nicer with you around." I beam and Aerick glances at me curiously. He must not be able to hear her over the loud music.

Paulo comes back with a tray of shots and drinks. "Alright, party people, shots up." He picks up a shot and tries to hand it to me. My eyes find Aerick, trying to figure out which one of us is going to be driving home.

"You can go ahead and drink, I'll drive home," I tell him and wave off Paulo. It's only fair, since he drove home on our first date.

"Oh no, you don't. We can call a cab if I drink too much," he tells me grabbing the shot from Paulo and gives it to me as Paulo hands out the rest of the shots.

"Here's to a good time tonight!" Paulo bellows out. We all raise our shots and then drink them down.

* * * *

There's a grin plastered on my face as Aerick discreetly runs his thumb along the inside of my thigh where his hand is resting as he waits to take his shot. My head is a little fuzzy and the room we're in has become much more crowded in the last few hours. Aerick hasn't been overbearing at showing that I'm not available, which has surprised me just a little, but if someone were to watch him, they would see. He's made it a point to be touching me in some little way all night, when he's not taking his shot on the pool table. Most the time he's standing next to me, touching his arm to mine, but sometimes he will covertly run his fingers across my lower back while standing behind me or touch my legs in some way like he's doing now. Not that I'm complaining – it's oddly pleasurable. I'm starting to believe this is his game, driving me crazy by slowly teasing me hour after hour. Seeing how long it will take before I break and just attack him, which is definitely on my agenda the minute we are back home.

He gives me his signature smirk as he removes his hand and walks over to the pool table. That look alone hits me hard between my legs. He is drop dead sexy in his designer jeans, and button up shirt with the sleeves rolled up. He hasn't shaved in a few days and you can clearly see the facial hair on his face now; it suits him well. I watch as he bends over the pool table, gripping the pool stick, causing the muscles in his arms to flex and his shirt to tighten around his back and shoulders. I cross my legs on the high bar stool I'm sitting on trying to ease the ache that has been slowly building.

After two successful shots he misses and comes back over to stand with me, but instead of sitting beside me, he comes to a stop in front of me. He picks up his beer off the table that I'm leaning on as Terrie and I talk while we watch the guys play. He has done this a couple of times, and is getting a bit more irritated each time he does it.

"I swear if that guy doesn't stop staring at you, he is going to meet my fist." *Now I get it.*

"Hey charming, my eyes are only on you. So, cool down there handsome." He glances over at me and his expression softens, his irritation taking a back burner.

"Well, well, well. Look who it is." Aerick turns around to the high cartoon-like voice coming from behind him. A pretty, skinny, tall brunette stands there with a massive smile on her face. "It has been far too long," she says as she steps closer to him. "And looking as hot as ever!" She places her hand on his chest and my irritation goes from zero to a hundred in a millisecond and by the way he bites on the inside of his cheek, he's noticed my change in mood.

"Uh, hi Jen. Good to see you." He moves a step back but can't move too much because our table is right behind him, so her fingers are still on his chest. "I didn't know you were back in town. I haven't heard from you." She runs her fingers down his chest and I'm two seconds from getting up and knocking her on her ass.

Aerick steps sideways so he is on the other side of me and puts his hand on my legs, successfully holding me down. *That bitch better keep her hands off him.* "Hey, Jen, I want you to meet my girlfriend, Nadalynn."

She glares at me with a raised eyebrow and shock on her face. "Really... you have a girlfriend? That's a first."

I hold in the urge to smack her and put out my hand. "Nice to meet you." My voice is dripping with sarcasm.

"Likewise," she tells me as she shakes my hand, but her tone says different. "Well, I have to get back to my friends. Call me sometime, Aerick," she tells him, with flirtatious eyes, and I swear if Aerick wasn't effectively holding me down that bitch wouldn't be smiling right now.

"Yeah, that's not going to happen," I bite out and she glances back at me with an irritated glare on her face before walking away.

I glance back to Aerick and he has that smirk on his face again. "Jealous much?" I just roll my eyes at him, not bothering to tell him what's really going through my head, like the fact that I would feel better if my fist were to meet her face. He leans over and starts kissing me lightly on the neck, working his way up to my ear.

"Don't worry princess, my eyes are only on you," he says before pulling back slightly and giving me a quick kiss on the lips as he taps his finger on the underside of my chin. My bad mood is instantly forgotten. "Better?" he questions.

"Much!"

Paulo calls him over to take his shot.

"Does that kind of stuff happen a lot?" I ask Terrie. She purses her lips.

"Don't think like that, Nadi. He has a past, you are his present and his future, and he is hell-bent on keeping it that way. I mean, he hasn't taken his eyes off you since you guys got here. You've changed him, you know. It's just the little things." I watch her curiously. "Like the way he isn't so tense all the time and that half-smirk, half-smile that is permanently etched on his face these days."

My eyes move to him and I see the that look she's talking about as he jokes around with Paulo. She's right, I need to stop letting these women get to me. He catches me staring at him and gives me a wink.

He lifts his bottle, questioning if I need another drink, and I nod 'yes'. He says something to Paulo and then hands him his pool stick before walking out toward the bar. As soon as he rounds the corner, Paulo turns back toward me and shouts,

"Okay, sis. You took my partner away, so now you have to stand in for him."

I'm more than happy to. I hop down from my stool and go over, taking the pool stick from him. I wait for his cousin to finish his shot. The shot goes just to the left of its intended target. He must be getting pretty drunk, because that's the first time he hasn't sunk at least one of his balls during his turn.

"You're up," Paulo tells me, nudging my arm.

My eyes study the table for a moment as I debate my options. We're solids, so my best bet is the number two ball. I line up my shot. "Damn!" I hear someone behind me say loudly. Out of reaction, I stand up and peak behind me and some guy at the table next to us is staring at me, licking his bottom lip. *What a pig!* I shake my head and go back to my shot.

It's taking a little more to really concentrate because my head is pretty fuzzy. I shoot and make the shot. "That's what I am talking about!" Paulo shouts out, shoving at his cousin, who doesn't look as enthusiastic.

Shaking of the slight embarrassment, I move to my next shot. Luckily, the cue ball set up a perfect shot on the six ball, but the only way to get the right angle on the shot is going to have to be behind my back. I'm glad that I played a lot of pool back home at the billiards hall by my house. I concentrate on my position, which has me perched on the side of the pool table, with the stick threaded through my arms behind me. My shot sinks the ball like a pro and I'm absolutely elated.

I send another grin over to Paulo, but he stands up straight quickly, gawking intently at something just past me, alerting me that there is something very wrong.

"Well, aren't you all kinds of talented?" someone says way too close to me.

My head snaps back in front of me and the guy that was checking me out a few minutes ago is now standing so close to me that I cannot move my ass off the pool table unless I want to be standing up against him. *Great!*

"Thanks, but I'm taken. Might I suggest you move back," I say forcefully as this guy has just totally ruined my mood. Out of the corner of my eye, I see Paulo start moving around the table toward me.

"I don't see a ring on that pretty little hand, so I would say my chances are still good." He runs his fingers down my arm and my chest starts to tighten a little. I focus on breathing through it; this guy is not going to ruin my night.

I put a hand up to stop Paulo as he reaches me. "I suggest you don't touch her without her permission," Paulo warns him and the guy gapes at him like he is crazy.

"That is your only warning," I tell him, holding in my emotion. Instead of what I was hoping, which was him to get afraid so he would back off, he has excitement in his eyes.

"Wow, that is hot. Please let me be the one that tames you." *As if, buddy!*

He moves his hand down and rubs it along my leg. My fist reacts in a second – I can no longer hold back. I hit him square in his jaw but, because I'm perched up on the pool table, it doesn't do as much damage. He merely stumbles back a few steps as his hand flies up to his jaw. In my defense, he is by no means a small guy, and I didn't have much leverage. I hear Paulo's cousins snickering at the guy that just got punched by a girl.

"Fucking bitch!" he says as the hand not holding his jaw clenches at his side and Paulo quickly steps in front of me before the guy can do anything else. Aerick is by my side in a second. Paulo quickly steps to the side, so he is in front of Aerick instead of me, but still facing the guy in case he tries something.

"I warned you, dumbass. She doesn't like to be touched. Now. I suggest you leave before I move aside and let my buddy, *her boyfriend,* kick your ass."

The guy stands up straighter and a few of his buddies step up behind him. Kalo and Poe both quickly step up behind Aerick. This is really not how I wanted this night to go and I have to stop it now before there's an all-out brawl. Now that there is a little room, I jump down between the guy and Paulo, pressing my hand to Paulo's chest.

"Come on boys, he isn't worth it. There is only one guy man enough for me." I push Paulo aside so I can get to my man and I move my hands around his neck, but he is still staring at the guy, and still as stone. "Hey handsome, I'm right here," I tell him putting my hand on his cheek to pull his gaze back to me. "Only you, babe. Remember?" I tell him sweetly.

After a minute he relaxes and leans down to kiss me very possessively as he encloses me in his arms. "Only you," he says back to me quietly and pecks me on the cheek before releasing me.

The other guy and his friend turn and walk away, going back to their table. "Now, if you don't mind, I have a game to win." I turn and walk to the end of the table, swaying my hips to keep his attention on me.

His smirk is back as he walks around and comes to a stop flush against by back. Leaning down, he moves my hair off my shoulder and kisses me just below my ear. "Keep teasing me and we aren't making it out of this bar," he threatens and then smacks me hard on the ass, causing me to let out a little yelp.

I focus back to him, smacking him on the chest lightly and pushing him back so I can shoot, but his eyes are not on me. They are staring mockingly at the guy across the room; typical Aerick, rubbing it in. I roll my eyes at him before turning back to the table.

"Eight ball corner pocket," I call out my last shot as I line it up, relieved our night wasn't ruined. It doesn't take a lot to concentrate now that the adrenaline has sobered me up a bit and I've somehow gotten extremely lucky that the shot on the eight ball is almost perfectly aligned. I slide the stick forward smoothly, hitting the cue ball so it hits the black ball flawlessly, sending it into the corner pocket.

"And that, boys, is how it is done." I hand my stick to Kalo and turn around, putting my arms around the neck of my man. He gives me a quick, passionate kiss before grabbing my thighs, lifting me up, causing me to instinctively wrap my legs around his waist. I squeal loudly, which turns into a giggle.

"You're amazing," he muses, being a bit over the top, but it doesn't bother me right now. I kiss him again since he is showing no sign of setting me down and he bites my lip. I open my mouth willingly and his tongue invades my mouth, exploring.

"Jesus, you two, get a room."

I pull away, giving Paulo a look of disapproval and Aerick sets me back on my bar stool but stays standing between my legs. "Fuck off, Paulo," he shouts over his shoulder, before turning back to me. "And you, young lady, shaking that ass at me in those tight jeans." I bite my lip as he leans forward, nipping at the base of my neck. "I think it is time I get you home so you can get your prize for winning our game."

I glance over his shoulder. The guy from earlier is sitting across the room sulking as he watches us. We better get out of here before anything else happens. "Well then, my prince, let's get out of here."

He licks his lips with a new determination. He turns to Terrie. "Make sure they don't drive drunk," he demands, and she nods at him. I hop off the stool as Aerick grabs my hips, stirring up the ache between my legs again.

"Your wish is my command, Princess," he growls, with clear intent in his eyes.

CHAPTER EIGHT

(Friday, November 6th)

WHAT THE BLAZES was I thinking?

I park the car at the testing center to take my second CLEP test this week. I have eighteen of these tests that I have to complete over the next few months, but Luther wanted me to do as many as possible before the next camp session, since I will have to take classes and intern for Tia while I'm there. When he called me and told me he had scheduled me to do two tests a week for three weeks in a row, I thought he was crazy. Of course, he just huffed at me, telling me he knew I could do it and to just do my best. I took my first two tests for math and science last week, which were pretty easy, but the tests this week were for history and American literature, which required a lot more studying. I moan to myself, trying not to focus on the fact that that I still have two more tests next week.

My life has turned into endless days of studying. In addition to all the tests, I'm taking six classes online for the fall quarter instead of the normal four. To make matters worse, I started a week late, which meant I had to play catch up. The last few weeks have been nothing but schoolwork and studying. Luther and Aerick have total confidence in me, but it's only been a few weeks and my brain is already feeling like a soggy mess of goo.

I didn't let Aerick come with me this time. He didn't enjoy sitting in the lounge for hours while I took my last few tests. I explained that now that I know where the place is, it isn't necessary for him to come. He was hesitant to let me go by myself at first, but after explaining to him he needs to let me have a little room, he eased up a bit.

I love him, but we have been together basically 24/7 since we got home. Other than the night he freaked out, the only time he has left me alone was a few times when he went to the gym without me. Each of those times, it took a heated conversation to get him to go by himself. He didn't need to stay home just because I needed to study. I've always been pretty independent and I don't want to make it seem like I can't do things when he isn't around. It took a while, but he finally agreed to give me a little room. Besides, he needs to get used to it because when we go back to camp, we are not going to be together all the time.

My phone buzzes with an incoming text.

Aerick: You there yet?

Me: Yes, I am here, and your car is in one piece.

Aerick: Why didn't you text me yet? IT BETTER BE!

Me: I just got here, keep your panties on.

Aerick: Christ Woman, the mere thought of your panties is making me hard. Stop talking about panties, or I just might come down there and remove those sexy black ones I saw you put on this morning.

Oh shit. Even in a text he sounds sexy as hell. I squirm in my seat reading his text. How on earth does he do that to me?

Me: You really need to stop talking to me like that, I am supposed to be focused.

Aerick: What's the matter babe? Miss me already? If I was there I could help relieve that ache I know is bothering you!

Damn, I hear his voice in my head and I can't help but be extremely turned on as a picture of him 'relieving my ache' starts playing in my head. *STOP!* I chastise myself. This is not the time or place; but my body is betraying me as I feel the wetness between my legs.

Me: STOP IT! I need to concentrate!

Aerick: LOL. Sorry babe. Good luck with your test!

Sorry my ass! He did that on purpose.

Me: Gee thanks! Love you too.

I can just see him there sitting on the couch laughing for getting me all riled up. I'd bet a hundred dollars he did that to get back at me for not letting him come. *Jerk!* I inhale a long deep breath, trying to get his voice out of my head. There are still a few minutes before the check-in time, so I decide to turn on some Linkin Park to calm myself and clear my head. I need to be able to concentrate on this test.

* * * *

Finally! My test is complete and go to the locker to retrieve my personal items that I wasn't allowed to bring into the testing room. I have a couple of texts from Aerick. *Figures.*

Aerick: Babe, Amar needs me to fill in for a couple of classes because someone is sick. I won't be home when you get there. See U later.

There is another one a few minutes later.

Aerick: Text me when you're home safe.

Elation tugs at my lips. His protective ways are so freaking cute sometimes. If he's working, then I should probably make some dinner. I start the car and head for home. We haven't gone grocery shopping for over a week, so a stop at the grocery store is going to be a necessity. Aerick gave me $40 before I left 'just in case', so I have enough to pick something. I think about it for a few minutes and decide on making steak and potatoes for dinner. We still have potatoes and green salad, which means we only need the steak.

Thankfully the traffic is still light since it is only one in the afternoon. The one thing I've come to dislike is the traffic here. The freeways are a traffic mess from two in the afternoon until seven. It's ridiculous. It's nice most of the places we need to go are all within a few blocks, because fighting the traffic is nerve-wracking. It takes no time at all to get to the grocery store near home.

Once there, I find the steak, and also grab a few other things we are out of like bread and eggs. It's probably good that Aerick gave me some money because over the past few weeks I've slowly whittled away at the small bit of money I had. I never realized how buying a few small things here and there can really add up. Aerick doesn't like letting me pay for things, but I've done it here and there and now I'm down to only $30 in the bank. It's okay though, because we will be going back soon so I can start saving up some money. Although, I don't have much I can spend it on, other than clothes.

Aerick has put his foot down and completely refuses to let me pay any bills. I talked about maybe getting a car of my own, but Aerick said that since he has a Charger and an Armada, it really isn't necessary, and that I'm free to use his cars anytime. After seeing my irritation though, he backed off, saying it was up to me and if I did want to get a car, he could always put one of his in storage so I could park my car in one of the two stalls that are assigned to our condo. That made me feel a little better, since his overwhelming need to control things can be a bit overbearing at times, but it's clear he's trying.

In the end, I pretty much decided he was right. Besides, if I get a car it is just going to sit there most of the time and then he would be paying for storage for his car. It just creates another bill for him to pay, and I don't want that either, since he won't let me pay for any of them. I'll just save up my money and I am sure there will come a time when it comes in handy, or maybe just buy a car outright instead of having to make payments.

Getting home, I text Aerick before he can freak out. He doesn't answer me right away, but if he's in the middle of teaching a class, he wouldn't be able to. I get busy to distract myself, putting the groceries away and putting the steak in a marinade to sit for a few hours. After finishing, I grab the laptop, turn on some music, and get comfortable at the dining room table to start another grueling outline to study for my next two tests.

When I focus up at the clock on the wall, it's almost four-thirty. It didn't seem like I'd been sitting here that long. I stand up and stretch. watching out over the water, the sun is beginning to set and is beautifully bouncing off the few clouds that are in the sky. My body is in need of at least a little exercise. I didn't go to the gym today because of my test, so a quick walk before it gets dark should work nicely. I save the paper I'm working on and write Aerick a quick note in case he comes home before me, letting him know where I went and that I will make dinner when I get back. It's better than a text because he won't have the option to argue with me. I grab my keys, debit card and my phone and head outside.

There is a nice little coffee stand up a few blocks, so I decide to go get a latte before walking down to the Marina Park. At the coffee stand, the barista Stacy already has my coffee ready, since she can see me coming from down the block. I've always admired the way people like her can just remember what people drink all the time. Especially since I only come here once or twice a week. She must have hundreds of customers a day. I thank her and give her a generous tip before taking my coffee and heading back down to the Marina.

Walking down the long dock that goes out over the water, I breath in the ocean air that no longer smells odd to me. The sun has almost sunk below the horizon and the colors in the sky are just phenomenal. I never understood people's obsessions for sunsets until moving here. It is so captivating; I could probably just stand here for hours gazing at the skyline as the movie of color moves across the sky.

After a little while of watching the sky change to several different colors, I resolve to at least walk to the other end of the park and back to work off the latte I just drank, before going back home to make our dinner. I follow the walkway into Beach Park and walk around the meadow, then back around the Founders Lodge, before finally heading down to the beach. It's getting a little chilly now that the sun is gone and the park is empty, but I don't mind. It is so serene here. I just love it. This place reminds me of everything that Chicago isn't. I pick up a few of the rocks and throw them out into the water, watching them drop into the water with a splash.

"You shouldn't do that!" A deep voice behind me startles me and I spin around. A tall, muscular man is standing several yards behind me. The sun disappeared a while ago and I can't see all his features clearly, but he has a smirk on his face, which eases my tension a bit.

"Sorry. I didn't know you aren't supposed to," I tell him sweetly, hoping I won't get into any trouble. "I've seen kids do it in the past and had no idea there was any rules against it."

"It's sort of an unsaid rule. If everyone that came down here did that, the rocks would gradually disappear, and it changes the landscape of the beautiful park." His voice isn't quite rude, but it is almost condescending.

I give him a polite smile just because I don't want to let him ruin my peaceful evening. "Like I said, I apologize. I will be sure not to do it again." He nods his head up and down slowly but when his eyes follow his nod, staring me up and down, it gives me the creeps. That's my cue to leave. It's getting pretty dark and it's noticeably cooler now. I only have a tight tee shirt and skinny jeans on. *Why didn't I bring a jacket?*

I give the gentlemen a nod and head back toward the front of the park to the Marina. After a minute, I chance a glance over my shoulder and the guy is still standing in the same place, staring out at the water. Okay, that was kind of creepy. Maybe now I understand why Aerick always insists on joining me for my walks. Once I get a little further away where I'm sure the guy can't hear me, I start humming and slow my walking to a leisurely pace, as I walk the path back around the meadow. Might as well enjoy this last part of my walk before having to get back home and do more studying. I really do hate school, even if I am good at it.

The park around me is so green, full of trees and bushes surrounding the lush green grass. This would be a cool place to have a birthday or even a wedding. There is often a small breeze, but it is so beautiful. Wedding pictures done here at sunset would be amazing. I can't help but wonder if Aerick and I will ever get married.

I'm startled again by that same voice and it sounds quite close to me. "Miss?" I turn quickly and the guy is standing only a few feet behind me. *How did I not hear him behind me?*

"Yes?" I ask warily.

"Do you live around here?"

The hair on my arms is standing on end and my body is tense with nerves. "Yes. I live just above the Marina."

His lip turns up in a unsettling grin. "Then you should really know that you shouldn't walk around in the dark alone. Maybe I should walk with you."

I huff. That has got to be the worst pickup line I've ever heard. I wonder how many times he has tried that. "I think I'll be just fine. Thank you," I say, a little sarcastically.

I'm about to turn around but he moves a step forward to bring him closer to me. "But there may be someone bad lurking around here." His tone sends chills down my spine. The sudden change in the atmosphere puts me on high alert. *Time to get out of here – like now.*

"I um... will be okay. I can defend myself," I try to say with confidence, but my voice betrays me.

"Good, because it's more fun when you fight back!" He jumps forward and grabs me by both my arms. *Shit!*

My chest reacts automatically, cutting off half of my oxygen supply. *This is not happening.* "Let me go, asshole!"

He grips my arms with bruising force as I try to pull out of his hands. "Come on. No need for the language sweetness." He starts dragging me to the side, toward the trees and bushes. *This cannot be happening.*

"I said fucking LET ME GO ASSHOLE!" I scream at him as my panic rises and then I feel a sharp sting across my cheek.

"I said watch your language, you little fucking whore." My vision is burred as the tears well up in my eyes from the sting of his hand and I feel myself getting dizzy from the lack of oxygen reaching my lungs as my panic attack is setting in. *Do something now!*

As he tugs me to the side again, I lung forward toward him, bringing my knee up, and it successfully connects with his groin.

"Bitch!" he yells as he releases me and bends over, grabbing himself. I quickly turn to run but I am stopped as he grabs a handful of my hair, pulling me back flush against him, and he wraps his arms around me tightly. Tears are streaming down my face and I can't believe this is happening to me. Before I move to try to get out of his hold, he throws me to the ground and kicks me hard in the ribs before sitting down on top of me, straddling my hips. He grabs my hands in one of his and pins them above my head and clamps his other hand over my mouth, muffling my shouts. Using the hand over my mouth, he pushes my head down forcefully, and the back of my head hits one of the scattered rocks that litter the grass, causing a sharp pain to shoot through my head. My body stills for a moment, stunned by the pain.

"You're mine now, sweetness." His words bring me out of my momentary trance, but he's much stronger the me and no matter how much I struggle, the only thing I can move is my legs. My legs flail around and I manage to push my hips up off the ground just a little, but he is too heavy for me to get them up enough to turn. "

"Ohh, feisty!" *Fuck, Fuck Fuck!*

My lungs burn. *BREATHE!*

I have to get free. *Fight Nadi!*

He pulls my face to the side and leans in, putting his disgusting lips on my neck. "Damn sweetness, you taste good!" I try to buck him off me again, but it's useless. There is another sharp sting on my cheek as he smacks me again, then moves his hand down to grip my neck. Both my hands shoot to his wrist, trying to pry it off. Blackness begins to edge its way across my vision, and I am suddenly reminded of Aerick's sulky face as I left to go take my test. *This can't be it.* That can't be the last time I see him.

The man yanks down the collar of my shirt with his other hand, ripping it, and he begins to touch me. *Fight Nadi!* I hear Aerick's words in my head and I am back at camp, watching him demonstrate ways to get away from an attacker. *Fight!* His words come again.

The man's hand is tugging to undo his pants. *Nadalynn, NOW!*

I react to Aerick's final demand in my head. My arm shoots up, encircling around his arm holding me down, breaking his hold on me as I buck and twist my hips at the same time. Pushing off with one leg and tucking the other, I use my other hand to push his shoulder all in one movement. We both roll to the side and I end up sitting on top of him.

His stunned expression is barely visible through my tears. Before he can react, I grab a rock lying in the grass next to me and hit him as hard as I can in his temple. He goes limp below me. *He's out, RUN!* I tell myself, and I am up in an instant, running toward the marina.

I stumble along the walkway, trying to catch my breath, but my chest is tight, my legs are rubber and my body is becoming numb. I have to keep going, but my body isn't listening. As soon as I reach the marina, I collapse onto my hands and knees. I'm not going to make it. He's going to catch me.

"Nadalynn?" I hear the sound of my angel, and I want to look at him, but I can't move. "Babe what...?" is the last thing I hear as my body collapses completely on to the concrete and the blackness pulls me down.

* * * *

"Baby, please wake up. Please." Aerick's panicked voice pulls me back up and sirens are getting louder and louder. "Nadalynn, baby, open your eyes, please!" After another moment my eyes cooperate; they open up and meet the most beautiful eyes.

"Thank God, babe. What happened? Are you okay? Who did this to you?" His words come out in a rush. He's holding me in his lap and there's a voice coming from the phone pinned between his shoulder and his ear. "She is awake. Where's the damn ambulance?" he shouts into the phone. "Nadi, tell me what happened," he says again – the panic clear in his eyes.

"A man in the park…" My voice is strained and it hurts, causing tears to stream down my cheeks.

"Christ, don't tell me he-" I shake my head 'no' quickly as checks over my body. "Did he touch you?" he asks, focusing down at my ripped shirt, but I can't answer him. "Fuck!" He pulls me tight against his chest. A police car comes to a screeching halt and two policemen get out and run over to us.

"Sir, Sir. What happened?" they ask him.

"Someone in the park attacked her." His eyes fall back to mine. "Babe, is he still there? Please tell me you knocked his ass out." My body is shaking uncontrollably and I try to pull Aerick closer to me. I nod my head, telling them yes, and the cop quickly pulls his gun out of the holster and tells us to stay here. He and his partner quickly run off toward the park entrance.

Another cop car pulls up and the man runs off toward the park behind the other two, while a policewoman comes over to us. "Ma'am, there is an ambulance on the way. Are you hurt?"

"No," I tell her in a whisper as I try to slow the river of tears flowing down my cheeks.

"Don't you lie Nadi, your face is swollen. Tell the truth – what happened?" Aerick is trying not to freak out in anger.

The officer glowers at him, irritated. "Sir, please calm down."

He just throws her his glare before turning his head back to study me. "Babe, you've got to tell me," he says softer as runs is fingers along my sore cheek. "Please."

My eyes squeeze shut hearing the sorrow in his voice. "A guy in the park. He attacked me." His grip around me tightens and I bury my face in his chest. "He tried to... to..."

"But he didn't, right?" he says, getting angry again.

I shake my head. "I knocked him off me and hit him with a rock and... and ran, but I couldn't breathe... I couldn't... I panicked... I..." My words stutter from my mouth, not allowing me to finish because my words turn into sobs. My chest begins to tighten again thinking about the guy's hands on me.

"Shh, shh. It's okay baby, I got you. I got you! You're safe now," he says gently to me as he holds me tightly and rocks me in his lap. His soothing words and actions push my oncoming panic attack back down. Several more police cars and an ambulance pull up and a flurry of noise starts around me. I just try to bury my face deeper into Aerick's chest. I don't want to be here; I just want to go home. I hear the officer's footsteps retreating and she starts talking, repeating what I said to someone.

Another pair of hands is suddenly on me and I jump and start squirming, knowing they don't belong to Aerick, but they disappear quickly. "Nadi, calm down!" Aerick's authoritative voice rings out and I still in his arms that are so tight around me they're cutting off my air. He relaxes his hold when I still.

"Ma'am, I need to check to make sure you're okay." The unfamiliar hand lightly touches me again and I flinch away from the touch. *Don't touch me!*

"Nadalynn, please let him check you over." My hands fist into Aerick's shirt. His finger pushes under my chin, forcing me to gaze up into his eyes. "Please – for me," he says softly with pleading eyes. He looks so mad, sad, and almost scared. My heart breaks and for a moment we are the only two there as I stare up at him. I draw in a few deep breaths and loosen my hold on him.

Aerick grabs my legs and slides them around so I'm sitting between his legs with my back to him, but he keeps his hold around my waist, and I keep my hold on his arms. I work to breathe like Christian taught me and focus on not freaking out again. There are too many people watching me right now.

"She gets panic attacks when she is touched. She has already had one and is on the verge of another, so try not to touch her, as much as possible," he tells the EMT sternly, and it pisses me off that a bunch of people just heard that, but I am grateful for his warning as well. The guy nods his head at Aerick before he brings his focus back to me. I see pity in his eyes, and I hate it. Anger quickly rises within me.

"Don't look at me like that," I snap at the guy, before glancing down so I don't have to see his face.

I feel Aerick humph from behind me. "There's my firecracker," he whispers in my ear. The feeling in my chest is gone now that my anger has pushed it completely away, and making me a little better.

"Were you hit in the face at all?" the EMT asks. The police lady stands behind him, watching.

"He just slapped me a few times." Aerick's arms tense.

"Does your head hurt anywhere?"

The question brings the throbbing in my head to the forefront of my thoughts. "I hit the back of my head on a rock or something when he threw me down," I say quietly and his face turns white as he focuses past me to Aerick. He must have that look on his face.

"Can I check your head?" I nod at him and lean forward, lowering my head. He presses around my head and when he hits the sore spot, I flinch away from his hand and groan. He pulls out a light and checks my eyes. "Did you lose consciousness?" I did, but only because of my panic attack.

"She passed out when I first found her," Aerick says when I hesitate.

"Were you hit anywhere else?" he asks after feeling around my head more.

"He kicked me in the ribs." Knowing what he is going to ask, I lift up my shirt just enough to expose the aching area on my side.

"Fucking Christ," Aerick says quietly behind me. My answers are just pissing him off more and more as he finds out what happened. The guy lightly touches my side and my hand clamps down on Aerick's leg as I try to keep myself under control. I try not to groan at the pain, but my face still crunches up and I'm relieved when he quickly removes his hand.

"Anything else?" he asks hesitantly, glancing down toward my pants.

"No, it happened pretty quickly. He didn't have time to do anything else," I say him quickly and a bit of relief flashes across his face.

"Well, overall I would say you are pretty lucky. I don't think your ribs are broken, although there is a chance you may have a concussion. You will need to get that checked out at the hospital."

"Ma'am, you have blood on your hand and shirt," the woman cop interrupts. "If it isn't yours, then my guess is that it belongs to your attacker." I glance down and see what she is talking about. *Did I hit him that hard?*

"I don't know… I hit him with a rock in the head and ran." Aerick kiss presses down on the top of my head.

"I'm sorry. I know you have been through a lot, but I need to get a sample of that from your hand, and we'll need your shirt." I nod at her as someone brings her a large case.

She opens it, taking out a camera, an empty vial, and several long cotton swabs. "First, I have to snap a few pictures, okay?" she says softly. She has me hold out my hand so she can take a picture of it. She continues taking pictures of my face, my torn shirt and my ribs. Then she collects samples of the blood on my hand. I hate this, I just want to go home.

"We can get the shirt from you at the hospital." Her voice is soft, but it just pisses me off more, because I hear the pity. I have had enough.

"I'm not going to the hospital," I tell her firmly.

"Nadi, you need–"

"I said I don't want to go." I stop him before he can say anything else.

"I would recommend you be checked out," the EMT says.

I glare at him and stand up quickly, making me a little dizzy, but I hide it successfully. "I'm fine, I just want to go home." Aerick stands up behind me.

"Ma'am, you really should–" The lady starts up, but I am not listening to another word.

"I said I'm not going. He didn't rape me; he just beat me up. NOW LEAVE ME THE FUCK ALONE!" My voice turns into a shout and Aerick's arms are around me in a second.

I turn in his arms and bury my face in his chest. "Come on, babe, listen to them," he urges me, and my will begins to falter. *Shit.*

"Please, please, just take me home. I just want to go home," I plead quietly. Tears fill my eyes and spill over. "I just want to go home, please."

He holds me tightly to him. "Okay," he says in defeat.

"But ma'am," I hear the lady say again but Aerick shakes his head 'no'. I hear her sigh behind me. "That's your choice, but please know I advise against it. We'll still need your shirt. You can change in the ambulance."

Aerick releases me and removes his shirt. "Here: put this on."

I follow the lady officer and the EMT to the ambulance. He lets me in, and she follows as he closes the door behind us. I quickly remove the shirt but when I pull the shirt over my head, I get a shooting pain in my ribs. *Christ!* I don't know why bad stuff always has to happen to me.

"Sir! Sir! Stop!" I hear people yelling outside the ambulance. I quickly put on Aerick's shirt despite my ribs protesting and jump out of the ambulance. "You fucking asshole. I'll kill you!" Aerick is yelling and there are several police officers pinning Aerick to the ground yelling at him to 'calm down' and 'stop'.

"Aerick!" I shout but then I see his eyes move and mine follow. I turn my head and see a policeman putting someone in the back of his car. I'm frozen in place and the noise fades into the background.

"Nadi... Nadi... Let me... needs me..." I half-hear Aerick's struggled words, but I can't stop staring into the face of my attacker and suddenly can't breathe again. They found him. They got him. More tears escape my eyes. Then Aerick is in front of me, cutting off my view. I feel his hands on my face and see his lips moving but I can't focus. He wipes the tears from my eyes and his voice comes into focus.

"Breathe, baby. Look at me and breathe." His words break through and I inhale a deep breath into my aching lungs. "That's right, breathe. It's okay, I'm here. You're safe." He pulls me in his arms again, bringing me the comfort I desperately need. I squeeze my eyes shut. *I just want to go home.*

Unfortunately, I have to stay for another hour answering questions, before they allow Aerick take me home. He never lets go of me once and I'm extremely grateful. Feeling him against me gives me comfort and strength as I recount exactly what happened again for my statement. I'm so grateful when we finally get to go home.

Standing in front of the bathroom mirror, I feel so cold now. Not because it is cold in here, but because I lack his touch. My eyes roam over my naked body. My skin is all red from my overly aggressive scrubbing in the shower. It made sense that if I could just scrub hard enough, it would make the ghost feeling go away, but even after washing myself over and over, it is still there. There are several bruises on my arms and a large bruise on my ribs. My cheek is swollen, and my eyes are all red and puffy. I want to get dressed but I am dreading the pain of having to move. All my muscles are sore, and my head is pounding despite the pain medication Aerick had me take already.

There is a light knock on the door. If I hadn't locked it, I'm sure he wouldn't have bothered, he would have just come in, but he doesn't need to see the bruises. I slip on my underwear and shorts and then pull on Aerick's shirt, jerking and wincing as the pain shoots through me. I open the door and see his guarded eyes.

"You okay?" he asks cautiously, and I give him a nod. He draws in a deep breath, not believing my words for a second. "Babe..."

I thought I could be strong, but my composure breaks in an instant hearing his voice, and tears well up in my eyes again. I cover my face with my hands. I'm so weak. How does he love someone as broken as me? I sink to my knees.

"Hey," he says softly as he comes over and holds me. "It's okay, babe." My tears turn to sobs. His strong arms fold around me, lifting me as he carries me into our room. He perches himself on the end of the bed with me in his lap and holds me tight as I release everything I've been trying to hold back the last few hours.

Once my tears have dried up, he stands and lays me in bed, pulling the covers up. "Please don't leave me," I whisper, completely exhausted. I need him, even if it is selfish of me.

"I'm not going anywhere." He slips on a pair of sweats and a shirt. I hadn't even realized he still didn't have one on. He crawls into bed next to me and pulls me tightly to him. My fatigued body relaxes in his embrace. A kiss presses into the top of my head. I just want to forget today. A song begins to play in my head, pushing away all other thoughts.

"Hold me now. 'Til the fear is leaving, I am barely breathing… Crying out. These tired wings are falling, I need you to catch me…"

"I am so sorry, I failed you again. Please forgive me." I scarcely register his sad words and I try to answer him, but I'm too far gone and exhausted as my sleep takes me.

CHAPTER NINE

(Sunday, November 15th)

THUD, THUD, THUD... The boots pound the ground moving toward me. I'm all by myself in a small room, with just a bed and small desk. He's coming to get me.

Aerick where are you? I need you!

Thud, Thud, Thud... It's getting louder. No one's here to help me, I'm all alone. He is going to get me because I'm all alone. A small whimper escapes me as I pull the blanket tight to my chest and curl up in the corner of the bed to make myself as small as possible.

Thud, Thud, Thud... Oh God! Please don't let him come in here.

"Oh, Sweetness. I hear you." He knows I'm here. Oh, please someone help me. Please, please, please! The heavy boots stop just outside the door. He isn't going to pass me up – he's coming for me. I can't breathe. This isn't fair – why me, why me?

"Sweeetnnness," his sickening voice calls out to me. The door slowly starts to open, and I pull the blanket over my head to hide myself, even though I know it won't do any good. His heavy steps enter the room. "Don't hide from me, sweetness. I just want one more taste." His hand finds my shoulder...

"NO!" I sit up, breathing hard. The room is dark. My hand searches the bed to my side but there is no one there. Just as I come to that realization I'm alone, Aerick opens the bedroom door.

"Hey, you okay?" he asks as he comes to sit beside me.

I concentrate on slowing my breathing. "Yeah, I'm fine." Sweat is dripping down my face and back – it feels disgusting. That is only the second nightmare I've had in the last week, so they're getting better, but it still worries me. I throw myself back on the pillow and Aerick's hand finds my hair as he stretches out beside me and begins running his fingers through my hair.

"Babe, I have about had enough hearing those words out of your mouth. You're not fine. You had another nightmare." His low growl makes me flinch away from him. He draws in a deep breath to calm himself. "Do you want to talk about it?" he asks, in a much lighter voice.

He means well but I also know he doesn't like hearing what my dreams are about. I've seen the way he's been sneaking peeks at me when he thinks I'm not paying attention. He blames himself for what happened to me a few weeks ago. It isn't his fault, but no matter how much I tell him, it doesn't ease his feelings.

Several nights I've woken up to feel him running his fingers along the scar on my stomach where Liz stabbed me. I haven't been able to convince him that one wasn't his fault either. There's got to be something I can do to make him understand my bad luck isn't his fault.

"Nadi, are you listening to me?"

"Sorry babe." I move to snuggle into his side.

He inhales another deep breath. "What were you dreaming about?" His tone is now soft and soothing, but telling him anything isn't going to help him.

"Don't remember. I just have a creepy feeling now," I lie. His fingers pause for moment but then he continues stroking my hair. He probably knows it's a lie as he has an uncanny way of knowing when I do.

"I love you, Aerick," I reassure him, running my hand along his stomach, hoping he will let it be.

After a moment of hesitation, he leans over and kisses me on the head. "I know, Princess. I know."

We lie like that in silence for a while until his breaths even out and I know he has fallen asleep. Watching at the handsome man lying beside me, I just don't get it. How can he love me so much? I'm hardly pretty. Yes, I can be strong-willed, but that is only because my past has made me a broken and sad person who hides behind the persona of a much stronger person. He sees past that facade and knows the true me, so it makes no sense how he can love me. As much as I know he deserves better than me, I can't find it in my heart to push him away. I'm too selfish to let him go.

The large black and white clock beside the bed clicks another minute down, landing it at six in the morning. Going back to sleep at this point is useless so I decide to get up and take a shower before making us some breakfast. As carefully as possible, I slide away from Aerick, freezing for a moment when he stirs, but he just huffs and turns his head away. When I'm sure he hasn't woken up, I grab one of his clean shirts and some panties and head into the bathroom.

The dry sweat causes the shirt to stick to my back as I pull it over my head. Gross. The bruises on my hip are still there but are now faded. All the other bruises have gone away and my ribs are still a little sore sometimes but it's bearable.

The day after I was attacked, the bruise on my ribs had grown and turned several different shades of purple, green and yellow, that ran along my entire side. It's much lighter now and is mostly just an outline on my lower side but it is still there, reminding me, and Aerick, of what happened. Shaking my head, I pull my eyes away from the reminder and get into the hot shower.

Aerick has been absolutely frustrating when it comes to sex. He has refused to make love to me since it happened because he says he doesn't want to hurt me. I'm starting to wonder if it is that, or if it's just that he doesn't want someone as tainted as me anymore.

It's stupid and I try to tell myself that isn't the truth but the more time that goes by, the harder it is to push the feelings away that Aerick might not what me anymore. I've tried several times the last few days to instigate it but anytime I do anything other than kissing him, he pushes me back and tells me 'I need time to heal' and that he 'doesn't want to hurt me'.

It has left me not just wanting him, but wanting a release. I never knew women craved sex until now, but I suppose when you enjoy mind-blowing sex nearly every day, it becomes an addiction. I have a half a mind to relieve my own ache, but it's not something I've ever done, and it probably won't help much anyway – it's him I want. *Stop thinking about it!* I silently yell at myself – just thinking about it is making it worse. Letting out a sigh, I rinse the conditioner out of my hair. I'm so tired of everything in my life being so difficult. My whole life is one big struggle of emotions and it isn't getting better anytime soon.

Tomorrow we are going back to camp for the winter session, so things are going to change. No more strong arms slung around me as I sleep. We won't be able to be openly affectionately when the cadets get there, and yet again I will be adjusting to a new home. I'm not even sure where I'll be sleeping. There really isn't anywhere else for them to put Jeff and I, but Luther told us not to worry about it, and things would be ready when we got back.

I wonder if Aerick's over-protectiveness will ease a little when we get back there. Being in a more controlled type of environment might ease him off a little. I thought I'd been prepared for his overbearing behavior after the attack, but he has hit an all new limit. He refuses to do anything or go anywhere without me. Geez, other than when I'd gone to take my test this last week, he hardly leaves me in a room by myself for more than a few minutes, but once we get back to camp he isn't going to be able to be with me 24/7. Then again, it wouldn't be surprised if he asked me to wear a tracker at this point. There is no way he can keep all bad things from happening to me. The sooner he realizes that, the better off we will both be. Like he has told me in the past, I always seem to find trouble.

Exiting the bathroom, I see that Aerick is lying on his back with his arm stretched over the place I should be. He's still lying uncovered and my eyes roam greedily down the body that is fit for a god. Every perfectly defined muscle in his stomach, all the way down to the V where his low hanging shorts start. The ache between my legs starts again and an idea hits me. If this doesn't work, then nothing will. I change into a tight cami tank top so my bruises are still covered but it still shows off my body shape.

I carefully crawl up the end of the bed to straddle his legs and place a light kiss on his happy trail. He shifts a little and lets out a moan. I give him a second because if he wakes up right now it will ruin my plans. Pulling the string on his basketball shorts, I untie them and pull the front of them down, along with his boxer briefs, until he is fully exposed. The sight of him is sweet. Slowly, I wrap my hand around and massage him, causing him to twitch in my hand. After a few moments, he begins to stir under me.

"Fuck, babe." He's still half asleep, so I continue. "Nadalynn." His eyes are still closed, and I am elated, knowing that at least he knows it's me and he isn't dreaming of someone else. I lean down, waiting for him to open his eyes. It only takes another minute before his moans stop suddenly and his eyes fly open.

The minute his eyes find mine, I take his hardened length in my mouth. "Ahh fuck!" he moans loudly but I don't give him any time to stop me. I suck on him hard, pushing him to the back of my throat. His hand finds my head, but he doesn't stop me. My tongue swirls around him as I pull him in and out of my mouth. After a lack of sex the past few weeks, it's only a few minutes before he reaches his climax. He doesn't bother warning me anymore, knowing I wouldn't stop anyway. His warm fluid fills my mouth while a flurry of curses around my name stagger out of his mouth, but I'm not finished with him yet.

"Princess," he moans harshly. "What are you doing?" He's still breathless from his orgasm. I hum, knowing the vibrations drive him crazy. "Fucking Christ." His words push my need for him almost to an unbearable place.

Finally stopping now that he is ready again, I climb up his body and kiss him with every ounce of passion in me. His lips move against mine without hesitation, letting me know he wants this too. I just pray that getting him this excited is enough to make him forget about his aversion regarding my pain, but I have to admit that my ribs are screaming at me for leaning down in my current position.

He must sense it after a moment because before I know it, he rolls me onto my back, so he is half lying over me on my good side. "Babe." He tries to break our kiss but my grip around his neck tightens, keeping his lips to mine.

"Nadalynn," he tries again but I am not having this, I want him so bad right now. "I don't want to hurt you," he pleads against my lips and I stop kissing him but don't let him move back away from my lips.

"Please, Aerick," I beg him. "I need you Aerick, please." A tear escapes my closed eyes. I can't handle being rejected by him again. This is what I need this right now. He pulls back just slightly. "Please," I plead softly one last time and more tears fall.

Another second passes before I feel his lips begin to kiss me from the side of my eye down to my ear, following the trail of tears. I can't help the tears that continue to fall, knowing he is giving himself to me finally. His lips find mine again. "Please don't cry, babe. I'm yours, all yours," he whispers into my lips and his words hit my heart hard. This is what I've been craving, to feel him, and it is such sweet bliss as he kisses down my neck and removes my panties before shedding his own clothing.

As he positions himself between my legs, he holds himself higher than normal, barely putting any weight on me, but thoughts are washed away quickly as he slowly slides into me until he is fully sheathed. "I've missed this so much," he whispers in my ear as he begins moving at a very comfortable, slow pace.

"You are my world and I love you so much." His pace picks up as his frenzied words sink in. I love this man so much it hurts, but I am so overwhelmed with emotion and the feeling of him inside me, that I'm speechless. I pull his lips back to my own, hoping it will be enough for now.

* * * *

After two mind blowing orgasms rip me apart, he finds his release again and then collapses beside me, trying to catch his breath. I curl into him and he wraps his arm around me tightly. "Can we wake up like that every day?" he jokes and for the first time in weeks, *my Aerick* is back.

"That would be lovely," I admit as I kiss him on his chest.

"You appear to be feeling better." He almost sounds smug about it and I wrinkle my nose up.

"Sorry. Perhaps it would help if my Prince Charming wouldn't leave me so sexually frustrated." I meant to say it as a joke, but my irritation is peeking through.

"Nadalynn, I just didn't want you to hurt any more than you already were."

I prop myself up on my elbow so I can gaze down at him. "I am a big girl and can deal with the physical pain. Especially if I'm getting that kind of pleasure out of it."

"But I can't deal with hurting you." The frustration is clearly painted on his face now.

"I'd much rather the physical pain then the emotional pain."

"What do you mean emotional pain?"

"Aerick, are you really that blind that you don't see?"

"Apparently, because I have no idea what you are talking about."

How can he not understand this? "Aerick, you've spent almost two weeks treating me as if I were a bubble ready to break. Until this morning, you refused to have sex, you barely kiss me, and the only time you hold me tightly is when we are asleep."

"Because I don't want to fucking hurt you!"

"But you are hurting me. It's starting to feel like you don't want me anymore," I confess, closing my eyes to hold back the tears.

His finger slides under my chin, pulling it up, and he waits until my eyes find his. "How could you think that? I tell you all the time how much I care for you." His eyes are overflowing with sincerity, but he still doesn't get it.

"Just telling me isn't enough, Aerick. Haven't you ever heard the saying, 'actions are louder than words'? I need to feel you dammit – I need you!" I sit up, throwing my hands up in frustration, as a tear escapes my hold.

"Okay, okay, I get it. Calm down. I'm sorry."

A small amount of relief flows over me but I'm not done yet. Might as well get this all out of the way. "And you have to stop beating yourself up over this." His eyes drop away from mine. "It isn't your fault, Aerick."

"I should have been there," he murmurs quietly.

"No, Aerick, you can't be with me every minute of every day, and you can't blame yourself when bad things happen to me. That's my life in a nutshell – a string of bad shit that always lands at my feet."

He sits up so he's eye to eye with me. "But now I'm with you. It's my job to protect you." His lips press into a line as he tries to control his anger.

My hands clasp his face. "And you do," I tell him softly, trying to get through to him.

"It doesn't seem like it. I've failed you so many times."

"That's not true. You may have not stopped what happened, but you were always there for me after. Like I said, I'm a big girl and can protect myself. There may be times I'm don't come out on the other side completely unscathed, but I'm alive."

"Barely," he grumbles but his anger is mostly gone.

"Seriously, babe. I don't know what I would have done if you weren't there for me after those things happened. My whole life I've always wanted what we have now. To have someone that could hold me, someone I felt safe with, someone who would accept that I'm broken and doesn't look at me with pity. And now that I have you, that is what I need; you to continue to be that rock for me, no matter what happens." He closes his eyes, taking a deep breath. "Aerick, please don't push me away physically because the emotional pain it causes is worse than anything else I've ever felt." His eyes fly open again and he stares at me, deep in thought. He goes to talk but hesitates for a moment and I wait, letting him have the time he needs.

"I'm sorry. It's just that, the way I feel about you, it's something I'd never thought I would have. For the first time in my life I'm afraid of something, like so afraid it gives me nightmares. I honestly wouldn't be able to live with myself if I lost you. Twice now, in only a few months, my nightmare has almost come true. Nadalynn, I refuse to live without you. You're mine and it is my job to protect you; you can't tell me not to protect you."

"Fine then, protect me from the outside world. Stop trying to protect me from you!" I yell at him, completely frustrated.

He stares at me, shocked at my outburst, and then his lips are crushing to mine, rough and demanding. He pulls my legs over his lap so I am straddling him. I moan as our still naked cores meet and he hardens against me. He lifts me slightly, positioning himself under me and even though my ribs scream at me, I'm lost as he pushes me down, burying himself into me.

* * * *

"Nadi..." Aerick's whispered voice wakes me. Light kisses float across my shoulder and arm. "Princess, time to get up." I don't even bother opening my eyes because right now I'm content and would be happy to just stay right here in our bed for the rest of the day. My stomach growl; it obviously doesn't agree with my mind, and I hear Aerick chuckle next to me.

"Why?" I question him sleepily.

"As much as I'd love to stay here in bed with you all day, I'm hungry. Come on, it's our last day by ourselves and I want to take you somewhere."

"It isn't the gym, is it? Because I already got enough of a work out today." I giggle at him and he laughs.

"No, I just thought we could go eat and show you one of my favorite places to go when I was a kid."

I perk up at the thought of seeing something he did as a kid. "Okay."

"Nice, now get dressed, my stomach is killing me. It's a little chilly, so grab a sweater." He gets off the bed, grabbing his sweater, as I realize he is freshly showered, dressed in jeans and a shirt. He must have been up for a while.

He stops in the doorway. "You got five minutes, hurry up or we'll go in what you have on." I glare at him, since I'm only in a cami, and he feigns innocent before continuing out of our room. I jump up quickly and throw on a pair of cute jeans and a shirt before grabbing my Donnelly Bootcamp hoodie.

Aerick is waiting for me with a smile. I notice the sweater he grabbed is the same one I've put on. It is kind of corny to match, but who cares. We head down to the garage and he surprises me by opening the passenger door to his Armada instead of the Charger. I mean, he told me it was his, but we never use it. I give him a confused look.

"I want to stop and get the oil changed, since we're taking it tomorrow." It baffled me at first that he had two cars, but he explained that he got it last year because he needed a 'winter car'. Apparently, a Charger is not the greatest thing to drive in the snowy Washington mountains.

The SUV is amazingly comfortable and has all kinds of electronic things on the dash, just like his Charger. He pulls out of the garage, but he surprises me when we only drive two blocks away and he parks at Wally's Chowder House. "I'm too hungry to wait," he explains with an adorable smirk and I laugh; men and their stomachs. Then again, my stomach is telling me it's not funny.

* * * *

Aerick exits the freeway just past Seattle. We had a delicious lunch, then went up to the car shop so he could have the Armada's oil changed and everything checked over before we leave tomorrow. Aerick's mood is a bit lighter, which really has made me feel better. I've just wanted things to go back to normal and hopefully they're starting to.

"So, are you going to tell me where we are going?" I ask curiously as he drives down what appears to be a residential street.

"Nope, I'm going to show you." He suddenly pulls over on the side of the road and parks the car. I gawk at him with a raised eyebrow.

"Come on," he says as he gets out of the car. I follow him and he takes my hand. We don't walk long before I notice people gathering under the bridge we are walking toward. My curiosity is piqued. *What are we doing?*

As we go under the bridge, my eyes follow his and my mouth

drops. Against the wall under the bridge is a huge dirt troll sculpture that looks like he is crawling out from under the bridge. It's absolutely massive and is one of the craziest things I've ever seen.

"Pretty amazing isn't it?"

I nod my head.

"That's an actual VW beetle that he's holding." I just stand there admiring the artwork before me.

He moves to stand behind me, moving his arm around my waist. "I used to come here as a kid," he tells me softly in my ear. "I was always fascinated with odd pieces of art and I remember reading 'Three Billy Goats Gruff' when I was really little. I particularly remember reading it because my dad got mad at me, telling me it was a waste of time to read fairy tales." He pauses and my heart sinks a little thinking how horrible it must have been for him.

"My grandfather brought me here when I was about ten. After that, I found any reason I could to come back. It was my way of defying my father and his idiotic beliefs. It was almost comforting to me to sit here and watch parents bring their kids. It showed me that not all families are as dreadful as mine. I would dream about what it would be like to have different parents."

I scan everything around, seeing what he means. There are kids running around, crawling on the troll, laughing and playing while the tourists snap pictures. I turn and gaze at him. He has the most daydreaming smile on his face. It's a look I don't think I've ever seen before.

"You want to take a picture with it?"

We go closer to the troll and Aerick ask a guy who is clearly a tourist to take our picture with his phone. We stand back toward the statue and Aerick squeezes my side, causing me to grin widely as our moment is captured in time. The gentleman hands Aerick the phone back and I peek at the picture. We are both smiling like crazy fools; I love it. Aerick thanks the guy and we admire the troll for a few more minutes, watching everyone around us.

"I miss him already. It's a stupid notion, since I really didn't see him that often, but just knowing I can't call and talk to him, it makes me miss him." He's talking about his grandfather and my body sags in sadness for him.

"Did you see the note I sent with the check I signed over?"

I shake my head. "No, I didn't want to intrude."

He huffs behind me, holding me tighter. "You're never intruding, Princess." He kisses the top of my head. "I wrote that the money was to pay for my real father's funeral expenses and that as his son, I was proud to pay for it. I told him I no longer have a father and to never contact me again."

I don't know what to say to that so instead I turn in his arms and just hold onto him tightly.

We walk down back to the car and I try to lighten the mood again. "There's a lot to see in this city, isn't there?"

"Yeah, I guess. I've lived here for so long, I just have never really thought about it. How about I show you a little more of it?" he asks me with his signature smirk.

"Sounds good to me. Where to?" He begins driving and seems to be thinking about where he wants to go. "How about the Seattle Center? We can catch dinner before we go back home."

This man and food. I gaze at him in amusement. "Okay."

It only takes us a few minutes to get to the Seattle Center. Aerick pulls me around, showing me the different things, like Key Area where some basketball team named the 'Super Sonics' used to play before they moved to Oklahoma, and the Experience Music Project museum which he promised to bring me back to when we had more time since he knows I love music. We walk over and he shows me where the Seattle Science Center is and again promises to bring me back to see it since it is too late to go now. He stops in front of the gate and reads the board on the ticket booth. I can almost see the wheels turning in his head.

"What?" I question, raising my eyebrow at him.

"I'll show you after dinner," he says, as he starts pulling me toward the Space Needle that is just to the side of us.

"Wow. That's where we're going for dinner?" Aerick just nods in response.

We wait in line to ride the elevator up to the top. When we get up there, the view is breathtaking. Of course, the ever-knowledgeable Aerick tells me about the history of the Space Needle and I listen, fascinated. I could listen to him for days.

After I've gotten my fill of the view, we go to the restaurant. I feel a little underdressed but it doesn't appear to bother Aerick, so I just ignore it. We have a wonderful dinner and I love that Aerick is smiling again. He keeps finding ways to touch me and keeps a hold of my hand. The problems of the past two weeks melt away as the evening wears on.

Once we make it back outside, it's dark, but the city is lit up in artificial light. Aerick clutches my side and we walk back to where the science center was. A line has formed; we go to the ticket box where Aerick simply buys two tickets but never says what they are for.

We get in the line and the suspense is killing me. "Okay, tell me, what the heck are we doing?" An absolutely adorable smirk plasters across his face.

"We are going to see Laser Linkin Park." I love the sound of my favorite band, but I am still confused.

"Um, what is that exactly?" The line starts moving before he can answer me, and we are ushered through the courtyard into the side of a building and into a large room. Aerick leads me over to the center and pulls me down so we are lying on the floor on our backs. I peer around us, feeling a little odd, but everyone one else is doing the same. After a several minutes the lights go out and music starts playing. It's deafeningly loud. Laser lights start dancing around the room to the music. This has to be the coolest thing I've ever seen.

I squeeze Aerick's hand that is still in mine. He pulls me over to lie on his shoulder. He kisses me on the head and begins running his hand through my hair as I listen to my favorite band's music bumping through the air to the light show. This man has completely blown me away, again!

* * * *

On our way home, I get a text. It's from Terrie.

Terrie: Hey Nadi, hope you are feeling better.

Aerick told Paulo about what happened, so naturally Terrie found out. She has asked if she could come visit but I haven't felt up to seeing people with the tension that was between Aerick and me. I ended up telling her that I was okay, but that I wasn't feeling well and would see her when we got to camp. I decide to text her back.

Nadi: Feeling much better. Can't wait to see you tomorrow.

"Who is it?"

"Terrie, she's just checking up on me. I can't wait to see her tomorrow." He huffs and goes back to concentrating on driving. Something tells me he isn't completely happy about going back, but I don't want to ask because right now I am floating in the clouds from the day we have had. It is getting late, so I don't expect a text back, but after a minute, my phone buzzes.

Terrie: Good to hear. Can't wait to see you, too. We can have a little girl time finally :)

Girl time, huh? Not really my thing, but I really like Terrie. I guess she's like me a little. She's strong, doesn't like girl drama, and is straightforward. I admire those qualities, so if I'm going to have a close girlfriend, she would be a pretty good fit. My phone buzzes again.

Terrie: I almost forgot. Make sure to see me in my office tomorrow.

It has been 13 weeks, so I need to do a pregnancy test and give you your shot.

My stomach falls and my whole world goes numb.

Pregnancy test?

CHAPTER TEN

(Monday, November 16th)

"SOMEHOW, I FOUND a way to get lost in you..."

I'm momentarily pulled from my thoughts as Aerick starts humming the song playing through the speakers. I don't know if I have ever heard him do that and if I had, it could have only been once or twice. He loves to listen to music just like me, but he usually only moves his head to the music. Not wanting him to stop, I keep myself from peeking at him and continue focusing out the window. We're close to camp and I'm just getting more and more nervous.

Terrie's text has been repeating over and over in my head. Aerick of course has noticed my change in mood, despite me trying to hide it. He's asked several times what's wrong, but I play it off as if it's nerves because we're going back to camp. Like always, he knows there is something else, but he hasn't pushed me any further.

Aerick tugs on my hand that he's holding causing me to turn toward him and he kisses the back of my hand. "*I'm nothing without you,*" he says, singing along to the song as he gazes into my eyes. I can't help but allow the joy to spread across my lip. That was so corny but just too freaking cute. He kisses my hand again, mirroring my smile. "We're almost there. You still nervous?"

"Yeah, a little." I bite the inside of my cheek and immediately regret it because again, he knows I'm holding something back, but I don't want to worry him about it so don't bother elaborating. It's probably fine; it has to be.

"Are you sure you don't want to tell me what else is bothering you?" *Why does he have to be so damn observant?*

"It's just nerves, babe. That's all."

He rolls his eyes at me before going back to concentrate on his driving. It's the truth, it really is nerves; it's just not about camp. Maybe a little fear as well. Seriously, I can't be pregnant. I'm barely eighteen and we have only been together for a few months. I don't even know if Aerick wants kids. I certainly haven't ever seen him around them. Having kids is such a big deal and honestly, I kind of wanted to be married before having kids - something I don't think Aerick and I are even close to yet.

If I was pregnant and Aerick didn't want it, ending the pregnancy would never be an option. I just wouldn't be able to live with myself doing something like that. But how could I raise a kid all by myself? And if Aerick and I split up, there is no way I would be able to stay at the camp or live with him. That only leaves me going back to Chicago, pregnant and alone. This is always my luck: just as things start to look up just a little, something has to go and screw it up.

We finally exit the freeway and make our way to the back road that goes to the camp. The knot in my stomach tightens with every mile we get closer. *It's going to be fine. It has to be.* I try to convince myself to ease my nerves but it's useless. As we turn to pull into the long driveway, Aerick squeezes my hand again.

Pulling up to the front of camp, there are only a few cars in the parking spots. We still have another hour before we are supposed to be here. Luther sent everyone a group text early this morning telling us to stop by his office once we get there, so that needs to be our first stop. Aerick gets out without a word and gets both of our large bags out of the back before we head to Luther's office.

"Good morning Aerick, Nadi. Welcome back," Luther greets us. "Nadi, you will be in cabin two with Terrie. We've added a few cabins and there are some extra things going on this session, but I would like to wait until everyone to get here, so I don't have to repeat myself. Aerick, the instructor cabin dorm will remain the same. Why don't you guys go get your things put away. I want everyone in the mess hall by eight for our welcome breakfast." With that he nods, effectively dismissing us.

Aerick nods and leads us outside but I notice he's a little upset. "You okay?" I ask as we walk.

"I just don't like being out of the loop. He never said anything about changes." Always wanting to be in control.

"So does Luther always run things by you first?" I question curiously. *How close are they?*

He glares at me. "No, not everything, but usually anything that effects myself or the other instructors."

I giggle at his pouty face, earning me another glare. "I'm glad it takes me being irritated to get you out of your little mood." His lips press into a line. It shouldn't be funny to me, but it is. Pouty Aerick's facial expression is priceless and I let out another giggle as his irritation radiates off him.

"Sorry babe, but I can't help but think of the irony. That pout of your is fit for a Prince," I tease, and we stop at the door in front of my cabin.

Suddenly he drops our bags and pushes me up against the door with his body. "Keep laughing at me, Princess, and see what happens." His voice is completely serious as he puts his hands on my hips, gripping them tightly, sending a tingling feeling through my body.

"In that case, stop distracting me so I can do it some more, because that sounds fun to me."

His lips are on mine, soft yet demanding, and I am lost in his touch. A muffled moan escapes my lips and his fingers clamp around me even tighter. "We still have a while before we have to start work." His whispers vibrate on my lips and right now that sounds like the best thing I've heard in days. All of a sudden, the hard surface behind me is gone and I'm falling backward. Aerick's hands on my hips keep my feet in place so only my top half falls back. I grab his shirt and pull myself back up. "Or not..." he grumbles, sneering over my shoulder, irritated again.

"Sorry to interrupt, but I didn't care to hear what I think was going to happen next," Terrie says in a way too peppy voice.

"Terrie, you are on thin ice right now," he tells her. I go to face her but he holds me in place.

It takes a moment to realize his hardness is pressed against my stomach and he is probably trying to hide it from her, so I just put my hand on his chest. "Easy tiger."

His glare shoots to me but I ignore it and slightly turn my upper body toward her as much as possible with him holding me in place. "Hey, Terrie. Sorry about that."

"What are you sorry for? She interrupted us!" He retorts and I slap his chest for being rude.

"Well, there is the Aerick we all know and love. I knew he wouldn't be too far away," Terrie jokes, obviously oblivious to the death glare she is getting right now. "Anyways, sorry Aerick, but I need to steal Nadi away for a few minutes. I need her in the clinic." She grabs my hand and yanks me away from him before he can protest. "You can just put her bag on her bed, and I promise to return her soon," she yells over her shoulder as she hurries us through the courtyard to the infirmary. I glance back in time to see Aerick shake his head and adjust his pants before picking up my bag.

"Do you love tormenting my boyfriend?" I question irritated.

"Sometimes." She acts as if it is nothing.

"Do you have a death wish or something?" She gawks at me like I have two heads.

"Please, I could see past that 'I'm the biggest badass' facade he puts on a long time ago. He doesn't scare me." I stare at her in disbelief. "Okay, so he can be a little scary sometimes, but I know he would never hurt me."

At least she admits it, because he kind of scares me sometimes too. My mind flits back to the night he got the phone call from his mom. Thinking back, it was pretty terrifying watching him in the kitchen.

We get into the building and she goes straight to a urine cup on her desk. "Here you go. Just pee in this and leave it on the sink when you're done." She hands it to me, giving me a shove me toward the bathroom. *Damn.*

All my previous worries that had been momentarily forgotten, spring to the front of my thoughts. *Breathe, just breathe.* I quickly do what she asks before my body has time to completely freak out.

As soon as I walk out, she walks in without focusing on me. I'm frozen standing next to her desk as I watch her move around. She put on some gloves and I have to turn away, I can't watch what she is doing for some reason. I start biting on my nails as she comes back out and starts unlocking her cabinets. "It'll take a few minutes. So-." She tries to start a conversation, but it is drowned out by my thoughts. All I can do is gape at the floor

Please say not pregnant, please say not pregnant. It seems like I'm going to die here. Why can't the stupid test be instantaneous? For the first time, I feel like I'm having a panic attack that has nothing to do with someone touching me.

"Nadi? Nadi, what do you think?" I glance up and Terrie is standing in front of me holding the test. "Have you heard anything I've been saying?" Her brows pull together and I regretfully shake my head no and glance down at the test. She studies to the test and then glances back to me. "Were you worried about this?" She gestures to the test in her hand, but I don't answer.

Her lips press in a line. "I'm sorry. I didn't mean to worry you. It's negative." I let out a staggered breath and lean down, putting my hands on my thighs. "Jesus, Nadi. Were you really that freaked out about it?"

I glower at her like that was the stupidest question on the planet. "Um, yeah, Terrie. I don't think me being pregnant right now would be a good thing," I snap at her and instantly regret it when her face falls. "Sorry. It's just that I've been freaking out since I got your text last night. I mean, kids in the future is great but right now I don't think I could handle that!" My words begin to rush out. "With everything that has been going on, and all the things that have happened in the last six months, it just..."

"Hey, slow down," She throws the test away and disposes of her gloves before she places her hands on my shoulders and stare me in my eyes. "Stop freaking out. You're not pregnant. It's just procedure to do a pregnancy test before each shot. As with any birth control, it isn't one hundred percent, but it has one of the best prevention rates of any birth control option. So, don't worry about it." I draw in a deep breath. "Sorry. It never occurred to me that you would react like that."

I shake out the lingering panicked feeling. "It's okay. I was overreacting." She puts on a clean pair of gloves and picks up the shot on the table. I turn and pull down the edge of my pants.

"Did you hear me say that Paulo and I are going to get a place together?"

I glance up, surprised and she chooses that exact moment to stick me with the needle. "Ouch!" She lets out a little chuckle. "And to answer your question, no. I didn't hear you the first time, but that's awesome.

You guys are actually really cute together. Where are you guys moving?"

"We have the next couple of months to figure it out and find a place. My lease is up next month, so I've spent the last few days packing, and my brother is going to put it all in storage for me. My apartment is just a small studio, so there isn't much."

I hope they decide on a place near us. I've come to like her a lot and she's one of the only 'girlfriends' I have. "That is nice of your brother. Do you really think you can put up with Paulo 24/7? I mean, that man doesn't take anything seriously."

She lets out an exaggerated huff. "Please. Tell me how that is any better than that man of yours that wouldn't know how to take a joke if it hit him in the head."

We both giggle because she is so right. "Speak of the devil," she says as she walks over to dispose of the needle in an orange box.

Aerick walks in and his eyes immediately fall to my hand that is still rubbing my backside where she gave me the shot. He raises an eyebrow, looking between us. "Should I come back another time?" he asks, causing me to giggle.

"He may not be able to take a joke, but he sure knows how to dish them out," I say, and Terrie and I both fall against each other laughing as Aerick just stands there looking confused.

"Okay, if you two are done now," he says, irritated, after a minute of us just laughing at him – which just makes us double over in a new fit of laughter. I feel so much lighter now that all those stupid ideas are out of my head. Getting fed up, Aerick finally just clasps my hand and pulls me outside. I wave back at Terrie, telling her we'll see her in a bit, and follow behind him.

When I calm down a little, Aerick stops and turns toward me. "If you don't tell me what is going on right now, I swear I am going to absolutely lose it. You have been all over the place since last night and it's driving me nuts. What is going on with you?"

I sober up seeing the expression on his face. I didn't realize it was bothering him that much and now I feel like crap for being the cause of his anxiety. The fact that Luther has left him out of the loop, and he doesn't know what is going on with me, has pushed his overwhelming need to control things to the limit.

"It was nothing, really. Terrie just caught me off guard, but everything is fine now."

"You call that an explanation?" He glares at me more intensely.

He's in instructor mode and it irritates me just a little. "Aerick, stop looking at me like that. I am not a cadet that you can intimidate." His jaw tenses and after a moment his features soften a little. "It's just Terrie had mentioned needing to take a pregnancy test before she gave me my next birth control shot, and it kind of freaked me out thinking that it was a possibility, because we stopped using condoms after I got the first shot."

He pales as pure shock turns his body stone solid. His hands tighten on me and it reminds me of when I saw him on the phone with his mom. "Babe!" I say, trying to shake him out of the little trance he just fell into, but it doesn't work, and it puts me on edge. "Aerick!" I shout slightly as my hand tightens round his arm.

"You're not –"

"No, I'm not. It was nothing, really. Just a routine test." I don't move my eyes off of him and after a second, my words must sink in. He quickly pulls me into a tight hug, and I feel his body relax.

"Thank fuck." He mummers in my ear. Guess I was right when I thought he may not even want kids. It's not a subject we need to broach right now, but I file it away so we can have that conversation in the near future, at a more appropriate time.

"Nadi!" I hear one of the best voices in my world call out to me. I spin around to see Jeff walking up to me fast and I wriggle out of

Aerick's arms and throw myself at him. He catches me in his arms and gives me a quick bear hug before setting me back down and moving his hands to hold my own.

"Well, you look, the same," he observes, and I'm not sure that should offend me so I ignore it.

"Yeah I missed you too."

A loud noise comes from beside us as Aerick clears his throat. Jeff immediately drops my hands when he sees Aerick staring at our joined hands with a murderous expression on his face. "Oh, ah, hey Aerick."

Overjoyed despite Aerick's less that welcoming scowl, I go to stand in front of Aerick just for good measure, effectively placing myself between the two. "Did you just get here?"

"I actually got here a little bit ago and took my stuff to my cabin."

"Cabin? I thought Luther was putting you in with us," Aerick's confused voice comes from behind me.

Jeff shrugs at him. "I don't know. Luther said I'm in cabin four with the other guy that Ayla picked up from the airport."

The tension radiating off Aerick is suffocating. It's clear he's itching to ask more but he doesn't. He probably doesn't want to hear that the new kid knows more than he does.

"I was just heading over to the breakfast. You guys coming?" Jeff asks after a moment of awkward silence.

"Yeah, sure," I tell him and grab Aerick's hand, who follows but pulls me to his side so he can hold me around my waist. *Great, here we go again.* The jealousy thing really needs to stop, but I try to ignore his possessiveness to avoid irritating him further.

We walk into the mess hall and several people in uniforms are setting up breakfast. Luther must have had it catered. I see Paulo and Trent as Aerick pulls me to the side toward them. Aerick lets go to grab Paulo's hand and do their little back slap hug guys always do.

"S'up, little sister?" Paulo says before lifting me up into a tight hug.

My body tenses but he doesn't hold on long and Aerick immediately grabs my waist when he puts me back down.

"You know dude, one of these days she is going to hit you in the face," Aerick says matter-of-factly.

"Oh, come on. She would never do that to me. She loves me," he teases.

Aerick's fist clenches at his words. "Well, if she doesn't, I might," he threatens, and I give him a warning glare. Paulo is only playing around, no reason to be an ass. Jeff looks at me, seemingly comfortable with the banter.

Truth be told, I'm actually slowly getting use to Paulo's touch, similar to the way I am toward Patrick and Jeff. Like with them, as long as I see or know it's him touching me, and it doesn't last more than a few seconds, I don't panic. I'm ecstatic at the thought that he would be the first since it happened, other than Aerick's unique hold over me. For the first time, I'm starting to believe Christian's words that it will get better.

We continue to make our way around the room as everyone greets and catches up with each other. I am surprised to see that even Christian is here, especially as he'd just been at the forefront of my mind. He greets me with a kiss on the cheek, much to Aerick's irritation, and we talk for a few minutes. He informs me it is just for the day, since he only has to be here for the pre-camp meeting. He makes sure to remind me he would like to start seeing me again while we are in camp, and that he has arranged with Luther to have a session with me after he finishes with the cadets each week. We greet Laura, who has also joined us for the meeting. Everyone appears to be here already, with the exception of Brayden.

Just before eight o'clock, Luther walks in with another man I've never seen before and it's hard to not notice how hot he is. He must be in his late twenties and is wearing a gorgeous half-smirk that is peeking through his short, well-kept goatee. His longer dirty-blond hair is brushed back, falling to the middle of his neck, and boy does that tight white shirt show off his well-sculpted upper half.

My eyes quickly divert to the floor, feeling a little guilty for my wayward thoughts. I suddenly feel a little exposed as Aerick steps slightly to the side of me, dropping his arm from my waist, and secures his hands behind his back, so I am no longer hidden from the two men by Aerick's massive form. I suspect Aerick's action is because Luther has walked into the room and Aerick is attempting to move into professional mode. In fact, most of the staff have stood up a little straighter. It appears that everyone looks up to Luther as much as I do. For my part, I'm grateful for all he's done for me. He gave me a chance, despite my attitude and ridiculous past. I would venture to say that he has done that for most of us. He's truly a stand-up man.

"Good morning, staff. If everyone wants to dish up their plates and have a seat at the table, we can get started." Everyone immediately moves toward one of the long tables that has a huge assortment of food in warming plates. We all get our food quickly and move to sit down at the table. A couple of people murmur about the guy that walked in with Luther, but no one happens to know who he is.

Once we are all settled, with Luther at the center of the table with Mr. Mystery, Luther stands up to address everyone. "Alright everyone, quiet down." The room immediately gets quiet enough to hear a pin drop.

"Welcome back to camp. It is great to see everyone." Luther's eyes roam over everyone at the table and an irritated look crosses his face. As if he was expecting it, Brayden walks in the door and everyone turns to him.

"You're late," Luther chides. "I will be docking your pay for one hour, Brayden."

"Ahh come on, Luther, I'm barely fifteen minutes late."

Aerick shakes his head slightly and mutters to himself, "Dumbass."

"Rules are rules, Brayden. Did you want to make it two hours?" He raises a questioning eyebrow.

"No. Sorry, Luther," Brayden concedes with a sigh.

"Get your breakfast and join us," Luther speaks, dismissing him. I guess Luther tends to be just as hard on his staff as they were on us. This camp means a lot to him, so it only makes sense that he wants the best for it.

"For you newbies, let this be a lesson. I don't like tardiness or half-ass work. I have expectations and you'll be made aware of them. They are to be followed to a T if you want to keep your job here." His eyes stay on Jeff and me as he is talking, and we nod at him when he is finished.

"Now, since Brayden has made me be an asshole this morning, let's get back to our meeting." Brayden sits down in the last seat at the table next to Trent and Trent punches him in the arm. "Today I have a little news for everyone." He motions for the guy next to him to stand. "This is Gavin. I am excited to report that Chicago has decided to open their own camp a little quicker than previously planned. Gavin here owns an old education summer camp just outside Chicago that is currently undergoing renovation to become the new bootcamp. Gavin will be joining us for this session to observe how things are run. He will be joining daily tasks and rotating around to learn every part of how we do things. I expect each and every one of you to show him the same respect you show me and help him learn, just as I have taught you."

Luther introduces all of us, going around the table telling Gavin who we are and our position in the camp. He then motions to Gavin, giving him the floor, and moves to his seat.

"Good morning, everyone. It's a pleasure to meet each of you," he declares in with a slight British accent. All the girls' mouths drop open, including mine and a grin cross his face like that is a normal reaction.

I'm quick to compose myself before Aerick notices, but Terrie is not so quick, and Paulo gives her a dirty look from across the table.

Gavin continues, "I appreciate you letting me into your camp, Luther. I only hope I can learn enough to be as successful as you've been. I look forward to working with you all over the next few months." He sits back down, and Luther stands again.

"I have a few more things to announce. To help Chicago's camp to be successful, I've agreed to help out with staff a little as well. So, after this session, Ayla, Jack, and Laura are all relocating to Chicago to work for Gavin." Several of us glance to Ayla, who is sitting on Luther's other side. "That also means I have a position opening for Operations Manager. Aerick and Brand, I'd like one of you to take that position. Please think about it and I would like to talk to each of you later today about it." Aerick has tensed beside me.

"With Gavin, Nadi and Jeff all here training and learning, I'm going to need all you veteran staff to pick up the slack. Laura will also be helping out more with this session to refresh her before she leaves us. Ayla has made up a training schedule for this week that she will be passing out in a few minutes. We want to get them up to date as quick as possible with vital information before the cadets get here. In addition to training, we need to prepare for the cadets' arrival. Supplies need to be stocked, the camp needs to be cleaned up and put in order. I will have information packets for everyone by Thursday so you can read up on all the new cadets. We have one week to get everything in tip-top shape. Go ahead and finish up your breakfast and then we can go into everything in more detail." He looks around again at all of us. "Welcome back staff; and, Nadi and Jeff, welcome to the other side."

* * * *

By the time I make it back to my cabin, it is just after six in the evening. Our meeting lasted the entire day, right up to when dinner was delivered at five, and only stopped occasionally to allow everyone a bathroom break. We went over some updated statistics from previous sessions, and over the entire week to come, day by day. Luther explained what he expected of us, going into detail for the sake of Jeff, Gavin and me. We worked through lunch and by the time the pizza was delivered for dinner, I felt exhausted from the overload of information. The stack of papers in my hand are just a reminder of everything we went over.

I throw them down on the neatly made bed with my bag on it. Strong arms circle around me from behind and it is such a welcomed feeling. I hum, leaning my head back against Aerick's chest. He hardly touched me all day other than squeezing my leg here and there under the table. I cover his arms with my own. It has been months since I had to go all day without touching him whenever I felt like it, but Aerick would never be anything less than completely professional here, especially with outsiders around.

When we are technically on the clock, we are not to be perceived as a couple, which Aerick has already explained to me. I thought I was prepared for that, but after just one day, I miss his touch so much. I turn around and cuddle into his chest. "I have been waiting hours to be wrapped in your arms," I tell him honestly.

He untangles one of his arms to clutch my cheek in his hand. "And I have been waiting all day to do this." He leans down and captures my lips with his own. I moan at his contact. I never get tired of feeling his expert lips, that always seem to be able to take my breath away.

"Hey guys." Terrie and Paulo walk in and we break apart. Aerick leans his forehead against mine. "I have to go meet with Luther. I'll see you later." He kisses my forehead and releases me. Man, this whole roommate thing kind of sucks.

"Aerick, are we working out tonight?" Paulo asks before Aerick gets out the door.

Aerick's eyes find mine, asking me silently, and I give a slight shrug. I could use it after sitting all day. "Sure, I'll meet you here in an hour."

"Sounds good, man."

Aerick leaves, closing the door behind him.

I open up my bag and start unpacking, needing to do something to keep busy until he gets back, or I'm going to go stir crazy.

"We are really going to have to make some kind of schedule so we can have some private time with our others," Terrie says and it mirrors my feeling exactly.

"I couldn't agree with you more," I tell her and Paulo lips turn up in amusement, flopping down on her bed. "Dammit Paulo, get your grubby shoes off my bed or I'm going to kick you ass out of it."

I giggle to myself. I just like her more and more.

"Okay, sister – some ground rules." I turn to her, raising an eyebrow. "Well, I am a fairly clean person and Luther doesn't like our cabins to be messy, so no leaving your stuff everywhere."

"That's easy enough. You may get tired of my OCD," I warn.

"Second, if you and Aerick need private time, warn me first, because it's the last thing I want to walk in on."

I try to stifle my laugh. "Back at you!"

"Yeah right, Nadi. You know you would enjoy seeing all of this." Paulo gestures his hand up and down his body and I turn so he can't see me blush.

"Please, Paulo, don't make me vomit," I say and see Terrie roll her eyes.

"Here." She walks over to the door and puts a small silver bracelet around the door handle. "If this is on the outside doorknob, we know not to enter. Okay?" I nod; that makes things a little easier.

"Anything else, Terrie?" I ask, before Paulo can say anything else.

"Nope, not that I can think of. I'm pretty simple." There are still things I need to talk to her about, but not while Paulo is here, so I go back to putting my stuff away.

"Hey, my darling. I'm going to go finish unpacking real quick so we can play cards tonight. I'll see you in a bit," Paulo tells Terrie as he gets up off the bed. When he is gone, I turn to her while we have a moment alone.

"Hey, Terrie. I need to warn you about something."

She stops, going through her paperwork. "What's up?"

It's embarrassing to admit it, so I buck up and just tell her before I lose my nerve. "I sort of get nightmares. Not usually often, but after what happened a few weeks ago, they've been coming a little more often."

She gives me a warm smile. "No problem. It's no big deal."

I'm grateful for her playing it down. "Well, if they are ever bad enough you feel you need to wake me, just be careful. Aerick made the mistake of not watching himself when I was a cadet and ended up getting hit in the face."

She teases loudly. "I would have paid to see that." I join in the laughter.

We continue on after that, putting things away and straightening up. We split the desk drawers and shelving so that we each know whose stuff is whose. I have just enough time to finish and change before Aerick is knocking on our door.

When I open it, he is in workout pants and a tight tee shirt, almost mirroring what I have on. "Ready?" he asks. I give him a nod and we head out to the path.

It is weird to be out here this time around because it is so dark already. Last time we were here, it was light until around eight or nine. Now it's getting dark by five. There are lights on all the buildings that go around the courtyard, lighting it to a dim glow. Paulo is already out there waiting for us.

"Anything new?" Paulo asks Aerick and Aerick gets a sour look on his face.

"Luther says everyone needs to sleep in their own beds this week because Gavin is here."

"Dude, are you serious? " Aerick nods his head yes.

"Man, that sucks."

"My thoughts exactly," I tell them both and they laugh at me.

"Hey guys," Jeff says, running up behind us. "Going for a run?"

"Yep. Are you joining us?" Paulo asks him.

"Yeah, if that's cool with you guys. I need to get back into shape. I haven't really worked out much the last few weeks."

Aerick joins in the laughter and I glare at him. "Knock it off, Princess, I'm not trying to be mean. I'm guessing no one told you two about this Friday."

I raise an eyebrow at him. "No, I'm sorry. My boyfriend failed to mention it." The sarcasm oozes out of me.

Paulo turns his face to hide his snickering. "Well, you should really get on him about that. Anyway, the whole staff gets together, and we have MMA style fights on the Friday before the cadets get here. So, you better get up to par kid," Paulo tells us, smacking Jeff on the shoulder harder than necessary.

I roll my eyes at them and start jogging. "Well, let's get going then."

I hear Aerick chuckle at me.

"You sure you can handle that one?" Paulo questions him.

"Fuck off," he volleys back and takes off to catch up to me, with Jeff and Paulo close behind.

We run in a comfortable silence for almost thirty minutes before we are all sweating and breathing heavily.

"Alright, are we ready for a race? Loser buys the winner a bottle of their choice," Paulo asks and we all slow to a stop.

"You're on, man," Aerick answers quickly.

"I'll get in on that," I say, with just as much confidence.

"Not me man, you all are clearly in better shape," Jeff says.

"Alright, one lap. Jeff can be the judge."

We take another minute and then line up. "Ready, set, go!" Jeff calls out to us and we're off.

My shorter legs have to work twice as hard to keep up with the guys, but I hang back just behind the boys so that I don't tire too quickly. "Come on, Aerick, your girl's making you weak?" Paulo taunts and Aerick picks up the pace, forcing both of us to follow.

Once we get halfway around the path, I know I need to pick it up. There is no way I'm losing, so I start pulling up to the outside of Paulo, who is barely behind Aerick. I even up with Paulo as we reach the three-quarter mark.

"Not happening, sister," Paulo says breathlessly and with my endorphins in full swing, I push myself to the limits to start moving in front of him.

We are all in a full sprint for the last part of the run. We're all really close and even though my legs are screaming and I'm out of breath, it's still going to take one last push to get past Paulo. I wait until we are about fifteen feet from our makeshift finish line. Pushing myself into maximum overdrive, I'm able to pull just ahead of Paulo before we cross the finish line, all within a foot or two of each other.

We all double over, putting our hands on our knees. "Aerick, Nadi, Paulo," Jeff shouts out our placing.

"Make it a bottle of Crown, dumbass," Aerick says, shoving Paulo's arm as they both stand up, but I can't just yet. That run made me a little dizzy.

"I'll beat you one day," he tells Aerick, making him chuckle.

"Man, you can't even beat a girl," Jeff busts out laughing. "Dude, I don't know why you're laughing, you didn't even try," Aerick throws at Jeff, earning him a smack on the arm from me.

"Be nice."

Gavin, who is standing against the cabin that he is sharing with Jeff, pushes off and walks over to us. "Not bad. Another few feet and she may have beat you both."

I'd never admit it out loud, but a few more feet and I would have collapsed. "Yeah, one day," I say, still out of breath, and notice a smile tugging at Gavin's lips. Aerick is still watching me with a concerned look, probably because I'm still not breathing normally. He snaps out of it hearing my words and raises his eyebrow at me.

"Keep dreaming, Princess."

"So, do you guys all work out everyday, even when you don't have cadets here?"

Of course, Aerick stands a little straighter like he is in charge. "The instructors are expected to be in better shape than the cadets at all times. So yes, most of us work out daily. The rest of the staff are encouraged to keep up the physical training and will often join in the workouts."

Gavin seems impressed. "Yes, you all do appear to be in good shape. I'm pretty big on fitness myself. Mind if I join you guys occasionally?"

"Anytime. We usually run or hit the gym most evenings, even once camp starts." I swear Aerick was made for this job. He sounds so confident and carries himself like this is second nature to him.

"I'm going to hit the gym now; you guys have a good night." With a nod he heads to the gym.

"Well, I need a shower," I tell the guys and Aerick leans over to whisper in my ear.

"Can I join you?" I roll my eyes at him.

"You don't have clothes over there yet, so you're going to have to accept a rain check," I tell him, but obviously not quiet enough because Paulo chuckles to himself.

"Fine," he says, getting all pissy and staring into my eyes but I don't back down, I just stare right back at him.

"Come on, Aerick. Poker in thirty. Jeff, you in?" Paulo says, breaking Aerick and I out of our little bubble.

"Poker. Hell yeah!"

"Meet us back in Nadi's cabin." We all nod and Aerick gives me one last glance before we all split up, going our separate ways.

* * * *

I am lying on my bed, freshly showered, with my feet on Jeff's lap, who is sitting at the end of my bed. There's a knock on the and Aerick and Paulo walk in with their chest rumbling in amusement. Aerick walks over and drops a small stack of clothing on my stomach. "Put them in your drawers," he tells me, before sending an irritated look to Jeff, who picks up on the issue right away.

"Hey, don't look at me like that. Your girlfriend is the one that thinks I'm a foot stool."

Aerick's irritated gaze smooths out a little. "Yeah, she seems to do whatever she wants. Maybe you should try standing up to her."

"I found life is easier if you just go along with it," Jeff chuckles.

Aerick glances over at me. "Oh, I don't know, I kind of like it when she gets feisty."

He quickly closes the two steps to my bed and grabs me by my waist, picking me up off the bed, causing me to grab his neck and wrap my legs around his waist as I let out a loud squeal. "Aerick!" I shout, smacking him on the chest, rewarding me with his cute smirk. I can't help but to give him a chastising kiss, he is so adorable when he is playful.

"See?" he tells Jeff as he lets me down and everyone laughs.

We gather around the table and again we are one chair short, so I end up sitting on Aerick's lap while they play. I don't really mind because I would much rather be sitting here with him playing over my shoulder, touching and kissing me, than playing myself. It reminds me a lot of the first night I joined them for poker. But I will have to talk to Terrie to see what we can do to get a few folding chairs, because I have a feeling this isn't going to be the last time.

CHAPTER ELEVEN

(Tuesday, November 17th)

Aerick POV

I JUST DON'T understand why in the world my life has decided to become so complicated. Six months ago, I was in this same spot, preparing for a new session with a new group of cadets. My life at that point had become an easy routine of simple back and forth – work, home, work, home. Work was my only commitment and my day to day life rarely changed. There was nothing to irritate, bother, or anger me, which was the way I liked it. It took a lot of hard work to create that life and I was more than comfortable with it.

Then she came into my life, and it's like my world has been turned upside down ever since. None of it's her fault; I don't blame her for it – not directly, anyway. Bad luck happens to find that girl wherever she goes.

A big part of it is her uncanny ability to attract men, which only compounds the other problems in her life. It took me a while to figure out exactly why that was. She isn't one of those overly beautiful, sex goddess-type women that gets every man's attention the minute she walks into the room. Yes, she has an athletic body, long dark hair, gorgeous eyes, and the cutest smile ever, but it isn't those looks that attract men. Well, maybe it attracts a few – she is beautiful – but it's everything else about her that makes her so noticeable to men.

It's the way she carries herself. She doesn't throw herself at guys. She comes across as a strong, confident, and fearless person who is just as comfortable being in a room full of men as she is in a room full of women. Assuming none of them touch her, that is. She rejects all the whiny drama that most other girls are attracted to. Drama that all men quietly curse and hate.

Everything about her personality pulls in what feels like every man around her. In the beginning, it's what attracted me. Then I figured out that part of her is that way to hide her past. At one time, I thought her whole act was a facade, but the more I got to know her, the more she proved that theory wrong. She used the bad in her life to create rock solid walls within her, but those walls just made other parts within her shine that much brighter. Her personality drew me in, but it was her heart, her bravery, and her selflessness that I fell in love with. I meant it every time I said how amazing she is.

She's an addiction. Ever since the first time I dreamt about her, the second night she was at camp. Her coming into my room, and me silencing that smart mouth of hers as she pleasured me on command. It was a little embarrassing telling Paulo about such a provocative dream about a cadet, but we just laughed it off to my lack of sex at the time. I was hooked even then, whether I wanted to admit it to myself or not.

This addiction has brought her troubled life into mine. Not only that, but it's like ever since I fell for her, my life has become more complicated. I know the timing is nothing more than a coincidence and, in a way, I'm grateful to have her with me to deal with it. She was there for me when my grandfather passed and surely, she will be here for me to help me deal with all the changes Luther is making.

It's still confusing me why Luther didn't keep me in the loop about all of these changes, and I'm absolutely livid that Luther is even considering Brand for this new leadership position. I've worked my ass off the last few years to prove to Luther that I'm better than Brand. That's why he appointed me lead instructor, and now it's like a slap in the face that he is making me prove it all over again. I've considered the possibility that he thinks Nadi is too much of a distraction for me to take on the new position, but if he wants me to prove it again, then that is what I'm going to do.

I peek at my watch. Thirty minutes before we have to be at the stage. I need to get up and shower before going to wake up Nadi. She'll probably be up already, but I'm dying to feel her lips on mine before we start the day. It sucked not being able to show my feelings toward her for the better part of yesterday, and not being able to wrap her in my arms at night kept me tossing and turning. She's become my nightly sleep aid and without her I'm screwed. A groan settles in my chest at the thought of her in my bed. I quickly jump out of bed and grab my clothes, needing to see her sooner rather than later. *I'm addicted!*

After a quick shower, I head back into the dorm where Brand and the other guys are just getting up. "Hurry up, guys. Let's not be late on the first day," I command as I finish putting on my boots and head out the door. Brand rolls his eyes, but I decide not to start my day arguing with him about respect, and just head for Nadi's cabin. I stop at Andi and Tia's cabin, pounding on their door to let them know we have ten minutes, and then continue to Nadi's cabin. I knock instead of pounding on the door.

Nadi answers the door already dressed in her uniform and brushing out her hair. The shower is still on in the other room – Terrie must be in there. I push Nadi back inside, closing the door quickly, and push her up against it.

She glares up at me amused. "Can I help you with something?"

She barely finishes her question before my lips descend, kissing her roughly and letting her feel my demand for her. My body immediately explodes with fire at the contact between us. My hands find her hair as hers find my neck, and ecstasy shoots through me when she moans into my mouth. My need for her becomes even more apparent as my pants begin to get too tight in the front. She is definitely an addiction.

Terrie chooses that moment to come out of the bathroom covered only in a towel and I break our kiss. Terrie gives me a pointed stare as I glare at her in frustration, but it's probably a good thing she interrupted us anyway, before things got too carried away. I need to go make sure everyone else is up, anyway – I have a job to do.

Looking back to Nadi, I give her another quick peck. "Maybe later," I whisper into her ear, before I pull the door open and leave her standing there breathless. I smile knowing I have the same affect on her as she has on me.

My fist pounds on Jake and Brayden's door and then I quickly move to the last cabin where Jeff and Gavin are. Luther and Ayla are in the two new cabins that are behind the four existing staff cabins, but there's no need to go there; they're undoubtedly awake. In an out-of-character gesture, I wait at the last cabin for someone to open up, since Jeff is new to this. Unfortunately, it's Gavin who opens the door only in his boxers. Clearly, it woke him up, but his actions piss me off – it could have been one of the girls at the door.

"Wake up calls part of the package?" he questions sarcastically.

"Excuse me, Gavin. Jeff needs to be outside in the next five minutes for our staff workout. Luther wanted me to let you know that you are welcome to join us." He stands there for a few moments, seemingly pondering something.

"Does everyone participate?"

"It's not a requirement but Luther frowns on lack of participation, so basically yes, all staff participate." He huffs and opens the door a little more before walking to the bathroom.

Jeff is sitting up in bed now. "Be out at the stage by six, Jeff." He falls back on his bed. "I highly advise not being late," I tell him, before reaching in and closing the cabin door.

Gavin appears to be a cocky jerk. The way he walked in here yesterday like he was already part of this place didn't sit well with me. He caught all of the girls' attention right away and several of them seemed to catch his. Initially Nadi wasn't one of them – much to my enjoyment – but that appeared to change throughout the day. It didn't go unnoticed, the way he looked at her after he witnessed our race. All I know is that he better keep his distance from her.

I'm met at the stage by Luther. He appears to be in a good mood this morning. "Morning, Luther."

"Morning, Aerick. Everyone up?"

I answer with a nod as several of them make their way over to us. "Yes sir. I've also extended an invitation Gavin, as you asked."

"Good. Thank you!"

I lean up against the stage as we wait for everyone else to join us. My eyes catch sight of and follow Nadi from under my eyelashes as I fiddle with a coin in my hand. My lip twitches as she beams, walking beside Terrie. Being back here with everyone should help her feel more comfortable about being around other people again.

She's still a little wary after what happened to her. Every once in a while, when she thinks I'm not paying attention, she gets that sad expression on her face, but it hasn't gone unnoticed. It pains me to my core that not only does she feel like that, but that there's nothing I can do for her. She's used to dealing with bad stuff on her own and it's taken a long time for her to let me in enough to help her deal with those feelings. I hate the fact that she still tries to bury it deep down. It isn't healthy. I'm trying to be patient with her but it's proving difficult. Hopefully with more people around, she'll open up a little, and as much as I hate to admit it, her being around Jeff should help too.

Jeff is following Gavin and bringing up the rear of the group. *Great.* I was secretly hoping Gavin wouldn't come. Pushing off the stage, I take several steps out before turning around to face the stage. Nadi falls in step next to me and it settles me just having her close. Luther clears his throat to get everyone's attention and we get the day started.

* * * *

I've been sitting here staring at this computer screen for the last three hours. Luther has Nadi, Jeff and Gavin training with Jake today, learning about the software program we use to track the cadets so they will be comfortable using it. Unfortunately for me, it means I've only gotten to see her while we ate breakfast and lunch. Both times, there were people around, so I haven't been able to touch her, and kissing was definitely out of the question.

I'm itching to see her later. Although, Jake's supposed to be giving her a new laptop today so she can keep up with her online classes, which probably means she's going to be distracted with homework tonight. Glancing back at my computer screen, I have a lot of the groupings and scheduling done. Part of the task Luther has given me, in addition to my normal duties, is to schedule in Jeff, Laura, Nadi and Gavin, rotating them around so that they can all participate in the different classes and work with Tia, Jake, and each of the instructors. The scheduling for the instructors is the same as last session, ensuring I don't have to work with Brand very often. Once Luther gets the list of cadets, I'll just need to group them into instructor groups and the computer program will automatically create their schedules based on my criteria.

My phone vibrates suddenly, making me jump, and I almost knock over my water. *Thank the stars no one is here.* I pull it out of my back pocket and to my surprise, it's from Casey. Other than me asking him to use his cabin, I haven't heard from him much in the last six months or so. Normally, he has several parties out there and he always extends an invitation to me. Then again, the point of going to those parties was always to get laid, something I've made clear I'm no longer interested in now that I've got Nadi. Shaking my head, I click to open the text and read it.

Casey: Hey man, what's up?

Ok, how generic can he be?

Aerick: Not much, you?

Casey: Heard you were back in Cle Elum?!

Aerick: Yeah, we're on prep-week.

Casey: I'm having a party on Friday, need you there, man.

I had a feeling it was something like that, but I'm not sure I want to bring Nadi to one of his parties. Hanging out with him sounds good, but I'd prefer Nadi not hear about my colorful past. Liz has tainted her enough with that crap, and a drunk Casey is a loud, annoying, and forthcoming Casey.

Aerick: I dunno, we got a lot going on here.

Casey: Seriously?

Aerick: Yeah, not sure if I'm up for partying.

Casey: Again SERIOUSLY? Since when do you turn down my parties? Does it have something to do with that new girl of yours?

It isn't her fault and the last thing I need is him thinking of her like that. She'd never stop me from hanging out with friends.

Aerick: No, just other stuff going on here at camp. Luther is changing things around and it's irritating the crap out of me.

Casey: All the more reason to come party. Besides, it's about time I get to meet the woman that managed to tame the ever so sex-crazed, non-committal Aerick.

Aerick: Fuck Off!

Casey: No! Dude. I ain't taking no for an answer. I expect to see you (and her) at my place at 9pm on Friday! Paulo, Trent and the other guys are already coming.

Lord, he isn't going to stop until I say yes. I don't answer him, but I get another text after a minute.

Casey: Understood?

Dammit. Whatever, it could be fun, and we have our fights on Friday, so it will be nice to go drink afterwards. It will be cool for him to get to meet Nadi, too. He's one of my few good friends. If it gets to be too much, we can always leave.

Casey: Hello?

Aerick: Fine!

Casey: That's what I'm talking about. I'll see you there!

I put my phone down with a sigh. I can only hope Friday goes off without a hitch. Then again, with Nadi, nothing ever seems to go that way. Oh well, she's definitely worth it.

* * * *

I'm finding it difficult to not stare at Nadi as we sit in the courtyard stretching before our evening run. Normally I'd have done the gym tonight, but Nadi said she has been sitting all day and really wanted to stretch her legs, so I agreed to run again tonight. Paulo, Terrie, Jeff and Gavin all decided to join us, while Brand and the other guys all headed to the gym.

At dinner, Nadi appeared a little overwhelmed, but she perked up pretty quickly when I quietly told her we were going to go to a party on Friday. She's overeager to meet more of my friends. I don't share her enthusiasm, but it should be good for both of us.

She bends far to the side, stretching her arm out as far as she can over her head, exposing her midsection, making me groan internally. Her body shape has changed subtly since she first came here. Her abs and arms are more defined, making her appear stronger on the outside to match her attitude on the inside. My eyes are having a hard time peeling away from her luscious curves.

Unfortunately, I'm not the only one. Gavin is watching both her and Terrie. At some point soon, we're going to have to talk to him about eyeing our women; or maybe I'll just wait until Paulo gets sick of it and gives him a piece of his fist. The thought of Paulo punching him in the stomach makes me content. For now, I've had enough of his ogling.

"Let's go," I say, quickly jumping up. My irritation must be showing a little because Nadi gives me a questioning stare but doesn't say anything. She just follows me over to the path and we start running. Nadi falls into step next to me as she puts her ear buds in, and Jeff comes up on her other side.

After a few laps she removes one and glances sideways at me, asking hesitantly, "You okay?"

Jeff has his ear buds in too, hopefully keeping him from hearing us. "Yeah."

"You're lying." She gets that worried expression on her face.

I hate when she does that. "It's nothing, babe. I just don't like the way Gavin stares at you."

She tries to hide her smile. "Well, he can do it all he wants. There's only one man I'm looking at and that's all that matters."

My heart warms but the irritation doesn't let up. "The feeling is mutual, Princess." She beams as she puts her ear buds back in and we finish our laps in silence. She manages to keep up with me the entire run, while Jeff falls back with the others halfway through.

As we cool down in the courtyard, Jeff jokes about Patrick whining that he couldn't come back and that he misses Nadi. I'll probably never get used to her closest friends being male. Gavin picks up on the fact that her and Jeff are old friends all too quickly.

"You two knew each other from back in Chicago?"

"Yep. I'm from Chicago and just moved here a few months ago. I, uh, got into some trouble back home and was a cadet here last session. After finishing in the top position for the session, Luther kindly offered me a position here along with this fool." She punches Jeff in the arm, and he laughs, pushing her back as she joins in his laughter. *Man, I wish he'd keep his hands off her.*

"That's great. So, are you guys, you know, together?"

"No," Jeff says quickly as he glances at me.

"He's just my best friend. We've known each other for a long time," Nadi tells him nonchalantly, and Gavin's eyes light up.

I'm just about to say something when Paulo butts in. "Yeah, I hear her boyfriend is this big, strong, overconfident, pig-headed jerk." Luther told those of us dating that we needed to keep our personal relationships on the downlow, so that we can maintain professionalism – or some bullshit like that. This is Paulo's way of telling Gavin she's taken without telling him it's me – and saving me from my own mouth.

"Really, Paulo? He is not." He's standing next to her and she kicks him in the side of the leg lightly.

I raise my eyebrow at her. Surely part of that statement was true. Her eye's find mine and her face suddenly gets a bit red. I love being able to do that to her. "Okay, well maybe he's big and strong but the rest of that statement is pile of horse shit." We all break out into laughter, except Gavin, who is clueless. *Good, you imprudent prick.*

"Hate to cut this short, guys, but I've a ton of studying to get done," Nadi says, crushing my mood. I knew she was going to do this. *This sucks!*

"Aren't we playing poker tonight?" Paulo whines.

"Not in my cabin, you're not. My schoolwork has been put on the back burner for the last two days, I need some peace and quiet." In other words, that means no 'us' time, as well. Paulo peeks over to Terrie, but she seems to be in agreement with Nadi.

"Well hey, if you guys don't mind me joining in, we can play in our cabin," Gavin offers.

Spending time around him is not on the top of my list, but if I'm not going to be able to spend some time with Nadi, keeping my head busy is going to be a necessity. Paulo and Jeff both focus on me and once Gavin notices them, he studies me with a confused stare. *Yeah, asshole, they look to me for leadership.*

I shrug my shoulders. "I guess that works." Luther only said no poker in the dorms and the mess hall. I don't think it was because he wanted to hide the fact that we play poker from Gavin. That would be pretty impossible, since it is one of our only outlets outside of the cadets.

"We'll be there in about thirty minutes," I tell him before turning to walk back toward my dorm. I catch Nadi's eye and she has a slight grin on her lips, so I give her a wink. "Night, Nadi," I say over my shoulder. I'll make sure to stop by later and say goodnight properly.

* * * *

Terrie causes us to arrive at Jeff and Gavin's cabin late, since she took forever to meet us in front of her cabin. I didn't go in to get her because then I'd be too tempted to stay. As we walk in, the guys are sitting at the table, talking with none other than Luther. Well, this is going to be interesting. At least Luther's to be in a good mood.

"Hey guys, hope you don't mind me joining you," Luther says to us as we come in. Everyone else shrugs at him and I can't believe he is even asking.

"It's your camp, Luther," I say and sit down next to him.

Gavin goes over to his fridge and pulls out some beers. He goes to hand one to me, but I glance to Luther first. I don't know how he feels about this. He shrugs at me, so I accept the beer, and Gavin hands one to Paulo and Terrie. Luther is glaring at Jeff as he goes to accept one, but then he has second thoughts and tells Gavin 'no'. *Wise choice, kid.*

Terrie excuses herself, pulling Jeff with her to go get some more chairs.

"Luther, I'm really liking the set-up you've got here. It seems like you have some top-notch employees."

Luther's face tilts up, showing his pride. "Yeah, they are a really great bunch."

"Do you think I could convince you to let me take a few more off your hands? There's a lot of potential in several of your younger ones." *Dick.* That prick is talking about Nadi, and apparently Luther realizes it too, because he speaks up before I do.

"No way Gavin, I'm already giving Ayla up. I refuse to let you rob me of my new recruits, too. Besides, something tells me they have reasons to stay." Luther gaze doesn't meet mine, but Paulo discreetly glances in my direction.

"I don't know, Luther. Nadi and Jeff are from Chicago; are you sure they wouldn't like to be closer to home?"

My fists clenches under the table.

"Sorry, Gavin. No more picking off my staff," Luther tells him a little more seriously.

"Okay, okay. I can take a hint. In all seriousness though, thanks for letting me sit in for the session. It's much appreciated, and I promise, I'll stop trying to take your staff away." Him and Luther chuckle as Terrie and Jeff walk back in with a few more chairs, and everyone sits down to play.

This fucker is ticking away at my last nerve and he just confirmed what I already knew. *Always attracting attention.* I'll have to watch her closely when he's around. It isn't that I don't trust her – it's him I don't trust!

CHAPTER TWELVE

(Friday, November 20th)

"AERICK SEEMS LIKE a really good teacher," Gavin says to me as we sit in the office and comb over the new cadet files. I just nod my head, keeping my eyes on informational packets. It's our job to know them all by name and face before they arrive. This week has flown by and I've been so busy between camp stuff, training with Aerick, and trying to keep up with school.

Gavin, Jeff and I have been stuck together for a good portion of the week, training on all different stuff. It's been great hanging out with Jeff again and I'm really starting to get along with Gavin. He's a little older than Aerick, but it can't be by much. He told me about the camp he inherited from his mother back in the suburbs of Chicago. He explained that this new camp is a good opportunity, since the old camp is pretty run down, and that the state is co-signing the loan to renovate it – something he wouldn't have had the ability to do otherwise.

He's sweet, funny, and made it onto my good side rather easily. He's been joining us for workouts and is in excellent shape his body almost rivals Aerick's, though Aerick has been pushing himself a little harder than normal in an effort to show his dominance. *Men!*

Aerick has been working out with me in the evenings and has been teaching me different boxing techniques. He teaches Jeff too, but I think that's more for my benefit. Aerick has managed to keep his hands off me most of the time, but as the week has gone on, it's gotten harder and harder. We haven't been able to have any alone time since we got here, and it's driving us both nuts. Not from a lack of trying though. I've wanted to spend time with him. But between our daily jobs, working out and trying to get all my schoolwork done and ahead a little so that we can go out tonight, it's left no time.

Aerick told me a few days ago that we were invited to his friends' cabin for a party. The same cabin he took me to when I was a cadet. I figured it would be a good chance to spend some time with Aerick before the cadets get here and get away from camp, where we can actually be together. Hopefully we can have some actual alone time, whether it be at the party or after. My body has been dying to be intimate with him, but timing has been an issue, and my drive to do good is overtaking my days. I need to show Luther that putting faith in me to do all this was the right choice. I want someone to finally have a reason to be proud of me.

"You know, that wasn't very convincing."

I glance over to Gavin as he breaks me out of my thoughts. We're the only ones in here right now. Jeff and the guys are cleaning up the trails and I wasn't allowed to help. Luther has specifically scheduled everything this week so the couples aren't together.

"No, he's a really good teacher. I learned a lot from him back when I was a cadet. I suppose he feels a need to continue to teach me and Jeff." I hold back the snicker bubbling up at the thought that he has taught me a lot more than just stuff at camp, but that's totally not appropriate for this conversation.

"So, you really haven't said much about your boyfriend, other than the other night when everyone else brought him up." I shrug my shoulders. If he only knew that it's because we're not supposed to talk about it.

He gets a smirk on his face. "So, do you really have a boyfriend, or do you just tell people that so guys don't hit on you?" *Did he really just go there?*

"Yes, I really have a boyfriend! I don't talk about him because Luther expects us to be professional at all times and that includes not bringing our personal relationships to work. If you haven't noticed, most of us don't talk about our significant others, even though many of us have them." He still appears a little unconvinced.

"Does he live back in Chicago?" My eyes fall back down at my papers. It's almost funny that he doesn't realize it's Aerick. Anyone who watches Aerick would see that he looks at me all the time. We also spend a lot of time together when we're not working. Then again, so do Jeff and I; only we don't seem so tense around each other.

"No, he lives around here."

"You haven't been with him for very long then, huh?"

I study him, wondering where he's going with this. "We started dating a few months ago. Right after my eighteenth birthday." Actually, it was basically the night of my eighteenth birthday. The night Aerick and I spent sitting under the stars. My face flushes at the thought of that night. It seems like it was so long ago, it's amazing that it really only has been just a few months.

"I'm sorry. I didn't mean to make you feel uncomfortable," He says to me and I realize he must think his questioning made be blush.

"No, it's fine, we just really aren't supposed to talk about those things."

"You and Jeff appear really close. It's not him is it?"

I chuckle at the thought because it isn't the first time someone has thought that.

"No, Jeff is just a good friend of mine. I've known him for about as long as I can remember, and he's always been there for me." I don't want to talk about me anymore. "So, what about you, some special girl waiting for you in Chicago?"

His lips press in a line, obviously he doesn't like it either. "No, I really haven't had a girlfriend for the last few years."

This news surprises me. He's hot and appears to have half a brain. How can he not have a girlfriend? "Really? That's surprising."

"Why's that exactly?" he questions with a dazzling smile.

"Well, you seem to be doing good for yourself, you're sweet, and you're um..." I can't finish my sentence.

"I'm what?"

I feel my face get flushed. "You're, um, you know… you look really good."

The corner of his lips tug upward, "Is that your way of telling me I'm hot?" I just glare at him, making him laugh again. "It's okay. You don't have to say it. You know, you aren't too bad looking yourself. Your boyfriend's a lucky man." I glance away not willing to validate that statement because he's not the lucky one, I am.

We sit in silence for another minute before he speaks up again. "I'm starving, and the smell of food is going straight to my stomach. Should we go to dinner?"

I examine down at my watch: it's pretty much dinner time. I'm surprised the guys aren't back yet. "Sure," I say standing up and stretching my arms above my head. My body is sore from sitting for the last few hours. Gavin gets up too, leaving his folders scattered, while I put mine in a neat pile.

We walk over to the mess hall and the smell is floating all around the camp. Tia and Andi are setting the food on the bar, so I go over to help and Gavin follows me. We help finish up and I peak at my watch. Dinner officially started five minutes ago. I'm about to get worried, when all the guys come walking into the hall. Brayden and Trent are both dirtier than the others.

"What did you guys do this time?" I ask and Jeff starts laughing.

"Trent said something to piss off Brayden," Jeff says, trying to hold in his amusement. That sounds typical.

"What was that?" Gavin asks him.

"That he was a pussy for whining about breaking up with his girlfriend."

"It's been almost two months; he needs to get over it already." Trent says and Brayden glares at him.

"I'm sorry, Brayden, I hadn't heard you and Laura broke up," I say to him. It makes more sense now why she agreed to go to Chicago.

"Laura, as in the Laura that works here?" Gavin asks and Aerick sends me a cold glare. *Oops.*

"Yeah, that's her," Brayden answers him in a sad tone.

"Dude, I said enough whining or I'm going to throw you into the river," Trent scolds him, and we all laugh at him.

"Trent, leave him be," I say, standing up for him since no one else is going to. Grabbing his arm, I pull Brayden toward the food. "Come on Bray, let's eat before I'm forced to kick your brother's ass." I hear some of the guys snicker.

"Keep dreaming, Nadi," Trent yells behind me.

"I don't know, Trent, I'd be careful. She might be a good match for you," Brand says to Trent as he shoves and I see Aerick out of the corner of my eye holding in a grin.

"Maybe we'll find out tonight!" I say over my shoulder while Brayden and I start dishing up our food.

I sit down next to Brayden and Aerick sits on the other side, while Gavin sits across from me. "So, how does this fighting thing work tonight?" Gavin asks. Aerick doesn't look at him but starts explaining.

"We split everyone into two groups: lower weight class and upper weight class. The names go into a jar and two are drawn out. Fights can either be boxing or MMA style, whichever both opponents agree on. Winner of each round gets a hundred dollar bonus, and you can fight in up to two rounds."

"You only split it by weight, not gender?" He glances at me, and then to Tia, who is sitting on the other side of Brayden.

Aerick shakes his head. "No, just like when camp starts, we don't differentiate by gender. We believe a woman can be just as strong as a man. But we do believe in fair play, which is why it is split up by weight class. You and Luther, if you guys fight, Brand, Trent, Paulo and I will be in the upper weight class. Jake, Brayden, Jeff and the women will all be in the lower weight class," Aerick explains.

"That's a little insulting," Jeff says.

Aerick glances up at him and there's a ghost of a smile tugging at his lips. "You're right, after Nadi kicked Paulo's ass last session, maybe we should move her to the upper weight class," Aerick tells him and Gavin almost spits out his food.

"Kiss off, dude," Paulo complains and Gavin turns to scrutinize him.

"Seriously, she kicked your ass?"

Everyone starts laughing as I try to hold my in. "She didn't kick my ass. She had a major adrenaline rush and caught me off guard. She may be stronger than she appears, but she is still a little runt."

"Hey! Don't take it out on me," I complain, throwing my biscuit to make my point. "I didn't say a thing. Pick on them."

He huffs, throwing it back, but as I glance over at Jeff, his face is solemn makes me freeze. He's gazing at me nervously. I guess he didn't see it either, but he knows exactly what we're talking about. It only takes a second from the time my gaze lands on him before he catches himself. Quickly he plasters a mask of joy on his face as he shakes himself out of the daze he's in. The others are still carrying on when I feel Aerick squeeze my leg under the table. I peek up and see the nervousness in his gaze, like he's worried about what I'm thinking. I give him a reassuring grin and go back to my food, trying to ignore the circumstances behind the conversation.

"Oh, and on that note, just a word of advice, Gavin. This one doesn't like to be touched," Brayden says, bringing me back out of my bubble as he messes up my hair, earning him an immediate punch in the arm, a little harder than I intended to.

"OUCH!" he says loudly causing everyone to start up again. Luther and Ayla walk in just as I hit Brayden.

"Nadi, hands to yourself," Luther scolds.

"Um, sorry, Luther. Someone else hasn't learned to keep his hands to himself," I sulk and his focus moves to Brayden.

"Brayden, you better be careful. You don't want to end up like Paulo!" Everyone busts up laughing again.

"Seriously, Luther? Come on," Paulo whines again as he glances at me. I throw my hands up in defense. *I didn't say it!* I'm glad to see that Jeff has joined in. Luther and Ayla dish up their dinner before sitting down at the table.

Luther is a little more relaxed compared to the rest of the week. I wonder if he's always so uptight, or if it's just because Gavin is here. He wasn't this way the week after the cadets left. He did make sure we stayed professional during the day, but he seems a little more stressed this week.

"Everyone excited to tonight?" Luther asks and everyone quiets down a little, nodding their heads. "Gavin, are you joining the fights tonight?"

"Heck yeah. Looking forward to it. You?"

He beams. "Yep, I don't always, but it has been a stressful week, so it will do me some good." Gavin studies Luther a little more seriously.

"You really think letting these guys box it out is helpful?"

"Yes, as long as it stays in good fun. I don't let any of the fights get out of control, and we have Terrie here just in case. No one is required to fight, and it tends to boost moral right before we settle down into the long haul. Not to mention, it's a healthy outlet for those of them that struggle with emotional issues." Laughter threatens to spill from me.

Gavin nods his head. "You sure do have an interesting dynamic here."

"It's really about knowing what's needed to keep everyone cohesive. I try to keep things as professional as possible, but let them have a little fun, too."

Gavin peeks over at Tia, who has developed a bit of roundness in her stomach, to the point you can tell she's clearly pregnant. "What about relationships that build between employees?"

"It happens, and I don't necessarily discourage it, but we have strict rules about how staff conduct themselves. If they happen to develop relationships between each other, they're still expected to stay professional at all times, especially once the cadets get here. I also make it a point to split up any couple when necessary to make sure the cadets are the number one priority at all times." Gavin nods his head, agreeing with Luther's words. Glancing around, most of us are clearly trying to keep the emotion off our faces.

"What about staff members and cadets?"

I force myself not to react and Aerick tenses beside me.

Luther draws in a deep breath. "Well, technically I don't have any rules against it, but I discourage it, and I definitely don't allow anything illegal." I peek up at Gavin through my eyelashes and see his brows pull together.

"Why wouldn't you make rules against it?" he asks curiously.

"With the closeness in age between the cadets and staff, it's bound to happen eventually. And in very rare circumstances, I've found it can actually turn out to be a good thing." His lip turns up slightly and it seems like everyone has stopped talking to listen to Luther.

"So, it has happened before?" He peers around the room, but everyone is concentrating entirely too hard on their food – a few holding their lips in a tight line to keep from exposing the truth.

"Yes," Luther says simply.

"And it turned out okay?" I hold my breath, feeling as if it was him asking my father if he approves.

"I think it turned out to be a blessing to both of them." Relief spreads through me and Aerick's whole body relaxes.

* * * *

"Alright, first fight, Andi and Terrie," Luther bellows as he reads the names on the two pieces of paper. They both step up on the mat and put on gloves. I'm getting more and more excited as Tia says they agree on MMA style fight. When they are both ready, Luther begins the fight.

They circle each other, sending punches and kicks here and there. Terrie may be stronger but Andi is quick. After a few minutes, Andi is able to knock Terrie off her feet by sweeping her legs out from under her. Andi pounces on top of her, sending several hits to her sides. On the third hit, Terrie catches Andi's hand and twists her arm around. Within seconds, Terrie is able to whip her body around and lock her in a choke hold. Andi ends up tapping out and Luther calls the fight. Terrie is a little smug but they both get up and give each other a hug.

Luther goes to the other bowl and draws out two pieces of paper. "Trent and Paulo." They step up to the mat and both seem overly excited. "Rematch time!" Trent says and I turn to Aerick with a questioning glare.

"They fought last session and Trent lost." I'm surprised when they choose boxing style; I figured Trent for more of a mixed martial arts kind of guy. They begin and it's a pretty good match of back and forth. Both get in some pretty good punches but then Paulo makes the perfect connection and Trent goes down dazed, making Luther call the fight. Paulo picks Trent up and helps him over to the side, laughing at him for being so cocky. Terrie automatically goes over to check him out.

"Nadi and Brayden." I turn back to the ring as Luther calls out my name. In an instant both Aerick and Jeff are in front of me.

"Are you sure you want to do this?" Jeff asks me. "You can still back out."

"Have a little faith in me Jeff, geez." Aerick's scowl is cold as ice. He doesn't like this any more than Jeff, but he knows better than to question my strength. "I'll be fine, boys!" I tell them as I start to push past.

Aerick grabs my arm. "He jumps around a lot, let him tire himself out. Then attack and don't let up until he goes down." I nod slightly to him and pull away to step up on the mat.

"Boxing!" I say to Brayden quickly, because I know there's no way I'll be able to do MMA style. He shrugs his shoulders and we put our gloves on. He glances worriedly between Aerick and I as we go to shake hands before we start our fight.

I lean in close to him. "I promise, he won't touch you." I move a few steps back and speak up. "Don't go easy on me Brayden! I want to be able to say I won this fair and square." I beam at him, stretching my neck out, moving my head from side to side. He narrows his eyes at me. "Don't worry, I won't hurt you – too bad," I say to him, trying to egg him on, and a bunch of people chuckle around us.

"Brayden, if you let her beat you, we'll never let you live it down," Trent shouts at him and I see determination take over the worried expression on his face. *Good*. Now this should be a good fight. He starts dancing around on his toes, moving back and forth.

I slowly circle but without the bouncing, keeping Aerick's advice in my head. He makes the first move and tries to hit me in the face, but I bring up my hand, blocking his fist to the side, and move out of his way. He quickly gets back into stance, bouncing around. I try to hold in my amusement because he's like a bobble head moving like that. He tries again a second time and then a third. I narrowly miss the last one but it's clear he's trying to find my weakness. Aerick's words echo in my head, as he's told me countless times about finding your opponent's weakness.

Brayden goes for me again but this time toward my side and I'm not quick enough. He gets me right in the ribs with a solid jab, causing me to lose my breath momentarily. I jump to the side out of his reach again.

"Come on Nadi, aren't you going to fight back?" Brayden cocky words try to goad me, but glee spreads through me as I noticed that when he went for the low jab, he left his face wide open.

We start circling again. I find my rhythm as I watch him closely. He swings wide for my jaw and I'm able to duck and lay a hard one into his stomach, making him step back.

"Christ!" he says as he grabs his stomach. Several of the guys standing around the mats are now rowdy with joy, but Aerick's face is a stone wall as he tries to hide all of his emotions.

Getting back into position, Brayden isn't quite as bouncy as he has been. I decide to try to go on the offense to see what I can do, but Brayden blocks my first punch and then when I swing in again, he takes one from my book and gets me in the stomach hard, knocking the wind out of me.

I stumble back just as Brayden throws another punch to my face and it connects with my chin but barely skims me because I was already moving back. "Dammit," I groan. Out of the corner of my eye I notice Jeff step in front of Aerick and I try to shake it off. *Good thing Brayden didn't see that.* He'd probably forfeit.

"Giving up, Nadi?" Brayden asks me with way too much confidence.

"You kidding me? You hit like a girl," I tell him, getting a chuckle out of a few people. We set up again and both get serious. Brayden is slowing down more; his bouncing around so excessively is starting to take a toll on him, especially since he's not big on running. He has no endurance. We punch back and forth a few times, but both block each other.

"You know, we always knew that thing with Paulo was a fluke!" he taunts and it pisses me off. I need to draw him in and end this. I pull my arm up a little, exposing my side, hoping he takes the bait and he does. He punches at me with his right arm to my side and I shoot my left hand straight into his face just as he gets me in my ribs and I connect squarely to his jaw, causing him to momentarily be stunned and let down his guard, so I swing out around with my right with all my strength and hit him hard on the side of his face. He goes down and I grab my side that he had just hit and stand, a little stunned that I just knocked him down. Everyone is momentarily quiet.

Then the whole gym erupts in cheers and howls as Luther calls the fight. I try to help Brayden get back up. He's still a little dazed, but shrugs me off him and heads off the mat, insisting that he's okay. Paulo runs up to me and gives me a bear hug, but releases me quickly, and then Jeff does the same. I'm so high on adrenaline right now I don't even care. Aerick comes up to me, still trying to hide his emotion, but fails miserably.

"Nice combo," he says, giving me a side hug, making my pride swell.

"Thanks. I guess all that training finally paid off."

I'm on cloud nine as Luther calls out Aerick and Brand's names. I silently wonder if that was fixed somehow. That's a dream matchup for Aerick. Brayden steps up next to me as soon as Aerick leaves my side, looking all glum.

I nudge him with my shoulder. "You okay there, Tiger?" He stares at me, confused.

"You jumping around like that, it reminds me of Tigger. You know, from Winnie the Pooh. You should really cut that down a little, because it only wears you out."

He huffs. "Yeah, I'll keep that in mind."

"Still friends?" I ask as Aerick and Brand start boxing.

I turn to glare at Brayden with a raised eyebrow when he doesn't answer, and he finally nods. "Yeah of course, let's just keep this on the D.L." I turn the rest of the way to give him a quick hug and move back just as quickly, before his closeness starts to bother me.

"I can promise you *I* won't say anything. If I were you, I'd be more worried about your brother."

Turning back to the current fight, I wince slightly as Brand connects a punch to Aerick's face like he hadn't been expecting it. They continue to go back and forth for several minutes, each landing a few blows. Even though Brand is smaller, he sure is holding his own. They're pretty evenly matched.

Aerick lands another hard one to Brand's ribs, causing him to grunt loudly. Aerick's confidence is growing by the second as he taunts Brand. He really shouldn't do that, it will cause him to fight harder, just like I did. As if reading my thoughts, Brand goes for a combo shot, landing the second shot to Aerick's ribs. *Come on, Aerick!*

I notice Gavin move to my side, I'm sure to congratulate me. He leans a little closer to me and I try to keep calm at his closeness. "I have to say, that was impressive."

Another wide grin crosses my face. "What can I say? I have a good teacher," I say, watching Aerick, and he glances at me for a moment, giving Brand a chance to connect one to his kidney. Aerick's anger goes from two to ten in an instant and before Brand can get back into his stance, Aerick goes at him with several punches, landing the last one right to his nose. Blood starts streaming out of it as he stumbles and falls to one knee. Luther calls the fight, naming Aerick the winner.

* * * *

I exit the car and go stand next to Aerick. There's loud music coming from the house and parked cars scattered everywhere. Last time I was here, it was so quiet, peaceful and warm! I'm already regretting letting Terrie talk me into wearing this dress, even if it is totally cute. It comes just above my knees and clings to my lower body while the top hangs loosely, but the material is thin and it's cold out here.

Aerick grasps my hand and pulls me tightly to him. "I've missed you." He brings his lips down to mine and warmth shoots through my body when he makes contact. His lips move quickly over mine and instantly the wetness pooled between my legs.

"I've missed this," I tell him as we pull back a little.

"Are you guys going to actually make it into the party?" Paulo questions us as he gets out of the other car. Aerick focus moves back at me.

"Tempting, but I don't think she would be interested in giving these people a show." I hum because right now, I might not care. He bites the inside of his cheek before smirking at me. Maybe he's thinking the same thing.

Aerick steps to the side and circles his arm around me. "Ok, let's go inside." We fall in line behind Trent, Paulo and Terrie while Brayden, Jeff, Brand, and Tia trail behind us. Jake and Andi decided to stay back at camp since Luther, Gavin and Ayla were going to go out for drinks. I think they needed some alone time themselves.

As we get inside people start to greet the guys. This obviously isn't the first time they've been here. There are people everywhere, but Aerick and Paulo head straight for the kitchen. There's a guy in his mid-twenties setting up a line of shots, with several females standing around him. He says something I can't quite catch over the loud music and him and the four girls all gulp down the shots he poured.

"Casey, my man!" Paulo shouts out and the guy turns toward Paulo's voice.

"Whoohoo! You guys made it," he says, sounding like he's already had a few drinks. He greets Paulo and then turns to us. "Aerick, man, glad you showed up." He talks to Aerick but doesn't take his eyes off me.

"Case, this is Nadalynn. Nadalynn, this is my good friend Casey. He's the one that owns this place."

I beam at him and he shakes my offered hand before glancing at Aerick with a raised eyebrow. "Well, it's a pleasure to finally meet you. What's mine is yours, make yourself at home," he tells me, and I blush as his eyebrows jump up and down toward Aerick.

Aerick introduces Jeff, and then Casey says hello to Brand and Tia. Tia stiffens a little when Casey puts his hand on her stomach, congratulating them on the pregnancy. "Alright, let's do a round of shots and then you guys can enjoy the party." He pours a bunch more shots and we stand around. "Here's to a good time tonight," he says, raising his shot and we all follow as he pours it down his throat.

Everyone scatters off to their own thing, but Casey doesn't let me and Aerick leave just yet. He grabs my hand, pulling me closer to him, and I hold tightly to Aerick, bringing him with me. "Wait, you can't go just yet. What kind of host would I be if I didn't give another shot to my main man and his woman?" He pours more shots and I glance at Aerick, who is shaking his head.

"Here is to the woman who managed to tame the untamable man," he announces, and I study Aerick again, who gives Casey an aggravated scowl before throwing back his shot. I drink mine quickly, not sure of what to make of that comment. The alcohol burns going down, but the shots have warmed me up a little.

Casey leans in and gives me a quick kiss on the cheek, trying to hide the fact that he was passing something to Aerick. "Have a good time, kids!" he says as he pulls away and turns to join his other party guests.

"Sorry, he's a little crazy," Aerick tells me, and I shrug, letting it roll off my shoulders. He grabs two beers from a big bucket on the counter and opens one before handing it to me.

"So, what was that all about?" I ask him, wanting to know what Casey gave him.

He gives me a dark stare before whispering in my ear. "You'll find out later." He swallows down a long drink of his beer and grabs my hand. "Come on, dance with me."

He pulls me over to where a bunch of people are dancing to loud music. I'm careful not to touch any of them. As we reach the center of the room, Aerick starts moving around, keeping his hands on me, and I just follow his lead. I never knew he could dance like this. *Damn, he's good at it!* The rest of the room starts to fall away from us until I can only see him. Feeling him moving against me is mesmerizing.

I turn my back to him and move my body against him as he starts kissing my shoulder and rubbing his hands across my stomach. *Sweet Jesus!* He's making me so hot. Then I feel him harden against me. Obviously, the feeling is mutual. I grab his neck and pull his head down so I can kiss him, and it instantly turns lustful. He pulls me tighter against him, so his hardness is digging into my back. I moan into his mouth, feeling his need for me.

He breaks the kiss. "I can't wait any longer." He releases me and starts pulling me through the house before I can ask him what he's talking about. We go upstairs and stop outside a room – the same room. He pulls out a key and unlocks the door as I gaze at him confused, but he doesn't give me time to ask where he got it.

Pulling me into the room he quickly shuts the door and locks it before his lips are on mine again. "I need you, babe," he mumbles on my lips. There is such a yearning in his voice.

"I need you too, Aerick."

His lips press against mine once more as he pins me up against the wall with his body. His fingers slide my thong to the side, and they enter me quickly, causing another moan to escape.

"Babe, you are so wet for me already." He moves his fingers in and out of me quickly as his lips attack my neck.

Circling his thumb around my bundle of nerves, it only takes a few minutes before I'm teetering on the edge. All of a sudden, he pulls his fingers out of me and undoes his pants. He reaches down, pulling my leg up around him and rips the lacey material of my underwear before he slams into me.

"Holy Fuck!" he groans loudly, resting his forehead on mine. As he starts to move in and out of me, I quickly get lost in his touch. I've missed feeling him inside me, his hands and lips on me. This is what I've been yearning for all week.

"Faster, baby," I moan, needing to feel more of him.

He grabs my other thigh, picking me up, and I wrap my legs around him. He moves us around and my back hits the bed, but he remains standing. I feel the pressure of him push up on my walls and it's amazing as he resumes moving in and out of me. His speed picks up just as I requested, and his thrusts get rough as he inches closer to his release. I'm right at the edge. He moans my name, letting me know he's almost there, and the rawness of it sends me over as I scream out his name. He continues thrusting into me, extending my orgasm, before finally giving in to his own release.

As we both come down from our highs, the music makes its way back to my ears and I'm suddenly grateful that it has covered up our noises. "A little presumptuous, your friend is," I remark as he straightens up to button his pants.

"What do you mean?"

"He gave you that key when he kissed me on the cheek."

A flash of irritation crosses his face. "Yeah, he better not do that again; and no, he didn't presume anything. I texted him earlier and asked for it." He leans down with his adorable smirk. "Like I said, I needed you. I've been dreaming about doing that all week." He kisses me softly, cupping his hand around my face.

"I guess we need to find some time to be alone more often," he says sourly, but I'm unsure why he's had such a change in mood. I question him with my stare, and he gazes down, messing with his clothes. "Or I guess I should say, maybe you could find some time to be alone with me."

I stand up, putting my hand on his chest, making him stop straightening his clothes and look at me. "Hey, I just have a lot on my plate right now. Please try to be understanding." I'm not trying to push him away, there's just so much that needs to get done.

He purses his lips. "I know. Just don't forget, I'd like some of your attention too." He's so serious. It's obvious that he feels put out by my lack of attention, which was never my intention.

"Sorry babe, I'll try to make more time for us, okay?"

"Sorry. I just miss you, that's all."

"I know, and now that things are settling down, I promise to kick Terrie out and spend some time with you!" I pull him down to kiss him and he finally smirks. I feel something tickling the inside of my thigh and I remember that he tore my underwear.

I glare up at him.

"What?" He stares at me concerned.

"You know what!" I tell him as I step back and remove what's left of them.

He smirks at me. "Oh, yeah. Sorry about that. I guess I got a little carried away."

"Mhmm." I pull him back to me and tuck them in his pocket, since I don't have a purse with me. "Come on, lover boy. Let's go back to the party before they send a search party."

Giving me one last kiss, he grabs my hand and leads us out of the room.

* * * *

I giggle, sitting with my legs crossed on one of the counters, drinking a beer with Jeff and a few other guys that are around me. Sean and Eddie showed up and I remembered them from the day Aerick took me out for lunch when I was a cadet. Sean is telling us about some of the wild parties that have gone on at the cabin.

I've been hearing a lot about Aerick's 'wild side' but do my best to ignore the 'other woman' comments that keep popping up – it's his past. Sean is telling me about some crazy dares he's gotten Aerick to do. Some of them are pretty funny, like climbing a tree naked. I can just imagine him looking like Tarzan.

My eyes find Aerick again, who's now on the other side of the kitchen taking more shots with Paulo and Casey. He's gotten pretty drunk in just a few hours, but he appears to be happy and relaxed, which is rare for him when we're around other people. Another girl comes up from behind him and puts her arms around him, but he pulls away quickly and says 'hi', giving her a kiss on the cheek before moving out of her reach. It's probably a good thing I'm not a jealous person, and he's clearly not interested in her like that.

I turn back to Sean talking and squirm slightly because my bladder is about to explode from the amount of alcohol I've consumed. I'm dreading getting down with these high heels on. I scoot to the edge of the counter and go to let myself down but suddenly Sean is in front of me, grabbing under my arms, and helping me down carefully. I freeze at his touch and my feet hit the ground. "Wouldn't want you to ruin your shoes there," he says playfully, obviously trying to be a gentleman, and goes to step back, but Aerick's behind him. *Shit.* He pushes him to the side slightly and grabs my hand.

"Come on, let's go," he tells me and starts pulling me away. *What the hell?*

"Aerick, what's your problem?"

"His hands on you is my problem." *Really?*

"Aerick, he just helped me off the counter. No reason to get all worked up."

"Whatever. I didn't like it. We're going." He's clearly drunk and I don't want to fight, even though he's being ridiculous. I follow him out to the car, and he downs the rest of the beer in his hand before opening the passenger door. I glare up at him, frowning. *I know he isn't planning on driving.*

"Get in," he commands and his tone gets under my skin.

"Give me the keys. I'll drive," I say, rolling my eyes and reaching for the keys, but he pulls his hand away.

"I'm fine. Just get in."

I draw in a deep breath. I'm not going to let him drive like this. "Aerick, give me the keys. You've had way too much to drink." I put my hand out, expecting him to give me the keys.

"Stop talking to me like I'm a fucking child," he says coldly, and he's really starting to annoy the shit out of me. Paulo and a few others have made their way out to the front of the house.

"Then stop acting like one and give me the damn keys so we can go," I say quietly, trying to keep the others from hearing me.

"Get in the damn car, Nadi," he shouts at me and my anger lashes backs.

"Don't you fucking yell at me. What the hell is your problem, Aerick?"

"My *fucking* problem is you need to do as you're told."

My hand flies up before I realize what I'm doing, and I feel the sting as I slap him hard in the face.

"I'm not a cadet that you can command." The anger leaves his face and he reaches for my hand, but I pull away from him. "Don't touch me. You want to act like idiot, fine. I'll walk back."

I walk over to Paulo, who's made his way closer to us, probably to jump in the middle if it got too heated. "You talk to him, since my opinion doesn't seem to mean anything to him. If he drives home like that, I'll personally kick your ass. I'm going home." I turn away.

"Um, I'll give you a ride back," Casey says, looking at me concerned – at least someone is concerned.

"Like hell you will," Aerick growls. "She isn't fucking leaving here with you."

I'm so outraged and I've had enough of his overpowering jealousy. "You know what? It isn't your choice. Casey, can you please take me back to the camp?"

"Nadi don't –"

I glare at him as I cut him off. "I swear Aerick, if you try to order me around one more fucking time…" I don't finish my sentence because even though I'm seething right now, I'd never be able to get those next few words out of my mouth. "Casey, can we please go now?"

"She better get home safe, or your ass is mine," Paulo tells Casey, and now he appears nervous.

"Of course, man."

I follow Casey to his car and see Aerick start to walk forward, but Paulo steps in front of him and starts talking to him really quietly. Casey starts up the car and goes to pull out. I watch as Aerick throws his empty beer bottle at the tree.

"Fuuuuuck!" he screams and I turn, staring down at my lap.

"Christ, woman! You got some serious guts," Casey says quietly.

"What am I supposed to do? Just let him walk all over me?" I snap.

"No, no. He's just, you know. He's a little scary, and you just stood up to him like you were twice his size."

Aerick doesn't scare me. He would never hurt me and there was no way I was going to sit there and let him talk to me like that. He's used to getting whatever he wants because he's so damn intimidating, but I refuse to be that little cowering girl that lets herself be disrespected.

"You did the right thing though. He was way too drunk to drive and you don't deserve to be talked to like that."

I gaze out the window into the darkness. "I know," I say quietly and a single tear rolls down my cheek as I realize this is the first time we've really fought. My hands begin to shake, and I still feel the sting on my hand.

"Just let him sleep it off. I'm sure he'll be apologizing at your feet in the morning." I nod, not wanting to talk anymore.

He pulls up to the office and I thank him for the ride. The camp is quiet as I walk through it. It feels empty, just like the feeling in my chest. More tears are beginning to fall down my cheeks. I feel bad for leaving him there, but I know this wasn't my fault. He needs to stop trying to be so controlling. But it still hurts. I don't like being apart from him and I really don't like fighting with him.

Once in my cabin, I shower quickly throwing on my night shorts and a cami. A quiet knock sounds at the door as I'm brushing my hair out about to get in bed. *Please don't be Aerick.* I'm not ready to face him.

I open the door to a worried-looking Jeff. "Hey, you okay?"

"Yeah, I'm just tired and it's been a long day."

The irritation is clear on his face. "I heard you and Aerick got into an argument."

"Is he here?" My heart leaps, betraying my thoughts. I really want to know he got home safe.

"No, Paulo and Casey were trying to calm him down when we left, but Paulo got the keys from him. Tia, Brand and I snuck out." That's good at least. Paulo can halfway handle him when he's drunk. "Alrighty then. I guess I'll see you in the morning," he tells me and I nod as he walks away.

I sit down on the couch and stare out the window. *I hate this.* I just want him to be home, holding me in his arms. My tears return and I grab the couch pillow, hugging it tightly to me as I cry myself to sleep.

CHAPTER THIRTEEN

(Saturday, November 21st)

"NO!"

I scream, waking myself up. A thin layer of sweat is covering me and I'm still trying to catch my breath. Glancing over, Terrie still isn't in her bed. *Thank goodness.* I always found having nightmares a little embarrassing. To me, it's a little childish that I still have them after all these years.

I attempt to rub the creepy feeling of my nightmare off my arms and legs, but it's hard to forget. I want to go sleep in bed with Aerick, but if Terrie isn't back yet, then he must not be either. The red light coming from the nightstand says it's two in the morning, so I've only been asleep for an hour. I wonder how late they're going to stay out. Then again, after our argument, I'm not sure if I really do want to see him right now. That leaves me with two options: I can try to go back to bed on my own, which probably won't work, or I can go see Jeff.

After a moment of hesitation, I slide my shoes on and head to Jeff's cabin. Aerick will probably be pissed, but who cares – not me right now. If he wasn't such an ass, I would have stayed at the party with him and wouldn't have gone to bed so upset.

It's freezing outside. *Why didn't I grab my sweater?* When I get to the door I knock softly. *Please, Jeff, answer the door.*

My thought is cut off as Gavin opens the door in only his boxers. "Oh... ahh..." *Christ!* I glance down at the ground quickly, trying to avoid staring at his next-to-perfect physique.

"Can I help you with something?" he asks sleepily. I glance up to see him resting his forearm on the door and he raises his eyebrow at me. He really needs to take that smirk off his face. Then again, I'm standing at his door in the middle of the night wearing next to nothing when the temperature is probably barely above freezing.

"Nadi?" Jeff's voice comes from behind Gavin, who opens the door wider so I can see Jeff, but doesn't remove his arm from the door.

"Um..." *Why do I feel so weird with this?* It has to be the fact that Gavin is standing here.

"Come here," Jeff says as he sits up, putting a pillow in his lap. Gavin raises an eyebrow at me again. I duck under his arm and go over to Jeff, crawling into his bed.

Gavin shuts the door and sits down on his bed. "You okay? Did something happen?"

"Yeah, I just, um... I had a nightmare," I stutter quietly. A shudder runs through my body and I'm not sure if it was from the cold or the thought of my dream. I pull the covers over my shoulders tightly like it's shielding me from everything, including his questioning. I hate feeling weak, I hate the fact that I feel the need to seek out comfort, and I really hate that I just had to admit that.

Jeff starts stroking my hair and Gavin glances up to Jeff with a question in his eyes. His gaze turns to confusion and then he lies down without another word. I'm grateful that he's dropping it because it's not something we need to talk about, not with Jeff and definitely not with him. It still feels like a piece of me is missing and all I want is to forget it.

With Gavin here, I try to hold my tears in, but one manages to escape. *I miss Aerick.* It's his absence in my dream that's making me feel so vulnerable, and it's him I want right now. I draws in a deep breath, pulling back the rest of my unshed tears. Jeff's hand on my hair is calming and my eyes close, trying to block out the feeling of the dream that woke me. I finally start to feel better after a while of comfortable silence, slowly relaxing until my breathing evens out and I'm half asleep.

"Just friends, huh?" Gavin says quietly, causing my consciousness to return slightly and keep me from falling completely asleep.

"Yes. She's just a friend," Jeff says defensively in a loud whisper. They both must think I'm asleep.

"You said you've known her for a long time. Did you ever want it to go beyond friendship?"

Jeff ponders the question for a minute before he answers back. "Yeah, I did, but I screwed it up. I never told her how I felt until it was too late, but it's okay. I'm happy knowing she's is. It took me a while to get over her, but I'll always love her, and as long as she has someone who loves her and takes care of her, I'm good with that. She will always be my best friend and I'm satisfied just being there for her when she needs me."

"Like tonight," Gavin says, before pausing for a minute. "What happened? It seems this isn't the first time." I wish they would end this conversation but I'm too tired and too embarrassed to stop it now. They think I'm asleep and I'd rather keep it that way.

"Some bad shit happened to her when we were kids. It caused her to get really bad nightmares, among other things. She always felt safe with me and when she would get upset or scared, she would sneak into my room at camp or she would sneak up the fire escape to my room in our apartment block."

"And then what?"

Jeff lets out a soft chuckle. "Just this. I run my fingers through her hair until she falls back to sleep or cries herself back to sleep."

"Cry?" *Dammit, Jeff!*

He inhales a deep breath, still running his fingers through my hair. "Like I said, it was some bad shit and she's had more things happen to her recently, causing her nightmares to resurface more often. She would probably kick my ass right now if she knew I was telling you this, so please don't say anything to her about it." He tries to laugh it off but there's a sadness in his voice.

"I heard about that. Luther told me that she was stabbed out of jealousy by another staff member a few months ago when she was still a cadet. I guess you can say that was pretty screwed up. It sucks that she's been through so much. Though, you wouldn't realize it by looking at her. She seems so strong."

"Yeah, well, even as stubborn and tough as she is, she has this soft, vulnerable side to her that she rarely shows because she thinks people see it as a weakness. She doesn't like people looking down on her. Most of the time she holds in all of her pain and sadness. On rare nights like tonight, when it's too much for her, she lets me comfort her. Sometimes she just needs someone to be strong for her."

It's quiet for a minute. "Did something happen tonight? Is that why she had a nightmare?" *Please don't tell him, Jeff.*

He draws in a deep breath. "Her and her boyfriend got into an argument."

"Her boyfriend was at the party? I was really starting to think she was making that up." *Dick!* Like that's something I'd make up. I wasn't the first one that mentioned him. It was everyone else.

Jeff chuckles. "No, he's real, and yes, he was at the party, but they got into an argument about something and she left. I'd gone off to hang out with Brayden and we found some girls to talk to. We went outside when we heard some commotion and Paulo was out there trying to calm down her boyfriend. He told me what happened, so I came back here to check on her. Being Nadi, of course, she played it off like she was okay, but obviously whatever he said or did hurt her deep down."

"So what? Did he get physical with her?" *That's not happening.* I would never be with someone who hit me.

"No, nothing like that. I would murder him if he ever touched her out of anger. I honestly don't think he would ever do that, but with her, words can do just as much damage, and it's not the first time he's done something to upset her."

"I have to give it to you, kid. You're a really good friend to be there for her like you are. I couldn't imagine being in your spot."

"I'll always love her in one way or another. I'd do anything for her, and I just want her to be happy." He's so sweet.

"Do you like him? Her boyfriend?"

Jeff chest rises as his lung expand fully. "It's complicated. I mean, he can be the biggest asshole sometimes. He's so jealous and controlling, and it pisses me off when he upsets her over petty stuff like tonight. He was completely out of line. Her on the other hand. She is strong, loving, smart, and selfless, despite everything she's been through. There are times when I think she can do so much better than him, but then seeing them together and how content she is just being with him, it's like a light erupts in her that was never there before. " He pauses for a moment and then lets out a chuckle.

"They actually balance each other out well. She pulls him down off the pedestal he pretends to be on and he's not such an ass when she's around. When he's around her, she lets down her guard and you can see true happiness within her. No one has ever been able to get close to her like he has. Not even me." He lowers his voice as he says the last part.

"I don't know, you two seem pretty close."

Jeff lightly runs his thumb across my cheek as he lets out a sigh. "Not like they are. Even I have to be careful around her sometimes." He sounds so sad and I sigh internally.

I'm sorry, Jeff. I wish it wasn't like that. I don't mean to be like that with him.

"She seems pretty amazing." Gavin's voice is full of wonder.

"Amazing is one word to describe her. She's definitely one of a kind," Jeff tells him with pride. I hear Gavin's bed move and footsteps going toward the bathroom. *Good!* I'm glad that conversation is finally over. I feel Jeff kiss the top of my head and I let the darkness finally pull me down.

* * * *

I wake up to pounding at the door. Opening my eyes, I see that Jeff is propped up against the wall, just waking up, and I'm still lying on his lap. Gavin is on his feet going to the door. When he opens it, I hear the voice I was dreading.

"I need to talk to Jeff." Aerick's commanding voice fills the room.

"Is everything okay?" Gavin asks and I notice he put on basketball shorts sometime after I arrived last night. That's probably a good thing. Just imagining what Aerick would have thought if he was still in boxers like he was last night sends a chill through me. Probably something not to tell Aerick anytime soon.

"I'm not sure, Terrie just told me Nadi isn't in their cabin and that her bed looks like she never came home. Nobody has seen her since last night." He sounds extremely worried, but his voice is hard, almost like he's scolding me without even knowing that I'm here.

"Didn't she go to a party with you guys last night?" Gavin questions him, even though he knows the answer to that question.

Aerick pauses before answering him. "Yes, she did, but she got upset about something and left with some guy she barely knows, and now she doesn't appear to be here, which is unlike her."

"So, wait, you let her leave a party, probably drunk, with some guy?" There's an accusation in his voice. It's clear he thinks Aerick should have stopped me, which pisses me off a little. I'm not a damn kid that needs looking after.

"First of all, I didn't *let* her do anything. She is stubborn and does what she wants, when she wants. I tried to stop her last night, but she really doesn't like people bossing her around. Second, I don't need *you* questioning *me*."

He is beyond pissed and I need to intervene before he does something he regrets. I jump up and go to the door. His eyes widen in shock and relief when he sees me. Gavin steps back as soon as I get to the door and goes back over to his bed. "I'm right here, safe and sound. No need to flip out," I snap at him, so he realizes I'm still pissed off at him. His eyes glance up at Gavin and then back to mine.

"Why are you in the guy's cabin? That's against the rules, you know that." His voice is steady, void of any emotion other than disapproval, so as not to reveal his true feelings, but I can see the anger in his eyes. By the way he just scowled at Gavin, I would venture to say he thinks I came here to see him. His need to keep his composure is the only thing keeping him from outright accusing me of sleeping with Gavin. *Dick!*

I'm not in the mood for this right now. "Look, I had... a difficult time sleeping, and I sought out my best friend. I know it's against the rules, but I didn't think it would be a big deal. I was obviously mistaken, and I'll make sure it doesn't happen again. Satisfied?" Confusion crosses his face and then realization.

"What –" he begins, but I cut him off, knowing exactly what he's going to say. It's not a conversation to have right now.

"Thanks for your concern, Aerick, but as you can see, I'm here and alive." I glance down at my watch making a show of it. "I've had a long, irritating night, and need to get cleaned up. I'll see you at P.T. in twenty minutes."

His face falls and there's regret plastered on it for a moment before he composes himself again. I'll forgive him for last night, but right now I'm not ready to. I shut the door softly before he can say anymore. Walking over to Jeff's bed, I see the concern in his eyes. I fall back on the bed, bouncing a little before putting my arm under my head and letting out a loud sigh. Gavin is staring at me too, looking completely dumbfounded.

"Wow, I think you're the first person that I've seen talk to him that way."

I want to roll my eyes. That's because no one else has the guts too. "Well, as he said, I don't like to be bossed around and I surely don't need him checking up on me like a five-year-old," I snap.

"Easy there, tiger. Just making an observation," he says with a chuckle, and a smile finds its way back to my lips. I need to chill out.

"Some things never change. You should have seen her stand up to him when she was a cadet. She never backed down then either, and it used to piss him off like crazy," Jeff muses.

"I can't help that you all are a bunch of pussies too afraid to speak up," I throw back at him.

"I wasn't afraid; I was being smart. Something you would do well to remember. It isn't always about being the strongest."

I glare at him.

"Well, I might as well get in the shower real quick. You good?" Jeff asks and I nod standing up with him.

"Yeah, I'm fine. Thanks for being there for me last night."

He grins at me. "No problem, I always enjoy you climbing into my bed in the middle of the night." I smack him playfully and he snickers. "I was joking. No need to be violent!"

"I need to go shower, too. I'll see you out there."

Jeff gives me a hug and kisses me on the forehead.

"Hey, all kidding aside, I'm always here if you need me." My heart warms at his words. He really is the best friend I could ever ask for.

"I know." I give him a kiss on the cheek and turn to Gavin.

"Sorry your sleep was interrupted on my account," I apologize, feeling a little bad that he got caught in the middle of this.

He shakes his head with a smirk on his face. "No problem at all. We all need a good friend sometimes." I nod in agreement before slipping on my shoes and leaving to get ready for my day.

* * * *

I punch the bag with all my might as sweat drips down my back. I concentrate hard on my form while music blares in my ears. *"This is my answer to everything... This is my place to hide from everything... Now you know, this could never be justified. Now you know, I could never be satisfied... Now you know..."*

I stop punching the bag, pull my earbuds out and put my hands on my knees, trying to catch my breath. It's amazing how much I relate to some music.

My anger hadn't let up from this morning and I figured beating the crap out of a bag would help. As always, it has done wonders, and my anger is slowly dissipating. I haven't talked to Aerick, since he is clearly giving me some time to cool off, which is very wise of him. It's annoying being so conflicted about this. On one hand I want to run and jump in his arms, but on the other I want to just hit him over the head for being such a jealous, controlling asshole.

It's a good thing we have the second half of the day off because I'm not in the mood to deal with being around people right now. I've been here for over an hour and it has helped a little. Something at the corner of my eye catches my attention. I stand up, turning my body toward the door, and Gavin is leaning against it with a troubled expression on his face.

"How long have you been standing there?" I ask, a little annoyed at myself for not noticing him earlier.

"Only a few minutes. To be honest, the way you were hitting that bag, I was afraid to interrupt you." He seems amused by that, but I'm not.

"Then why are you still here?" I snap at him and his lips press into a line.

"I know you're a grown woman and all, but I thought I should check up on you. Everyone else is shying away from you today."

"That's because they know me well." I glance down to my gloves. Everyone knows I like my space when I'm upset.

"That can be dangerous, you know." I nod, knowing full well it can be. I've been told on several occasions by Christian and once by that bitch Liz, but it's what I know. Being alone with loud music or exercise or both, until I feel better. It's how I cope.

He walks over and sits on the bench near the bags. "So, do you want to talk about it? You were pretty upset last night."

"Really? I'm not talking to anyone else, why do you think I would want to talk to you?" That came out a little harsher than I meant it to.

"Ouch. I'm not trying to intrude, I just wanted to offer my ear and maybe a word of advice. You know, from an outside perspective. Unlike everyone else, I have no emotional attachment to you, so I could give you an unbiased opinion. Or, if you're more interested in just forgetting life for a while, we could just talk about anything else to keep your mind off of it. You don't have to, I just wanted to let you know it's an option." He stands up and walks toward the door.

"Gavin, just to be clear, I seriously do have a boyfriend, and I have no interest in getting that close with anyone else." By the way he has been asking about my boyfriend constantly, he has to know I noticed he was interested in me.

He grins at me. "As much as I wouldn't mind that, I swear that's not my intention here. You have a boyfriend and I'm not like that. I respect the fact that you're committed to someone and I'd never do anything to cause problems between you two." He seems pretty sincere. Maybe he's really just trying to be helpful.

"Thank God, because that's the last thing I need right now," I say out loud, but not really to him.

"Well, if you change your mind and want to just chat, come find me." He walks out before I can respond. That was kind of weird, but at least I don't have to worry about him hitting on me now.

* * * *

"Is she here?" I hear Aerick's guarded voice at the door. Terrie answered it, but only opened it a crack so he couldn't see me. She peeks over to me. I suppose it's now or never. I'm sure he's worried that I skipped dinner and our evening workout, but I really needed some me-time. After Gavin left me in the gym, I ended up just running laps inside until I collapsed to my knees from exhaustion. By then dinner was done, so I came back to my room to shower and do my schoolwork.

I inhale a deep calming breath and nod to Terrie. She opens the door wide and he steps in. "I'm going to get you something to eat, Nadi. I'll be back." Before I can tell her it isn't necessary, she leaves without looking at either of us and shuts the door behind her.

Aerick's eyes are still on the floor and I move back up against the headboard with my legs crossed so he has room to sit. He takes the hint and comes over to sit on the edge of the bed, putting his elbows on his knees, still not taking his eyes off the floor. I wait to let him speak first.

"Nadalynn, I can't tell you how sorry I am about last night. It was out of line and I let my emotions get the better of me. I was being stupid, and you didn't deserve that. I'm so sorry." He closes his eyes, lowering his head into his hands. My heart breaks at the sadness in his voice.

I crawl over to sit next to him. "Aerick, I know it's in your nature to be controlling, but you need to understand that if you want to be with me, I'll only stand beside you – I will not sit below you. Even as screwed up as I am, I deserve that much respect."

He draws in a deep breath and then gets down, kneeling between my legs. He pulls on my face, gently to gaze into his eyes. "You're not screwed up, but you are right that you deserve respect. I had no right to talk to you like that last night and I definitely would never, ever consider you to be below me. You're my life. My days start and end with you on my mind. If anything, I hold you above me." He sits on his heels so I have to look down at him. He circles my waist with his arms, pulling me tightly to him as he lays his head on my chest. "Please forgive me, babe."

I slide my arms around his neck. Listening and seeing his emotion makes me feel like I have a hundred-pound weight on my chest. I push him back a little and bring his face back up to mine to place a soft kiss on his lips. "I love you, Aerick."

He closes his eyes, swallowing loudly before he pulls my lips back to his own. "I love you too, and I promise to try to keep my emotions in check from now on," he murmurs against my lips, and pulls me back into a tight hug. This is what I've craved since last night. To be in his arms, to feel safe, to feel loved and comforted.

"Aerick?"

"Yeah?"

"You know that I'd never cheat on you, right? There's no reason for you to be so jealous."

He holds in a long breath for a moment. "Deep down I know that. I just have a hard time seeing other men touching you."

"You know, I saw that girl at the party put her hands on you but didn't freak out. I waited and watched. I saw you move away from her and knew you had no interest in her. That was me giving you my trust and confidence. That's something I need you to learn to do. The majority of my friends are guys, and while only very few can comfortably touch me, that may not always be the case. You need to learn to trust me that I'd never, ever do that to you."

"I do trust you. It just makes me uncomfortable. I promise I'll try my best to not overreact in the future." Finally pulling back, he gives me a hesitant smile. "So, do you forgive me?"

I roll my eyes at him. "Yes, you big knucklehead, just don't let it happen again." He smirks from ear to ear before he places a passionate kiss on my lips that quickly deepens. Our need for each other explodes.

Terrie walks in, making us break apart. "There wasn't much, but I got you a sandwich and some cookies." She stops and stares at him still holding me in his arms, clearly flushed from our lust-filled kiss. "Forgave him so quickly, huh? I would have let him writhe in his guilt for at least another day."

"Terrie, lay off," I tell her before she can make him feel any worse. I know he feels bad about what he did, and he has suffered enough. "I'm not really hungry."

Aerick glares at me. "You didn't eat dinner and you hardly ate anything at breakfast or lunch. You should really eat something. Tomorrow is going to be a long day."

"I hate to say it, but he's right."

I glare at Terrie for taking his side, but I know they're right.

"Please eat something, babe."

"Fine!"

"That a girl," Aerick says playfully, placing a kiss on my forehead.

"Don't push it," I tell him. He cups my face in his hands, pulling me to his lips once more before he gets up and moves behind me, sitting on the bed against the wall. He pulls me back to sit between his legs. Terrie sets my food on my lap before going to sit on her own bed. Now that we've made up, I am a little hungry.

After a few minutes, Paulo shows up. "So, who's ready for

tomorrow?"

"Is that a joke? Of course we're ready," Aerick says confidently.

"Who do you think are going to be the troublemakers?" Terrie asks.

"My money is on Skyler and Ryan. They have the most history of problems. That's why I assigned them to me," Aerick says, as if it's nothing.

"Do you always do that? Assign the ones you think are trouble to yourself?" I ask him, and his smirk answers my question.

"Yes. I assumed last session that it would be you and Mike, although I thought he would be more trouble than you. Boy, was I wrong!"

"Hey!" I say slapping the arm that's around my waist still.

He kisses my neck, whispering in my ear. "Hmmm. Feisty as always."

CHAPTER FOURTEEN

(Sunday, November 22nd)

"GEEZ, TERRIE, THIS braid is so tight, it hurts."

"Stop your whining. The first day is always important. We need to make a good impression of what's expected. Don't touch it!" she shouts as Tia French braids her hair in the bathroom. I drop my hands and stare back in the mirror at her. I'd have much rather just put my hair back in a ponytail like I normally do, but somehow Terrie talked me and the other girls into braiding our hair today.

I slide out of my shorts and into my uniform pants, before grabbing my boots. "Next time, remind me not to blindly agree to letting you get me ready," I mumble, just loud enough for her to hear, and Andi giggles. At least our clothes are comfortable. It took me a while as a cadet to get used to wearing boots every day, but now it's like second nature having them on. I brought my runners with me but most days, I choose to workout in my boots.

I grab out my new camp zip-up hoodie that matches the uniform. The weather has gotten chilly the last few days, making me glad that the cadets are arriving in the afternoon, when it's just a little warmer.

It's definitely time to dress warmer. I regretted only wearing a tank top out to P.T. this morning because I froze my butt off. Thankfully our uniforms this session include extra hoodies, long sleeve shirts, and a warm jacket. We even got long johns and wool socks. I've never been in the mountains for winter, but I'm guessing it gets really cold here.

Looking at myself in the full-length mirror, it appears like I just stepped off a military base. My hair is perfectly pulled back into a tight braid that runs down my back, my makeup is light and almost unnoticeable – thank goodness for that – and my clothes are perfectly fitted to my body, showing off my fit physique. All that's needed is to stand up straight and put on my 'no bullshit' face and I'm set.

I can't help but be amused because standing next to Aerick right now would actually make us both look like two of the biggest hard-asses. I always thought we appeared a little odd together because we're so different. Just looking at him, he's so handsome and has the body of a god. When I'm not around, he's a hard-ass that no one would dare stand up to. As for me, I'm pretty average. While my body is a bit more defined these days, I'll never be that girl with the perfect boobs or ass. My attitude is a little withdrawn, but I'm generally nice to most people, as long as they don't piss me off. It's almost like we're complete opposites; I may never understand what he sees in me. At least for today, I can imagine that we are more alike than we typically are.

Thinking back to my first day here, I did think everyone looked like a bunch of uptight hard-asses, not just Aerick. They had all been perfectly done up, just like we are today, making me feel like I was walking into something much worse than juvey. I suppose now I understand why the first impression is important.

Someone knocks on the door, so I move to answer it, since the other two are still finishing up. I open the door and see Tia standing there, already done up. Tia's jacket is just a little looser than ours, but I suspect that it's to make her baby bump less noticeable. At four months pregnant, it's only noticeable when she wears tight shirts. Luther pressed that her safety is one of our main priorities this session while the cadets are here. We'll be hiding her pregnancy as much as possible and, once it's more noticeable, she isn't to be left alone with any cadet. That isn't going to be too hard since, I'm shadowing her. We'll be together almost all day, every day. I've had Luther, Brand, and even Aerick lecture me on keeping an eye on her during the day – something I'm more than happy to do. We aren't the greatest friends, but I'd never let anything happen to her, and I'm honored to know that everyone trusts me enough to look after her. Although, between Tia and I, we don't think it's a big deal. Tia's a rather good fighter and could probably handle anything without me.

"We need to get out there. Did I ever mention how much I hate being around Aerick on arrival day?" she says to all of us, adding, "No offense Nadi." I shrug it off. Aerick has been extremely uptight today, I'll admit; he's even getting on my nerves. He's been running around all morning barking orders at everyone, including me – though I know it's nothing personal. He's just trying to do his job well, but it really wouldn't hurt for him to lighten up just a bit.

Terrie grabs her jacket and we head out to the stage, where everyone else is already standing around. Luther, Ayla, Aerick and Gavin are standing on the stage talking and we join all the other guys standing in front of the stage. At least most of them appear pretty upbeat. Brand is glancing at Tia with worry, but he lightens up when she beams at him. I glance up to Aerick, who's watching me from the corner of his eye while he talks to Luther. I allow my lips to turn up slightly before turning to the guys.

"Hey guys!" I say as we reach them. Naturally, I find myself standing between Jeff and Paulo. They're the two I usually gravitate toward when I cannot be close to Aerick.

Jeff hits my shoulder with his own and joy fills me. "At least your attitude is better than Aerick's."

Paulo hits my other shoulder with his. "Yeah, you should really do something about that," he says quietly, with a mischievous smile.

"He's his own person guys, don't think there's much I can do."

Paulo chuckles, "Who are you trying to kid? You say jump, and he says how high."

I shoot a glare at him – that's not true. "I may stand up to Aerick, but when have you ever seen me order Aerick around?"

"The night he got into the bar fight."

Jeff gives me a questioning stare and I shake my head at him.

"He was drunk. That doesn't count." Besides, all I really did was calm him down.

"Of course it does. Even more so because he doesn't listen to anyone when he's drunk." I stare up to the stage again and shake my head.

"Two minutes!" Aerick shouts as he jumps down and comes over to our group. "Everyone, line up. Let's go, Brand!" Aerick's 'hard ass face' breaks for a second as he passes me. His lips turn up slightly and he gives me a quick wink. As soon as he passes the group, Brand joins him, and they head out front.

Paulo leans close into me. "See?" I push him away from me and walk toward the other girls, who have already moved to one side.

"I'd be interested in hearing about that story," Jeff says quietly, before he goes to stand with the other guys.

"Alright, you guys know the drill. Girls on one side, guys on the other. Nadi, stand next to Tia; and Jeff, you need to be on the end with the instructors," Luther tells us, and we all get into position. The squealing of the brakes alerts us as the bus pulls up – they're here.

"I want everyone to put on their serious faces. If anything out of the norm happens, let Aerick or I deal with it." *Yeah, just like Aerick did with me.* Although, all I did was smile. Knowing now that Aerick thought I was going to be one of the troubled ones, I find myself wondering if he did that on purpose to show me who was boss.

We all stand up straighter and put our hands behind our backs. We're perfectly spaced; everyone's uniforms are nicely pressed, and we all appear like we just got out of bootcamp ourselves. The cadets start filing between the two buildings and I stand a little straighter. I take in their faces and try to remember their names. I studied the files one last time this morning for good measure. With all the schoolwork and learning the ins and outs of camp, it's been information overload.

The guy in front is Asa. I think he's the easiest to remember, because his name is so unusual. He's followed closely by two girls who have hard glares on their faces, but you can see they're really trying to hide the worry. Something tells me they're going to be trouble anyway. As the last of the new cadets clear the buildings, Aerick barks at them to hurry up. These poor kids have no idea what they're in for. The first two weeks were the hardest for me, and it will probably be the same for them.

Some of them look pissed, some appear scared, but one of the guys looks indifferent. The kid's name is Skyler and he's one of Aerick's group. I think he was one of the ones that Aerick believed was going to cause trouble – I guess we'll see.

They finally all get to the stage, and Brand and Aerick fall in with the rest of us as Luther starts in on his speech. It's pretty much identical to the one that we got last session, with the exception of me, Jeff and Gavin, in which he explained we're training but have just as much power to punish as the others. As he finishes up, Aerick, Paulo, Brand and Trent move to make a square around the cadets. Jake hands a tablet to Luther, who gives out the instructor and dorm assignments.

"You will all be split into four groups. You will be paired with an instructor, who will be your lead instructor. When your name is called, go stand next to your instructor. Clarrisa, Vincent and Alex, your lead instructor is Trent. Eve, Charlie and Reid, your lead instructor is Brand.

Amanda, Skyler and Ryan, your lead instructor is Aerick." I have to concentrate hard to keep a straight face as I remember my name being called out a few months ago. I was so irritated to be put with Aerick. "Crystal, Asa and Martin, your lead instructor is Paulo."

When they're all situated around their instructors, Luther continues. "Behind me are the main dorms. If you are in Paulo and Aerick's groups, you will be in dorm A; if you're in Brand or Trent's groups, you are in dorm B." Glancing around at their faces, it only takes a second to see realization cross their faces. "Your instructors are in dorm C, on the back side of this building."

"You're kidding me," one of the girls spits out. I think her name is Crystal. Only a few people seem upset at the sleeping arrangements. That is, until Luther goes into his speech and gives a warning to all of them, at which their faces fall. Again, it takes everything in me to keep myself from laughing at my sense of deja vu.

When no one else has anything to say, the instructors moved the cadets into the dorms. Jeff follows Brand and Gavin follows Aerick. Aerick isn't too thrilled about Gavin having to tag along with him, because it leaves less time for us to be around each other, but he'll do whatever it takes to prove to Luther he deserves Ayla's position. I'm hoping he'll have time to stop by tonight, because I miss being around him. Last night I was so tempted to ask him to stay, but as much as he would have wanted to, he would follow the rules.

As soon as the cadets are in the dorms, Luther dismisses us and lets us know that everyone needs to be at dinner and be on time. Tia and I don't have much to do because of our positions, so I figure it's a perfect time to get some schoolwork done. Terrie has to be in the clinic, so I'll have some peace and quiet until dinner.

The moment I step foot in the cabin, my fingers attempt to move the braid on my head up and down with the hope of loosening it just a little. She did the braid way too tight, but it's pointless to take it out because she'll just insist on redoing it for dinner. I throw my jacket on the bed and get comfortable at the desk. *Time to focus.*

* * * *

Holy Crap?

I'm startled, nearly falling out of my seat, by a sudden tapping on the window above my night table. *Who in the world is that?* I get up from the desk and walk over to the window. Throwing the curtain open, Aerick is standing there smirking at me. I try to hide the emotion threatening my lips and give him a disapproving glare. I unlock the window and slide it sideways so that it's all the way open.

"What are you doing?" I ask him, trying to act unamused.

"What does it look like? I'm sneaking around to see my girlfriend. Just like old times, huh?"

Elation bubbles up in me. Him acting like a teenage boy is so out of character for him, and so freaking adorable.

"You do know there's a front door, right?"

"Yeah, but that defeats the purpose of the 'sneaking around' – and someone might see me. There's no cameras back here, remember, and I'm able to get through the blind spot on the one attached to the dorm."

I chuckle a little and bend down to his level. "Really? So, what exactly did you need to see your girlfriend for?"

He hums and grabs onto my face with both of his hands. "Well, you're all alone in here, and I couldn't help but think how extremely hot you looked standing out there. I figured I'd sneak away and maybe steal a kiss." He pulls me the rest of the way to him and kisses me gently. One of my hands moves from the windowsill and wraps around his neck. All too soon he breaks away, putting his forehead to mine.

"Ugh, I hate this." My whisper is raw, and he pulls back to gaze into my eyes.

"Hate what?" He almost looks hurt, although I can't imagine why.

"Not having access to you whenever I want."

His face immediately perks up. "Ahh, what's the matter, Princess? Miss me?" I hum in agreement, making his lips turn up. "Do you miss me, or do you miss my friend?" My eyebrows pull together in confusion and he glances down.

Not only does it dawn on me what he's talking about, but there's a clear outline of excitement in his pants. My cheeks get hot. "Hmm, maybe both," I tell him, using up the little bit of bravery I've saved for a moment like this.

A low groan rumbles from his chest. "Move back."

I raise an eyebrow but do as he asks. Grabbing onto the windowsill, he springs himself up before grabbing the side of the window so he can swing his legs inside. *Impressive!* He quickly closes the gap between us, as I stand there, stunned by how easily he just did that.

"Which one do you miss more?" he asks, grabbing my waist and pulling me tight to him so I can feel his need for me.

An ache erupts between my legs. "Hmm, I can't decide," I whisper, teasing him as I stare into his beautiful eyes. He pulls my face to his again but this time his kiss is much more passionate and lustful.

"Well, why don't I give you both and then you can decide," he says in a low, breathy voice and lust explodes inside of me. His lips crush down to mine again and he walks us backwards until my legs hit the bed. He lays me down without breaking contact and his hands quickly undo the buttons on my pants.

"I don't have long, Princess," he whispers as he moves his lips down to my neck. None of that matters right now. All I know is I want him right this minute.

"Then you better make it good." I have no idea where that boldness came from, but he clearly enjoys it. He groans against my neck and the vibration from his lips travels down, hitting me between my legs just as his fingers enter me. "Aerick," I whimper, grabbing his shoulders tightly.

"You like that, huh?" I feel his grin against my neck as he continues to kiss and bite at me. His fingers move quicker and quicker in me and I'm dying to feel him inside me. "Aerick, I need you."

"Impatient as ever, Princess." He pulls me up off the bed and quickly pulls me over to the table. "Put your hands on the table," he whispers in my ear from behind me. Aerick talents have no end and in no time, we are both breathless as we find our release.

My chest relaxes onto the table as I come down and Aerick's chest presses against my back, pining me between him and the table. "Fuck, babe. You never cease to amaze me," he tells me, as he places kisses across my back and shoulders.

"I think the same can be said about you."

He chuckles and his weight disappears. I straighten up as well and pull my pants back up before turning around to face him. He's staring at me with as smirk on his face.

"What?"

He shakes his head. "Nothing. I just love the sight of you bent over that table." My face flushes. Great, that will probably be the only thing I will think about the next time we're sitting around the table playing poker.

"I have to get going. I told Paulo I would only be a few minutes." He kisses me quickly before going over and jumping out the window.

"Well, feel free to do that anytime," I call out to him and he turns back to give me a heart-stopping smirk. There's no possible way anyone could love someone as much as I love this man.

He quickly disappears and I turn toward the front door. It's a good thing Terrie didn't stop by, because I hadn't even locked the door. I'm also glad the blinds on the front window just happened to be closed. I swear, all rational thoughts evade me when he's around.

Dinner is almost ready, so I save the paper I'm working on and go to see if they need any help. I quickly glance in the mirror and am surprised to see my hair is still almost perfect. I fix the few little hairs that are out of place and put on a little powder in an attempt to cover my flushed skin. It doesn't really work, but hopefully people just think I was exercising or something. In a way I was, but that's beside the point. After putting on some chapstick, I grab my jacket and keys before heading out the door.

The dining hall is already buzzing when I get there. All the staff are already there, with the exception of the instructors. I go and make sure Andi doesn't need any help, but she insists it's all done and tells me to dish up. We're having baked chicken, fried rice and mixed vegetables – it looks mouthwatering. I get my plate and sit down next to Luther, since the instructors will likely sit together at the other table today.

"Where did you disappear to?" Gavin asks as he sits down across from me.

I peek up at his face; he appears like he's just trying to start a conversation, so I try my hardest not to flush. "I was working on a paper that's due next week," I mumble, concentrating on my food.

"That reminds me. I've been meaning to ask you, how is school going?" Luther asks.

"It's going good. I've managed to maintain a three point nine so far this quarter, so it's going okay. It's just taking a little bit of time to get used to adding work into the demand of my schoolwork, but I'm up for the challenge."

"I heard you passed the first half of your CLEP tests with flying colors." *Aerick!* Him and I are the only ones that know, so it must have been him. "I want you to know I'm proud of you, and if you need to study for a test or something, just let me know. We'll cut out some time for you, alright?" Luther is really the best.

"Thanks Luther. For everything. You've been too generous already."

He's more upbeat for probably the first time today. "Nonsense. I know talent when I see it." Heat rises on my cheeks and I glance over to see Gavin smiling as well.

"I heard you were going to school. What are you getting your degree in?" he asks me before I can look back down.

"I'm getting my teaching degree."

"And you're going to school and working here?" I nod but keep my eyes down. It's not a big deal.

"Don't let her fool you," Luther pipes up. "She's doing a fast track program to get her teaching degree in one year and so far, not only has she done well, but she has exceeded any expectations I've had. Her school workload is enough to overwhelm anyone, let alone someone who's working too. Anyone who can take on that much stress and still smile deserves some recognition." He bumps my shoulder with his own and I'm sure my face is the shade of a rose, but I'm smiling. If I didn't know any better, it would sound like he's praising his own child.

"Well, looks like you found a really great girl here, Luther.

"I know!" His confidence reminds me of Aerick, and it is exhilarating.

The door opens and the first of the cadets start wandering in. Luther tells them to get some dinner and take a seat. Once they have all filed in, the instructors come in too. As expected, all the instructors sit together at the other table behind Gavin.

* * * *

The rest of dinner was fairly uneventful. We showed the new cadets how to clean up properly after dinner and then Aerick left to finish showing them around. I had gotten a little nervous when Luther asked me back to his office. When I got there, he sat down with me on his couch, instead of at the desk, which clued me in that it wasn't going to be anything good.

He went on to give me an update on the case against Liz. Apparently, my lawyer and the prosecuting attorney have been able to build a pretty strong case, showing motive and premeditation. Both lawyers seem to think they have enough grounds to try to plead it out, so we won't have to go to trial.

Luther was very supportive in telling me that it was completely up to me; if I wanted it to go to trial, because she would receive a harsher sentence, he would completely understand. Given he's footing the bill for my lawyer, I would have thought he would have pushed me to settle, but he did nothing of the sort. After he explained the possible outcomes of both sides, I agreed that I would rather settle it out of court.

Of course, he praised me for being so strong throughout this whole ordeal and even gave me a quick hug, which totally threw me off. As I was leaving, he said he would call my lawyer in the morning to give him my input, since he had a meeting with the prosecutor this week. They will be pushing for seven to ten years if she pleads guilty to aggravated assault, which would cut out the extra two and a half years for the deadly weapons charge. So, at a minimum, she would get seven years. I suppose giving up a few years on her sentence will be worth not having to go to court and testify.

The whole situation infuriated me, even just having to think about it. I immediately went to the back field behind the cabins and ran sprints between the cabin and the fire pit until the sweat ran down my back. I stopped by my cabin and changed into a tank top and grabbed a hand towel before heading to the gym so that I could see Aerick. Not that we could be openly together, but even working out with him makes me feel calmer.

I reach the gym and there are a couple of people inside. Gavin and Brayden are both punching at the bags, while Jeff lifts weights.

"You okay, Nadi?" Of course, Jeff is the first to notice my foul mood.

"Yeah. Where's Aerick and Paulo? I thought they would be here by now." They're usually here about an hour after dinner, even when the cadets are here.

"There was an incident with the cadets. They should be here in a little bit. Now, you want to tell me why you look like you just ran a marathon?"

I notice Gavin and Brayden have both stopped and are listening. "Because I was running sprints out back. I needed to work through some things in my head." He nods, getting the hint I don't want to talk about it.

"So, what happened in the cabins?" Brayden asks, coming up behind me.

"I don't know. I was talking to Trent in the courtyard a little bit ago, and he got an urgent text from Brand telling him to get back to the dorm." Jeff shrugs.

"Well, crap. Aerick and I were supposed to work on boxing today," I say, hoping Jeff will want to work with me until Aerick gets here.

"I can work with you until he gets here?" I turn around at the voice behind me to see Gavin walking toward me.

"I'm not Aerick, but I'm pretty good." I watched his fight with Luther the other night. Gavin is a great fighter. Good enough that he would be a pretty even match for Aerick, even though he's a bit shorter.

"Yeah, okay."

He nods and picks up the boxing hand pads while I put on my gloves. We step onto the mats and agree to stick to basic combo punches. He starts calling out punches and I follow as quick as the word leaves his mouth. "Right, right... left, right... right, left, uppercut."

After a few minutes, he stops. "Okay, now I'm going to go faster and after each combo, I will send one to you. Make sure to block or duck." I nod in understanding. This is the same thing Aerick and I normally do, and we start again. He begins slow but speeds up with each set until we are at full speed. When I miss the block, Gavin hits me quite a bit harder than Aerick does. Not that I mind, but I can't help but notice Aerick must hold back a bit. He must be afraid to hurt me. As much as I love him, I really wish he wouldn't take it easy on me.

After a good fifteen minutes, I'm sweating again, and slowing down a little. Gavin keeps encouraging me, which helps me to keep pushing on.

The door opens and I lose my concentration just enough that Gavin hits me hard in the shoulder. Aerick and Paulo walk in and Aerick's already irritated face turns pissed as he watched me move a step back to keep my balance from the blow.

"You okay?" Gavin asks; his back is to the door. He didn't see them come in and the music playing in the background drowned out the noise.

"Uh, yeah, that was my fault. I got distracted." He frowns and then he turns to see where I'm staring. Aerick quickly gets his emotions in check before Gavin can see him.

"Is everything in the dorms okay?" I ask Aerick, trying to divert his attention.

"It's fine. One of the cadets wanted to try and start a fight. I intervened when he shoved another cadet."

"Who was it?" Jeff asks.

"Skyler." I huff – guess he was right.

"And how did you deal with him?" I ask, a little curious.

"Made him do push-ups." I glare at him, not because I'm surprised that's all he got, but also his tone with me is cold and I don't like it.

"That's it?" I try to cover up my irritation with him.

"Actually, he did push-ups until he dropped in exhaustion," Paulo tells me with a little chuckle.

"Yeah, that sounds more like it," I joke, still looking toward Aerick.

"You want to take over?" Gavin offers Aerick the pads.

"Actually, I have some frustrations I need to get out. If you don't mind, Nadalynn, I'm going to just hit the bags." I shrug my shoulders, trying to appear indifferent to it, but he's upset. Gavin puts the gloves back on and turns back to me as Aerick and Paulo walk away.

"Don't let anything break your concentration. When you're fighting, the only thing in the room is you and the person you're fighting. Alright?" Nodding my head yes, I get back into stance. I attempt to block out everything else as we start again.

After another fifteen minutes I'm exhausted. Gavin doesn't let up on me for one minute. Between boxing, sprints, and my little rendezvous with Aerick, my body is spent. "Okay, okay. I'm done," I say to Gavin, trying to catch my breath.

"Tired so soon, little sister?" Paulo says as he glances at Aerick, who's trying to keep his mask composed. *Damn him.* Why do boys have to air out their business to each other? It never bothered me before, but when I'm the subject of conversation, it definitely does. Gavin is looking at me a little oddly.

"Give me a break. I was running sprints before coming in here." Aerick stops hitting the bag and turns toward me, probably realizing that our little time together earlier was not the reason why I'm so tired.

"Why? Something happen?"

I realize that was probably something I should have kept to myself. He won't back off like Jeff did, so I keep my words as vague as possible. "Luther got a call from Mr. Walker. He called me into his office to give me an update and get my opinion."

Aerick continues to gaze at me for a minute. "Everything is okay, right?" he finally asks.

"Yep. I just needed to get out my extra energy afterward."

"Okay." He turns back to the bag and starts punching again, so I turn back to Gavin.

"Thanks for your help tonight."

He nods his head. "Anytime."

I go and pick up my towel and wipe the sweat off my neck and face. "Night, guys! See you tomorrow," I say to everyone, but really, I just want to say it to Aerick. Everyone chimes in with their goodnights, but I see Aerick's lip twitch when he says his.

Satisfied with that, I turn and head home to shower. Today has been a long and busy day. Glancing up, I stop just outside my cabin. The sky is clear, and the stars are bright in the sky, with the moon not currently present. It's so beautiful out here at night. So quiet and calming, I don't even mind the cold that is quickly chilling my skin.

My phone buzzes in my back pocket and I pull it out to see who it is. It's from Aerick.

Aerick: Are you really okay?

Me: Yes! I really just wanted to get the situation out of my head.

Aerick: K but if you need me, I'm here and sorry about my mood. It really wasn't you, I just have a lot on my mind as well. See you in the morning. Sleep well princess!

I let out a big sigh. He can be so sweet sometimes.

Me: As long as my dreams are of you, I will most certainly sleep well :) Good night my prince. Love you!

I grin, thinking of the face he probably would have made as he read that message.

Aerick: Stop! You are going to make me need another cold shower and just an FYI... secret rendezvous, now a high priority!

I let out my amusement. I wonder how often he's had to take a cold shower since we came here. We've only been together a few times, including today. The whole secret rendezvous sounds good to me and if anyone can make it happen, it will be him.

CHAPTER FIFTEEN

(Thursday, November 26th)

BANG, BANG, BANG...

"What the hell?" I mumble, jumping out of bed still half asleep and swinging the door open to see who's pounding on the door like like they are the police at two in the morning. "Someone better be dead."

"Um, sorry." Brand embarrassed gaze quickly falls to the ground and it reminds me that I only have on my lace boy-short panties and the matching camisole top. I quickly move behind the door to hide my lower half and he seems to be speechless.

"What, Brand?" I try to say as if it's nothing, but surely my face is as red as his.

"I need Terrie. A cadet tried to escape, and his tracker was activated."

I turn to the noise behind me and Terrie is already getting out of bed, starting to put on her pants over sleep shorts. "Be there in a minute, Brand."

"Who was it?" I ask.

"Skyler. Aerick's in the infirmary with him now." Well, that doesn't surprise me one bit. He has been awfully mouthy since the day he got here. He even started a fight that first night. Aerick worked him really hard on Monday and I would have thought that he got the point.

"Is he okay?" I know they check all the cadets that end up setting off their trackers to make sure there aren't any adverse reactions. It's very rare but it can happen.

"Yeah, he's fine. Just precautionary." He still seems rather uncomfortable. *Great!*

Terrie slips pas me. "Let's go!" He nods and quickly turns around to follow her.

I watch them walk toward the infirmary for a minute before closing the door and slipping back into my bed. *Shit.* I really hope Brand doesn't say anything to Aerick about me answering the door in my damn underwear. Maybe it would be a good idea to wear shorts to bed from now on. I normally do wear them, but Terrie keeps our heat up kind of high and sometimes it's too hot at night. I'm not really complaining though, because I like it to be warm, especially when I don't have Aerick to sleep next to.

I let out a heavy sigh. I really need to get some sleep. I just went to bed two hours ago because I was working on a paper for school that's due by tomorrow. I wanted to finish it, so I didn't have to worry about it tonight. I really hope Aerick drives Skyler into the ground for pulling this.

* * * *

"Hmm." My body heats as my face is peppered with kisses.

"Wake up, Princess." My eyes don't want to open – I'm way too tired. There's no way it's already time to get up.

"What time is it?" I groan as he moves his way down my neck, over my chest and to the exposed bare skin on my stomach. His lips feel so amazing.

"It's four-thirty." He mumbles on my skin. "I thought maybe we could spend a few minutes together before everyone gets up, while Terrie is occupied in the infirmary."

"Uhh, babe," I whine. I've only been asleep for two and a half hours. He stops kissing me and I glance down to see his beautiful eyes staring into mine with a questioning look. Not once since we've been together have I ever told him no. Mostly because I enjoy sex just as much as he does, and he always seems to know how to work me up when I'm not quite in the mood. Oh well, it was bound to happen eventually. "Babe, I haven't even gotten four hours of sleep. I'm too tired."

He groans. "Come on, Princess. It's been four days – four days! I miss you." He kisses my stomach again and pulls at the top of my panties with his teeth. I love it when he does that, but I'm just way too tired for that right now.

I put my hands on his head and he lays down on my stomach so that I can see his sad eyes. "I will kick Terrie out tonight, I promise. Please just let me sleep."

He groans again. "Fine." He goes to get up but I pull on his arm, stopping him.

"Stay with me, just until I fall asleep. Please."

He inhales a deep breath, thinking about it for a moment. "Move over," he finally says. I quickly move toward the wall and he lies on the bed next to me. I notice he has removed his boots and socks. He really did think he was getting some. *Poor guy.* I cuddle into his side as he folds his arm around me, pulling me tighter to him.

"Ugh, as if telling me *no* wasn't bad enough, you have to torture me too."

I hold in my teasing and sigh deeply. I miss this so much. Being wrapped in his arms as I fall asleep. Even if he is grumpy, I want to stay like this forever. "I love you, babe."

I feel him kiss the top of my head. "I love you, too, Princess. Now sleep, before I change my mind." I chuckle this time and close my eyes, letting sleep find me again.

* * * *

I wake to up to my alarm. As I turn it off, I'm startled to see it's six fifty-five. *Seriously?* My alarm should have gone off at five forty-five so I could get in a run before breakfast. It had to be Aerick. He must have changed it before he left. I'm not sure how long he stayed, because it took me all of two minutes cuddled up to him to fall back asleep. Considering it took me over thirty minutes to go back to sleep when Brand woke us up this morning, it was an improvement. Having him next to me is just so much better. With a deep sigh, I get up and grab some clothes quickly so I can get to breakfast on time.

Stepping into the mess hall, it's after seven and everyone is already here. A bunch of people turn my way, but I just ignore them and go dish up my food. The staff have gone back to mixing between the two tables, and most of the seats next to the staff are already occupied. No one is sitting next to Aerick, which gives me the perfect opportunity to sit next to him. I sit down between Aerick and Jeff. *Just like old times!* If I didn't know any better, I would think they did that on purpose.

Brayden and Paulo are sitting across the table from us. "Nice of you to join us, little sister," Paulo says pinching his lips in a line. Something tells me he already knows why I'm late.

"Well, it seems my alarm clock didn't go off when I expected it to." I kick Aerick under the table and I see a smirk pull at his lips, but he manages to keep a straight face.

"You should really have that checked," he tells me, trying to give the impression like it's nothing.

"Yeah, I'll get right on that. Or maybe I should just make sure people don't sneak into my cabin anymore," I say quietly, so only the people sitting closest to me can hear. Jeff, Brayden and Paulo all laugh.

The staff at the other table stares at us like we're crazy.

"So, what did I miss at P.T. this morning?" I ask no one in particular, but I know exactly who will answer me.

"We're having a Thanksgiving dinner tonight. Luther wants you to help out Andi today. Everything else is business as usual," Aerick tells me in his 'all business' voice. "Well, except Skyler. I will be running his ass into the ground today."

A chuckle escapes my mouth. "You do that. That little punk interrupted what little sleep I was supposed to get last night."

"Yeah," Aerick says quietly, looking deep in thought. I really hope he isn't too disappointed about this morning when he woke me up.

"You know Nadi, I think Aerick here is rubbing off on you a little too much. You're starting to sound a little sadistic." I don't bother replying to that, I just roll my eyes at Brayden.

I turn back to Aerick and lean close to whisper as a thought hits me. "What about Tia?" I've been trying not to leave Tia in the classroom by herself with the cadets, and especially not all day.

"We have it covered." I know we can't get into it with the cadets there, so I just nod for now and put it in the back of my head to ask him later.

Aerick pushes his leg against mine, making me smile, before he leans in to talk in my ear. "And in the future, try and not embarrass her pansy ass man, okay?" He pulls away and I see his eyes glowing with humor before he switches back into instructor mode.

"Skyler!" he shouts, making half of the cadets jump in their seats, and I have to try hard to hold in my laugh. "Outside, now!" Skyler appears just a little worried as he empties his tray and follows Aerick outside.

Wow. So much for keeping what happened this morning between me and Brand. Though that's certainly not how I expected him to react. At least that's an improvement, but I'm sure that it has to do with the fact that he knows Brand is with Tia and that he probably was more embarrassed than I am.

Gavin comes over and sits in Aerick's empty seat. "So, Paulo, apparently I'm stuck with you today, since Jeff is taking over Aerick's spot for the day." Paulo nods his head as he inhales another bite of his bacon. "What's the kid's punishment?"

"Running," Paulo and I both answer at the same time. We beam at each other before Paulo continues. "Aerick will make him run for all of his spare time today."

"So, he will still go to his classes?" Gavin questions.

"Yeah, only the really bad ones get out of class too," Paulo says as he glancing to me, and I glare at him.

Gavin picks up on our exchanges. "And I take it you experienced that?" he asks, looking at me. I glare at Paulo again before gazing down at my food.

"I sure did."

"What did you do?"

I can't help but show my cheerfulness. "I basically told him he couldn't control me." I grin, remembering his expression when I told him he couldn't make me eat. "He didn't take it too well. He made me run until I collapsed from exhaustion." Some of the cadets glance over at me in shock.

"Actually, I think it was the fact that you told him to *fuck off* that really pissed him off," Paulo says with a goofy-happy look on his face.

"Well, that took some guts," Gavin says, appearing a little shocked.

"Yeah, probably not one of my smarter moments. He definitely is not one you want to piss off. I spent the rest of the day in the infirmary." I speak a little louder so I know the cadets can hear me. Maybe they will think twice before they do something stupid.

"So Nadi, I heard you gave Brand a little show this morning," Paulo says a little quieter, trying to hold in his amusement. I glare up at him and then over to Brand at the other table. He hasn't looked at me once since I walked in. He just keeps his head down, staring at his food. Gavin, Brayden and Jeff all raise their eyebrows at me.

"Shut up, before I hit you. I was half asleep," I tell him quickly as I feel my face heat up, and he starts laughing.

"Ahh, don't be embarrassed. I'm sure he enjoyed it."

"Paulo, I swear if you don't shut up, I'm going to stab you with my fork."

"Whoa, whoa, whoa. Now you have to tell me what happened this morning?" Brayden asks, getting all jumpy, and Paulo's face brightens.

"Apparently, sleepyhead over here doesn't like getting woken up, and temporarily forgot she went to sleep in just her underwear." *What the fuck?*

"Hey, I wasn't just in my underwear, you ass. I had my sleep shirt on."

"You mean that tight, barely-there tank top that leaves nothing to the imagination?" Gavin says, trying to hold his grin back. It occurs to me that he saw me in an almost identical one the other night when I went to their cabin looking for Jeff. I don't think my face could possibly get any redder. At least I had shorts on that night.

"I'd like to have seen that. Brand probably didn't even appreciate it," Brayden says jokingly and all four of them start laughing. *What the hell is this, pick on Nadi day?*

I lower my voice to just above a whisper. "Oh my god, you guys are hopeless. Look: I know being here, you're all extremely sex-deprived. So please, go out and find some ass, so you can stop jacking off to the thoughts of mine." I quickly stand up with my tray, not even caring that I haven't finished my food

"Oh, come on Nadi, we're just messing with you," Paulo tells me, trying to stop his giggles.

"Whatever, I'm going for a quick run before it's time to start cooking. See you guys later."

I turn and leave with them all giggling and whispering to each other still. I don't even want to know what they're saying.

Outside, Aerick is running alongside Skyler, barking orders at him. I give him a grin as they pass me. He slyly winks at me before continuing with his verbal assault on Skyler. I hurry to my cabin to pick up my iPod. Since Aerick is running Skyler, the gym will have to do – it's much warmer in there.

As I'm reaching for the handle to the gym, someone calls my name. Turning to the voice, I watch as Gavin jogs up to me. "Hey, I just want to apologize for what I said at breakfast." *Seriously?* I didn't care, just preferred not to stick around and listen to them talk about me.

"It isn't a big deal. Most of my friends are guys. It's normal, and to be honest, I've heard much worse."

"Well, not that it wasn't true but still, wasn't very gentlemanly of me to say it and I just wanted to make sure you weren't mad at me." I grin at him. He didn't start it, Paulo did; and besides, his comment wasn't really that bad.

"Like I said, you're a guy. It's to be expected. All the guys here pick on me because they know I can take it."

"Yeah, so I've noticed. You really are something different."

"I know." No point in denying it. "Anyway, I want to get in a quick run before I have to get to work."

"By all means. Don't let me stop you," he says with a cute little smirk.

"See you later," I tell him, and turn to go inside.

* * * *

Finishing up P.T. this evening was a little difficult. Between missing this morning's P.T., being on my feet all day, and stuffing my stomach with heaps of food, exercising at all was a challenge. Andi went all out for Thanksgiving and cooking a big-ass dinner for twenty-six people is no small feat. Especially when the majority are young adult males. We spent a good part of the day cooking, except the little break I got earlier in the day before lunch, since we got all the desserts done plus all the prep work.

Spending time with Andi today was surprisingly very relaxing. She had me cracking up all day long as we cooked. By the time dinner rolled around, we had a buffet of all kinds of delicious foods. Andi baked a huge turkey with stuffing, and we made all the traditional food you would normally see on the table for Thanksgiving. We even made pumpkin and apple pies for dessert. It truly reminded me of home.

It was sort of a family tradition with my family to have a big dinner. Mom is an incredible cook and is great at putting on holiday parties. There wasn't one year that we didn't have over a mass of people for Thanksgiving dinner. Our home was always open to anyone in our family that didn't have anywhere to go, and there were always those that came every year. Of course, that usually meant me and my sisters in the kitchen for two days helping her cook because with my mom, it was never 'just dinner'. We cooked all kinds of candies, made dips and snack trays, everything needed to keep a bunch of people happy and having fun all day long. I loved helping her cook, and seeing everyone happily enjoying all the food always made the hard work worth it.

This year is the first time I haven't been home for Thanksgiving. A bit of sadness stuck in my gut as more memories flooded me, but I was able to put on a brave face. After spacing out a few times thinking of everyone back in Chicago, I decided after lunch to do a Skype chat with everyone back home. It was refreshing to see my parents and brother again. Several of my uncles were already at the house and they were all curious about what was going on in my life. Mom went off and started bragging about how well I was doing and how she was so proud of me. Even my dad looked as if his head was up higher. After the call I felt a whole lot better.

I'm brought out of my thoughts as Aerick dismisses everyone. I give him a quick smile before turning and heading back to my cabin to shower, with Gavin following close behind me. He's been a little weird this afternoon, which struck me as odd, since he was trying to be all nice this morning. At lunch and dinner, he glanced over a few times, looking almost confused. It sort of reminded me of how Aerick use to regard me when he knew I was keeping a secret from him, which is a little unnerving. Jeff kind of hinted that I had issues the night I stayed in their cabin, and I just hope he doesn't push me to tell him, like Aerick did.

I hear him closing the distance on me and nervousness starts spreading down my spine. "Hey, Nadi." I just keep walking with my head down, trying to shake the awkward feeling. "Can I ask you a question?"

"You just did." *Man, I am starting to sound like Aerick.* I don't mean to sound rude, but I just don't have a good feeling about this.

"No, seriously. Can I ask you something?"

I stop and turn around. The cabin is right in front of me and it would be rude to just walk inside. Besides, something about his tone sounds off, and it's piquing my curiosity. "Fine, what is it?"

"What did you and your boyfriend get into a fight about the other night?" *What?*

I let out an audible huff. "Are you serious? I'm not sure how any of that is your business."

He gives me an odd look, like he's debating what his next words are going to be. "I mean, was it because of another guy?" *Holy shit.*

First off, how could he possibly know that? Second, what is it to him that me and Aerick were fighting about another guy? My mind is totally at a loss for what to say right now.

"Does he suspect there is something going on between you and Aerick?"

My mouth drops open as my brain scrambles to comprehend what the fuck he just said. What does he mean? Does he think I'm cheating on my boyfriend with Aerick? *Aerick is my boyfriend.* How does he even know there's something between me and Aerick? I glance over to the dorms and all the instructors and cadets are already back inside.

He continues when I don't answer. "I know you've been sneaking around with Aerick. It was a little odd how you appear so comfortable and playful with every guy here except him. Although, until recently I never thought it was because of that. I suppose the fact that you two always happen to disappear at the same time makes sense now. Honestly, I just never thought you would be that kind of girl."

I'm shocked speechless and just stand there staring at him. After a moment, he shakes his head, turns toward his cabin, and walks away without another word.

What the actual fuck?!

CHAPTER SIXTEEN

(Sunday, November 29th)

THE LAST FEW days have been really irritating. It's been difficult to get that conversation with Gavin out of my head – well, if you can call it a conversation. Really, it was just him spouting off, not knowing what he's talking about. He's been avoiding me the last few days and my internal dialogue has been working overtime trying to decide what to do.

On one hand, my personal life is really none of his business. It's even a little funny that he thinks I'm cheating on my boyfriend; if he had any common sense, he'd realize that Aerick *is* my boyfriend. Yes, it's true, I act different around him because we're trying to keep our relationship strictly professional, which is not something we can do halfway. Either we're cute and touchy, or we're serious and controlled at all times. As much as I'd like to just tell him we're together, it's a bad idea. Aerick is trying to prove to Luther that at work, he can put his personal feelings aside and focus solely on his job. Last session he got in a lot of trouble because of everything that went on between us and I feel like now Luther is testing him.

Although I understand Luther's reasoning, I still don't like it. Brand doesn't even want Ayla's position. Tia told me that he doesn't care if Aerick gets it. When I told Aerick that, it didn't change his attitude or reasoning one bit. If he's anything, it's one hundred percent committed to doing his job. That being the case, I'm going along with him in his decision to keep our relationship to ourselves. The others have done pretty well at not showing theirs, as well. Brand and Tia were never really the PDA type to begin with, but their relationship had to be exposed during training for safety reasons and with her growing belly, she could only hide it for so long anyway. As for Terrie and Paulo, I don't think anyone knows besides me, Aerick and Jeff. They've been hiding it from Luther for quite some time so that it wouldn't inhibit their time together here at camp. They're much better at hiding it than Aerick and I are, but for the life of me, I don't know how they do it.

On the other hand, I don't like the fact that Gavin's words insinuated that I was some kind of slut. I'm most definitely not a hoe, and the thought that someone would actually think that low of me is even more insulting. I wanted to just smack him in the face after he said that, and if he'd continued to stand in front of me, my rage would probably have gotten the better of me. He has no idea what I've been through in my life and doesn't have any right to judge me. Part of me questions if he may be jealous, since he obviously was checking me out the first week we were here. He's probably upset that it was Aerick instead of him.

The other thing bothering me is how the heck he figured it out. He was fine at breakfast that day. Then all of a sudden, at lunch, he was acting weird. Aerick and I have been careful to limit our contact to only when we're alone or when we're around Terrie and Paulo. Granted, Aerick has snuck into my cabin several times while it was just me, but he's always careful not to be seen by anyone. He knows all the camera blind spots, which he uses to his advantage. He's even gone as far as jumping through the back window, so people don't see him coming into the cabin when I'm here alone, like he did Thursday.

I'm not sure how, but Gavin had to have seen Aerick coming through the window, or maybe back out of it. None of it makes sense, because no one ever goes behind the cabins, except maybe me, and now there's another cabin behind mine, making it even harder to see. Ayla's cabin is behind mine, but the side of her cabin faces the back of mine, and there are no windows on the side, so you can't see in mine from hers. My mind just keeps replaying Aerick's visit, trying to figure out how Gavin could have seen him.

Flashback to Thursday

Walking back to my cabin, Aerick catches my attention. He seems a little annoyed but as soon as his eyes find mine the expression on his face softens and he walks over to me. "Hey, Princess."

"Hey babe. What are you up to?"

He rolls his eyes letting the irritation show again. "I was checking on Jeff and the cadets. Trent is teaching today's class, but I still wanted to make sure everything was going okay. You know, kind of like Ayla does throughout the day. Just wanted to check up on everyone. What are you doing out here? Shouldn't you be in the kitchen or something?" He smirks at me, almost letting it bloom into a smile.

I let out a humph. *Really - in the kitchen?* "Ha, ha, ha. Do you think I'm going to be that barefoot and pregnant in the kitchen type of wife?"

His smirk grows wider. "That would be something to see," he jokes, but clearly, he's half-serious.

"Keep dreaming, buddy." He bites his bottom lip, staring at me for a minute before letting out a soft grunt, but wisely doesn't say anything else on the subject. It suddenly occurs to me that I just insinuated that one day we'll get married and have kids, and he didn't bother to say anything to the contrary. Not wanting to sour his playful mood, I just push that thought aside.

"So anyway, where are you going?" he asks instead.

"Andi and I finished pretty much all we can until after lunch. She suggested I go work on my schoolwork, since we have an hour until lunch still." I see the wheels start turning in his head.

"Well, isn't that a coincidence, because I don't have nothing to do for the next thirty minutes. Maybe I should cash in that rain check that you gave me this morning." His suddenly low, seductive voice stirs up my body and it's instantly on fire.

"Well, maybe you better hurry up and find a way to sneak off to my cabin," I tease him, waggling my eyebrows suggestively.

As I reach my door, I see him walking swiftly to the instructor's dorm with clear intent on his face. I continue inside and lock the door behind me to make sure we aren't interrupted if someone does show up. Within a few minutes, there's a tapping at my window. Smiling, I go and unlock it. These little meetings make me feel like a little kid trying not to get caught breaking the rules. He slides the window open and jumps through it almost before I can step back to give him room. It's a treat in itself to see how young and playful he seems at this moment.

"Miss me, did you?" I ask. He doesn't answer me, just grabs my hand to lead me to my bed, where he sits down and pulls me to him so that I'm standing between his legs. "I'll take that as a yes!"

As I giggle, he gets that adorable smile on his face. His face slowly turns serious as he begins pulling up my shirt slowly, untucking it from my pants without taking his eyes off mine. As soon as the skin of my stomach is exposed, he kisses it just like he did this morning, causing a moan to escape from my mouth and my hands find their way into his hair.

"You know, not that I'm saying it should happen anytime soon or anything, but the thought of you barefoot and pregnant is making me hard as fuck." He kisses my stomach again and then adjusts his pants as if trying to prove his point. His comment is a little shocking to say the least, considering his reaction when I told him about the pregnancy test the day we got here.

"So, you do want kids?" I ask skeptically.

"Um, maybe *a kid,* and like I said, not right now – but yeah. In the future, having a kid with you would be ideal." Just the thought of being his wife stirs every emotion in me possible. He's telling me that he wants to marry me someday and even have a baby. He's right – that's such a turn on. Smiling, I push him down on the bed and crawl over him.

"Sounds good to me."

Our lips crash together with overheated passion and we don't stop until we're both lying naked and breathless.

End Flashback

That was truly unforgettable. I'd worried for the last several weeks that maybe he didn't want kids at all. It isn't that I was dying to have kids anytime soon, but I did always want them. His words were like a weight off my shoulders and it was so comforting to know that he thought about our relationship in terms of our distant future.

After Aerick made love to me, he dressed quickly, grabbed his coat, and jumped back out the window to go make Skyler run before lunch. After getting cleaned up and fixing my hair again, I set off for lunch. I even made sure to remove the grin off my face before I walked out the door, in case someone saw me. I'm just dumbfounded how he could possibly have known Aerick was here.

I did attempt to approach Gavin yesterday, but he just gave me a dirty sneer and walked away. It was my intention to politely explain the situation, but after that, he obviously doesn't deserve to know the truth.

"So, are you going to tell me why you're trying to kill that punching bag?" Aerick asks me, pulling me out of my thoughts as he hits the bag next to me. I'm speechless. I wasn't even aware of it, but now that he's mentioned it, there is a dull ache in my knuckles. "You've seemed... a little off for a few days. What's bothering you?"

I chose not to tell him about the conversation with Gavin. Mostly because I didn't want him to worry about it, but I'm certainly not going to lie about it, and now is as good a time as any. I draw in a deep breath and resume punching the bag. "Gavin stopped me the other day and said something that didn't sit well with me."

He raises an eyebrow. "And what was that exactly?" He stops punching the bag and glances around the gym before returning his gaze to me. Paulo, Jeff and Brayden are all around us working out, but aren't paying attention.

"He thinks I'm cheating on my boyfriend." He frowns, confused. "He thinks I'm cheating on my boyfriend, with you!"

His face changes into a smirk and he actually laughs, confusing me even further.

"What are you laughing at?" I ask, as the heat of anger rises in my neck.

"What a dumbass," he says, going back to punching his bag.

"That's all you have to say?"

"What do you want me to say? If that's what he wants to think, then screw him. He's an idiot. Don't mind him."

He seems to genuinely not care. *He doesn't get it.* Putting my hands on my hips, I glare at him even harder. "Do you realize that by him assuming that, he's insinuating I'm a slut? I'm so pleased you're perfectly fine with that." I turn to walk away from him. He's unbelievable right now. So glad he doesn't mind people thinking of me that way.

He grabs my wrist, stopping me. "Babe. I don't mean it like that."

Glaring back into his eyes, something occurs to me. "You know, you don't appear too surprised that he knew. Did you have something to do with him finding out that we're together?"

He takes about one second too long to answer me. "Why would you ask me that?" He's deflecting. *Guilty!*

"Why are you answering my question with a question?" Now I know he had something to do with it.

"I don't know what you are talking about," he tells me, but there is no conviction in his words.

"Sure you don't. First, you somehow let him know that we're together. Then you're going to sit there and be okay with him thinking I, your girlfriend, am a slut. Real nice, Aerick." I shake my head in disbelief. I need to be by myself; he's pissing me off just as much as Gavin.

"Come on, Princess, don't be mad at me."

I glare at him and pull my wrist out of his hand. "You know what, I'm going to go for a run on the trails."

"Babe, seriously. Don't be mad over this." The smugness on his face turns to concern.

"I'm not. I just need to run out some of my frustrations."

"I can't leave, I'm on dorm duty in twenty minutes. Why don't we go run on the path?"

"Don't bother. I want to run by myself. You finish here and I'll see you at dinner."

He seems uncomfortable but with the glare I'm giving him right now, he knows not to argue with me. "Fine, don't be too long and make sure you take your phone." I roll my eyes – him and his damn controlling nature.

"Don't worry, I have an appointment with Christian right before dinner." I start turning to walk away and he immediately wraps his arm around my stomach, pulling me back against his chest.

"Hey, please don't be mad at me."

It's so hard to deny his pleading tone. I breathe in deeply. I feel his lips brush across my shoulder. "Like I said, I'm not mad. Just frustrated that my boyfriend has a habit of being devious at my expense."

"Nadi..."

I don't want to hear it, especially when he calls me by that name, so I interrupt him before he can say anymore. "Like I said, I just need to get these frustrations out. I'll be back in time for my session with Christian."

"Sunset is just after four tonight, it'll be dark before your appointment. Please be back before dark."

I hold in the laughter threatening to escape my throat and settle for just rolling my eyes even though he can't see me. At least he's asking. "Fine." I don't turn back as he releases me, because looking into his eyes will just make me fall under his spell. I leave without another word.

"Uh-oh, trouble in paradise," Paulo says teasing me.

"Fuck off, dude." Aerick volleys back, and his tone satisfies me because he knows he messed up.

The door closes behind me and I quickly put my jacket on. There's an icy chill in the air. Peeking at my watch, there's about two and a half hours before my meeting with Christian. I could probably run up to the charcoal tree in less than an hour, and with it being downhill on the way back, it'll take less than that to get back. As I'm crossing the courtyard, slipping my earbuds in, I see Gavin leaving the dorms out of the corner of my eye. Great, the last person I want to see right now.

The expression on my face must be pretty bad, because his expression when he glances up at me turns to pure worry. He seems like he's going to ask me something, but before he has a chance, I turn my music up and start running toward the back trail. I pass right by him and don't glance back.

Hopefully the run will help me shake these feelings. It shouldn't bother me what Gavin thinks, but it does. Not to mention the fact that Aerick did something to let Gavin know we're together. I'd still like to know what in the world it was, but with my growing frustration for both of them right now, there's no point in trying to talk to him about it.

Maybe Christian can help me out. In fact, maybe Christian could invite Aerick into the session so he can help me explain all these frustrations I've had with him lately. He can be the sweetest man on the planet, and then he gets around other people or something insignificant happens, and he starts acting like a possessive, overbearing jerk – or maybe, I'm just an over-emotional and clingy girlfriend. Maybe I just need to stop over thinking all this.

Christian and I have already talked about me not letting myself overthink things, but it's getting harder and harder. Work, school, boyfriend, new home, it's all just overwhelming to the point that I want to get away from it all and be by myself. Like right now. I can just hear Christian standing next to me, telling me that 'running away from your problems won't solve them'. He's probably right, but right now, in this moment, this is where I need to be. I push my legs harder, continuing deeper and deeper into the woods. Stretching my legs out here is soothing. Yes, this is where I need to be. Lost in nature, where there's no need to worry about anybody or anything.

I inhale the air around me. The forest smells of the crisp, fresh rain that fell early this morning. Even though the cold is settling in for the season, many of the trees here are pine and their colors are still a brilliant green that mix in with the other trees that are a beautiful rainbow of red, orange and brown tones.

This place is amazing. I finally allow myself to melt into my surroundings and enjoy the setting while it last. I feel like when everything else in the world is wrong, I'll be able to count on this place to make me feel right. I turn up my music up louder to drown out the rest of my thoughts while I'm still content and concentrate on pushing my legs as fast as possible while I sing the words of the song in my head.

"Try to find out, what makes you tick, as I lie down, sore and sick. Do ya like that? Do ya like that? There's a fine line, between love and hate, and I don't mind..."

Oh shit...

What the...

"Fuckkk..."

Crack!

"Uhhhh." I try to move but my body is a ball of pain. Something wet is dripping down my neck, and then there's only darkness.

CHAPTER SEVENTEEN

(Sunday, November 29th)

Aerick POV

I FUCKING HATE when Nadi is pissed at me. I know she's mad, even though she insists she is just 'frustrated'. With her, it's basically the same thing. *Talk about frustrating.* I huff at the thought and notice both Gavin and Jeff glance up at me. I ignore them and continue staring at the weekly schedule I'm working on.

She's the one who is so damn frustrating. There is really no reason to be mad at me. I only put Gavin in his place, in my own way. Yeah, maybe we were supposed to keep it under wraps, but my patience with Gavin hitting on her was spent, and I couldn't pass up the opportunity.

Flashback to Thursday

I jump out of her window and straighten out my shirt. Her giggle follows from behind me and it's hard to stay straight-faced hearing that sound. I used to say she was amazing, but she's so much more than just amazing. I don't even have a word to describe her – and that doesn't even include the sex. That's in a whole category of indescribable all by itself.

She always feels so damn good. Being buried in her is the best place in the world and I swear I'll never get enough of her. Every time with her is like the first, and the way she says my name as she tightens around me is mind-blowing. I love the thought that she is mine and *only mine.*

Watching Gavin around her the last few weeks has pushed me to think a lot about our future. It has crossed my mind that if there was a ring on her finger, it might keep guys from always throwing themselves at her. It would be a permanent claim on her and would show everyone that she's taken.

It's not only that though, it is something that I truly want. It has only been a few months and I can already see myself being with her for the rest of my life – maybe even have a kid with her someday. Before her, that wasn't even something I'd let myself consider. Now, being with her, nothing would make me happier than to have a baby that would be a piece of both of us, bonding us together, forever. Thankfully, now I know that is something she wants too, which fills me with overwhelming joy.

I cut through between Nadi's and Tia's cabins on the new path that leads to the two new cabins belonging to Luther and Ayla. If anyone was to ask, I'll say that I went to see if Ayla was in her cabin, even though I saw her leave for town earlier. I emerge between the cabins and put my jacket back on. There's a biting chill in the air today and it's seeping all the way into my pants. I bite my lip at the thought that I didn't clean myself up, so my boxers are a bit damp from our activities.

Gavin comes out of the mess hall right about the same time I glance down to see my pants are still unzipped, causing the cold chill in my pants. That fucker has been a never-ending pain in my ass. I have had enough of his flirting and his 'I just want to be friends' act with Nadi. It's easy to see right through his sweet and innocent act and I know that look he gives her all the time. It's the same one other guys around here give her. The same way Jeff used to look at her – sometimes still does, but he knows better and I trust him never to overstep his bounds.

Gavin stopped her again this morning when she was on her way to the gym. She seemed frustrated but when they finished, she ended up smiling at him. I didn't like it one bit. That should be me putting a smile on her face.

I stare right at him and zip up my pants. He raises up a questioning eyebrow, and the smirk on my face gets even bigger as I glance over to Nadi's cabin. Looking back to him, I raise both of my eyebrows silently telling him, 'yeah I just came from her cabin' and the realization soon floats across his face. Satisfaction fills me. Let's see what he thinks about that. Maybe now he'll leave her the alone.

I hurry to the gym to grab Skyler and run laps. I want to see the color in her cheeks when she leaves. I love knowing that I'm the cause of it.

End Flashback

Apparently, he got the message loud and clear. Unfortunately for me, his dumbass took it the wrong way, thinking she was actually screwing around with me while she had a boyfriend somewhere else. I mean, is it really that hard to believe that she is with me? I know we are complete opposites and that she is probably way too good for me, but she's mine.

I'm certain jealousy played a part in his conclusion. Anyone with a half a brain can see he wants her, and something tells me this is another one of his games. I think he's secretly hoping that's the case, because then he would have a small chance of getting in her pants. If I was the boyfriend and not a fling, he would have no chance and he knows it. Well, he can fuck off. *She's mine.*

I check my watch, getting a little antsy to see her. It bothers me that she went running up in the woods alone. There's really nothing to worry about, but it still makes me nervous. Shit, just not seeing her for a few hours makes me nervous. The only time I feel right is when she's in my sights. Any other time, it's like part of me is missing and it's a feeling I hate. Another deep breath fills my lungs.

"Are you okay man?" Jeff asks.

I glare at him, but not because he's irritating me, I'm just preoccupied with the thought that I can see her soon, and not happy that I'm stuck in this room with Gavin. "I'm fine!" I tell him, hoping he will back off. With another glare he gets the point.

The door to the office swings open and a flustered Christian walks in. That expression on his face puts my nerves on high alert. He glances at me before he even closes the door. *Great*, their session must not have gone well and with that worried expression, something tells me I'm not going to like what I hear. *She must be more pissed than I realized.*

"Aerick, have you seen Nadi?"

Huh? "What do you mean? She had an appointment with you." Realization hits me before he can even respond. *She never showed up.*

"She didn't make it to her appointment. I've spent the last fifteen minutes searching around the camp for her, but she isn't anywhere."

"You're just now checking with me?!" I nearly shout and pull out my phone to call Jake. "Get your ass to the office now!" I growl into the phone, trying to keep my control, but it's fading fast. I glance outside and the sun has completely set. The only light is coming from the floodlights on the buildings. Christian is on his phone, but I ignore him. I start pulling up the application on the computer, but I have to wait for Jake to log in. We don't have access to other employees; only Luther, Ayla and Jake do.

"Aerick, what's going on?" Jeff asks, obviously picking up that something is not right with Nadi.

Jake comes rushing into the office. "What the heck is wrong?"

"Track Nadi's phone and hurry up!" He stares at me, confused, making me want to knock him into next week. "Now!" I shout and that finally gets him moving. He sits down quickly and logs in.

"Aerick, what in God's name is going on?" I hear Jeff ask again, and the heat of everyone's eyes are burning into me. Luther comes into the office, looking as worried as I feel. *Fuck.* Christian must have been on the phone with him.

"What is going on?" Luther asks, but my eyes are glued on the GPS searching for her phone signal. Thank the stars, there are trackers in our phones.

"I don't know, Aerick is going crazy and won't say anything," Jeff says. *Fucking application, hurry up!*

"Aerick?" Words abandon me. Something is wrong, I know it. "Aerick!" Luther is losing his patience, but I don't care. If this thing doesn't hurry, I'm going to fucking go insane.

A hand falls on my shoulder and I shake it off, but it returns more firmly this time, so I turn around about to knock out whoever it belongs too. Christian is standing there with a load of concern on his face.

"Aerick, we need you to tell us what's going on so we can help her." His firm voice and the words 'help her' bring me back to the fact that there are four sets of eyes staring at me like I'm a caged lion that is about to escape, while another is just gawking at me like I'm crazy. I breathe in a calming breath and collect my thoughts.

"She was pissed earlier." I send a quick glare to Gavin because this is partly his damn fault. "She decided to go for a run on the trails. I tried to keep her here but..." I shake my head because there is no controlling that girl. She does what she wants, when she wants, especially if she is upset. "That was hours ago. She promised me she would be back before dark. She wouldn't miss her appointment with Christian, and if she isn't here, something is wrong."

"Why would you let her go by herself?" Gavin asks me, and I'm one second from beating him into the ground.

"How long is it going to take you to get it through thick ass head of yours that *no one* controls her but *her* – not even me?" I growl.

"Aerick, control yourself!" Luther says sternly and Christian's hand clamps down tighter on my shoulder. I realize my hands are fisted so tight, I'm fairly certain my nails digging into my hands are drawing blood. *Calm Down Aerick, Fucking Calm Down!* I let another deep breath in and out and loosen my hands.

"I got her!" Jake shouts and my eyes shoot back to the screen as everyone gathers around the desk. "She is almost five miles up trail eight," Jake says, but I'm already grabbing my jacket and putting on.

"Jake, send the coordinates to my phone!"

"I'll go with you," Gavin says quickly and I turn on my heels.

"No!"

Luther steps in front of me. "Someone needs to go with you. He's the only one in the room that can keep up with you. Do you want to waste time waiting for me to go get someone?"

Damn, he's right. "Fine. You better be able to keep up."

I go to the supply locker, grabbing two flashlights, throwing one at him without looking back. I also grab one of the hiking backpacks that we normally bring in case of emergencies on hiking days and pray we don't need the medical supplies inside. Swinging it onto my back, I dart out of the office not waiting for Gavin, but I hear his feet pounding hot on my heels.

"Aerick?" Brand questions as we run past the dorms to the trail.

"I don't have time. Talk to Luther."

Trail eight, that would be the trail to the tree. Of course, she would pick one of the steeper trails, and on a day that it has been raining. *No sense of self-preservation.* Crossing into the tree line, I notice everything is damp again. It must have rained again sometime in the last hour. Hopefully I'll be able to see her boot prints when I get closer. I need to pace myself; the GPS indicates she made it almost to the top of the trail.

It's irritating that my mind is going to the worst possible thing that could have happened. There's almost no chance of her running into someone up here, which means she had to have fallen. She is strong and determined. If she didn't show at camp, it means she is too injured to move. *Please be alive.* My jaw clenches at my thoughts and I feel my eyes burning. *Stop!* I can't think like that. She's alive and she is just hurt; she has to be. I need her.

Hopefully, we meet her on the way up. Maybe it isn't as bad as I think. Maybe she just got hurt and she had to slowly make her way back down, but facing reality, I know the chances of that are slim to none. Her cell phone is sending out a signal, so it's on and working. If she was okay, she would have called.

Calling! Why didn't I think about that first? Pulling my phone out of my pocket, my finger quickly hits her number from the recent calls list.

Ring, ring, ring, ring…

I count the rings as I hear them; one, two, three, four.

Ring, ring, ring, ring…

"You have reached five-zero-nine, six-seven-four…"

"Fuck!" I end the call as the voicemail message continues.

"Were you calling her phone?"

I completely forgot Gavin was behind me. He's the last person I want following me right now but, all things considered, I may need help. There are some steep ridges along this trail, if she... I don't even want to think about it anymore. *Just get to her.*

"Yes. It went to voicemail," I tell him, mostly to stop my other thoughts.

"Don't assume it's the worst. It may not be a big deal and all you'll do is drive yourself crazy."

I shake my head. He knows nothing about her. "Trust me, with her, it is always the worst. She's a magnet for bad things." And that is the absolute truth.

"You really care about her, don't you?"

About time you figured that out, asshole! "Yes, I do!"

We run in silence for a few more minutes and the burning in my legs is becoming more noticeable. *Why did it have to be this trail?* If this was the one that goes through the valley, I would have already been there by now; but we have to be getting close.

I pull my phone out again and call Luther – he picks up on the first ring. "Has she moved?" The knot in my stomach tightens.

"No, the signal is stagnant." The bile rises in my throat and my eyes blur. "Aerick? Aerick?"

"What?" I must have spaced out for a second.

"You need to focus, son."

"I'm focused! I'll let you know when we reach the signal. We should be getting close." An audible sigh comes through the speaker before I end the call.

The coordinates from Jake pop up in a text and I plug them into my GPS application. I'm close, really close.

"We're almost there," I tell Gavin. Both of us are breathing hard, but I push my legs harder and ignore the heat now burning through my whole body. My eyes flicker back and forth between the trail and the phone. I know these trails like the back of my hand, but it's dark and caution is a must. Nature can throw things all over the trails. It will do no good if I get hurt before I reach her.

The GPS zooms in again as we close in on the signal. *Closer.* I start shining my light further ahead, searching for anything to give me a sign she is there.

I'm almost right on the signal. "Nadi!" I shout out, hoping to get a response. I listen carefully but don't hear anything. "Nadi!" *Come on baby, answer me.* I check my phone and come to a sliding stop. We're right at the signal. I'm having a hard time breathing but it has nothing to do with sprinting uphill five miles. Gavin stops next to me.

"She has to be right here somewhere." We both start moving our lights around to search for her. "Nadalynn, where are you?!" I move my flashlight in a sweeping motion, looking up and down the trail and along the ridge. My hand is shaking and the more we glance around, the more nervous I get. The trail seems perfect, nothing is disturbed. *What if someone took her?*

"Dammit, Nadalynn. Where the fuck are you?!" I yell as loud as my vocal cords will allow. *Please, please, please.*

"Nadi!" Gavin yells gazing down at the steep ridge beside the trail. She has to be here. The signal is right here. "Aerick!"

My eyes flash up to him and his light is fixed down the ridge. Before I can even comprehend it, I'm by his side and my eyes follow his light. *Holy shit!*

Not caring, my feet leap forward. They slip and slide as I make my way down the steep ridge. It's wet and muddy, leaving very little chance of traction. It takes everything in me not to fall forward and tumble down the hill myself. In a less than a minute I'm down to where she's slumped up against a tree. I stare at her chest and I let out the breath I'd been holding when I see her chest is moving steadily.

Thank you, Lord!

"Babe? Babe, can you hear me?" I shake her lightly, but she doesn't respond.

"Aerick, her neck." I didn't even realize he followed me. My eyes move up to her neck. There is a long streak of dried blood running all the way down her neck. *Shit, her head.*

I move my fingers to follow the blood. "Careful," Gavin tells me as I feel around the back of her head.

"She has a large bump on the back of her head, but I think it has stopped bleeding." I begin looking and feeling along her body. There are a few small cuts, but most of it seems superficial. "We need to get her back."

"The hill is too steep for just one of us to carry her up. We'll have to do it together." For once, I actually agree with something he's saying.

"Agreed. Grab one of her arms." I'm worried about her neck, but there is nothing we can do about that now. I hesitate for just a second. It's risky moving her without knowing the extent of her injuries, but there's not much of a choice here. She needs medical help, but it would take at least thirty minutes to get Terrie or some EMTs up here, and there is no way I'm leaving without her.

I grab one of her arms and brace her head to keep it against her shoulder where it is now; Gavin follows suit. Carefully, we start back up the hill, but it isn't easy. The rain has made just enough mud that my boots keep slipping with every step. Gavin is struggling just as much as me, as we try grabbing little bushes and small trees to get some leverage.

"Give her to me," I tell him once we make it to the top and I kneel down with her lying against me.

"She's a little pale and cold," he says, but I'm already removing my jacket to put on her. The rain has soaked her clothes.

"Grab the backpack," I say, tossing it to him, and he hands his jacket down to me as he takes the pack. "Call Luther, tell him the situation. We're going to need warm packs and blankets." I finish pulling my jacket onto her and then I lay his jacket over her lower half. Pulling her up into my arms, I stand and don't pause as I start running back to camp, holding her as tightly as possible to my chest. Gavin falls in behind me, talking to Luther, but his words are only a mumble in the background. The only thing that matters right now is getting back to camp as soon as possible.

After sprinting uphill for five miles, it only takes another mile or two before I begin slowing down. "Do you want me to carry her for a few minutes?" Gavin asks, right at my side.

"No. Just keep that light in front of us, so I can see where I'm going."

All of a sudden a groan escapes her mouth and her head moves back and forth slightly. "Baby, hey can you hear me?" I slow down just a little as I try to look down to her face. "Come on, please open up your eyes for me. You've got to open your eyes and look at me." She lets out another small whimper and then tries answering me,

"My... prin..." Her eyes flutter but don't fully open.

"That's it. Talk to me." I push my legs faster. She's talking, that is a good sign.

"arming..."

It takes me a minute to figure out what she is trying to say and when it clicks, I let out a laugh. For the first time since I figured out she was missing, I feel like things just might be okay. "What could possibly be so funny right now?" Gavin asks, sounding irritated.

I kiss her on the top of her head. "That's right, Princess. Your Prince Charming is here to save you." Gavin gawks at me like I've completely lost my mind, but the hope in my heart gives me the extra rush of energy I need.

As we break the tree line into camp, Luther and Paulo are waiting at the edge of the field. I slow down but don't stop until they step in front of me. My legs and arms feel like jello.

"Give her to me," Paulo says, but I go to move around him.

"I've got her."

"Dammit, give her to me before you collapse and hurt her worse!" he demands. "It's alright Aerick, you got her back here, now let us help."

I growl at Paulo but only because he's right. My whole body is shot and feels like it's going to collapse at any second. He carefully pulls her from my arms and darts off toward the infirmary. I start to follow but I stumble just a little, until my arm is pulled around Luther's shoulder and we jog after Paulo.

We get into the infirmary and she is already on the bed, where Terrie is taking her vitals. "Has she been out the whole time?" she asks.

"She woke up for a minute as we were on our way back," I tell her, still trying to catch my breath.

"Lucid?"

"She called me Prince Charming... what do you take that as?" She lets out a quick chuckle and I smirk at Gavin's confused expression.

"Her blood pressure and heart rate are okay, but her body temperature is too low. Aerick, start taking off her wet clothes, Luther, help him put those sweats on her. Paulo, go get the blankets out of the dryer. Keep them as warm as possible."

Luther and I start taking off her boots. "

What can I do?" Gavin asks.

"We got this." The last thing I want is for him to see her naked. He needs to leave.

"Should I call someone for her or something?" He better not be thinking what I think he's thinking.

"Who exactly would you call? Her family lives in Chicago and I would prefer not to alarm them until we know the extent of her injuries."

"What about her boyfriend?" he asks smugly. *What a dick!* Terrie and Luther both gape at me. *Time to teach this fucker a lesson.* "You know what, go ahead and call him. Terrie, give him the number."

"Aerick?" Luther says, concerned.

"No, Luther, it's fine." He doesn't appear mad and he can clearly see my irritation. Gavin pulls out his phone and Terrie gives him the number. "Five-zero-nine, six-seven-four." I watch him dial the number as she finishes giving him the number. My phone starts ringing in my back pocket and Gavin's eyes fly up to meet mine. I eye him waiting for it to click in his head.

"You? You're her boyfriend."

Yep, that's right you dumbass idiot. "Oh, you mean the big, strong, overconfident, pig-headed jerk that everyone talks about her dating. Yes, that's me! And for the record, you basically calling her a slut was a good part of her irritation today."

"You called her a slut?" Luther bellows as he spins around, clearly pissed off. *Ha!*

"No! I didn't call her a slut. Not really."

"Not really? I suggest you elaborate on that." That's right Luther, get him! I try to hold in my enjoyment.

"I assumed she was cheating on her boyfriend with Aerick. Apparently, my assumption wasn't correct."

"Can we focus on her for right now?" Terrie asks, getting quite pissy herself. Paulo walks in with the blankets.

"Gavin, Luther and Paulo, wait outside the room for a moment so we can get her dressed."

The guys move outside the door, shutting it behind them.

"Where's Jeff?" I ask Terrie, just now noticing he isn't here. That is completely unlike him. I expected him to be the first one here.

"Luther made him go back to the cabin. He was driving him nuts."

We get her pants and shirt off. There are a few bruises, and she has some scratches, but nothing looks too bad. The worst part is the large bump on her head, but Terrie insists she will be fine. After we clean her up and dress her, Terrie lets everyone back in the room.

"I think she'll be okay. I'll have to keep monitoring her. She probably has a concussion from hitting her head and she's hypothermic, but other than that, she seems to be okay. It could have been a lot worse."

Yes, it could have been much worse, but I'm still wondering how it happened at all. She loves to hike, and she has been on that trail several times; she should have known to stay away from that ridge. It was wet, but not overly muddy, so it's hard to believe she just tripped and fell over the side. Something just doesn't quite add up.

I pick up her hand. It still feels cold, but it is warmer than it was earlier. She needs to wake up soon, because I need some answers.

CHAPTER EIGHTEEN

(Monday, November 30th)

OH MY GOD.

Just kill me now. My head feels like it's being split in two. The moan that escapes my chest only spurs on the pounding that's not letting up. My hand moves to feel the source of the throbbing pain on the back of my head, but my hand is pushed back down. "Hey, hey, just relax." Not the voice I was expecting to hear.

I slowly open my eyes but the brightness coming in through the window just throws another hammer at the throbbing and I only manage to open them halfway. "What the hell happened?" I ask Luther, as quietly as my voice will allow.

He lets out a little huff and gives me a half-smile. "Well, that's something we were hoping you could answer for us." At least he's speaking softly. I close my eyes again, trying to remember what happened.

"All I remember is running up the middle of the trail and the next thing I knew, everything was spinning and then that's it. I don't remember anything else. How did I get back here?"

I study my clothes. "Who changed my clothes? How long have I been out?" It's light outside, no way it's only been an hour. My head and my whole body ache, but something tells me the stiffness I feel is from sleeping for a long time.

"One question at a time, kid. Aerick tracked your phone. He and Gavin went after you."

"Gavin?"

"Yes, he was the only one there when we figured out you were missing that I thought could keep up with Aerick." My brows draw together. "I know you're upset with Gavin right now, but trust me, he feels just as bad." *I doubt that.*

"That wasn't what I was thinking, but it's good to know. I was wondering where Aerick is." He was the one I expected to wake up to, and oddly enough I can smell him, so I know he's been here.

"He stayed the night in here with you, but he was up early, so I made him go teach his class. I knew you would be okay, and it was better than watching him burn a hole in the floor with his constant pacing. To answer your other questions, it is just after nine in the morning, and Aerick and Terrie had to change you out of your wet clothing. Your body temperature dropped, and we had to get you warmed back up. Other than that, you have a possible concussion from that bump on your head, but you should be okay."

"Easy for you to say, my head feels like it's going to explode." He turns quickly hiding his reaction and walks to the door. "Terrie, would you please get her something for the headache?"

Terrie comes in a minute later and gives me two pills along with a glass of water. "You know, I think Luther is going to have to keep me on staff just to take care of you," she jokes as she checks over my vitals and assesses the bump on my head.

"Ha, ha, ha, very funny." Though, she's not wrong by any means.

"You're actually pretty lucky. There's a few scrapes and bruises, but nothing too bad. Aerick said they found you up against a tree, which probably stopped you from falling the rest of the way down the ridge. Unfortunately for you, it was your thick head that took the brunt of the force. That bump on the back of your head is pretty nasty. Do you remember anything right before you fell?"

"No. Nothing." Actually, I'd be happy just to know how I managed to fall into the ridge to begin with. Pressing my temples, I try to get a glimpse of what happened just before falling, but there's only blackness – I'm running, then I'm falling. It's so frustrating not to be able to piece this thing together. I'm so stupid, I should have just stayed in camp or, at the very least, stuck to the trails in the valley.

"Aerick said you were talking coherently on the way back down, so that's a good sign. Hitting your head can cause the loss of memory, but I think you'll be okay. You'll need to take it easy for a few days, but you should be fine. Just let me know if you start getting dizzy, nauseous or if you develop any other symptoms." I nod my head and she walks out of the room. I know the symptoms to watch for. In addition to the school classes, when Aerick and I were back home, I took first aid and sports medicine classes. Aerick said they were a requirement to help watch after the cadets.

"You know kid, you really need to stop doing this to me." I turn my head back to face Luther. His tone is sad, and his face intensifies the dreadful feeling that has planted itself in the pit of my stomach. He's completely serious. "You really scared all of us... again. I've found myself in this room more this year than I'd like to, and more times than not, you're the one in that bed." His eyes are cast down and his words sit heavy on my shoulders.

"I swear Luther, I'm not out looking for trouble and I didn't mean for this to happen. It's never my intention to end up here," I plead, hoping he believes me.

"I know you don't mean to. It's just..." He pauses, biting on the inside of his cheek as if contemplating something, and I just keep quiet, not knowing what else to do. He comes over and sits on a chair next to the bed.

"Did Aerick ever tell you I had a son?" He focuses on me with sad eyes.

"Yes, he did, but that's all he told me. He said it wasn't his place to tell me what happened."

A slight smile tugs at his mouth. "Yeah, Aerick is good at keeping things to himself. Very few people here know about my son, Chance. This place, the reason I do this, it's for him; in his memory.

"He was a good kid, most of his life. I did my best, trying to raise him without his mom around. She passed away from breast cancer when he was only six. Thankfully he was too young to remember what she went through that last year." He pauses and his hands come up so he can rest his head in his hands as his elbows rest on his knees.

"Of course, he wasn't perfect, but he never really got into trouble until he was about fifteen. It started out so simple. He would skip school or stay out after curfew. I tried to keep him in line, but being gone working so much, there was only so much I could do. Soon, I found out that he had a new group of friends, and he began pulling away from me. Over the next few years, he got into a little trouble with the law here and there. Getting caught with small amounts of drugs and getting into fights. He somehow managed to do good in school, but his drug use kept him off the sports teams." He shakes his head, dropping his hands and fisting them together in front of him. *Why he is telling me this?*

"He ended up doing a few small stints in juvenile detention. I didn't know what to do. I tried to keep him away from his friends and get him to stop smoking pot but the more I tried, the more he pulled away from me. Two weeks after he graduated and one month after his eighteenth birthday, he was caught with a significant amount of marijuana and was charged with distribution. Because of his several juvenile convictions, the judge gave him the maximum sentence of five years in prison. He was just a young man who made a few bad decisions that ended up deciding the rest of his short life." A single tear rolls down his cheek and my own are threatening to spill over.

"When I visited him in jail, he swore to me he was done, and he was going to clean up his act. He promised me that he was going to do his time and when he got out, he would make up for the bad things he had done. It was a promise he never got to keep." More tears spill from his eyes and I can no longer hold back mine. The sight of a strong man like Luther brought to tears is just too much.

"Six months into his sentence, he got into a fight. It happened to be with the head of a local gang who was mad that he wouldn't join his click. He was trying to lay low and stay out of trouble. Unfortunately, the guy he crossed didn't take kindly to not getting his way." He pauses and his eyes screw shut.

"He tried to teach my son a lesson by having three guys beat him within an inch of his life. He spent three weeks in a coma before his body finally gave out. He never had a chance to prove that he could be good, but I know in my heart that he was good on the inside." He covers his face with his hands again and his shoulders heave as he holds in his quiet sobs.

"Luther, I'm so sorry." I put my hand on his shoulder, trying to comfort him, but I feel so helpless right now. He covers my hand with one of his own and he quickly tries to get a hold on his emotions.

"It's okay. I know he's in a better place with his momma. After it happened, it gave me a revelation of sorts. I honestly believe it would have only taken someone reaching out to him and he would still be here today. That's when I bought this place. I'm determined to help as many kids as I can. To give them the chance my son never got. Our justice system is broken, and this is my way of trying to fix it. Even if it is just for the small amount of the kids that end up there." He shakes his head and I know exactly what he's saying. Juvie doesn't help anyone, it's just a scare tactic and these days, it doesn't scare anyone.

"Every time I hear about the kids that come through here turning their lives around, it gives me the strength and happiness to continue on. Even though I wasn't able to save my son, I've been able to save so many others. I just hope one day when it's finally my time to join my son, he can forgive me for not helping him."

"Oh, Luther. How could he not? You're one of the most honest, caring, and compassionate people I've ever met. I'm certain your son is extremely proud of you."

"I can only hope. You know, I see so much of him in Aerick. From the minute Aerick got here, it was like we had an unspeakable connection. It came to light during his time here that he had a rough childhood, in a way that most people would never know. I never knew how much emotional abuse could affect a kid until I met him. Although he hides it well, it's caused so much turmoil in his mind. I was so determined to help him, and he makes me so proud every day.

"Which brings me to you. It's that determination, that fight, that stubbornness that you both share. Traits that you both shared with my Chance. I've grown so attached to Aerick, it's like he's my own son, and now I find myself becoming very attached to you. Not only because you remind me of Chance, too, but because you've made my other son so happy, and I'm grateful for that." He stops and turns toward me, gazing into my eyes as he puts his hands over my own.

"What I'm trying to say, Nadi, is that I've begun to think of you as a daughter-in-law if you will. Which makes it hurt so much worse when something like this happens to you. The last thing I want is to see someone too young go before their time. I've seen more than enough of that in my life. You need to be more careful kiddo. Can you please promise me that you'll try to be more careful?"

The tears are streaming down my face. I almost can't believe what he's just told me. I jump to the edge of the bed and throw my arms around his neck. "I promise, Luther. I'm so sorry for making you worry." He gives me a tight squeeze before trying to release me, but my grip is like steel and after a moment, he gives in, letting me hug him. This man is a saint. Everything that he's been through, and what he's chosen to dedicate his life to, is the bravest thing I can ever imagine.

"Am I interrupting something?" I glance up and see Aerick standing in the door, looking extremely worried. I let Luther go and quickly wipe the tears from my face.

"Everything is fine," Luther tells Aerick and then turns to gaze at me again. "You get some rest, okay?" I give him a nod and then give him one more quick hug, which appears to take him by surprise, because he tenses up under my hold for a moment before he relaxes and hugs me back.

"I'll give you guys some time alone. Aerick, make sure you get to your afternoon class and let our girl here get some rest." He pushes me back down onto the bed and gives me a kiss on my head. "Get well kid, and I'll be holding you to that promise." I give him another nod and he turns, leaving the room and giving Aerick a strong pat on the shoulder as he exits.

Aerick makes his way over to me and sits on the bed behind me, pulling me back to lie against his chest. "Is everything okay?" He sounds almost nervous. Something tells me Luther rarely shows his emotional side.

"He told me about Chance."

"Really?" His voice is so low I can barely hear him.

"He also told me that he cares a lot about us. I guess me getting hurt all the time has weighed heavily on him. I feel terrible. He's been through so much without my drama."

"Well that makes two of us. Babe, I was so worried about you. What the heck happened?" His voice is still soft and apparently this impacted him as well. Why is it that I seem to hurt those I love so much?

"I'm not sure. I was running and then I was rolling down the hill – that's it. It's all kind of fuzzy and I'm not sure what happened. I don't remember tripping, but it's all kind of spotty in my head. Next thing I know, I wake up here." Aerick's quiet, but he clearly has his mind on something. "So, Luther found out that Gavin knows?" Luther knew I was mad at Gavin, it's the only thing that makes sense.

"Yes, and he was pissed that Gavin said that to you. He gave him a long earful once we got you stable and situated."

Good, he deserved it. Aerick's arms tighten around me. "Babe?"

I lay my head back against his shoulder. "Huh?"

"I need you to promise me that you will be more careful." I let out a chuckle. "What could possibly be funny?" he asks; obviously he doesn't see the humor in this.

"Luther just made me promise him the same thing."

"Oh." I scoot my head to the side so I can gaze at him. His expression is puzzled and then his lip turns up slightly. "Well, maybe you will listen to him." Geez, it isn't like I plan for all this to happen to me. I roll my eyes and shake my head slightly.

"You know you scared the crap out of me again?"

I divert my eyes and pick at the fuzz on my shirt. "I know. I'm sorry, Aerick." I put my arms around his. Being wrapped up in him is like no other feeling I can describe.

It makes me feel so damn vulnerable when I'm with him. My eyes began to blur again, and it makes me angry that I can't control myself.

"Hey, why are you shaking?" *I didn't realize I was.* I shake my head, letting him know it's nothing, even though I know that's a lie.

"Dammit Nadi, you need to stop shutting me out. Please talk to me!" I turn and circle his waist with my arms, and he holds me tightly. Why can't we just be happy? Why do I have to be the unluckiest person on the planet? In the last few months, I've managed to almost kill myself, have someone almost kill me, almost be raped, and then almost kill myself again. How long is it going to be before he gets tired of worrying about me? Tears begin to fall down my cheeks, making me even more mad that I can't control my stupid emotions.

"Baby, it's okay – you're okay. I'm here for you," he says, trying to soothe me, but I'm not stupid. One day he's going to get tired of saving me. One day he's going to get tired of my endless streak of bad luck. One day, he'll realize that he deserves better and he'll leave. All I can do now is enjoy being here with him until he figures out that I'm not worth it.

CHAPTER NINETEEN

(Saturday, December 5th)

"HEY GUYS, SETTLE down. Tia isn't feeling well, so I'll be teaching classes today."

Every day brings something different. Today, my day started with a message that Tia has managed to come down with the flu, and can't get out of bed. She started feeling lousy a few days ago and tried to tough it out, but today it got the better of her. Terrie says it's worse because she's pregnant, so her immune system isn't as strong as it normally would be. Not only is Tia out of commission for the day, since Brand can't stay with her during the day, he's being grumpy as hell. It's dragging down everyone's mood today, including mine.

"Please take out your nutritional charts and complete the worksheet I placed on your desk. You have fifteen minutes to complete it." Grumbles of displeasure echo throughout the room and I note that it's Skyler and Alex at the center of them – doesn't surprise me one bit. I'll have to mark that down.

The point system we use to track cadets' daily activities is becoming more familiar to me. Lately, I've been hanging back and watching how

Tia handles the classes when different scenarios arise. Afterwards, we sit, and she explains the score she marks for everyone and how she came to that number based on the point matrix. When I was a cadet, they told us we were scored on everything, and boy – they weren't lying. Even simple things like voicing your displeasure during activities or being rude to fellow cadets during meal periods can cause you to lose points.

Skyler and Alex start talking; clearly, they are testing me. "This activity does not require you to talk, so be quiet and get it done," I tell everyone in a stern tone, hoping they get the point; I'm not taking any of their shit. Skyler rolls his eyes and keeps on talking. I raise my eyebrow and start walking toward him. "I said be quiet – and do your work!" I say little more forcefully. He laughs and whispers something to Alex before I come to stop right in front of his desk.

"And what are you going to do about it?" he sneers at me.

There's no way I'm going to let this fly. "I'm telling you right now, you *do not* want to go there with me, cadet." He's taller and bigger than me, but there's no chance I'm backing down. I'll be fine as long as he doesn't touch me, and if he's stupid enough to do that, he'll get what he deserves.

He stands up to the side of his desk but makes no move to come forward. However, he's effectively showing he's got several inches on me. "Well, I can tell you where I *would* like to go with you," he responds, glancing me up and down making his intentions clear. Both of my eyebrows shoot up at his audacity and his stupid grin gets wider. Just then, the door opens and Aerick walks in.

It only takes him a second to assess the situation, but before he can react, I speak up. "Perfect timing, Aerick!" I say, my lips to turn up slyly and Aerick immediately looks confused. "Like I said, you do not want to fuck with me." I say in a low menacing tone, before speaking up so everyone including Aerick can hear me. "Aerick, Skyler here asked me if he could go run with you for an hour, and I was just telling him I think that would be a great idea!" Aerick's eyebrow shoots up.

"I didn't say that!" Skyler quickly backtracks and he moves a step back.

"Oh, I think you did. Now get out of my classroom, and next time maybe you'll learn to keep your mouth shut." A warmth of satisfaction spreads through me at how this played out as I about-face and return to my desk.

"Let's go, Skyler. Trust me, you don't want to piss her off even more," Aerick says, barely loud enough for me to hear. I glance over my shoulder to Aerick as he's pulling Skyler out the door and he gives me a wink, his eyes shining with pride.

Once they're gone, I glance around at the five that are left and they're all staring at me. I immediately harden my face. "Anyone else got something to say?" I stare directly to Alex, who has managed to keep quiet during the whole conversation that just transpired. They all shake their heads 'no'. "Then get back to work! You have ten minutes to finish and everyone better have it done or you'll all be running."

I move to the large dry erase board at the front of the room and start writing down the chart that we're going to be discussing. I can't help but smile at myself – so none of them can see, of course. I don't even think Aerick could have handled it better. Although he did help a little, and to his credit, he did it without questioning me, which also made me happy. He's not normally one to do things without an explanation, especially when it basically sounded like I was giving him an order. *Yep, I'm definitely where I'm supposed to be.*

When Skyler finally drags himself back into the classroom, he smartly sinks into his seat and is quiet for the rest of class. The second class goes much smoother, but to my surprise Aerick never comes back in. I don't get a chance to ask him why he'd come in to begin with, and he wouldn't have interrupted if it wasn't important.

After the second class, I head back to the cabin to get some schoolwork done. Teaching the classes today made me realize that teaching is my calling and gave me even more motivation to finish my degree. This setting and work environment just make it all the more fitting. I doubt it would feel the same if I had to listen to a bunch of spoiled and disrespectful high schoolers in a normal school. At least here when they're disrespectful, I can do something about it.

It never ceases to amaze me how much kids get away with in high school. Kids have absolutely no respect for anyone these days. The world is so worried about the rights of "kids" they have let all common sense go right out the window. I have no problem with trying to protect kids, but they have taken things too far. Then they wonder why parents can't control their kids anymore.

I slam the laptop shut. My head just isn't in the right space to concentrate enough to work on anything right now. I still have about forty-five minutes before lunch starts, but before I can think of what to do, there's a knock at the door. Since Terrie is in the clinic, it doesn't require a genius to figure out who it is.

I swing the door open to the smirk I know and love. "If I ask to come in, are you going to make me run laps too?" *Smart ass!*

Letting him in, I move back to sit on my bed as his stifled laughter follows behind me. "So, are going to tell me what this morning was all about?" he asks, trying to be nonchalant.

"It was nothing, really. He was testing my boundaries and I wasn't having any of it."

I glance at him and he's staring at me with his lips pressed into a line. "Well, I hope he wasn't pushing physical boundaries." I glare at him. I cannot believe him sometimes.

"Of course he wasn't, and if he was, I'm sure I could have handled myself." Hopefully he won't watch the video feed, because while he didn't push physical boundaries, he did insinuate pushing them, but I'm not about to tell him that. Besides, I handled myself just fine, and there's no reason for him to get mad.

He stares at me for just a few more seconds before his face changes and I can instantly see what is going through his head. He begins looking me up and down as he runs his fingers down my arm. "I have to admit, seeing you so controlling is fucking hot. What I would have given to kick all those little piss ants out of the room and have my way with you." His voice is so seductively sexy my panties are instantly wet.

I gaze up to him, biting my lip. "Well, we're alone now." Without giving him time to react, I push him down on the bed and crawl over the top of him. He thinks controlling is hot – I can show him that.

His chest rumbles in silent laughter below my hands as I attach my lips to his neck. He tastes like sweat, which is all my fault, but it does nothing to dampen my mood. It's been a few days since we've had some alone time. There's only the day spent in bed after my accident while running. The injuries weren't that bad, and Terrie said there was a possible concussion, but there wasn't much they could do besides watch me and make sure I was okay. Aerick and Jeff gladly volunteered to keep an eye on me when Terrie wasn't around.

After a few days of those three hovering over me, I was pulling my hair out in frustration and told them to back off. Aerick objected but after receiving the look of death, he finally agreed that I was okay and gave me a little more space. Space that was quickly filled covering for a sick Tia, and schoolwork that has to get in by the end of the quarter.

Aerick sits up quickly, bringing me out of my thoughts, and takes over control – something I gladly give up. The control he shows when we are intimate makes my heart beat a mile a minute. He makes me feel so loved and cherished. His hands are always so warm and comforting as the move all over me.

His lips connect to mine again and he stands up quickly, causing me to encircle his waist with my legs so I don't feel like I'm going to fall, though he would never let that happen. He starts walking toward the other side of the room. "Where are we going?" I mumble in between kisses.

"I need a shower and since you volunteered me to run, I'm volunteering you to help me get clean again." I feel his smirk on my lips.

"With pleasure," I tell him before intensifying my kiss. I feel him turn on the shower before he pulls my shirt up and over my head, our kiss only breaking for a second. My legs tighten around his waist as he starts removing my bra and then his own shirt. His body is so warm and the smell of sweat lingers on his skin. It reminds me of all the workouts we did together back home, which usually were followed by mind-shattering shower sex.

Aerick grabs my hips and squeezes me hard so that I release my legs from around him, but I don't allow him to pull his lips away from mine. I pull his hair hard as he keeps his grip on me so I'm forced to slide down him slowly before my feet hit the ground. He groans loudly as the already hard bulge in his pants rubs up my descending body. We both begin to unbutton each other's pants and within a few seconds we're both pushing them to the floor. The moment I'm out of mine, Aerick grabs under my ass, picking me up again as he walks into the steamy hot shower.

The space isn't very big, but it's enough for us both to fit comfortably, and the smaller space has allowed the area to be fully engulfed by steam already. I don't know why, but it seems to just intensify everything. Aerick presses my back against the wall as he kisses down my neck and the temperature difference between his hot body and the cool tiles is exhilarating, making the sensation so much more intense. I let out a loud moan, but it's muffled when he moves his lips over mine. The familiar build deep in me stirs and I'm instantly yearning for more.

Suddenly he stops and pulls away from me, setting me back on my feet. I glance up at him with a questioning look. It's not in his nature to turn down sex, and definitely not to stop it. "I do believe you are supposed to be washing me up," he says with a devious tone.

Okay, I'm very familiar with this game he's playing. I bite my lip, grinning at him as I grab the washcloth and soap off the holder. "Fine. Turn around so I can wash you up." His lips twitch slightly as he complies with my request. I lather the soap on the washcloth and then slowly begin to wash the top of his back and shoulders with one hand as I run my other hand over his skin more lightly to tease him. He places his hands on the wall in front of him and lets his head fall forward under the streaming water. His muscles are tense under my hands, so I begin to massage his back as I'm washing it, giving his entire back my full attention. After several minutes Aerick lets out a relaxing deep breath and his muscles begin to loosen.

When I'm satisfied he's more relaxed, I move on. Putting more soap on the cloth, I begin washing his tight ass. In a moment of inspiration, I move my hands around him to grab his length firmly. His previous erection has disappeared along with the tension in his muscles but the minute my hands find him, he begins to harden again. He lets me continue for a minute before he puts his hands over mine, pushing them away.

"Come on!" I whine at him. I want him, and his hard dick is telling me the feeling is mutual.

"You're not done, Princess. Right now, it is time to take care of your prince." His playful tone is irresistible

"Fine," I say, trying to sound upset, but failing miserably. I move the cloth back to his ass and then move down his legs, making sure to go as slow as I can stand.

"Turn," I tell him when I finish the back but stay crouched down and when he turns, his hardened length is right in front of me. I attempt to ignore it as I wash the front of his legs.

Once finished, I peek at it again before standing and then gaze into his eyes. My mind really wants me to just take him into my mouth right now but he's reading my mind and shakes his head 'no'. I stand up again, pouting. He's trying hard not to show his amusement at my pouting but he's successful in keeping it in. I resume washing him, running the cloth slowly over his chest and stomach, hoping that he'll finally give in and take me, because I'm getting really impatient. Finally finished, I pull his head down so I can kiss him, but again he pulls away and turns me around, taking the cloth out of my hand.

"My turn," he whispers in my ear. I'm so ready to explode. He's torturing me, and what's worse is that he's doing it on purpose. He washes my back from top to bottom, going painfully slow, mimicking what I did, only I have nothing near his control. "Aerick..." I whine.

"What, Princess?" he says in a teasing tone. "Is going slow driving you crazy?" he questions as he runs his lips along my neck.

His arm enclose around me and he begins running his hand over my stomach and then over my breast. "Yes," I whisper, barely able to concentrate as his hands massage my chest. His lips stretch into a grin on my neck and he pulls my hair back and to the side, forcing my head into a position where his lips can connect with mine. When they finally do, my desire catapults to the sky. I reach up, pulling his face impossibly closer to mine. His finger travels down my stomach and over my folds, eliciting another moan from me. It seems to push his own sexual need, because his fingers are in me so quickly, I can't help but gasp. They begin to move quickly in and out of me as his thumb circles my bundle of nerves.

His foot spreads my feet apart as he pulls me back from the wall slightly. His fingers pull out of me and he breaks our kiss. His lips move down my neck for a moment before pushing my back down and I place my hands on the wall, knowing what is coming. He spreads my legs a little further apart as he slowly runs his hardened length against the outside of my most sensitive area.

The water is pounding against my back as he slowly inserts himself into me with incredible control. His hands tighten on my hips so that I cannot move, even though I'm dying to push back against him. Once he's fully sheathed, he lets out a satisfied hum and then begins to move in and out at a leisurely pace. "The best place in the world is buried in you," he says breathily. I love hearing those words out of his mouth. I want so bad to move my hips, but he hasn't let up his grip on me, and he's still showing his controlling side. I'm completely turned on as I try to move back against his thrusting, even though it's doing no good.

He finally begins to move faster as my pull builds slowly but intensely. He moves one hand to the center of my back and moves it lightly up and down my spine. It feels so incredible, right now I could scream, but I resist. In and out, he continues to pound into me with incredible force. His remaining hand on my hip is the only thing keeping me in place. He pushes my oncoming orgasm higher and higher, but just as I come to my tipping point, he stops again. Before I can complain, he turns me around quickly and picks me up. I wrap my legs around him and in a second, he buries himself in me, but pauses when he's fully inside me. "Open your eyes," he says softly. "I want to see you."

I open my eyes to see his lust-filled eyes staring into mine. He begins to move slowly at first and then faster and faster. At that moment I see more. I see the worry, and the sadness, but most of all, I see the love and it pushes me over the edge I'd been teetering on. The overwhelming intensity forces my eyes to close as the feeling overtakes my whole body. He continues slamming into me as my orgasm racks my body, pulling every last part out of me. As I finish coming down, his grip tightens, and I feel him empty himself into me. He stills himself and rests his head against my own.

"You are so incredible, woman," He says, shaking his head. He kisses my forehead before helping me stand up. He pins me against the wall and I'm grateful because my legs feel like they may collapse.

"You know, you're not too bad yourself," I tell him with a goofy grin. These stolen times away with him are always so satisfying. I pull him down and give him a sweet kiss, which he seems glad to return.

"Turn around."

I raise an eyebrow. "Again, so soon?" I question.

"Maybe later," he says with a smirk. "For now, I think my princess still needs her hair washed." Smiling, I oblige and he massages shampoo into my head, thoroughly washing and rinsing my hair.

We dry off and get dressed. Just as we finish, Terrie comes walking in and gives me a questioning look as her gaze roams over our freshly showered appearance. "Good thing I didn't come back earlier." I notice Aerick roll his eyes, but my cheeks heat up. He goes into the bathroom, probably to do his hair, and I sit on the bed and begin brushing mine out. "Have fun, did you?" she says, a little quieter.

"Maybe," I say, trying not to be embarrassed. It isn't as if she's never done it with Paulo or anything. I don't have anything to be embarrassed about.

Aerick comes out of the bathroom with his perfectly styled hair and comes over to give me a kiss. "See you guys at lunch," he says as he puts his serious face on, but he gives me a wink before he leaves.

"Man, I don't know if I'll ever get used to Aerick being so nice and sweet," Terrie says as soon as he walks out of the cabin. I ignore her comment and grab the hair tie off the table next to the bed and throw my hair up into a messy bun. "So, I actually came here because Luther says you need to find him before your next class. Apparently, you had an issue with a cadet this morning." I giggle.

"I guess you can say that. Skyler tried to get mouthy and made an inappropriate comment, but I shut him down quickly."

"I figured it was Skyler. I saw Aerick running him into the ground earlier. Wait, does he know?" I shake my head no. "That makes sense. If he knew, he probably would have ended up in the infirmary."

"Aerick just walked in at the end. It was my inspiration for his punishment. Running with Aerick is the worst punishment you can get."

She laughs. "You say that, but you're the one who runs with him most nights."

"Yeah, but he almost ran me to death once, remember?" I begin laughing with her.

"Yes, I don't think I'll ever forget that."

* * * *

"So, I hear you had some trouble today?" Luther says as he combs through some paperwork on his desk.

"It wasn't anything I couldn't handle." Standing straight, I try to show my confidence.

"That I saw for myself. I was keeping an eye on you earlier and you handled it perfectly. Just wanted to tell you to keep up the good work. I've told Tia to spend a few more days in bed, so you will be on your own until Tuesday."

"You got it, boss!" I say, turning for the door.

"Oh, and just one more thing." I stop and turn back, hoping it isn't anything bad. "No running on the trails by yourself tomorrow, alright?" he says, completely serious, his lips pressed into a tight line.

"Okay."

* * * *

I punch the bag in front of me, working out the little bit of frustration that has lingered in me today. Aerick helped a lot with his impromptu visit, but Skyler's attitude still bothers me a little. It doesn't help that he and Alex chose to work out tonight as well, although they're more messing around than actually working out. Paulo, who's spotting for Andi, is getting annoyed with their playing around. Most of the time when we're in here, we take things pretty seriously. This is the time of the day when we can work out all of our daily frustrations and it helps us keep it from building up.

Aerick continues to punch the bag on one side of me while Jeff is on the other. Aerick is going at the bag pretty hard. He must have seen the footage of earlier, because he's more tense than he was when he left me in my cabin earlier. If that's the case, Skyler better be careful. We don't need another incident that would end up getting back to Luther.

"Nadi, you're up," Paulo says to me.

Aerick goes to move with me but I stop him. "You seem like you could use some more time on that bag. Paulo can spot me," I tell him with a wink.

"You sure?"

"Yes, I'm sure. You need to work out whatever's bothering you." He shrugs his shoulders and starts punching again.

I offer my gloves to Andi, but she shakes her head. "I'm going to use the machine." I give her a nod as she steps aside to the leg press machine next to us. Paulo has already added some weight to each side of the bar, and I count it. "Come on, Paulo. I can do more than that." I hear the cadets snicker and Paulo glares at them, but he keeps quiet and adds five more pounds to each side. I lie down and pull the bar off the rest, beginning my reps. I've been able to build up to quite a bit of weight.

It doesn't take long for me to finish my ten reps. Andi finishes and steps over as I sit up. Paulo gives me a quick pat on the shoulder, telling me how great I did. He's always very encouraging when we work out. Not just to me, but everyone he works out with. Aside from Aerick, he's my favorite person to workout with.

The other boys at the bags seem to have had enough too, since they have pretty much stopped. Jeff goes over to grab a water out of the cooler in the corner. "Jeff, bring us some," Andi says sweetly and he nods, grabbing a few extra. Aerick walks over toward us.

"You guys up for a run tonight, too?"

"I'm exhausted," I tell him.

"Me too, I was moving boxes all day from the delivery we got," Andi says. Jeff comes over with water for me and Andi.

"Tomorrow?" I say, hoping to soften the blow. He lifts his eyes in agreement, but he doesn't appear upset.

"Punks," one of the cadets says with a laugh.

"What was that?" Jeff asks, getting into instructor mode. He sure is getting that down quickly.

"I was just saying that the guys here let these girls walk all over them like a bunch of pussy whipped little bitches," Alex says smugly. I immediately jump up and stand in front of Aerick, grabbing his and Jeff's shirts, and see that Andi has done the same with Paulo.

Skyler's lips turn up, "See, look at you." He points between the guys and me. I have to tighten my grip on both boys as they push against my hands.

"Don't you dare," I say just above a whisper, glaring at them. They both glance at me and see that I'm completely serious, but both are pushing with almost too much force. Any harder and I'm going to fall backward.

Unfortunately, Andi doesn't have that much of a hold over Paulo, and he's around her in a second and in their faces. "You want to say that again, you little piss-ants?"

"Paulo!" I say in a warning tone. While we're allowed to punish the cadets, we're not allowed to fight with them, especially out of anger.

He glances at me and then back at them. "We don't let them walk all over us. It's called respect for women, dumbass. Maybe if you tried acting like a gentleman, you could actually get some instead of trying to act like a badass, hoping you appear cool while doing it." Great, he must have seen the video too. "Guess what? Women don't want some troublemaking fool that can't even beat her in a fight."

Both the cadets seem completely insulted. "Are you trying to tell me they could kick my ass? Because if that's it, then you are seriously mistaken!" Alex says and Paulo outright laughs in their faces.

"You really think you could beat either of these women in a fight?" Paulo questions him, knowing damn well Andi and I can fight with the best of them. Skyler and Alex gawk at him like it's a stupid question. "Shit, you idiots are even more stupid than I thought. Either one of them could put you on your ass in less than thirty seconds." They both snicker. "Seriously. Nadi, you want to show them that I'm not joking?"

I feel Aerick tense under my hand. Although both him and Jeff have stopped pushing against me, I'm still holding them for good measure. I release them both and turn, but keep myself in front of Aerick. I know he doesn't want me to fight and if by some miracle I got hurt, there would be no one that could stop him from retaliating.

"You know what? It wouldn't be fair if I did it, why don't you let Andi do it this time?"

Aerick lets out a deep breath. That was definitely the right choice, although I would love the opportunity to hit Skyler square in the face. I pick up my gloves from where I dropped them and toss them to Andi. She seems excited.

Jeff removes his and throws them at Alex. "Go ahead, mouth. Going to back down to a girl? What's the matter, you afraid?" Jeff eggs him on, and that's enough to get him hooked.

"I ain't afraid of a girl, asshole."

"Well then, get in the ring."

Alex hesitates for a moment but Skyler nudges him and he gives in, walking over to the ring as we follow. Paulo whispers something to Andi before she steps into the ring. She looks super stoked. I hope we're still within the rules here. We fight in the ring sometimes, but normally instructors only fight with the cadets when they're in class.

Alex starts circling around the ring bouncing, up and down. The expression on his face is one of total contentment. He has no idea what's about to happen.

"Alright, fight!" Aerick shouts and I know he's going to enjoy this just as much as we are. Alex is easily twice Andi's size, but he doesn't know that we do this all the time. I've practiced with her several times and she is wicked quick.

He keeps bouncing around, just outside of her reach. "Come on little lady... don't be scared... I won't hurt you... much." He continues bouncing around.

"Stop playing and fight!" Aerick says, as if he's bored. Alex glances at him for a second and then bounces in and tries to hit her in the face. She quickly ducks and hits him in the side, but not too hard.

"That's one point for the little mouse," Paulo says with a toothy grin, and it clearly pisses off Alex. He recovers quickly and starts bouncing again, but now all joking has left his face and has been replaced by determination.

Circling her a few more times, he moves in and takes a hard swing and my breath hitches, but Andi moves to the side and puts all her weight into her swing, which connects perfectly with his jaw. He immediately goes down. I let out my breath. While he isn't knocked out, he's noticeably dazed. Andi moves back to the other side of the ring where we're standing.

When he gets his bearings back, he jumps up and begins to charge her, but Aerick is over the ropes and between them in a second. He grabs Alex by his shirt, effectively stopping him. "If I were you, I would stop before you really embarrass yourself." Alex stops struggling but Aerick doesn't release him, just glances over to Skyler. "And how about you? You want to go a quick round with Nadi? Because if she can put me and Paulo on our asses, I'm sure she would have no problem with you. Especially after you pissed her off in class." Skyler quickly shakes his head.

"Well then, I recommend you two learn how to show the women around here a little respect, or next time, I'll make you fight them in the presence of everyone else so they can see how pathetic you both are. Now get your asses back to the dorms!" He shoves Alex back; Alex stumbles but regains his balance, then takes off with Skyler out of the gym.

"Good job, little mouse," Paulo says, giving Andi a pat on the shoulder and I give her a hug.

"Great job, girl!" I tell her.

"Thanks. Paulo, don't call me that," she says, pushing at him.

"Nice right hook," Aerick tells her as Jeff hugs her and gives her a pat on the back. "I think this is cause for celebration. There's a freshly baked cake sitting in the kitchen."

"Sounds good to me," Paulo says, and we all laugh as we head to the mess hall.

CHAPTER TWENTY

(Sunday, December 6th)

"WOOHOO!"

All the guys hoot and holler as Baldwin catches a pass for a Seahawks touchdown. So far, Seattle has dominated this game as the field goal is good, pushing the score to twenty-one to zero against the Minnesota Vikings. Jake was able to hook up Aerick's tablet to the projector and we're now watching the game on the wall of the instructor's dorm. Since we really haven't been able to have many poker nights, it's kind of nice to just hang out with everyone.

Aerick is staring down at my tablet, with one earbud in, pretending to be working instead of watching the game, but I see the smile pulling at the corner of his mouth. He already told me he was a Seahawks fan. I mean, come on, we're streaming it on *his* tablet. He wants to be watching this just as much as the other guys, but he wants to pretend he's being responsible since the cadets are right in the other room. It's been raining pretty hard today, so no one is outside. A few cadets were in the gym earlier, but Aerick has informed me that everyone is back in the dorms.

Poor Andi and Terrie, though. They're the only ones that can't be here right now, because Andi is cooking, and Terrie has to stay in the infirmary on Sundays. No one is going to be happy when we have to turn off the game and go to lunch. The first half ends, and everyone starts talking all at once.

"Hey Nadi, think fast!" Jeff says loudly from the other side of the room and I glance up just in time to see a football flying right at my chest. Somehow, Aerick manages to reach his arm in front of me and catch the ball with one hand, pulling it back into his chest.

"Jeff, what the hell? If that had hit me in the chest, I would have kicked your ass."

Jeff teases. "You could try!"

"Boy, you know I'd have no problem laying your ass out."

"And if you didn't, I sure would," Aerick says quietly beside me as he sends death glares at Jeff.

"The only reason you'd win is because I'd never hit you. So, let's just say you would have an unfair advantage."

I roll my eyes; he's probably right. Jeff is one of those quiet guys that you have to be careful of. He could probably keep up with the best of them.

Aerick puts the ball down behind us on the bed, staring intently at the tablet again. Jeff is probably lucky because if that ball did hit me, I could just imagine Aerick retaliating.

Trent laughs and tackles Jeff back onto the bed, giving him a nuggie.

"Trent, you ass, get off me."

"Don't worry, Nadi, I'll take care of your light work," Trent howls over Jeff's shouts to get up. We all start laughing at them, but I stop immediately as I feel Aerick tense beside me.

"Fuck... Paulo!" Aerick says loudly, jumping up off his bed and heading quickly for the other dorms before I can even look at him. I scramble to my feet, following after him, as does Jeff, who pushes Trent off of him quickly, causing him to land hard on the floor. As soon as we hit the bathroom, I hear loud noises coming from one of the dorms. Aerick goes into dorm A, which houses his and Paulo's cadets. As I enter, Asa lands a punch to Alex's face and Skyler, who is behind Alex, immediately jumps at Asa.

We all quickly move into action, as Aerick is grabbing Skyler before he can reach Asa, Jeff grabs Asa. Asa is short, but still taller than me and would have probably been more ideal for me to get him, but Jeff was closer. So I grab Alex, who is much taller, by the back of his shirt before he can retaliate and pull with all my might so that he falls back onto his ass. He immediately goes to get back up, but I pull his shirt again, making him go back down, and then move in front of him. "Get up and I swear I'll make what he just did to you look like child's play," I say in a deadly serious tone. He seems to debate it internally, but decides to stay down.

"That's enough!" Aerick bellows as Skyler continues to struggle; he finally gets the point, becoming still in Aerick's grip. The room falls silent and Aerick glances around.

"Everyone to the gym now!" he shouts. Everyone is stunned, but they snap out of it when Aerick shoves Skyler toward the door. I pull Alex up and do the same, making sure to stay behind him.

"Trent, get the other cadets and tell Luther to meet us in the gym," Aerick says without turning around. Trent disappears through the bathroom doorway. I still don't know how he seems to know where everyone is without even checking. We go out in the rain, heading for the gym. The group gets larger as everyone else in the camp joins us.

By the time we file into the gym, Luther, Gavin and even Christian come through the doors. Aerick has led the group over to the boxing ring and everyone has created a sort of semi-circle around him. He steps up onto the side of the ring and faces everyone. I discreetly move to the edge of the circle, not feeling comfortable with so many people so close to me, and Luther and Gavin join me at the edge.

"What is this all about?" Luther whispers to me, but I'm at a loss and shrug my shoulders.

"Skyler, in the ring!" Aerick says. Skyler gives him a bit of a worried look but complies. Aerick watches him get into the center of the ring, and once he's there, turns back to the group.

"Brand, Trent, Paulo." All three move immediately, giving me the impression that this is another tactic that's been used before. The four of them create a square around Skyler, whose face has turned worried.

"Let's go, Skyler. You wanted to fight? Then let's fight," Aerick says, deadly serious.

"You want me to fight all four of you?" He says as his face morphs into fear.

"What's the matter? You don't like it when you're on the other side of it?" Skyler stares at him with a blank face. "We have told you. We watch everything you guys do. You want to bully and manipulate others, then I'll show you what it is like to be on the receiving side of it." All at once the four instructors begin to move in on him.

"It wasn't like that, I swear." Skyler says quickly as his eyes bulge out of his skull.

"I suggest you start speaking the truth," Paulo says as he grabs Skyler's shirt from behind, yanking him back on his ass. Trent quickly picks him up from the front of his shirt, standing him up and then pushing him into Brand, who pushes him back into the center of the circle they've formed around him.

"Come on, Skyler. You like to talk all big and bad, so show everyone how much of a badass you really are!" Aerick shouts in his face.

"I'm not stupid enough to fight all four of you!" Skyler growls back at him.

"Maybe not stupid, but you are a coward. Only a coward bullies people around." Aerick spits out.

"You mean, like you guys are doing to me right now. Let me bring a few others into this ring and I'll gladly fight you."

"You mean you're too scared to do it by yourself? You have to let others fight for you?" Aerick's words are calculated – he's doing it on purpose. Skyler glances around, debating the situation. "Let me make this easier for you," Aerick says, nodding to the other guys, and they exit the ring, leaving just Aerick and Skyler. Aerick removes his shirt to reveal his perfectly sculpted upper body and Paulo throws a pair of gloves at him, and a pair at Skyler, who barely catches them.

"The difference between you and me, Skyler, is I believe in a fair fight. I don't pit people against each other and try to jump in at my convenience. I don't gang up on people, creating an unfair advantage, and I sure as shit don't pick on those smaller than me."

I'm starting to get a little nervous and I move my gaze to Luther, but he's relaxed, with his arms crossed, watching this unfold like it was any normal day.

"Come on, I don't have all day," Aerick says, sounding aggravated.

Skyler looks him up and down, understanding that he's going to have to fight Aerick. "I'm not fighting you," he says, trying to stand up straighter, but his confidence is clearly shaken.

"Why not? Are you that much of a coward you won't fight me one on one?" Aerick huffs. His tactics are clearly working, as Skyler begins to get angry.

"I said I'm not a coward!"

"Then come on, fight me. Show everyone that you are not the pathetic little boy who is afraid of a fair fight..."

As Aerick gets the last word out, Skyler punches him across the face with bare hands, but Aerick isn't fazed – like he knew that would be his reaction. I move a step toward the ring, but Luther puts an arm out in front of me and shakes his head. I just hope Aerick keeps his emotions under control. Skyler has been pushing him from the day he got here.

"Good, now put your gloves on and let's fight. I will even let you get the first punch." But Skyler doesn't put on his gloves, he lunges toward him, hitting him in the face again and Aerick shoves him hard, causing him to fall back onto the ground. "The thing you fail to realize, Skyler, is I don't need a fair fight to win against a coward like you."

Skyler's face is one of pure hatred and anger as he jumps up and attempts to hit Aerick, but he moves to the side, shoving him slightly, and Skyler goes right by him, stumbling to the edge of the ring.

"Come on, badass. Show me what you're made of."

Skyler turns around and charges him once more. This time Aerick steps aside and sticks his foot out effectively tripping him. Skyler hits the ground hard, but again he's quickly on his feet.

"This isn't fair!"

"What's not fair, Skyler?" Aerick asks calmly.

"You're bigger, you have an unfair advantage."

Aerick lets out a chuckle. "Well, that is the first thing you need to learn today, and that goes for the rest of you," he says, looking at the rest of the cadets. "There is always going to be someone bigger and badder than you, and if you continue to bully people around, that person is going to find you." He glares back to Skyler. "But if you think this is unfair, then let's make it fairer. Nadi!"

I'm momentarily surprised but hide it and step forward toward the ring. It isn't like Aerick to put me into a situation where I could potentially get hurt, but he wouldn't do this if he didn't think I could win.

"Wait, you want me to fight *her*?"

"Yes! You wanted something fair, well, she is smaller than you and she is a girl. What is your complaint now?"

When Skyler says nothing, Aerick continues as he hands me his gloves. "Good, now put your gloves on, because you hit her with your bare fist, I'll show you how unfair this fight can be."

After a moment of hesitation, Skyler picks up the gloves that he had previously abandoned and begins to put them on.

"Do not let him hit you," Aerick whispers to me before giving me an encouraging nod.

I purse my lips. "Thanks for the advice." Slight amusement tugs at his lips and he exits the ring and goes to stand next to Luther, Gavin, and Christian, who all have amused expressions on their faces. Apparently, they all have faith in me as well. Luther gives me a nod and a reassuring wink.

"This will be a fair boxing match," Luther's voice booms from the edge of the crowd. "No pulling hair, no hits between the legs, and when I say stop, you stop!" We both nod toward Luther. "Good. First one to go down loses. Now, fight."

We turn toward each other and start circling. I bring my hands up and he mirrors me. I'm slightly curious if his hesitation a few minutes ago was because of him watching Andi's fight the other day, or if he really didn't want to fight a girl. Either way, I understand the point Aerick is trying to make, so it's important for me to win this and win it quickly. *I can do this!*

I move in to hit him, but he moves and I quickly backstep. He's a cocky little bastard and I know that's all it would take to get his confidence up. His lips turn up a little as comes at me. His fist flies for my face but I'm able to duck under it and spin away from him. He tries again and I easily dodge him, spinning away from him once again. He's starting to appear a little annoyed.

"Stop playing and fight!" Aerick shouts, and I'm pretty sure he meant that for me. He obviously doesn't feel completely comfortable with me in the ring and wants me to end it. He's right: the longer I'm in here, the more likely he is to connect a punch. He sends another punch at my side and barely misses me. His lack of ability to connect a punch seems to be irritating him just like with Aerick.

I let out a quiet chuckle to tease him. In anger he tries to punch me, but this time I lean back and, once his fist passes my face, I swing my arm around and connect my fist perfectly with his temple. He goes down onto his hands and knees.

"Enough!" Luther says, and I look to see pride on the face of every staff member, with the exception of Aerick who's already stepping back into the ring. He gives me a pat on the shoulder and then reaches down and pulls Skyler back to his feet by his arms, but not in an angry or malicious way. Skyler is a little dazed, but you can tell he's realizing that a girl just beat him. He shakes Aerick's hands off his arms, making him a little unsteady, and Aerick keeps his hands out slightly in case he falls.

Once he's sure Skyler will stay on his feet, he turns to the cadets instead of directly speaking to Skyler. "The second lesson you will learn today is that size doesn't matter. Don't assume, just because you are bigger, that you have the advantage." He nods at me and then continues.

"Fighting is not about size. It is about physical and mental skill. It doesn't matter if you are big, small, quiet or loud. It is about knowing your skill level and knowing how to outthink your opponent. The one thing I hope each of you takes away from this lesson today is that there is always someone better, someone bigger, someone stronger. Therefore, give yourself the advantage and don't put yourself in the situation at all. You can't lose a fight that never starts!

"With that being said, in this camp we fight fair. If you want to fight it out, it is to be done in this ring and it is to be a one-on-one fight. The next person to start a fight in my camp outside of this ring will be running laps until you can no longer walk. Do you all understand?" I hear a chorus of 'yes sir' come from the cadets and he turns to Skyler. "Do you understand?"

"Yes sir," he says, his eyes never leaving the floor.

"Good. Now tap gloves. What happens in the ring, stays in the ring. You don't harbor any grudges when you leave this ring. We learn lessons here, not defeat." I step forward and put my fist out. He glares at me for a minute before he hits my glove with his own.

"Good fight, Sky," I tell him, trying to be a good sport. He nods again but doesn't say anything.

"Alright, everyone back to the dorms. Lunch is in fifteen minutes," Luther shouts over the chatter that has started up and everyone disperses. Aerick gives me another pat on the shoulder and goes over to Luther.

I glance over to Skyler and he's still scowling at the ground, obviously upset. He let his emotions get in the way and they just ended up embarrassing him. Funny that I know exactly how he feels. I go up to him, but he doesn't acknowledge me.

"You know, you shouldn't let your emotions control your actions," I tell him in a soft voice, trying to keep him from feeling intimidated.

He huffs but doesn't glance up. "I don't think you have much room to talk." I'm not sure how much he knows about me, but surely there are rumors going around. It isn't like Paulo and Aerick haven't hinted toward it enough times.

"You're right," I say and he finally looks at me. "You know, we aren't too different when it comes to that. But it's also something I've been working on since I was a cadet here, and I've learned a lot since then."

He gives me a scowl of disbelief. "Yeah, like what?"

"Well, for starters, I've learned to breathe through my emotions before I act on them. It would do you a lot of good to learn the same. Most of your problem was you acted out of anger instead of thinking your moves through. Just remember, Aerick may come off as an asshole, but everything he does has a reason behind it." His eyes get big like he can't believe I just said that about Aerick. "Yes, even I can admit, he's an ass sometimes." Skyler chuckles a little.

"That's better. Just think about what he said, alright? You can learn a lot if you're just willing to listen." He gives me a tight nod before he walks away. I watch him until he's out the door. I make my way over to the small group still here that is made up of Luther, Gavin, Christian, Jeff and Aerick. All of their attention is transferred to me as I reach them.

"Nice right hook," Gavin congratulates me and Jeff nudges my shoulder in apparent agreement. It feels good to see so many people have confidence in me.

"Is everything okay?" Luther asks, glancing over to where Skyler has just exited the gym.

"Yep, just wanted to make sure the lesson sunk in and give him a little something extra to think about."

Christian smiles. "Another successful convert, Luther. The trainee has become the trainer."

* * * *

"So, how have things been?" Christian asks me as I sit down with him. I shrug my shoulders. "They've been okay."

"Word is, you're avoiding me," he jokes with me. "You know, if you didn't want to do your session you just had to say so. You didn't need to throw yourself down a ravine." The tug at his lips is the only thing that tells me he isn't serious.

"Ha, ha, ha. Yes, that's exactly what I did."

He snickerss for another second before getting a little more serious. "No, in all seriousness. How are you adjusting to things here? I haven't been able to talk to you for several weeks and I'd like to know how you're doing with all of this."

"I suppose things are getting better. It was kind of difficult at first. Things have changed so many times and so much in the last year that it's kind of surreal each time I go through another change."

"That's understandable. First you come here as a cadet, then you meet the man of your dreams, then you leave everything you know behind to start a whole new life." I can't help but be warmed at the, "meeting the man of my dreams" comment.

"That doesn't even include the millions of other things that have happened to me in between."

"Well, you are adjusting well to life here. If I didn't know better, I would say that you've been here for years. You handled yourself very well earlier. Even being put into a position I could tell you weren't entirely comfortable with." I raise my eyebrow at him because I tried to not let that show.

"Don't worry, I doubt anyone else noticed. It's my job to pay attention to the small details. For instance, you removed yourself from the center of the crowd to stand on the edge, which I'm guessing was to avoid physical contact. Then, when Aerick called you out, you hesitated for the slightest moment like you were questioning the situation, but then you immediately corrected yourself, showing trust in Aerick. I have to say, that was probably the first time I've seen you act in good faith at another person's commands. That says a lot about how far you've come. You should feel good about that."

I really don't know what to say about that, so I stay quiet, staring down at my lap.

"If we could, for a minute, talk about last week."

"Okay," I say, finally glancing up at him, pleased to move on from his praising. "What about it?" I ask, not sure if I actually want to talk about this either, but if I have to talk about it with someone, it might as well be him.

"I was curious as to why you felt the need to run. Were you mad, frustrated, upset?"

"Honestly, all three."

"How so?"

Great, here we go. "Well, I was mad at Gavin for insinuating I was a slut, I was frustrated with Aerick's need to always prove I'm his, and upset with the fact that we can't be open here, which would have allowed us to avoid the situation altogether," I get out in a rush.

"Well, you do have a valid point on all three counts, but in life we have to find ways to work around things when they don't go the way we want them to. I admit, I'm also proud of you for choosing to run instead of confronting those issues while you were still upset. So, what happened on your run?"

"Again, to be honest, I don't know. One minute I was running and then I was tumbling down the hill. After that there was nothing. I don't remember slipping or tripping or anything, but it's all kind of spotty."

"What do you mean by spotty?"

"Well, it's like my memories are in sections. I really don't remember the whole run, just pieces of it. Terrie says that can happen sometimes when you hit your head hard, that it can affect your memory, especially what happened right before the incident."

"That's correct, but people have been known to gain back those memories, too."

I shrug my shoulders. "I'm not too worried about it. I'm prone to bad crap happening. More than likely my dumbass slipped and I fell. I mean, really, it's the only explanation, so I'm not too worried about it." He nods in agreement, but a curious expression crosses his face.

"Something tells me that was a very loaded comment. Are you worried about something else?" *Should I tell him?* I can see he notices my internal struggle. "You know, whatever you tell me is confidential, and I'm not here to judge anyone. Just to help you understand your own situation and, if possible, improve it."

"I know." I draw in a deep breath. "It's just..." I pause and he stays quiet, giving me a minute to put my thoughts into order. "I just wonder how long before Aerick gets tired of my endless streak of bad luck," I say quietly staring down in shame. "I've had to learn to live with it, but he doesn't have to. He can walk away whenever he's had enough."

"Do you really think Aerick is going to leave you?" I look back into his eyes and release the breath I was holding.

Probably my biggest fear. "One day, yes. Yes, I do."

CHAPTER TWENTY-ONE

(Thursday, December 10th)

"YOU KNOW, I really could have driven myself," I tell Gavin as I get into the car.

I feel bad that Gavin has been sitting here waiting for me for over three hours while I took back-to-back CLEP tests. I've been studying all week for them in addition to trying to study for finals that start next week. Thankfully three of my finals are papers instead of actual tests, but that still leaves three tests that I have to study for. I'm glad the two tests I took weren't too hard, but it's been an overwhelming week.

Luther insisted that Gavin drive me to Ellensberg, since neither he or Aerick could come. Aerick had classes and Luther had a business lunch with investors in town. Gavin pulls out of the parking lot and heads for our next destination.

"It's okay, I don't mind. Besides, he didn't want you going to the lawyer's office by yourself. They're just trying to keep you safe."

"I can take care of myself." It's nice they want to watch out for me, but it often is at the expense of making me feel like an errant child. He gives me an pissed off glare and I realize how bad that came out. "I mean, they have my wellbeing at heart, but it's just all the attention irritates me," I quickly add on. At least he asked me if I wanted to drive, instead of just assuming he should. I suppose he deserves a little slack.

He shrugs his shoulders. "I didn't have anything else to do, anyway. Besides, while you were in doing your test, I decided to go to the Fred Meyers and picked up a few things I've been needing to get, so it worked out nicely." He gives me his charming smirk, making me feel a little better about having an escort on my trip today.

"I bet twenty dollars that your list included some alcohol," I say, a little smugly, since it annoys me that I'm not old enough to buy it yet. Then again, there's no real reason to be upset because Aerick can always buy it for me.

He laughs at me. "Not my idea. The guys found out I was coming and I was drafted to restock for a few of them."

"Figures." I can't say I'm not interested to know if Aerick is included in that. We decided to play poker tonight before I go into full-on study mode for the weekend.

We pull into the parking lot of the prosecuting attorney's office where I'm meeting my lawyer, Mr. Walker. I didn't want to come, but he called Luther yesterday and requested I come into the office in person to discuss the case. The jury selection is supposed to start Monday, which is also terrible timing, but the court doesn't make its schedule around me. It was my hope that Liz would just settle out of court so I wouldn't have to deal with this nightmare anymore. She continues to be a stubborn pain in the ass.

Gavin gets out of the car with me.

"You don't have to come in with me" I tell him.

"It's cold out here. I'd rather go inside where it's warmer." I roll my eyes – he can stay warm just as easily by keeping the heater in the car turned on, but Luther probably gave him orders. I decide to go easy on him, since it really isn't his fault he got stuck following me around today.

I continue walking into the building and after we get directions from the woman at the front desk, we head to the elevator. He presses the button and I anxiously bounce on my toes.

"So, was Aerick mad that he couldn't bring you today?" Gavin asks probably trying to ease the tension radiating off me.

"He was pretty pissed, but he'll get over it." Gavin teases. The door to the elevator opens and I freeze. *You have got to be kidding me!*

"Liz!" I say in distaste. She stares at me for a second in obvious shock, but quickly recovers as arrogance spreads across her face. *Stupid bitch!*

I step forward, ready to hit her in the face, but I'm stopped by Gavin, who must have picked up on the situation and firmly grasps my wrist, halting me before I can move more than a step. Liz walks out of the elevator and stops just out of my reach. "Oh, moved on from Aerick already, have you?" she asks, gawking at Gavin with lustful eyes.

I go to move at her again but Gavin tightens his grip on my wrist. "You stupid bitch! He's not my boyfriend, but you're lucky he's here or I'd kick your ass."

She huffs in disbelief. I lower my voice, trying to calm down. It won't help my case any if we get into a fight right now.

"I swear to God, Liz, you better fucking leave right now before I put *you* in the hospital."

"Oh, you mean like last time?" She tilts her head, mocking me.

"The only reason you got me last time was because you pulled a bitch move and blindsided me. Something that will never happen again!"

"Nadi, you need to calm down," Gavin whispers loudly into my ear and I'm suddenly aware that he's still holding my wrist.

"Gavin, you need to remove you hand from my wrist, now!" I hiss back as my chest begins to get heavy. I'm losing it and don't want to hurt him, but the way things are going, that just might happen.

"Yeah, Nadi. You should really listen to your boyfriend."

"You little..." I begin, but I'm cut off in an instant as Gavin moves in front of me so I can no longer see her. He keeps his hands out slightly like he's ready to catch me if I try to move around him.

"If I'm not mistaken, Nadi has a restraining order against you, and by continuing to stand here, you're violating that order. Should I inform security?" he says to her in a perfectly calm voice, reminding me a little of Luther. I don't hear her respond right away, but then she lets out a loud exaggerated sigh. A heavy clacking echoes through the hallway as she starts walking away.

"Mark my words. He'll get tired of you sooner or later," she chuckles out.

"Fuck off, bitch." I volley back. In the back of my mind, I know she's right. I let out a loud sigh of my own and Gavin turns around to face me, looking concerned.

"You okay?"

"I'm fine," I say, stepping to the side and pushing the elevator button again now that it's closed.

"So that was her, huh?" he asks after a second and the elevator dings just as the door opens.

"Yes, that was her," I answer and walk into the elevator. He follows, keeping his head down.

"She seems like a bit of a bitch."

I let out a snort. "You can say that again!"

We reach the office and I stepped up to the reception desk.

"I'm here to see Mr. Leeks and Mr. Walker."

The receptionist greets me warmly. "Your name?"

"Nadalynn."

"Yes, they're expecting you. You're a little early, but I'll let them know you're here. Please, take a seat."

I lighten my tone trying placate my foul mood. "Thank you."

Gavin follows me over to the group of chairs and we sit down. He kind of seems like he wants to ask me something but he just sits there, looking down and chewing on his lip. I wonder what's bothering him.

After a few minutes, Mr. Walker comes out and greets me. I'm not sure I like the expression on his face right now. He appears almost frustrated, and my guess can only be that Liz was leaving this office.

"Nadi, good to see you again. Thank you so much for coming down."

"It was no problem at all." Well, it was, but I'm trying to be polite.

"I wasn't expecting you for another thirty minutes."

"I finished up my previous appointment a little early so we just came right over. Although, I now wished I would have waited a few more minutes but I'm here so..." I trail off, not sure what else to say.

"I gather you ran into Liz." I nod my head slightly. "I was afraid of that and my apologies, I was hoping to keep you two apart. There wasn't any trouble, was there?"

"No, just a little talking." Lucky enough for her, Gavin kept me from doing anything stupid.

"Good. Well, let's go into Mr. Leeks' office and we can discuss this further."

I turn to Gavin. "I'll be back." I'm not sure why I told him that, but it felt weird leaving without saying something.

"I'll just be waiting here," he chuckles and picks up a magazine from the table next to him. Whatever he was thinking about has clearly passed out of his thoughts. Nodding, I follow Mr. Walker down the hall.

We stop at a large, heavy door at the end of the hall and like a gentleman, he opens it for me. Inside is a large room with a desk, a whole wall of what are probably law books, and a large, round meeting table which Mr. Walker leads me over to.

"Good afternoon, Nadi," Mr. Leeks greets me and comes over to join us at the table. "Thank you for coming in today." I nod my head. *Enough with the pleasantries already!*

Mr. Leeks is the first to speak once we're settled. "So Nadi, I have two purposes for wanting you to come in today. The first is to explain to you what's been happening the last few weeks. As I understand it, you talked to Luther in mid-November regarding the plea deal."

"Yes. We spoke about that."

"Well, we've been going back and forth with Liz and her lawyer. Like with any negotiation, we put the most harsh sentence on the table first to see if she would accept it. As you can probably imagine, she didn't, and her lawyer gave some terms of their own for us to consider. Let's just say, those terms would never be an option. So our next step was to give her and her lawyer some information about the case that we've managed to build against her and offer her another deal."

I inhale a deep breath, taking in what he's saying. "You mean what evidence you have against her?"

"That's correct. Liz's position is self-defense, so we're not trying to prove she stabbed you; that evidence is clear and established. We're trying to prove why she stabbed you."

"And do you think you have enough evidence to prove she did it on purpose?"

"Yes. That's part of the reason for trying to plea this instead of going to trial. We've managed to get enough evidence to convince almost any jury. Trials are time-consuming and expensive, something she needs to consider, too. It becomes in the best interest of both parties to settle. I don't wish for this to sound insensitive, but by pleading, she receives a lesser sentence and we save time, money, and usually the emotional trauma of the victims that trials can cause."

I suppose that makes sense, but his words only make me more curious about things. "Can I ask what evidence you have against her?"

They both exchange a glance at each other. "Are you sure you want to hear it?" Mr. Walker asks.

"Yes, I'm sure," I say confidently.

"Okay. Well, to start, we have talked in detail with Aerick regarding his previous relationship with her. The details of his interview were backed up by the interviews we did with several of his friends, who were all able to corroborate his story." Yeah, not details I care to know.

"We also have camera footage from the camp showing their interactions together on several occasions, which also backs up his story. Were you aware there are cameras in the buildings?"

"Yes, but I was told the classroom cameras are off on Sundays because of the counseling sessions, to make sure they stay confidential." He gives me a look that I just know is going to refute what I just said.

"That is partially correct." *WHAT?* "The cameras are on all the time, with the exception of when the counseling sessions are scheduled." I gape at him confused. *This matters how?* "Which means that things that go on in between sessions are actually on camera." He gives me a second and that's all it takes for me to realize what he's trying to tell me.

"So..." I say as my eyes widen in shock.

"Yes. Her meetings with Aerick, and the little get-together you guys had, it was all on the recordings." *Holy shit!*

"But Aerick said..."

"He didn't know. Those recordings are accessed only by the administrator, who is Luther. Aerick would have no idea they exist, and just so you know, Luther told us he doesn't normally check them unless there's a good reason to, but that isn't what matters. What really matters is the fact that it has backed up both of your stories."

I can't believe it. The damn camera caught us that day we snuck into the classroom! I suppose it also must have showed her watching us as well, and her leaving, pissed off. It would have also caught Aerick telling her off right before that. I'm not sure if I should be happy or pissed off about this news.

"What that proves is motive. We also were trying to prove premeditation. Something we believe we found more evidence on last week from a lead we've been following." He pauses and stares at Mr. Leeks again.

"And?" I prompt.

"We were able to obtain proof that Liz bought a knife a week before you were attacked. " *Oh no!* "While we don't have direct proof that she bought it with the intention of hurting you, with the other information, it is weighed more heavily than pure coincidence.

"If that isn't enough for premeditation, we also have our initial findings. When we interviewed Tia, she was adamant that the letter opener you were stabbed with was in the desk drawer. When the police processed the scene, they only found the tipped-over pen basket on the desk. None of the drawers were open. Since you said you were stabbed standing near the couch, she would have had to have it the whole time, since the desk is not near the couches. It also made her story that she grabbed it as you were attacking her less believable. Together, that's a pretty strong implication of premeditation."

I don't even know what to say to that, and the contents of my stomach are about two seconds from being all over this table. I really wish Aerick was here with me, or even Jeff, just someone to comfort me right now, but they're not. All I can do is work on trying to breathe and keep calm.

Mr. Leeks cuts in. "Getting back to our original conversation, Liz was here a little while ago because we offered her a final plea deal. If she accepts, she will be pleading guilty to aggravated assault and will serve the maximum sentence of ten years. She will be eligible to get out for good behavior after eight. Basically, we are agreeing to remove the deadly weapons enhancement charge which could have added an additional nine years if convicted, and pursue the maximum sentence on just the assault charge. With all the evidence against her, we think she'll accept it, despite the offer being the max sentence for the assault charge. She has until tomorrow afternoon at four to accept, or we will continue on to trial."

Hopefully she'll take the deal. It would make me ecstatic if I never have to see that conniving bitch again.

"That brings us to the second reason why we wanted you to stop by," Mr. Walker says. "If she doesn't accept this deal, we will have one week to prepare you for the trial. It's likely to bring in press, since this is such a small town and the nature of the crime is unusual, especially with your special situation at the camp. They are likely to bring up safety situations. I urge you to not speak to anyone in the media, and refer them to one of us if you are contacted. Okay?"

I nod my head. It's swimming with all the information they're laying out. It's probably a good thing I already did my test. At least I'll have a relaxing night tonight to try to deal with all the emotions running through my head.

"We don't want to go in depth with the details because we are pretty confident that she will accept this deal, but we just wanted to give you a heads up, just in case."

"I appreciate the update. Can you let me know as soon as you know tomorrow?" I ask quietly.

"Of course. That is my job."

* * * *

"You're being awfully quiet. Are you sure you're okay? What did the lawyers say?" Aerick asks me quietly so that the cadets can't hear him as we sit and eat dinner. This is the first time I've seen him since I got back. Luther brought me into the office to provide a debriefing of today, something Aerick wasn't invited to.

Our lack of alone time is probably for the best. If we end up alone, I'm likely to break down. I've been trying my best to just keep it together, at least until tonight.

"I'm fine," I tell him, but he gives me a dirty look.

"Gavin said you haven't really talked since you left the lawyers office." I glance across the table to Gavin as he shrugs his shoulders and gives me an apologetic smirk.

"So, what now? You and Gavin are BFFs? I said I'm fine," I spit at him and his eyebrows pull together.

"Funny. You don't have to be so grumpy. I'm just concerned." He scowls back down at his food, stabbing at his salad more violently than necessary.

"I don't want to talk about it right now."

"Whatever." *Ugh, why does he have to be so frustrating?* Now he's probably going to be pissy for the rest of the night. *Great!* I've lost what little appetite I had so I stand up to leave.

"Where are you going?" Jeff asks, and Aerick gives me a questioning look.

"There's somewhere I need to be. I'll see you guys later." Aerick figures it out pretty quickly and goes back to his food while Gavin and Jeff watch me in confusion as I empty my tray and leave.

Jeff should already know better. I head for the gym to work off my irritation, frustration, anger – whatever this is built up inside me. It's the only place I really want to be right now, other than in Aerick's arms, but with the way he's acting right now, I'm not sure I want that either. Inside, I put on a pair of gloves and go straight for the punching bag.

I put in my earbuds and put my music on shuffle. Breaking Benjamin comes on and I start punching away. This day has just been an emotionally draining one. Sometimes I wonder if my life will ever just be normal. A life where I don't have to worry about anything other than my job and my boyfriend. No pain, no irritation, no drama, and most of all, no fear. I'm so tired of it all. I punch the bag harder, hoping I will just wear myself out to the point that I'm numb to everything else around me. Tonight, I want to forget about everything else and have a nice relaxing night with Aerick and our friends.

He'll probably still be pissed at my attitude, though. Another thing that I've messed up, I suppose. Hopefully he'll forgive me, but it occurs to me for the hundredth time that I'm pushing him away again. I don't mean to do it; I'm just not used to having someone to lean on. All my life I've had to deal with everything mostly on my own. It's hard for me to let people in and, as much as I love Aerick, I forget sometimes that I can rely on him. *I messed up again, like always!*

I don't want to think about it anymore. I turn up my iPod to drown out my thoughts, unfortunately choosing the wrong time to do that.

"Time has had its way with me, my broken tired hands can't build a thing."

My arms slow down as the words sink into me. Why is it these songs always seem to be talking about my feelings?

"I need a heart that carries on through the pain, when the walls start collapsing again."

The words repeat again in my head. *I need him.* I need him and I pushed him away. *Why did I do that?* I'm so screw up.

Tears start to stream down my face as the realization of what I did hits me. Aerick was trying to be there for me and I walked away. *Is this how I'm going to lose him, by pushing him away?*

I stop punching and lean my forehead against the bag, holding onto the sides for support as my body goes weak with emotion. I knew this was going to come. Only now I'm here alone.

My silent tears turn into quiet sobs as I finally completely let go of everything I've been holding in. *How much can one person take?* I feel like my mind, my heart, and my soul are tearing themselves into pieces. I thought the things in my past were bad enough, but I'm not sure it compares to everything I've gone through these last six months, and my mind keeps going back to the meeting today.

She bought a knife. She meant to hurt me, hurt me badly. Maybe even to kill me, and I egged her on. I mocked her, invited her to hurt me, and that's exactly what she did. I always understood that I could have died that day, but it had never occurred to me that was what she really wanted. Someone hated me so much that they wanted me dead. *Am I really that bad a person?* My chest tightens more as another round of sobs rip through me. I'm a terrible person.

I feel strong arms fold around me tightly. The person I want, the person I need; I don't even have to see him to know it's him. He pulls out my earbuds.

"Babe, what's wrong?" The concern is weighted heavily in his words. I turn in his arms and cry into his chest. "Babe, what happened? Please talk to me. You are freaking me out a little right now."

"I'm a terrible person, Aerick."

His arms tighten around me even more. "You are not a terrible person."

"I am! I hurt everyone around me. Even the ones I love. I push them away, everyone, even you." I can barely get the words out.

"Nadi, stop. You don't push me away. You are just going through a lot right now, and I understand that. That's why I gave you some space to come in here and get it out on your own."

"But I didn't want to be alone. I wanted you and I'm so stubborn and stupid that I don't even realize what I really want until the damage is already done."

"Well, I agree you are stubborn, but you are far from stupid. You just aren't used to this yet. It's not in your nature to let others in. Of anyone, I'm the one person who can completely understand that. It isn't always easy for me to let you in. It's just what we have become so accustomed to, but we'll get better at it. We just need some time."

I inhale a long, deep breath to calm myself. He's amazing sometimes. I swear he always knows what to say. My tears slow to a trickle. "Aerick?"

"Yeah."

"I'm afraid I'm going to lose you," I whisper, trying to let him into my thoughts a little. Something I'm always afraid of doing, but he's right, we just need to get used to it, so I'm trying to put some faith in him. He lets out a small chuckle.

"Don't forget, I'm stubborn too! You aren't getting rid of me that easy and to be honest, I don't know if there is anything you could do to make me want to leave you. Really, you have nothing to be afraid of." *Not for now, anyway.* I bite my lip and resolve to do everything in my power to keep him for as long as I can.

"Stubborn, huh?" I say sarcastically, with the hopes of lightening up the mood. I hate being the weak, sobbing girlfriend.

"Definitely!" He teases loudly and I smack him lightly on the chest. "But I love you anyway," he adds.

"I love you too."

"Why don't you go get cleaned up and join me for P.T.?"

"Sounds good to me. Meet you out there," I tell him giving him a quick kiss. He pulls back, staring me in the eyes.

"You okay now?"

"Yes."

"You sure?" He still seems a little concerned.

"Yes. Thank you for being there for me, even when I push you away." I try to be sarcastic, but it doesn't feel that way in my heart.

"My pleasure. Now, I better go change my shirt since you soaked it with tears and nasty sweat," he jokes and I brighten, giving him one more quick kiss and hug.

CHAPTER TWENTY-TWO

(Saturday, December 12th)

AERICK POV

"WE'RE HERE," I shout out so everyone can hear, and they begin to gather around me as the stragglers come into the small clearing. "Cadets, this is the Fire Tree. It reminds us that there is always a force stronger than our own. Mother Nature is one of the most powerful forces on earth and sometimes she shows us just how powerful she can be. This tree caught fire and burned from the inside out when it was hit by a single bolt of lightning."

I have to admit, there is something that draws me to this tree. It stands alone in this clearing, black and charred. Ironically, cut off from the rest of the trees, as if showing it is the black sheep.

"Rest up for a few minutes and then we will start our trek back down to camp."

"You mean we walked all the way up here just to see a pathetic tree?" *This damn kid.* Skyler always has something to say.

"No, we came here to learn a lesson. Obviously, you are too dense to understand what I just said, so let me make it simple. Mother Nature is a bitch and if you piss her off, she will attack your dumbass!"

Everyone snickers at my remark. The look of shock on his face gives me pure joy. The little prick deserves it. Normally these badass type guys learn after a few weeks to stop pushing boundaries, but he is just thick-headed. Nothing we have done has deterred him and he is starting to piss me off.

I have actually been in a fairly good mood today. Yesterday, Nadi got a call from her lawyer saying Liz took the deal and that she was turning herself in on Monday. The great news was definitely in my favor. Last night Terrie gave us some time alone in the cabin and Nadi's enthusiasm made for some mind-blowing sex.

Nadi is normally distracted quite easily when it comes to anything sexual, but I have noticed she has been almost reserved lately. Like she just has too much on her mind, but last night, she was completely into it like she used to be, and it was amazing to see her like that again.

I am pulled out of my thoughts as I notice Skyler standing by himself at the edge of the group, which is unusual for him. I keep an eye on him without glancing up, not wanting him to see that I'm watching him. That look of contemplation on his face tells me he is up to something. He turns away from me and stares down a small trail that leads parallel to the ridge we are on and away from camp. I hope he isn't stupid enough to try running again. The bracelet will stop him.

I keep watching. *What the hell is he doing?* All of a sudden he darts off. I draw in a deep breath and shake my head as I stand up. Brand and I share a glance and his face reflects my thoughts. *Dumbass!*

We both glance back toward him; his tracker should take him down anytime now. The seconds continue to tick by. He is far enough now that it should have injected him by now. "Shit!" I say, as I realize he has gotten too far.

"Stay with them!" I yell to Brand, taking off after him. *Little prick.* He is fast, but I'm faster. He had to know this was a useless attempt. I push my legs harder to close the distance between us. He had a pretty good head start and the ground is cold and slippery.

"Stop now or you're going to be even more sorry!" I tell him, trying to get him to stop but instead it seems to give him a little boost, and he speeds up. I let out a growl of irritation and push myself faster. I'm in way better shape than him – he has no chance.

I feel my foot slip a little, but a few more feet and I finally catch him, grabbing the back of his shirt and stopping as quick as I can, throwing him backwards onto the ground. "You little prick. Did you really think you could outrun me?" I ask, not even out of breath.

"Fuck you, dickhead." He tries to get up and I place my boot over his chest, pushing him back down.

"Stay down!" I grab his wrist with the tracker, since he still has it on. I thought he'd figured out how to get it off. It's pretty rare for a cadet to figure out how to get the tracker off, but it does happen. One of the cadets, the one who kissed Nadi, managed to get it off last session by dislocating his thumb and pulling it off. Clearly this idiot wasn't smart enough to figure that out.

I inspect the bracelet. Maybe he isn't as much of an idiot as I thought. There is a penny wedged between his wrist and the bracelet, right under the pin hole that the needle comes out of. I have no idea where he could have gotten a coin. We make sure to keep all change or anything small and metal out of the hands of the cadets for this very reason.

"Where did you get this?" I ask as I pull the penny out.

"Kiss off!"

I roll my eyes and ask him again, but this time he doesn't answer me. He just glares at me, pissed off.

"I will ask you one more time, where the hell did you get it?" I am losing my patience with him.

"What are going to do, hit me? No, because you can't, can you?"

Well, not technically, but this ass is pushing my last nerve. "Didn't think so, prick!"

"There are things worse than my fist kid – which, by the way, I still may use." I hide a smirk that threatens at the idea that just popped in my head.

He huffs, "Yeah, like what?" At his words, I take off running.

"What the hell are you doing?" He screams behind me, but before he makes it on his feet, I hit the boundary distance and I hear him inhale a sharp breath as the needle pierces his wrist. I turn around to see his dumbfounded face.

"You crazy bastard."

He staggers toward me but only makes it a few steps before he collapses.

"Yes, yes I am!" I can't help but say out loud. I walk back to him and check his pulse. It's steady and strong.

Crap. Maybe I didn't think this through all the way. He is going to be down for at least a few minutes and pretty groggy for several more. Well, I did this, now I have to pay for it. I drag his upper body up to a sitting position and then pull him the rest of the way up. *Christ, he's heavy.*

I manage to get him up over my shoulder and I start walking back to the others. I walk quicker than normal because he really is heavy. When we get back to camp, I am going to make him pay for this crap. I'll show him crazy.

"What the did you do this time, Aerick?" Brand asks as we get close. I hear Skyler groan quietly as he starts to come around again. I dump him off my shoulder onto the ground and don't bother to be gentle about it.

"Aerick!" Brand scolds me like a little old lady.

"Lay off, Brand. The cocky bastard got what he deserved." The other cadets look at me, half in fear and half in shock. Brand kneels down to check his vitals. "He's fine, I already made sure," I tell him but he checks him over anyway, so I ignore him. More groans and movements start coming out of Skyler. When Brand is satisfied he is okay, he gets up and pulls me to the side.

I give him a pointed glare at his touch and he wisely drops his hand from my arm. "How'd he do it?" he asks me quietly. I show him the penny in my hand. "Where did he get that?!"

"I'm not sure, or I would have told you already."

"Well, did you ask?"

"Of course, I asked asshole. I'm not new at this." I try not to smirk. "When he refused to tell me, his bracelet malfunctioned and went off." Brand gives me a dirty look. "What? I can't help that these things tend to malfunction around me." It takes everything in me to keep a straight face. This isn't the first time I have pulled that little stunt.

"You know, Aerick, one of these days, you aren't going to get away with these little accidents. I'm sure I don't need to remind you what happened when your temper got the best of you with Nadi when she was a cadet."

My blood boils in less than a second and it takes everything in me not to hit him. How dare he bring that up. I get an inch from his face and try to keep my voice low, so the cadets don't hear me. "You better watch it, you little piss-ant! I'm still your superior." He debates something for a moment and then backs off. *That's what I thought!*

Skyler sits up, letting out another moan as he starts to become coherent again. I crouch down beside him and smack his cheek lightly. "Cadet, what's your name?"

He glances at me confused. "Huh?"

I smack his cheek a little harder a few times. "Hey!" I say louder. "What is your name, cadet?"

"Um, Skyler. What just happened?"

"You just found out the consequences for not answering my

questions. Hope that lesson was heard loud and clear. Now stand your ass up." I stand up and when he doesn't get up right away, I grab his shirt and stand him up. I release him but don't drop my hands until I am sure he isn't going to fall over.

"We should let him rest for a few minutes," Brand says.

He is probably right, but I really don't care. This is the last class of the day and I'm ready for it to be done. It is only precautionary that we do that anyway. "He'll be fine. Cadets, let's go, and unless you want to end up like him, I suggest you stay close." Everyone gathers in a loose group and we start walking back down the trail that leads to camp.

* * * *

"Hey, sexy!" I whisper in Nadi's ear as I come up behind her in the dinner line. Gavin is the only other one in line and I really don't care if he heard me. The tops of her ears turn red and I'm sure her face is a pretty shade of pink. She turns toward the wall, trying to hide it from everyone. I love being able to make her blush like that.

Once she has her color under control, she turns to me. "Good afternoon, Aerick. How was your day?" She is trying hide the affectionate smile that pulls at her gorgeous lips. She still has a harder time not showing affection in front of people that shouldn't see it.

"It was alright."

She raises an eyebrow. "Alright, huh? I heard you had some trouble with Skyler."

"How did you find out already?"

"Brand came to the classroom when you guys got back. We were working on scoring the cadets for today's classes. He told me you took Skyler to the infirmary and then you had to go tell Luther what happened."

Thankfully we are able to sit at the end of the table, away from the cadets. "What did he tell you?"

"Stop sulking. He said you took off running after him. Then you came back with him over your shoulder and he was knocked out from the tracker."

I fill my lungs and explain it all to her, not leaving out any details, other than Brand's smartass comment to me about her.

"So, did you find out how he got the penny?"

"Yes, I got him to tell me while he was in the infirmary. He found it on the trail right before we reached the tree. Who knows how long it was on the ground before he found it. It was pretty tarnished, it could have been there for years." I give her leg a squeeze under the table. "I've got to go."

She gives me a quizzical look. "You hardly ate."

"I have to run, and don't want to get sick. I'll eat again later." She gives me a tight nod and I stand. "See you at P.T," I say, and give her a wink while no one is paying attention to us. She stares down knowingly at her food trying to hide her reaction. God, she is so adorable sometimes. I give her one last glance before walking over to Skyler and grabbing him by his shirt, pulling him into a standing position.

"What gives, man?" he says and turns to face me.

"Follow me," I say sternly, hoping I don't have to deal with his smart mouth. Unfortunately, that's too much to ask.

"I haven't finished my food."

"Well, you have now. Jeff, dump his tray." He gives me a nod in agreement, and I grab Skyler's shirt again, dragging him toward the door. Once outside, I let go and he wisely follows me. We come to a stop on the track and I turn to face him.

"Now what?"

"Now, we run."

We run until he ends up puking on the side of the building. It's probably better I don't push my luck and it's getting close to time for P.T. After informing him he will be cleaning the puck after P.T, I pull him into the infirmary to let Terrie check him over.

We get inside and Terrie seems to be thinking hard about something. She glances up, first at Skyler then at me. "Can you check him out and clear him for P.T.?" She comes over, grabbing his arm, and leads him into the room to sit on the bed before she goes about checking all his vitals. "Can we make it quick? I only have a few minutes to get out there."

She turns, giving me a threatening look. Damn, it must be that time of the month or something. I hold my hands up and move a step back, showing that I don't want to start shit with her right now. I don't need Paulo bitching at me that she's being pissy. Knowing him, he will get me back by pissing off Nadi, and I definitely don't want that.

After a few minutes, she gets a bottle of water out of the mini fridge and gives it to him, telling him to drink it. "He's fine. He needs to drink that to make sure he doesn't become dehydrated, and I want to see him again after P.T." I roll my eyes at her and grab him off the bed to take him outside. We only have two minutes and it is my day to lead our workout tonight.

By the time I reach the stage, all the cadets have reached the stage along with a few of the staff, but I don't see Nadi. She probably got caught up doing something, so I get started. She will show up, she always does – well, when she isn't mad at me, anyway.

I shake my head quickly, trying to get my thoughts in order and focus on what we are doing. I am pretty tired already because of the run, but that is when I love working out the most. Feeling the burn of my muscles lets me know I am pushing myself to be better and to work harder.

As I continue with our workout, I'm sure to push Skyler harder than the others. Trent and Paulo pick up on it and join in on the harassment. Brand, however, stays back and just works everyone else. He really gets on my nerves sometimes. It's like he is blaming me for what happened today. *What did he want me to do?*

* * * *

We finish up P.T. and I'm a little surprised that Nadi didn't show up. I was going to make Skyler clean up his mess from earlier, but I'm a little worried about her.

"Skyler, go take a shower – you stink. You will be cleaning up your mess in the morning." He doesn't even look at me, just walks away toward the dorm.

I go over to Andi and Jake, who are standing near the stage talking to Paulo. Andi has been hanging out with Nadi and Terrie more and more lately. Tia is usually pretty tired at night and doesn't feel like doing much, so Andi has gravitated more toward Nadi. "Andi, have you seen Nadi?"

"She told me after we cleaned up dinner that she was going to walk around the back field, since you were running on the track." I shake my head and unsuccessfully try to hold in my elation. *Of course she is.* She's probably out there running or walking, listening to her music. I swear she gets lost when she does that. I don't know how many times I've had to pull her back to reality, even when she was a cadet here.

I give her a nod in thanks and head for the field. It is pretty dark back there now, but there are some lights on in the cabins that provide some dim light out there. Maybe I can even walk a few laps with her. It is nice to have time alone with her, even if walking is all we're doing. Maybe we can sneak to the outer edge of the woods and steal a few kisses. My lips turn up at the thought.

I round the corner of the cabins and glance around the field. It takes my eyes a minute to adjust to the dimmer lighting conditions but when they do, I scan carefully across the whole field. *Where is she?*

I turn and head for her cabin. Maybe she already finished and figured it was too late to join P.T. I knock on her door and wait. When she doesn't answer, I knock again. My heart is starting to race slightly. *Nothing*. I try the door, but it's locked. If she was here, it would be unlocked. *Shit.*

Now I'm worried. I pull out my phone and trying calling her. It goes straight to voicemail, so I go to Jeff's cabin. I am grateful that he opens immediately. "Jeff, have you seen Nadi?"

His eyebrows pull together. "Not since dinner, why?"

Gavin jumps up and comes to the door. Hate for this man is burning through me, but right now my priority is finding her. Even if it means getting help from him.

"I'm not sure. She was supposed to be running in the back field, but she isn't there or in her cabin."

"She has to be here somewhere," Jeff says.

"Can you guys check the other buildings and the cabins? I'm going to pull up her tracker if I don't find her in the gym.

"Sure!" Gavin says, and I don't wait for anything else.

I go over to the gym, but it's empty. I rub my face, unable to hide my frustration anymore, and start jogging for the office as I call Jake to meet me there. This cannot be happening again. She didn't leave the main camp. *How can she just disappear?*

Jake is already at the office with Andi when I get there. "What's up?" he asks.

"Track Nadi!"

"What, now?" He chuckles, but I no longer have any patience.

"Just do it!" I spit at him.

"Okay, okay." He starts pulling it up and the program begins searching for her. I begin pacing beside the desk as Jeff and Gavin come in. Both shake their heads.

"Aerick?" Jake says quietly. I glance down at the screen and read the error message, 'Signal Not Found'. Jake stare up to me. "The phone is off or dead."

"Check the cameras," I demand, and I sit down at my desk to start checking as well. "Andi, did you see her go back there?" My composure is starting to break as I realize this is not a fluke.

"I saw her walking between the cabins about a half hour after dinner ended."

I pull up the cameras on the cabins. They only cover part of the back field. I find the camera shot that shows her walking into the field. My heart races at the sight of her. She stops and puts in her ear buds before she jogs off out of the frame. This camera shows the furthest out, but it doesn't show the back half of the field. Pressing fast forward, I keep an eye out for her. She comes back into the frame as she jogs laps, once, twice, three times, and then nothing. My stomach drops as the time stamp keeps spinning with no more appearances.

"She did go for a run back there, but I don't see anything after three laps. I even went until you went back there," Jake says.

"Me neither." I check the other cameras on that side of the camp. I can't believe this is happening again.

"Gavin?" He glances over to me. "Can you do a quick lap around the field to make sure she isn't... over there?" I can't bring myself to say 'on the ground' out loud. He nods and sprints out the door.

"Why does bad crap always have to happen to her?" Jeff mumbles to himself.

"My thoughts exactly," I reply, although I don't think he was looking for one.

Luther walks in with Terrie and gives us all an odd expression. "Hey, everyone. What's going on?" He stares directly to me.

"We're not sure yet." I don't want him to freak out for no reason, but if Gavin comes back empty-handed, then I need to tell him. Unfortunately, my gut is telling me she's not there, or I would have checked myself.

Then it occurs to me that Luther wasn't called here. "What about you? Did you need something?" I ask. His lips press in a line.

"Actually, yes. I was trying to find Jake. I was needing to see the video from the infirmary today and to know if there were any interruption issues." We all stare to Jake at once.

"Um, the camera was static for a few minutes earlier. I went to check, and it was just a loose wire. Nothing too out of the ordinary. I put it in my daily report and reviewed the cameras around the infirmary to be sure. Why?" Only a few people know where the access points to the cameras are, but we do use them to our advantage when we want to, hence the 'not out of the ordinary' comment.

I'm surprised when Terrie speaks up. "I'm missing several doses of Methohexital." *What?*

"You mean the stuff we use in the trackers to knock out the cadets?" Jeff questions, realizing what she's saying.

"Yes!" the rest of us all say at once.

"Why?" Luther questions me again.

Gavin walks in out of breath. "She's not anywhere back there." he gets out after taking a few deep breaths.

"She who? What is going on, Aerick?" Luther all but yells at me.

"Nadi is missing... again!"

CHAPTER TWENTY-THREE

(Saturday, December 12th)

MY HEAD HURTS so much. I let out a groan and even that hurts. *What the hell happened?* I try to think back to the last thing I remember and after a second it comes to me.

Flashback

"Hey Nadi, Tia," Brand says as he walks in and over to Tia, giving her a passionate look. His hand finds its way to her stomach and he begins drawing small circles on her tummy. She stares up at him with such affection, I feel like I should leave, like I'm interrupting a special moment just by being here. She must sense my discomfort and breaks their eye contact.

"How was your hike?" she asks Brand, getting a little red as she glances at me.

"Very... eventful."

"What happened this time?" She doesn't even sound surprised.

"Skyler tried to escape. Aerick took off after him and I don't know what happened, but he came back with Skyler over his shoulder, passed out."

I let out a big sigh. "He hit him. What was he thinking?" I ask. *That's my Aerick.* I mentally shake my head. Always in the middle of chaos, but I expect him to show a little more restraint.

"Well, he didn't exactly hit him," Brand says as he presses his lips in a line.

I'm totally confused now. "But you said he was passed out."

"Yeah, well, he sort of made Skyler's tracker go off." *Oh.*

I glance down for a moment, trying to piece this together in my head. "So, he managed to try to escape but didn't remove his tracker. How did he do that?"

"He stuck a penny between his wrist and the tracker."

"We aren't allowed to carry change. How did he get a hold of a penny?"

He shakes his head. "Aerick's with him in the infirmary now trying to figure that out."

I let out a huff. "Do you really think that's a good idea?" I ask with a raised eyebrow.

"If anyone will be able to get him to talk, it'll be Aerick, but don't expect him to be in a good mood this evening. He had to tell Luther, too, and I'm sure he will be running him into the ground for the rest of the night." *Great!*

With one more quick look, Brand tells Tia goodbye and that he will see her at dinner. We finished up our paperwork and then I go back to my cabin. Studying every spare second that I have is getting old quickly. Lord knows I would be rather spending it with Aerick, but he's busy, and there's only one week left before winter break. One quarter down, two more to go, which means I'm that much closer to being to where I want to be.

Geez, it's like only yesterday I was wondering how I was going to get through all this, but this quarter had the heaviest workload, and now I'm one week away from finishing it. I shake the wayward thoughts out of my head and begin on the task at hand.

Dinner comes all too soon. Aerick didn't stop by, but I didn't expect him to, only hoped he would. I put my stuff away and head to the mess hall. I'm one of the last to enter, but Aerick isn't here yet. I get in line behind Gavin. Hopefully he'll at least stop in. He wasn't outside running Skyler yet so there's no telling what he's doing. My body is yelling to just be with him for a few minutes. It's as if these days, I only feel whole when he's in my sights.

"Hey, sexy." A whisper tickles my ear, and boy, the sound of his seductively low voice does all kinds of things to me. I love when he talks to me in that voice, especially when we're alone. *Hmmm.* Just the thought of him naked makes me blush and I quickly turn toward the wall so people can't see my face. Sometimes it's annoying that he can do that to me.

I breathe in a deep breath to calm myself before looking back at him. "Good afternoon Aerick. How was your day?" God, he's so freaking hot. What I wouldn't give to just be alone with him right now. I mentally smack myself and get my emotions under control.

"It was alright." He's trying to be sly, so I raise my eyebrow at him.

"Alright, huh? I heard you had some trouble with Skyler." Realization hits his face and I have to try hard to not show my emotion.

"How did you find out already?" He seems a little aggravated, like he was excited to tell me himself and now his plan is spoiled. I explain that we got a visit from Brand.

His face is definitely a picture of disappointment. "What did he say?" he asks as we sit down.

I explain what we were told and then he fills me in on the parts no one saw. He's almost proud of himself, his lips turn up slightly as he explains how he ran off and let the tracker activate. He can be so evil sometimes, but ever so resourceful. At least he didn't hit him; I sure would have wanted to.

"So, did you find out how he got the penny?" It's really the only part I'm still not sure of.

"Yes, I got him to tell me while he was in the infirmary. He found it on the trail right before we reached the tree. Who knows how long it was on the ground before he found it. It was pretty tarnished looking, it could have been there for years." Well, I guess that explains it. I still don't know how John managed to get his off, back when he escaped. I'll have to ask him some day.

I suddenly feel him squeeze my leg. "I have to go." *No!*

His plate is still mostly full. *What could be so important?* "You hardly ate."

"A lot of running and a full stomach don't go well together. I will eat again later." Of course, he's always the one who administers punishment. I give him a nod. "See you at P.T." he says, giving me that wink as a grin tugs at the corner of his mouth. *Man, that look does all kinds of things to me!* I glance down, trying to hold my emotions together, but I can't help but beam at the thought of him working out, or even better, him working me out.

"What the hell, man?" I hear Skyler ask, and my delight grows, knowing what's about to happen to the little punk. "I haven't finished my food." I silently rumble shakes my chest. *Trust me kid, you're going to regret eating at all.* Aerick tells Jeff to take care of his tray and Jeff nods at him as he drags Skyler outside.

Jeff gets up and puts the tray away before coming to sit next to me. "So, you gonna tell me what's going on?"

Andi raises an eyebrow. "Did I miss something?" she asks, and scoots closer to me to hear the gossip. At least if she hears the story, she'll gladly re-tell it to everyone, so I don't have to. I draw in a deep calming breath, pushing back the rest of the feelings Aerick stirred up, and quietly start to explain this afternoon's exciting event.

Andi's facial expressions are so animated I almost laugh at her. Jeff, on the other hand, keeps a straight face. When I finish, Jeff gazes up at me. "Damn, your man is a little psychotic. You know that, right?" A muffed giggle escapes my throat because he's sort of right, but I give him a light punch anyway – he shouldn't talk about Aerick that way.

He grabs his arm and rubs it. "Ouch!"

"Whatever, jerk. It wasn't that hard, but I can hit you harder if you want me to," I threaten and he puts his hands up in defense. His goofy behavior is a breath of fresh air. He always seems to know just how to make me laugh.

We continue going back and forth playfully until everyone is done eating. I decide to stay and help Andi supervise the cadets. I don't feel like studying right now. I've been glancing out the window and watching Aerick run Skyler. I should probably be disturbed that he enjoys it so much, but I'm not. In fact, right now I wish I was the one out there with him.

I could go out and run with them, but it wouldn't be very appropriate. He's trying to teach Skyler a lesson and it's not right for me to impede on that. He knows what he's doing.

We finish cleaning but it's done nothing to wane the energy built up inside me. I need to run, but the courtyard is a no-go, and I know that I'd never get away with running on the trails after what happened a few weeks ago. Andi turns out the main lights and we walk over to the door.

"You want to go hang out in my cabin?" she asks with pleading eyes. She's been craving some 'girl time' since Tia has been too tired to hang out lately. I hate to break her heart, but I'm just not in the mood.

"Sorry, Andi, but I really just want to go for a walk and get out some of these pre-final jitters." I give her an apologetic look, hoping she understands, even though my excuse is only half true. I really just want to be with Aerick and if I can't be there right now, I don't want to be around anyone.

"You going to go run with Aerick?"

"No, he's dealing with Skyler. I'll just go out in the back field. The lights on the building provide enough light if it gets dark.

"Okay. I'll see you later then." She plasters fake joy on her face and we walk outside, going our separate ways.

Grabbing my iPod and hoodie, I lock the cabin and head toward the field on a mission. As I'm slipping the hoodie over my head crossing between the cabins, Aerick's commands find my ears. "Pick it up!" My lips turn up and I turn around to see him pacing Skyler much closer than he needs to be. He's in his tee shirt but you can see all of his muscles flexing as he runs. *Damn, I could watch that man run for days!*

I take a calming breath and force myself to turn around and go about my own mission. I put in my earbuds once I enter the back to the field and start running. The sun is just below the horizon and the stars are starting to come, out creating a peaceful setting. I love running this time of night. My legs find a light, steady pace. There's no reason to rush, just need to kill some time and energy. I should be able to get in at least ten or so laps before P.T. starts. It'll be a good cardio warm up. My finger finds the volume up button and the loud music begins to clear my head. The only thing I focus on is counting my laps, so I'll know about when P.T. starts.

One lap down. Two laps down. Three laps down.

Almost halfway through the third lap I suddenly get a strange feeling that I'm being watched. It wouldn't surprise me if it's Aerick. I continue to run without searching for him, since I'll see him on my way back around.

Oomph. A hard knocked from behind me has me falling hard onto my stomach and then I'm pinned down as someone sits on my back. A sharp prick in my neck puts me on alert. *What the…*

My lungs go heavy with panic from the unfamiliar person touching me, and I try to turn but I'm still pinned down. The harder I struggle, the more I realize this is not someone's idea of a joke. A fuzzy feeling starts to creep over me, and my eyes go blurry. All my limbs are going numb and I register a faint laugh before the blackness overtakes me.

End Flashback

My body feels so weighted and tired, but other than my aching head, I don't feel physically hurt. I try to move my arms only find that they're tied together behind my back and attached to something. There isn't any give. I finally allow my eyes to open but it doesn't make a difference, it's dark – really dark. There's only a small amount of light coming from under a door. *Where in the world am I?*

I'm able to move my legs from under me and stretch them out. As I'm stretching, I accidentally kick something to my right; it sounds like a bucket as it echoes loudly in the space. Probably not the smartest thing in the world to do, considering my position. Not that I'm sure of anything right now. *Why am I tied up here and who would do this?* All my questions are answered in the next moment as the door opens and a light illuminates the room.

Liz!

"What the fuck?!"

"Now, now Nadi. We've talked about that anger, haven't we?"

"What are you doing, Liz?" My voice cracks a little as she lowers the lantern in her hand and I see her face. She doesn't appear so good. She looks like she hasn't slept in a week. Dark circles surround her eyes, her skin is pale, and her hair is a tangled mess. "How the hell did I get here? And where is here exactly?"

She continues to stare at me for another minute before she tilts her head to the side and answers. "Oh, I just thought it was time for us to have a little heart to heart, is all." *Is she really serious?*

"Are you high? I don't want to talk to you! Now, let me go!" I yell and start moving around to try to loosen whatever I'm tied up with.

"Nadi? Nadalynn, pay attention!" My eyes snap back up at her and she pulls something from her belt loop. All my limbs turn to ice as I focus on the large black hunting knife that she's holding in one hand, while a finger on the other lightly traces over the sharp edge of the blade. *Mother fucker!* "Now that's better. As I was saying, I thought we would have a little talk. Just us girls. You know, girl talk." *No, not really.* She must have forgotten, I'm not big on girl talk.

"As for how you got here, well that was pretty easy. Thanks to that hunk of a man Aerick, I've gotten fairly acquainted with the camp." She gets an amused expression on her face. "We used to have a lot of fun sneaking away, since Aerick doesn't like to mix business and pleasure, but I can tell you, he can give all kinds of pleasures. Take this place for example."

I glance around. We're in a small shack that can't be more than ten feet by ten feet. There are all kinds of outdoor things like shovels, chain saws and buckets. It has to be some kind of maintenance shed. We must be close to the camp still.

"HELP! PLEASE SOMEONE!" I shout as loud as my lungs can handle.

Liz comes up to me and heat explodes from my cheek as she slaps me hard across the face. "That's enough of that!" she shouts before smoothing out her shirt and continuing in a much calmer manner. "I really hate shouting and besides, we're too far away for them to hear you. As I was saying, this place was a little getaway shack that Aerick used to meet me at. There are a few of them placed along the trails throughout the property. You know, basic maintenance stuff to keep up the trails." Disgusting. They actually came out here just to have sex in a dirty old shack? A shiver runs through me at the thought.

"I would meet Aerick here and he would have his dirty little way with me. The things that man can do are enough to keep you on a high for a week straight." She shakes her head. Well at least she got the 'dirty' part right. "You don't deserve a man like him, you know. You can't please him like I can; you can't possibly understand what a broken man like him needs to stay sane." I feel like throwing up. I don't want to listen to this. She has no idea what he needs, and he's far from broken. Ugh, my pounding head is killing me already without having to listen to this.

"Why the hell does my head hurt so bad?" I ask, not really expecting an answer, since she hasn't bothered to answer any of my other questions.

"Oh, sorry about that. You were a little heavier than I expected, and you started to wake up before I could get you back here. I only had two doses to put you under. I may have hit your head on the ground when you woke up and started struggling. I had to let you go and you may have hit your head on a rock. Not that it matters, anyway. Back to what's important."

"Important?" I give her a quizzical look. I don't see how anything she has to say is important.

"Yes. I need to know," she whines.

"Need to know what exactly?" She's starting to sound like a crazy person. Well, she is crazy, but now she's sounding loony toons.

"I need to know what yours and Aerick's relationship is like. If I'm going to get him back, I need to know what you do to make him happy." Okay, she's officially gone off the deep end.

"Liz, you'll never be with Aerick. You're going to jail. You tried to kill me. What part of that doesn't compute?" It's probably stupid to irritate her more, but the pounding in my head is keeping me from thinking clearly.

"Well, you see, that's where you're wrong But we can come back to that. How do you get him to drop his guard with you? I've never seen him do that with anyone and trust me, I've seen him with a lot of women."

You've got to be kidding me. "I don't get him to do anything. He just does it."

She shakes her head again. "Come on Nadi, you can be honest with me. You have to have some kind of trick up your sleeve. Was it that whole, 'I can't be touched but I'll let you touch me because you're special' trick?"

"Trick? That wasn't a trick. I have a screwed up past. I've never lied about my panic attacks. I have no idea why I don't react the same way to him."

"Nadi, come on. Give up the pity routine."

"Pity! I don't want anyone to pity me!" I shout at her and she moves a step forward and another blow to my cheek leaves it aching. *Crap that hurts!*

"Now, I said there's no need to shout and if you do it again..." She puts the knife up to my face and runs it lightly over my cheek. "I might just decide to get rid of you before I get the information I want, and trust me, I have no qualms about killing you right now. I've almost succeeded twice now. I will not fail the third time."

She stands up and walks out of the shack, giving me a glimpse of the sky outside. It's completely dark, other than a small amount of moonlight. I have no idea what time it is, but the moon is still low on the horizon, so it can't be too late. I couldn't have been out for very long.

I just really hope Aerick finds me soon. He'll find me, he always does. I just need to hold her off until then. Something tells me she doesn't expect me to walk out of here alive. Part of that thought scares the crap out of me, but after everything I've been through, death really doesn't scare me so much anymore. Although I'll miss Aerick like crazy, I always figured my bad luck would end me at an early age, and now that I've had a chance to experience true happiness, at least I'll die content.

She comes back into the room, shutting the door and laying a blanket on the floor in front of me. She sits cross legged on the blanket with the knife on her lap. The only way this is going to work is to keep her talking. The longer we talk, the longer Aerick has to find me. The thought of him finding me lifeless sends a chill down my spine. He can't find me like that. I'm not sure if he'd be able to handle that after the last time. I don't want him doing anything stupid. I glare into her eyes and carefully decide what to say.

"What do you mean by twice?" I ask, curious about what other time she tried to kill me; the first time is obviously when she stabbed me.

She frowns at me. "You don't remember?" she asks, tilting her head to the side again. She looks bat-shit crazy when she does that. I shake my head no. "In the woods." She pauses and I continue to stare at her, still at a loss.

"When you were running. It was a coincidence, really. I like to go out on the trails and wander around. I didn't think I'd run into anyone, especially not you. I'm quite surprised Aerick let his precious little girlfriend out of his sight after what happened to you back in Des Moines. Now, I really didn't have anything to do with that, but I didn't bother to help, either. You see, I've been watching you and Aerick for a while now. It was easier when you guys went to the condo, because you were closer and there weren't as many people paying attention. I admit it's a bit of an obsession, but I just couldn't figure out how in the world you got him to open up. It was like you guys just fell into this normal couple routine. You got him to smile, to laugh, to be so relaxed. It's a side of him I've never seen until now." She stares off toward the wall for a moment, lost in thought, but she snaps out of it quickly with a shake of her head. "And now that I've seen it, I want it." Her expression turns hard for a moment and then softens.

"Anyways, back to what I was saying. I was up walking on the trail when I heard someone running. I hid behind a tree and when I saw it was you, I just couldn't help myself. When you passed me, I shoved into you as hard as I could, and you went tumbling down the ridge. It wasn't my intention to kill you, but it sure wouldn't have broken my heart if you'd died." I let out a huff. "Sorry sweets, you just don't mean anything to me."

"Apparently."

"You were out by the time you hit the tree. I thought about going down and checking to see if you were alive, but that ridge was so steep. No point risking me falling as well, so I left. Unfortunately for me, you lived. That's twice you've managed to avoid death despite my efforts."

I knew it. I knew I didn't just fall over that ridge. This stupid bitch tried to kill me. *AGAIN!*

CHAPTER TWENTY-FOUR

(Saturday, December 12th)

AERICK POV

"THIS IS A waste of time, Luther!"

"Aerick, you need to calm down, and don't forget who you're talking to. We need to be sure this isn't her trying to have some 'private time'. We all know how she can be, especially when you two are having *issues*." I can't believe he just went there.

"We weren't fighting. In fact, I had her happy and blushing at dinner. This time it isn't *my* fault," I say, trying not to yell. Gavin and Jeff both stare at me. Okay, so I just admitted that sometimes it's my fault, but not this time. She really was fine when I walked out. This isn't one of those times where she is pissed at me and takes off.

Luther has put the camp on lockdown and ordered Trent to watch over the cadets while we search for her. We have been over this whole camp with a fine-toothed comb and she is nowhere to be found. Paulo and Brand finally get back. "She's not out at the garage, and all the vehicles are here."

"I told you. She wouldn't just leave like that, and for the record,

Aerick is right," Jeff says. "She was happy at dinner. She wasn't mad or upset. We were joking around like we had no cares in the world."

"She was fine when we left the dining hall, too," Andi finally speaks up. "Maybe a little distracted, but not mad or upset at all."

"Besides, you saw the footage. She went running just like she told Andi. Why would she just leave all of the sudden?" Jeff asks Luther, clearly getting just as infuriated as me, but Luther doesn't like to be questioned.

He pauses a moment as he visibly calms himself. "It isn't like this is the first time she has up and disappeared, and we all know it. However, now that we know she's not in the main camp, we can take the next step." *Finally!*

"And what would that be exactly? Call the police?" Gavin asks and I think we all give him the same dumbfounded look.

"Why on God's green earth would we do that?" Paulo asks. "It isn't like they would help us do anything, anyway." Gavin doesn't seem to like his condescending tone.

"She's missing and we need to find her. Smart people call the police when someone goes missing. Otherwise you're likely to become the top suspect," he retorts, glancing to Luther.

"You're both right. We'll need to call sometime soon, but she's an adult with a record. Legally, they won't even consider her missing for twenty-four hours and with her record, it's unlikely they will consider this as being seriously unless we have some type of proof of foul play. That means we need to figure out what our next logical step is." Gavin still isn't pleased with Luther's answer, but Luther ignores him and continues.

"She didn't leave by any vehicle that we know of, so she's likely close by. I didn't want to say it earlier, but there's a possibility of some sicko just hanging out in those woods. We need to check the trails. For whatever reason, she isn't here at the camp and based on the camera footage, there are only two trails back there that she could have left by."

I try to push away the thought that someone actually took her, but nothing else makes sense right now.

"So, we divide into two groups," Paulo says, picking up on what I am thinking. "Both those trails divide into two. We do two groups of four people and when the trail splits, we split into twos." I nod. Luther glances from Paulo to me.

"I agree. It's getting late, so I want you guys to be careful. Aerick: you, Paulo, Jeff and Brand cover one trail. Gavin: you, Brayden, Andi and I will cover the other. Ayla, I need you to stay to help Trent with the cadets, and you can contact the police to make a missing person's report just in case. Jake, I want you checking at those camera's again. Search everything from this afternoon from all around camp. One of them had to catch something out of the ordinary. Tia, you stay and help Jake. I don't want something happening to you out there." Brand lets out a sigh of relief, which only seems to displease Tia.

"Luther, I can help!" she tries to say, but Luther quickly cuts her off.

"Tia, this is not up for discussion, and don't you start in with that insubordination shit either. These are my orders and I expect them to be followed. Understand?" She stares down, clearly pissed off, but gives him a quick nod. "Jake, you need to call me if you find anything. I want everyone's push-to-talk on your cell phones turned on. I want to know what's going on with everyone at all times. We don't need to take any more risks than what is necessary. Keep an eye on each other and for Christ sake be careful. Don't forget we're out in the woods. There are deadly animals out during the night, they are more likely to mistake you for prey." *Damn.* Another thing I didn't even think about.

Please let her be okay.

We all nod and I'm getting really antsy to get out of here already. Everyone heads for the lockers and several of us grab the black hiking backpacks. Someone tugs at me and I turn to see Jake pulling me to the side of the room. "I checked and her phone stopped pinging a signal around six o'clock, which means if someone does have her, they have one heck of a head start." I check my watch. It is just past eight-thirty already. *Shit!*

"Her signal was last seen at the far end of the field, so my guess is that she's up that trail." I give him a grateful nod and dart out the door with everyone else hot on my heels. I shake my head in irritation. We should have been doing this the minute we realized she was gone. *God, if you're up there, please let her be okay.*

I have a really bad feeling about this. We make it out to the field, and I start to push myself faster. "Aerick, wait for your group," Luther shouts.

"Then tell them to keep up." I say with a growl, but let up the slightest bit.

I hear Luther speak up again. "Gavin, stick with Brayden. He knows these woods like the back of his hand. Andi, you stay close to me at all times."

"Jeff, you stick with me." I don't know why I said it, but right now it just feels right that he is with me. Besides, Paulo and Brand will be okay on their own. "Luther, you guys take this first trail. We'll take the other one."

The back trail leads along the river and is pretty flat. If someone took her by force, there is no way she went easy. Since I never heard her yell or scream, it had to be someone strong enough to restrain her quickly. It's still hard to believe that anyone could do it without her making a sound, considering the immense strength she has shown in the past when she is attacked or restrained. That leaves only one other option, which is that they knocked her out. I shudder at the thought and my heart begins to race. But if someone did have to drag her or carry her, it would be easier on this back trail.

"Luther, you copy?" Ayla's voice comes over the speaker on my phone and I listen carefully.

"I copy, Ayla. What's going on?"

"I called the police. They're sending out an officer out."

"Thanks, Ayla. Let me know if you find out anything further, and make sure Trent has the cadets under control."

"Ten-four"

Great, Cle Elum and Roslyn's finest on the case. I bet we find her before they even make it to the camp. I glance back to make sure the others are all still with me. This trail splits and goes up the hill about another mile down. Something tells me I'm on the right track though. I'll be following this trail all the way to the road where it comes out about eight miles out. I just hope Jeff can stick with me the whole way. He is not in as good shape and even though we won't be going uphill, it's still a pretty good distance.

This still doesn't make sense to me. *Who would kidnap her? Why would they kidnap her?* I know she has a crazy way of attracting the wrong type of men, but it's pretty rare for anyone to be out on these trails. Most of them are camp property, and many of them aren't accessible from anywhere but the camp, unless you go off trail. This is one of the few that actually comes out on a road.

Jeff has surprisingly been keeping pace. I've been pushing a little harder, knowing Paulo and Brand are behind me. I know they can keep up, but Jeff has been on my heels since we stepped foot on the trail. We reach the split where there the other trail leads up the ridge and I signal with two fingers up the trail. Paulo and Brand silently split off, not bothering to say a word. The only sign that they are gone is the lack of pounding feet behind me.

Jeff mumbles something behind me. "What's that?" I ask.

"Nothing. I just... have a bad feeling about this. Something is off and none of it makes sense."

He's right. Like Luther said, there are people in these woods sometimes, but we never see them come to camp, let alone actually take someone. But there's no counting out Nadi's ridiculous amount of bad luck. It wouldn't surprise me if this is a first for the camp, that it would happen to her.

"I've had a bad feeling about this since the moment I watched the camera footage," I reply.

I also can't help but think Liz is behind this. Not that I'm willing to admit that to anyone right now, because if it is Liz, that would mean Nadi is in danger and it would be my fault, again. It would mean she might get hurt because of my fucked-up past, but it's the one thing that seems plausible right now. It's difficult to believe that anyone in camp would want to take the Methohexital, except maybe Gavin. I don't know him well enough to rule it out, but Liz knows the camp well. She would know how to disable the camera, and she would know how to sneak in and out of the camp. She has a doctoral degree and would be able to access information about the drug to know how much to use.

The one thing that doesn't make sense is why she would even bother. It makes sense to knock Nadi out because Liz wouldn't win in a fair fight, but then what? The only reason she would even do that is to hurt her or... *NO* ... I refuse to even think it, but she has motive. Without Nadi around, there would be no one to testify against her at trial. Nadi told me that her lawyer said the evidence was circumstantial but with the overwhelming amount of it, she would likely lose if it went to trial. If that was her intention, then why wouldn't she do it after knocking her out? Why would she move her anywhere? It doesn't benefit her in any way to stick around. That only would increase her chance of getting caught and going to jail for even longer.

If she did take her, she would have had to have had help. There is no way Liz could carry or even drag Nadi this many miles by herself, unless...

I shine the light on the ground and search carefully. The trail is too small for a car, but someone could drive an ATV on these trails. We have a few back at the camp in the garage in case of an emergency, but I don't see any tracks. I don't even see any drag marks, either. *Damn! Why can't I think this through?*

Maybe I'm just overthinking this whole thing. Maybe it is just a random thing, maybe Liz has nothing to do with this. I glance at Jeff, who is still pacing me, but he's clearly getting tired. We have been running for more than thirty minutes, so we must be getting close.

I don't even know what we are going to do if we don't find her. The radio has been silent, so no one has found anything. Not that I expect them to. I don't think she is down the other trails. Not to mention, it's eerily dark out here. The moon has disappeared into the clouds and I can barely see a foot or two into the tree line without shining the light at something specific. She could just be lying somewhere, and we could run right past her.

I have to stop thinking like that. She will be okay; she's a fighter – something that has become extremely clear in the short amount of time I've known her. I can't help but think about the first time I saw her hit that cadet in the face for touching her. The expression on her face was pure focus and, without ever having any training, she laid an almost perfect punch right to his face. I realize now that watching her those first few weeks was just pure fascination with a girl that was obviously different than any other I'd ever seen. As hard as she tried to fit in and seem normal, she was anything but.

We come to a sliding halt as we reach a dirt road. *Shit!* I didn't know what I expected to find, but I can't help the overwhelming amount of disappointment that is spreading through my body right now.

"Shit. What now?" Jeff asks.

"I don't know. Everything in me was telling me I would find her down this trail." She can't be gone. I try to shake the thought out of my head. "Maybe we missed her."

"Missed her where?"

"If I knew that, we wouldn't be standing here right now!" I snap at him, and he stares down. "She has to be here. I didn't see any sign of someone coming down this way." I run my flashlight back and forth over the dirt road. It has rained a little over the last few days, making the dirt soft, and there is no sign of fresh tire tracks. This back road is hardly ever used. Jeff follows my light and seems to understand my thoughts. "We should call out for her as we head back."

"What if whoever took her hears us? They might hurt her."

I inhale a staggered breath as I grab at my hair with both of my hands. "FUUUUUCCCK!" I scream as loud as my voice will allow, not able to hold it in anymore. "I don't have a clue Jeff. Do you have a better idea? If you do, speak up already, because I just don't fucking know!" I shout at him as I turn away, trying to hide my face as I begin to lose it. I'm out of ideas, and don't know what the hell to do. *Fuck, fuck, fuck!*

His hand presses down on my shoulder. "Dude, it's okay. We'll find her." I draw in some much need air, trying to reign in my rage. "If anyone can survive a bad situation, it's her." I nod my head in agreement because about that, he is absolutely right.

He gives me a hard slap on the shoulder. "Come on." I turn back, feeling the weight of his hand disappear from my shoulder, and see Jeff starting to jog back down the trail, yelling out to Nadi. I swallow the lump that is starting to form in my throat and follow him, yelling out for her as well.

I call Luther and let him know we didn't find anything and are on our way back. Gavin and Paulo call in that they are also on their way back. Luther must have taken the steeper trail, because he is the last to report that he is on his way back.

Jeff and I trade off calling out for her every fifteen seconds or so. I listen hard, hoping to hear her sweet voice, but there's nothing besides the quiet sounds of the forest creatures. I strain to see as deep into the forest as I can, hoping to catch a glimpse of something out of the ordinary, but all I can see are trees and plants.

We have slowed considerably due to Jeff. He's heavy with exhaustion but hasn't complained once. He just continues to push as hard as he can. However, his voice gives it away as he tries to yell for Nadi again and it comes out sounding like a sheep's broken whine. Something he and Nadi have in common. It would seem that him and Nadi actually have quite a bit in common.

My legs slow down until I'm barely jogging. I grab Jeff's shirt to slow him as he begins to pass me, and he gets the point. There was a tremendous need to get to the end of the trail as quick as possible, which we did. There really isn't such a need to hurry as fast back to the camp.

Jeff puts his hands on the back of his head as he tries to catch his breath, but we still continue to walk at a fast pace. After a few more feet I am stopped suddenly by a familiar, disgusting sound. I turn to see Jeff puking into a bush. He pushed himself too hard.

I pull the backpack off and pull out a bottle of water. I tap his shoulder with the bottle, and he grabs it before he starts another round of emptying his stomach contents. Yep, this is totally something she would have done. Not caring about herself, always putting everyone else first.

Giving him another minute to finish, I yell out for Nadi again, trying to drown out the nauseating sound of Jeff getting sick. He finally stands up and inhales a drink of water. "Don't drink too much too quickly."

"Sorry about that."

"It's fine. Ready?"

"Yeah."

I give him one last look before turning to continue, but I freeze in place. I put my hand out at once, stopping Jeff. "Did you hear that?" There was something, an odd noise, but I'm not sure where it came from. *Shit. Why wasn't I paying better attention?*

"I didn't hear anything. Are you sure you're okay?"

I glare at him. "I fucking heard something." We both look around.

"Aerick I don't hear..."

"That, I heard it again." I cut him off as I hear something again but this time, I distinctly hear it behind us. I spin around and Jeff mimics my actions. I swear that sounded like... I don't know, but it sure didn't sound like a damn animal. He must not have heard it, because he gives me a confused glare and shakes his head 'no'. I put my finger to my lips to tell him to stay quiet so we can hear it again. We stay silent for several minutes, dead still, but there is nothing. Maybe I'm hearing things.

Then I hear the distinct thud of foot falls. At least I know I'm not completely crazy, because Jeff glances at me with knowing eyes. It sounds like two sets. I have no idea how close we are to camp, but we have to be close to the trail split off. Walking several more feet, I shine my light to the left side. It only takes a few more moments for Paulo and Brand to come out onto the trail about thirty feet in front of us.

"Did you guys find anything?" The words gush out of my mouth before they even realize I'm behind them.

They both spin around quickly. "Aerick?" Brand questions.

"Did you find anything?" I demand again, a little more impatient.

"No, nothing," Paulo says, sounding defeated. Maybe, just maybe.

"Did you guys hear anything a minute ago?" They glance at each other before they look between me and Jeff, who has come to stand next to me.

"No, why? Did you guys?" Paulo says, with just a glimmer of hope in his eyes. *Shit.*

"I didn't, but Aerick thinks he did."

I pin him with my stare. "I heard something. I just don't know what it was."

"Are you sure it wasn't an animal?" Brand questions and it takes everything in me not to hit him. It wasn't an animal, at least I don't think so. I shine my light around once more, searching carefully into the tree line, but there's nothing. The trees and bushes are pretty dense down here in the valley.

My thoughts are interrupted by Ayla's voice. "Luther, you got a copy?"

"I'm here. Everything okay?" I freeze once more, waiting to get an update.

"The police have arrived. They would like to talk to everyone." *Great!*

"We are on our way back. Gavin, Aerick, Brand, give me your status."

Gavin answers before I can. "We just made it back. We will be in the office in a few minutes."

"Good. Aerick?"

If we are at the trail split, we are pretty close. "We're almost back. Brand's with us. Give us a few minutes." *Ugh.* I hate dealing with the police. I glance back down the trail one more time behind us.

Letting out a sigh, I turn back toward camp and start jogging. "Let's go!" I order and hear their boots fall in behind me, but I can't get that noise out of my head. I did hear it. Replaying it in my head though, I think it may have been just an animal. My emotions really are getting the best of me. They are making me hear things that are simply not there.

"Luther, you got a copy?" Gavin's voice crackles over the radio.

"Gavin, what is it?"

"Hurry back. We, uh, found something here." *No...*

CHAPTER TWENTY-FIVE

(Saturday, December 12th)

I HEARD HIM. It was him. Opening my eyes, there's only black again. I think she left, but I'm not sure. My head is pounding, that stupid bitch. We heard Aerick calling my name. I tried to yell back, but she hit me in the head with the handle of the knife. I can't even feel to see if my head is bleeding because I can barely move my hands still.

Aerick.

He was close. His voice sounded far away, but he was close enough for me to hear him. We must still be near the camp. I wasn't sure how far, or even where Liz brought me. I screamed earlier but she acted like she wasn't scared that someone would hear me. I figured we were pretty far away from camp. I had listened to her babble on for at least an hour before I heard Aerick calling me.

For a few seconds, I thought I was just hearing things, until a look of shock spread across her face. I barely got out a sound before her hand was on my mouth. I tried so hard, but I couldn't get my mouth uncovered. With my hands tied behind my back, it doesn't leave too many options. After struggling for a minute, I was able to move around enough to bite her hand and try to yell again, but then she hit me with the knife.

I wonder how long I've been out, or if she's even still around. It's probably stupid to try yelling for Aerick again, but it's on the tip of my tongue. Liz was pretty pissed when she hit me. I'm sure it had something to do with the bloody hand. I can still taste the damn blood in my mouth. *God, I hope she doesn't have any diseases.*

She was getting impatient before we even heard Aerick. I just don't know how many ways to tell her that I don't do anything special to keep Aerick's attention. I don't have to do anything, he just genuinely likes to be with me. I don't pretend to understand why. In fact, I keep waiting for the day he loses interest in me, because there really isn't anything special about me. I'm just, me.

Somehow, her questions and comments just happen to reflect my thoughts. She made it clear she doesn't see anything special about me, but she kept insisting there had to be something that I was hiding away from everyone. She's just a psycho, plain and simple.

I have to do something: I need to get out of here. "AERICK! AERICK!"

I hear a noise outside the door. My heart starts beating so loud, I wonder if whoever it is can hear it. *Please be you, Aerick. Please!* I'm frozen, not sure of what to expect. I see a small light from under the door. I want to call out but I'm afraid it isn't him. My gut says that it's her; if it was Aerick he would have come in tearing the door off its hinges to rescue me the minute he heard my voice.

Continuing to stare at the light under the door makes me more and more nervous. A minute later, it finally opens, and my stomach falls to the ground. My fear has come true. Liz comes walking in and she doesn't appear happy.

"Yell all you want, sweetie-pie, because they're gone and there's no one left to hear you. They all went back to camp. I'll admit, I'm surprised they didn't try harder. Seriously, it was hours before they even came searching for you, and then it's just a quick check of the trails and they head back to camp. Maybe you don't mean as much to him as I thought." Turning around, she walks back out the door, leaving it open, but she's disappeared out of sight.

Right now, I want nothing more than to hit this bitch in the face. Her stance and the expression on her face shows our time together is drawing to a close. I can only wonder what she plans to do with me. She has no reason to keep me alive. My chances of her just letting me go are pretty slim.

I pull at the ropes that bind my hands together. It seems like I'm going to have to rescue myself this time. The ropes are tight, and they bite into my hands as I try to get out of them. They're not budging.

Then I hear a voice. *Is she talking to herself?* I strain to listen closer. There are two voices. *What? She's not alone.* I try even harder to listen. The other voice sounds familiar, a male's voice, but I just can't place it.

"Liz, we need to end this. How long do you really think it's going to be before they figure out where we are?"

"Well if you were doing your part, they wouldn't have been so close. You were supposed to warn me when they were coming this way and she hasn't given me the information I need yet."

"They run too fast. There was no way for me to get here before they did without being caught. Besides, this is far enough off the trail that they would never see it in the dark. It's meant to blend in. What information are you trying to get from her exactly, and why don't you want to tell me? Is it about him? Because you told me you were over him."

"It's not about him, baby, I promise. You're the only man in my life." She purrs at the guy and it makes me sick. "I just need some answers, but right now I need to go check out the camp for a minute. I have to make sure everyone is still there and not out looking for her. Stay here, keep a lookout, and don't go in there!"

"Of course. Why would I want to go in there?"

"Just stay out here. I don't need her filling your head with lies, too." I can hear her heavy feet as she stomp off. It's quiet for a moment and I'm totally confused. Why would anyone help her? *What did I do to deserve this?* Maybe he'll help me. Probably not; I'm sure that manipulative bitch has him wrapped around her little finger.

After several minutes, footsteps start heading for me. *Shit!* A figure appears in the doorway and my mouth drops open – words fail me.

'Who is this fine little thing you got here?'

His words from the first time I met him float through my head. I can't believe he's here. That he's the one here helping her. *Sean!*

"Hmmm. The big, bad boyfriend isn't here to protect his little princess." He moves closer and squats down in front of me. The look in his eyes is making all my hairs stand on end.

"Didn't Liz tell you to stay out of here?"

"You dumb little bitch. You were listening, weren't you?" His voice is low and almost curious. He runs his fingers down my cheek before roughly grabbing my chin. "You know he doesn't love you, right? Aerick has been with almost every girl in this town, and most who have visited. Every time a new girl comes around, Aerick has to put his grubby little hands on her. Kind of selfish, don't you think?" I stay quiet, trying to ignore his little digs at Aerick.

"Even you. Of course, he would snatch up a pretty little thing like you and keep you for himself. Although, I'm surprised he's kept you around for so long. Other than Liz, I've never seen him stay interested in someone for any length of time. You must be one Grade A piece of ass."

I try to ignore the heaviness that's beginning to pull at my chest as his eyes roam up and down my body with a lustful look in his eyes.

"Shouldn't you be waiting outside for Liz?" I'm betrayed as my voice comes out much weaker than I intended. I've seen that look before and nothing good could ever come of it.

"Oh, don't you worry about me. I can handle Liz, but you? I've had an eye for you since the first day I met you, but no, Aerick had to get his dirty paws on you first." He finally releases my chin and runs his hand down my arm. I try to jerk away but he ignores me and continues. Whatever I'm tied to isn't allowing me to move very far.

"And you sure fooled everyone, didn't you?" My eyes fly up to his at his accusing tone. I have no idea what he's talking about. "Oh, don't give me those innocent eyes. Word has gotten out about you. You acted so sweet and innocent, but you're not, are you?" His hand grazes my stomach and I'm beginning to have a hard time breathing. *This shit is not happening again!*

"I... I don't know... what you're talking about," I stutter out.

He grabs my arms with bruising force and gives me a strong shake. "Oh, come on, screwing your boyfriend in the classroom in broad daylight while Liz watched from the next room? At the party a few weeks ago, in the bedroom upstairs while everyone else is downstairs drinking?" He lets out an exaggerated chuckle. "You even gave him head in the bathroom at the restaurant. Now, that one surprised me the most. You really didn't seem like that kind of girl." *What?*

"How does Aerick always manage to find the kinky ones?" he says quietly, still staring at me with those lustful eyes. I so badly want to cry right now. I know what he's thinking and there's no way out of this. For the first time, I'm hoping Liz will actually come back.

I don't understand; he was so nice to me the few times I've seen him. I never for a minute thought he was like this. Aerick didn't like him being near me, but I chalked it up to him being jealous. Then again, women can make men do crazy things, too. I'm sure that he and Liz have something going on, and my money is on Liz just using him. Otherwise, she wouldn't be so worried about getting the information about Aerick.

Suddenly he grabs both of my legs, pulling them straight out, and straddles them. *NO!* "Now, you're going to be a good little girl and let me have a sample of what Aerick gets every night." I try to move, but it only makes him tighten his legs around mine, and my chest tightens even more.

"Get the hell off me!" I scream at him, hoping Liz will hear me.

A hard smack burns across my face, causing me to fall to the side slightly, before he grabs my face with both his hands. "You fucking yell again and I won't wait for Liz to kill you, I'll kill you myself."

He kisses me with bruising force, and I try to struggle away again. "That's right baby, fight. It's more fun that way." He begins to kiss down my neck and a tear wets my cheek. I can't believe this is actually happening. *What the hell did I ever do to deserve this?*

"Ahh..." I cry out as he bites down on my shoulder.

"Oh yeah baby, let me hear you."

"Please, please, don't do this!"

"Come on baby, you'll enjoy this, I promise." I cry out again as he grabs at my breast roughly, sending pain through it. "Being with Aerick, you must like it rough. I know about him, heard the stories of what he's done to women straight from his own mouth. He always liked to brag about the things he's done," he says in between the sharp bites that he's spreading across my shoulders.

"Don't! Stop, please! Please don't do this to me!"

"Shh, shh. You'll probably enjoy it if you just relax." Pulling my legs forward more, I'm forced to lean back more toward whatever my hands are tied on behind me. He unbuttons my pants and it becomes clear that this is going to happen no matter what I do.

The lack of oxygen coming out of my lungs is threatening to make me pass out. That might be the best thing. I'm sure I won't want to remember this. *This is it.* The thing that turns Aerick away from me. The thing that repulses him so much that he never wants to touch me, or even look at me again.

* * * *

"Why is she lying down?" Liz asks. I can't see them, but they must be right outside.

"She was trying to escape. I hit her once or twice to get her to knock it off. Can we just kill her, or leave her, or whatever we're going to do? I'm tired of this game."

"We can't leave just yet. The police are at camp," she says, a little panicked. *What did she think was going to happen?* I hear her walking toward me and instinctively, I curl up as small as possible. I can't bring myself to open my eyes, and the tears are still running down my cheeks.

"I guess we can't leave her alive." She kicks me in my stomach. "What's the matter? Not going to beg for your life?" she asks with a cackle.

"No," I manage to get out in a small, weak voice. Right now, death looks pretty good.

"Oh, where's the strong, defiant little princess that managed to steal Aerick's heart? Giving up so easily?" There's not enough strength left to even answer her question.

"Wow, all it took was a man to smack you around a little and you turn right back into that sad, scared little girl that first came to camp. You're so pathetic." She kicks at my leg and lets out a huff. "Why are you giving in so easy? This isn't like you." She turns quickly and goes to the door.

"What did you do?" she says louder.

"Nothing, I slapped her a few times. She's just a pathetic little girl. Whatever Aerick even sees in her is beyond me."

"So, you didn't do anything other than that?" *She knows.* She walks back outside the door to him.

"No! Now I told you, get rid of her and let's get out of here."

"You liar!"

"Ow, what the fuck? You dumb bitch! That hurt. You made me bleed!" he screams at her. My eyes fly open to see him holding his arm. She still has the knife in her hand.

"What, I'm not enough for you, you needed to turn around and mess around with her too? What is it about her that everyone just falls over for? Just leave, you nasty-ass bastard!"

"Fine, you psycho bitch. Do this shit yourself!" He turns and walks away from her.

She stares after him for a minute before shaking her head. "Wait, wait, you can't leave me!" she whines. "Please, look, I'm sorry I cut you. I won't do it again. Please!" Her pleading is sickening.

"Forget you!" he shouts, no longer in my view.

"Fine. I don't need you anyway, and just for the record, you're a lame fuck. Aerick was a hundred times better than you."

"Whatever, psycho!"

"Dammit!" she screams as she comes back into the shack. "See what you did, you little whore! Always messing up my plans." My silence is rewarded with another kick to the ribs. I can't help but groan at the pain as my eyes screw shut.

"You stupid bitch, think you can outsmart me? What did you say to him?" she shouts, kicking me once more.

"Nothing, I swear," I choke out.

"Lies, lies, lies. That's all that ever comes out of your mouth, whore." I feel cold metal on my side where my shirt has risen up. I open one of my eyes to see her eyeing my stomach. "Hmmm, maybe I need to give you another scar to match this one." She runs her knife over to the other side of my stomach and presses it in slowly so just the tip pierces my skin. I scream as the blade penetrates my skin.

"Oh, I'm sorry. Did that hurt?" Her laughter sends the most chilling vibe down my back. She really has lost it. I'm dead, she's going to kill me this time. She moves the knife up to my cheek. "Maybe I should mark up your face a little while I'm at it. No open casket for you."

Something catches her eye. She stares at my shoulder and reaches down, pulling my shirt off my shoulder. "Looks like nothing has changed. Aerick still likes it rough, does he?" There's a longing in her voice. It makes me sick and what's worse, they aren't even from him. The overwhelming emotions cause a new set of tears pouring out of my eyes.

"Great, here we go again with the 'poor little me' act." She pushes at my face in disgust. "Whatever, let's get this over with. How do you wish for your life to end? I can either slit your throat or pierce your heart. You choose." This is it, my time is up and the reaper is here to collect.

"Liz, you..."

She places the knife over my lips, cutting off my words.

"Don't bother pleading with me. It isn't going to work. The only way I get out of this is for you to die, but don't worry." A unnerving grin spreads across her face. "I'll make sure Aerick is well taken care of. He will..."

She stops as we hear something outside. Her lips turn up in delight. "I knew you would come back, I'm irresistible. Well, you're out of time little girl. I guess it'll be your throat, then."

Everything seems to slow down for a moment. A shadow comes rushing through the door before my blurred eyes can focus on who it is. The figure pulls Liz backward by her shirt, quickly landing one punch to her face, and she's out. My vision clears and I finally focus on the figure gazing down at me.

Aerick!

Two other figures appear in the doorway.

Jeff and Paulo!

I bury my face in my chest. As glad as I am to see them, I can't look at them. Especially not Aerick.

I feel hands on me, and I shrink back from the touch. "Don't!" I shout.

"Babe, it's just me. You're okay." Tears wrack my body. It's over, they found me. He tries to grab me again.

"Don't touch me!" Curling up my body as small as I can, I try to bury my face into my body. I don't want anyone to look at me. He can't, not now. He'll never love me again. I'm sure of it.

"Baby, I'm sorry. I had to hit her, but I would never do that to you. I swear, you're safe now." *That isn't it.*

"Hey." Jeff whispers softly. I feel him stroke my head. "I'm going to untie you okay?" I nod my head but keep my eyes shut as tightly as possible. "Geez," he mumbles as I feel him tug on my raw wrist. An involuntary whimper escapes my mouth. "Sorry." There's a heavy sigh next to me. He'll try to hold me as soon as I'm free. I can't let him touch me.

"Hold on Nadi, I almost have it."

My whole body tenses up as I try to hold in another whimper.

"Almost, there..." he says quietly and as soon as I'm free I scramble up into Jeff's chest. Jeff freezes, only allowing one hand to touch my head. "You're okay," he whispers.

"Baby..." Aerick says again, but I curl into Jeff even more as I cry uncontrollably.

"Jeff," Aerick's concerned voices says quietly beside me.

"Jesus, Nadi your bleeding. Let me see," Jeff says, attempting to pull my shirt up to expose my stomach.

"Please Jeff, just get me out of here," I beg pulling my shirt back down before anyone can see.

"But Nadi..."

"Please!" I plead with him. Grabbing his shirt, I pull impossibly closer.

"Okay, okay." He shifts carefully, sliding his arms under my legs and arms. I feel momentarily weightless as he picks me up.

Aerick's face flashes into view out of the corner of my eye. So many emotions are plastered on his face: hurt, defeat, sadness, anger. His eyes are stuck to the floor as he must no longer be able to stand the sight of me. Jeff shifts me a little and I bury my face into his neck.

"Aerick... Aerick." Paulo beckons.

I feel something pull at the top of my shirt. "Don't, DON'T!" I shout trying to pull away and it knocks Jeff back a few steps.

"Calm down, Nadi. Please," Jeff begs and I freeze now that the tugging has stopped.

"What the hell happened to you?" Aerick's voice breaks at the last word. Again, I can't say anything, but the tightening in my chest begins to build. *The bite marks.* "What did she do to you, Nadalynn? For god sakes, please talk to me, look at me, something!" I flinch as his tone gets louder.

"Paulo," Jeff says quickly as my grip around his neck tightens.

"Aerick, man. Let's go for a walk."

"No, dammit. I need to know what the fuck happened!" he shouts, causing me to flinch again.

"Aerick," Paulo's powerful voice fills the small space. "You're scaring her even more." There's a heavy huff beside me, followed by a shuffling, which I can only guess is both of them vacating the room. After a moment I loosen my grip around Jeff and relax just slightly.

"Nadi, can you tell me what happened here?" Jeff's quiet voice fills in my ear.

I shake my head. "Not yet."

"How bad could she have been?"

"Not her."

"What do you mean, not her?" I shake my head. There's so much to say and no way to say it. Now that I'm rescued, I'm not sure if it was better than what may have happened if they were only a few minutes longer. "You know you can tell me anything, right?"

"Jeff..." More tears. "Not here, please. I just want to get out of here." My body rises and falls as he lets out a sigh.

"Okay. Let's go." I feel his lips against my hair for a moment as he begins to walk. He'll always be my rock. The one who's always there for me, no matter how screwed up I am, no matter how damaged I am. Jeff walks outside with me in his arms.

"Nadalynn?" Aerick whispers from beside me, but thankfully doesn't try to touch me.

"Let's just get her back to the camp," Jeff says, sensing my unwillingness to communicate with him.

"You got her?" he asks Jeff in defeat and Jeff nods his head.

"Paulo can you get... that," Aerick says with disgust.

"Yeah, man. I'll get that trash."

Our walk back to the camp is fairly silent, other than the quick call Aerick makes to Luther. I concentrate hard to stay as still as possible. My whole body hurts and each time Jeff tosses me up a little to get a better grip on me, I have to suppress the agony that jolts through me.

My mind is running rampant as well. *How do I explain what happened? Can I explain it? How do I go on from here?* I don't know what I'm going to do when I lose Aerick. He's become my whole world. The silence and tension rolling off him has been so intense the entire walk back. I think even Paulo knows something is off.

We reach the edge of the field and a slight sense of relief comes flooding over me. I made it back. By some miracle, I managed to make it back and mostly in one piece. Then again, I'm still questioning if that's a good thing or bad thing.

"How did you guys find me?" I ask quietly, finally finding a small voice within me.

"Aerick got upset with the cops' questions and came outside. Paulo, Brayden and I followed. We were standing outside and Brayden said something about rain coming and not having to clean up. Aerick swore under his breath and just took off. Paulo and I followed after him. We went to the first maintenance shack that was on the closer trail. When we didn't find you there, we went to the other one."

"Nadi, " Aerick's quiet and careful voice interrupts Jeff. "What did she mean when she said, "I knew you would come back?' There was no way she was expecting me." He's putting it together. Must be why he's been so quiet. I shake my head. *Not now.*

"Nadi, can I let you down?"

"I'll carry her," Aerick says quickly.

"No! I um... can walk."

"You're hurt, just let me carry you. I promise I won't hurt you." He sounds so desperate to do it, but there's no way I can handle being in his arms right now.

"No, it's okay. I'll walk." Jeff's arms are shaking. He's not as strong as Aerick and he just carried me for at least a mile. He must be exhausted. He lets me down slowly, keeping his arms around mine to steady me. I hurt but I can walk, sort of. I keep some of my weight on Jeff as we walk the rest of the way to the clinic.

I keep a hold on my stomach where she cut me. When he put me down, I felt the wound reopen and I don't want them to see it bleeding again or they won't let me walk. I need to be strong because it's going to take all my strength to deal with what's about to happen.

The cops are standing outside the clinic as we walk up. "You found her," one of them says.

"Yeah, no thanks to you," Aerick growls at him.

"Who's that?" he asks, ignoring Aerick's stare.

"She is the one who kidnapped her."

"What happened to her?"

"I had to knock her out before she slit Nadi's throat."

"Was that really necessary?"

"And what do you suggest I should have done?" Aerick's frustration is giving way to his anger.

"Come on," he says after a moment turning to Paulo, effectively breaking off his and Aerick's argument. "Put her in the back of my car and then we need someone to show me where you found her. Kerry, call this in and get some more units out here to process the scene. Then you can get her statement."

"Yes sir," the other officer says with a nod.

"I want Nadi inside, now. Before you question her, I want her looked at," Luther says, stepping in to take back control as I begin to sag more into Jeff's side. He grabs me and pulls me inside while Aerick follows. Jeff carefully helps me to the bed and Terrie starts barking out orders. She pushes me back on the bed and begins checking the cut on my stomach, since it is the most obvious wound.

"This is going to need stitches." She starts to pull up my shirt and I immediately pull it back down and turn away from her, glancing at everyone in the room. She gives me an irritated look as her eyebrows stitch together.

"Alright, everyone out." She shoos them away until only her and Aerick remain, but Aerick has stayed back in the corner with his eyes glued to the floor. He makes no move to leave and Terrie doesn't realize I want him gone, because she comes back over to me and attempts to inspect me again. I don't let her, and she gives me a curious look until I glance at Aerick.

Her eyes shoot up and confusion mars her face, but a second later she appears to understand. "Aerick, can you leave us for a minute?" His eyes fly up to me and mine fall in shame.

"Give me a minute with her first," he demands.

"Aerick, I really need to check over her."

"Just give us a minute!" he growls loudly, making me flinch. I close my eyes tight. *Please don't, Terrie.* But my silent plea goes unheard and she reluctantly leaves, closing the door behind her.

"Who was it?" he asks quietly, still rooted in the corner. I finally look up at him in horror. He figured it out.

"How?"

"You won't let me touch you, you have… bite marks on you, she was expecting someone else, not me, which means there was someone else there. Was it a man?" Staring back down, I try to hold in the sobs clawing at my chest. "So, it was a man." Sometimes I hate that he can read me so easy. He moves and comes to sit on the edge of the bed but doesn't touch or even look at me. "He's the one that left those marks?" There's no point in denying it; my head nods.

"What else did he do?" His tone surprises me. He almost sounds choked up. "Nadi, I need to know. Did he..." He doesn't finish his sentence and the tears spill over as the ache in my heart grows. His hands ball into fists. "What did he look like? Did you hear his name?" I glance up, hardly hearing his words as he's turned towards the wall and is barely audible.

I shut my eyes but it does nothing to stop the tears. *He knows.* I didn't even have to say it and he knows. Who cares who did it? It doesn't matter anymore.

The bed jolts suddenly and pain shoots through my arms as Aerick grabs me. "Dammit, talk to me!" My eyes fly open as he shouts at me. Anger, pure anger floods through his eyes and I freeze in fear. I open my mouth but nothing comes out. "Who? Fucking tell me!" he screams in my face.

"Sean," I cry out as he grips me harder. He freezes and Terrie throws the door open.

"Aerick!" she yells at him.

"Sean? You mean the Sean I know?" There's so much disbelief on his face. I nod, burying my head into the pillow.

"Aerick, your minute is up, now leave and let me do my job!" she orders, pulling him back.

His eyes glaze over. "He's dead," he seethes, before getting up, shrugging her off of him, and heading for the door.

He pauses in the doorway and his eyes find mine. "This is *NOT* your fault!" he says before storming out, closing the door with a slam, and I finally break down. Terrie comes to try and comfort me, but I shake her off. "Give me a minute, please just give me one... flipping... minute..." I sob.

The man of my dreams just left. Left me. I was so stupid thinking it would ever last.

* * * *

I feel better for the most part. Terrie gave me a shot of something and now I almost feel disconnected. Here, but not here. After I calmed down, she checked me over and determined that there was very little damage that needed attention, other than the stab wound. Although, her face contorted several times as she looked at the bite marks and the many bruises.

She numbed the area around my stab wound and used several stitches to close it up. She said I was pretty lucky nothing was injured too badly. Little does she know the real damage.

The cops have wanted to come and talk to me, but Luther insisted that Terrie finish first. She refused to let anyone else in either. It's very much appreciated. No one else needs to see the marks all over me. It would be too obvious, and I'm so exhausted. My body is begging me for sleep.

"Okay Nadi, I can't hold them off any longer. You're going to have to tell the officer what happened." I give her an understanding nod. She gets up and calls for Luther. He comes to the door and she steps out a little.

"I had to give her something to calm her down after she and Aerick talked. I don't know what he said to her, but she was hysterical. That cop needs to tread lightly." He nods at her. *Hello, I can still hear you, people!*

"I don't understand everything yet, but Aerick took off before I could stop him. I sent Paulo after him, and Jake is tracking him. Help them out and I'll take over here."

"I had to stitch up the wound in her stomach. She has some bruised ribs and likely has a concussion. There are several large bumps on her head, so she needs to stay reclined and relax as much as possible." He gives her another nod and she walks away.

"Jeff?" He walks over and joins Luther just outside the door. "I need you to help keep her calm." *Do they really think I can't hear them?*

"Yeah, okay," he says and comes into the room with worry all over his face. He removes his shoes off and lifts up my head as he crawls onto the top of the bed, placing a pillow in his lap. I gratefully lie back and he starts running his hands through my hair. Luther walks out of sight and I see several people in the other room just standing around. Gavin's worried eyes find mine, but he stays completely still, leaning up against the wall. "You okay to do this?" Jeff asks quietly in my ear.

My chest rises and falls with a deep breath. I feel so odd right now. "Yeah. Just please don't leave me." While I feel oddly calm, my head says I need him with me.

He kisses my hair. "I'll be right here. I'd never leave you."

Luther re-enters the room with one of the cops. He glares oddly at Jeff before taking a seat in the chair next to me. Luther closes the door and goes to stand in the corner of the room that Aerick vacated a little while ago.

"Hi, Nadi. My name is officer Kerry. I know this must be difficult, but I need you to tell me what happened. Can you do that for me?"

My head feels so weird right now and it's a second for me to get what he's asking. Taking a deep breath, I stare up at him. "I went out for an evening run in the back field. Everything was fine for the first couple of laps and then something hit me." I continue to explain waking up in the shack, and all of Liz's questioning. How she just seemed to get more and more angry. Then how we heard Aerick and scuffled around before she knocked me out again.

"Shit, he did hear you," Jeff mumbles, and we all turn to him. He describes how Aerick heard something when they were out looking for me.

"What happened when you woke up again?" Officer Kerry asks after writing down some notes.

This was the part I was wanting to avoid. But I can't be that weak little girl. If I do, then he'll get away with it. Free to do it again. It's time to be brave; or maybe it's whatever Terrie gave me that's making this feel like it isn't even me telling the story.

With a heavy sigh, I sit up, pulling my legs up to my chest and wrapping my arms around them tightly. Jeff tries to rub my shoulder, but I shrug it away. "Please don't touch me," I whisper as I scowl down to the floor and lay my head on my knees. I feel him lean away from me.

"When I woke up it was dark. I didn't know what to do so, I called out for Aerick. Liz came back in, telling me it was useless, before leaving out the door, but she left it open this time. After a minute I heard her talking to someone. I recognized his voice, but I couldn't think who it was. She blamed him for not warning her that the guys were out searching for me. He was supposed to be her lookout at the camp."

"You said he. So, was it a male? Did you figure out who it was?"

"Not until she left to come check on the camp. When she left, he came in, and I instantly recognized him. I first met him having lunch with Paulo and Aerick at the Cottage this summer. His name is Sean. I saw him again a few weeks ago at Casey's party. Him and Eddie had shown up. We were all drinking and talking. Nothing out of the ordinary. Sean helped me down off the counter and Aerick got upset, but I figured he was just being jealous."

"Sean and Eddie. You're talking about Sean Foster?"

"I don't know his last name," I admit.

"That's okay. Please continue."

"When he came in, he knew who I was. He admitted he had liked me since we met. He began touching my face and arms. I saw the change in his face. I asked, I begged him not to do it, but he just slapped me for it." *Calm down.* I try to slow my breathing as my tears fall onto my knees.

"Nadi, um, I need you to tell me. Did he hurt you?"

Without hardly moving I pull down the sleeve of my shirt to expose my neck and shoulder. He stands up and goes to touch me. "Don't touch her!" Jeff growls, making him jump back.

"Jeff!" Luther warns.

"Sorry, officer. She has a thing about being touched. It's in your best interests not to touch her." He's silent for a moment and my eyes are still stuck on the small mark on the floor that stuck out.

"Are those bite marks?" he asks softly and I nod, releasing my shirt. I hear him exhale loudly.

"Are there more?"

I nod yes again. "He told me that I was a bitch and he was going to treat me like one," I whisper through my tears.

"What else did he do?"

My chest hurts, all the crying and the pain today is just so much to handle.

"Nadi. I need you to continue. I need to know... to know if... he..."

"If he what? Can't you even say it? You want to know if he molested me, if he raped me. You can't even say the words, yet you want me to re-live it," I say, disconnected from myself, still unmoved, like it isn't even me talking. "The answer is 'yes'," I say, defeated, after a balloon of silence fills the room. Hurrying to get it over with, I give him a quick rundown of what the bastard did to me. It hurts just as much to say it out loud as it does thinking it.

"I prayed over and over that it would end, or that someone would find me, or even that I would just die so that my nightmare would end." Sobs rack through my body and I squeeze my legs as tight as I can, rocking myself back and forth trying to control them.

"I think she's had enough for now," Luther steps in again.

"No," I tell him through my cries.

"Nadi, just take a break for a minute," he says softly, like I'll break any second, and the thing is, I feel like I just might.

"I just want to be finished with this. Besides, there isn't much else to tell. " He steps back into the corner. I reign in my cries and continue. "When he finished, he dressed me and left me crying on the floor. He waited outside until Liz got back. She suspected he had done something, and they argued, causing him to take off. Then Liz came in and said she was going to kill me. She was about to cut my throat when Aerick showed up and knocked her out before she had a chance to." My sobs intensify again as my body starts shaking from exhaustion.

"Officer!" Luther barks.

"Okay, okay. I, uh, think I have what I need for now. We'll let you know if we need anything else." He gets up quickly and leaves, followed closely by Luther.

Jeff pats the pillow behind me. I gladly lie down on the pillow, curling into myself. Jeff's fingers find my hair and I feel myself relax as I cry myself to sleep. Just like I use to do almost ten years ago.

CHAPTER TWENTY-SIX

(Sunday, December 13th)

I'M JOLTED AWAKE by my dream.

"It is okay. You're safe," Aerick says quietly, and I'm confused by how he said it.

Jeff's gone and it's only us in the room. I wipe away the wetness from my face. I must have been crying in my sleep. Whatever or however horrible my dream was, I no longer remember what it was about, but I have that lingering, dreaded feeling like it was something bad. It's dark and I can only see the outline of Aerick's shadow, but it's enough to see that his face is buried in his hands.

"It's my fault," he says roughly.

"What is?" I ask confused.

"I was supposed to protect you. I promised to protect you and I failed."

"Aerick..." I try to stop him, but he doesn't let me finish.

"You were dreaming. You called out for me to save you. You pleaded for me to help you. Prayers that were never answered. I got there too late to save you from him."

"Aerick..."

"Don't!" he almost shouts, making me jump. He's quiet for a moment before continuing in a lower tone. "You don't have to explain anything. I heard your statement, the camera in the room was on. It was probably better I didn't see it until I got back." He lets out a deranged chuckle. He sounds off, like seriously off. I reach over and turn on the table lamp to see a gut-wrenching sight.

"Oh my god, Aerick. What did you do?" My voice is barely a whisper as horror fills my body.

He has blood all over him. His face is all bruised and nicked up, but there's no way all the blood is from him. I sit up, trying to grab his face, but he pushes my hands away. "Don't, I deserved it. What I don't deserve is you," he chokes out.

He gets up and leaves quickly. *What in the world just happened?* I don't get much time to think about it because suddenly police lights flood the room from outside the window. I kneel up on the bed to see what's going on. Two policemen get out of the car just in time to stop Aerick, who is walking out. *Oh no! What did he do?*

I jump out of bed and run right past Terrie, who's sitting at her desk. I ignore her shouts for me and run around the building to the front of camp. I have a terrible feeling about this.

I reach the front as Luther is exiting his office and I slow down to a fast walk as I see him. One of the police officers has Aerick up against the car and is searching him. "What's going on?" I almost shout as I rush toward them.

The other officer steps in front of me. "Miss, you have to..." I push him to the side and go around him, but he catches me by my arm.

I hear both Aerick and Luther shout in unison. "Don't touch her!" But it's too late, I hit him square in the jaw as he swings me back around by my arm. He falls to the ground but before I can get any further, strong arms appear from behind me, wrapping under my arms and back around behind my head, pinning me to whoever has a hold on me. I try to kick out as the heavy feeling in my chest quickly sets in, but it's no use, I can't move. I start shaking and the air in my lungs only move in, becoming gasping breaths.

Let go, please let go! I can't even speak the words out loud. *Stop, stop, stoooooopppp...*

"Nadi! Nadalynn look at me!" I try to breathe and stop struggling as I feel Aerick's hands on my face, pulling it up to gaze at him. "I need you to calm down." I try to comprehend what he said, but it's hard to focus as I feel myself hyperventilating. "Let her go, Luther." The stronghold releases and I fall to my knees as I try to breathe.

"Just breathe in and out. Come on, count, focus on breathing slowly," he coaxes, never removing his gaze from mine. I listen to his voice as he counts my breathing. "...in two, three, four. Out two, three, four." Luther is talking quickly in the background, something about a 'horrible trauma today,' but it sounds so far away. I just try to focus on Aerick's voice.

As I start to gain control of myself, Paulo and Jeff appear, one on each side of me. My attention turns back to Aerick when he goes quiet. "You need to stay calm now and just let what happens next, happen." I give him a confused stare and we both stand up. Aerick glances to my left, nodding his head, and I feel a familiar hand grab my arm.

Aerick gives me one last lingering look before he turns and walks away, but the empty space is immediately occupied by Luther. "If you can't stand here and be quiet, I'll have the guys take you inside." I nod in agreement and let out a deep breath. He turns and walks toward the car where the officer resumes searching Aerick. The other officer is standing between us, rubbing his jaw.

I feel like I should say something to him, even though I'm still half-distracted by what's going on over by the cop car. "Um, sorry about that. I kind of have a thing..."

He cuts me off. "With being touched. I get it now. I understand you have had a difficult day, but if you hit me again, you will be going to jail as well." The smug expression on his face is tempting me to let him meet my fist again, but then I fully process what he just said.

"What do you mean, *as well*?"

He raises an eyebrow at me. "You had to know that we were going to have to bring him in after what your boyfriend over there did."

"What exactly did he do?" I'm getting more and more impatient with this guy.

"He almost beat a man to death a few hours ago."

My hands fly up to my mouth. "Who?" The question is out of my mouth even though I know exactly who he's talking about. "Never mind, don't say his name," I whisper. "Just, please tell me what happened." I stare over to Aerick, who's now leaning up against the cop car, talking calmly to the other officer.

"From what we have been able to gather from witnesses, Aerick found Sean at the Old Number Three Bar in the next town over." Hearing his name sends shivers down my spine. The cop ignores me and continues. "They had a heated argument, and Sean pushed him, at which time Aerick proceeded to beat him within an inch of his life. Several of Sean's friends pulled Aerick off of him, and they began fighting with him as well. Aerick was able to inflict a lot of damage before the fight was stopped by the owner and several of Aerick's friends, who removed him from the bar. Sean was taken to the hospital in Ellensburg and they are not sure that he is going to make it. Several of the other guys also sustained severe injuries."

"But you just said that he pushed Aerick first. That's self-defense."

"Well, technically that is true. However, if Sean dies from the injuries that Aerick inflicted, he could be facing manslaughter charges. Taking into account that there is reason to believe Aerick went looking for Sean because of what happened to you, the charges could in fact be much more severe. "

Oh my god! This isn't happening. A small tear runs down my cheek as I see Aerick being handcuffed. *This is all my fault.*

"Please don't do this, this is my fault, not his, please!" I shout to the officer handcuffing Aerick.

"Nadalynn, stop!" Aerick says to me, frustrated. "Just fucking stop blaming all this shit on yourself." *What? How can I not?*

His eyes are so sad, and it tears me up inside. I can only stare as the cop puts Aerick in the back of the car. Jeff puts his arm around my shoulder to steady me. I feel a strong need to cry as the other cop gets into the car and they drive away from me, but so many tears have left my body in the last day, I don't think I can.

The only thing worse than him leaving me, is someone taking him away from me, and it's all because of my own stupid carelessness. I may never feel his arms around me again. I shrug off Jeff's arm from my shoulder; it doesn't feel right. I don't want him, or anyone, touching me. I stand still and quiet, feeling all alone.

I don't feel right. What do I do now? I don't know what to do. He's gone again, but it may be forever this time. I'm lost.

People around me are talking but their voices are just a hum in the background.

This should have gone differently, if I would have just let him touch me or hold me, maybe he would have stayed instead of taking off upset. Again, all my fault. He said not to blame myself but I'm the one who did everything wrong. I should have been more aware of my surroundings, I would have fought harder, and most importantly, I should have let him be there for me because he may never be there again.

I can't take my eyes off the darkness of the driveway where the taillights of the cop car have long ago disappeared.

The blackness represents everything in my life: dark, sad, and alone.

There is a sharp twinge in my shoulder, but I don't want to move.

Time seems to go on forever. My eyes start to feel heavy, but I still can't move. A final tear squeezes its way out of my dried tear duct as I succumb to the darkness.

* * * *

I wake up, dazed, to soft voices talking in the next room. There's an odd mixture of being completely refreshed but extremely sore all over my body. Flashes of yesterday's and this morning's events flood into my mind. For a moment, I almost thought it was all a dream, but I can't be that lucky. It happened, all of it.

Christ, Aerick is in jail!

I sit up but quickly stop when I realize I'm attached to an IV.

"Hey, you're awake," Terrie says as she comes into the room.

"Why do I have an IV?"

"It's just a precaution. With you sleeping most of the morning and afternoon, you needed some fluids in you." I glance out the window.

"How long have I been sleeping?" It must have been a long time, by the way I feel.

"It's almost four in the afternoon."

"What about Aerick? I need to know what's going on," I say in a rush, realizing how much time I have wasted.

"It's okay. Christian is here and he wants to talk to you. I'm sure..."

"I don't want to talk about it, not yet, please tell him I'm not ready." My voice gets more panicked.

"Now, would I ever make you talk about something you don't want to?" Christian says from the doorway. I scowl down at my hands that are tangling themselves together.

"Yes!"

"What if I promise not to make you talk about it until you ready?"

"Fine." There's no use arguing with him. He comes in and sits down in the chair next to the bed as Terrie leaves, shutting the door behind her. I draw in a deep breath, trying to prepare myself for this conversation.

"Well, first, I'm sure you want to know about Aerick. Should we start there?"

"Yes, please." His lips turn up slightly.

"I called the hospital a short while ago. Thankfully, I'm a doctor and was able to sweet talk the nurse that answered. She told me that Sean is doing better, but he's not out of the woods yet. The swelling in his brain has stopped luckily, so if he can hold on through tonight, he should be okay."

"And what does that mean for Aerick?"

"I was able to relay the information to the police." He pauses for a moment.

"And?"

"If Sean is downgraded, they're willing to release Aerick on bail, pending any charges he may face." I let out a heavy sigh of relief. Even a little good news is good to hear right now.

"Luther has offered to put up the bail to get him out in the morning, but Nadi, I really think the three of us should sit down and talk. I had hoped to get to visit with you more, but it seems that fate has other plans. You have a lot of things pent up inside you, and it's not healthy for you or Aerick to keep them locked away. With all this new stuff that's being stacked on top of the old stuff, there are going to be drastic consequences if you don't let someone help you."

"I don't need help, doc." I'm not a crazy person that needs her whole life psychoanalyzed. He frowns at me, not a fitting look for him.

"I think you do. Tell me, Nadi, what happened early this morning?"

A lot happened this morning. "What part?"

"Well, let's see. We could talk about how you hit the officer out of pure reaction, the part where you regressed at the touch of Luther trying to restrain you, the part where Aerick's touch seemed to calm you down, or the most troubling part, in which you became close to being in a catatonic state. Please let me know if I missed anything important."

I stare down at my hands again. I probably seemed crazy last night, but that look in Aerick's eye as they put him in the car, it was as if he had given up. It didn't just worry me, it scared me.

"Look, this is just as much for Aerick as it is for you. Luther and I had a long conversation this morning. Aerick is blaming this all on himself and that can be dangerous. Obviously dangerous for others, but also himself. He has a troubled past just like you and the stress of all this is weighing heavily on him." I gaze up at him and the urge to cry returns as Christian's words fall in line with my worries, but I have other worries as well.

"Do you think we can get past this? I mean, is there a chance he'll still want to be with someone as broken as me?" I'm not sure I really want to know the answer, but I need to hear it from someone.

"Nadi, the love you and Aerick share is very strong. You two are really lucky to have found each other." *I don't think luck is anywhere in my vocabulary.*

"You guys share a bond that few others ever experience. Love comes on many levels. The strongest of them all is what most may refer to as soul mates. I honestly believe that is what you two have and if I'm right, soul mates can survive nearly anything. It's a bond that is almost unbreakable. That's why I want to help you two. You belong together, and I don't want the stubbornness in both of you to ruin something so rare."

I flop back onto my pillow, exhaling loudly. "Fine, but I'm still not talking until I'm ready!" I hate how he always seems to talk me into getting what he wants. He claps his hands together and stands up.

"Great. I'll be staying in town tonight, and I'll be here when he gets back."

"How do you know he's being released?" He still doesn't know for sure what's going to happen.

"Oh, I have a gut feeling about this, and I think things will turn out okay. I'll see you in the morning."

So freaking confident, sometimes it drives me crazy. "Tell Terrie to get in here and remove this damn IV out," I order, trying to regain a little bit of the dignity that he pretty much just trampled down completely. I need to talk to Luther.

Terrie walks in, shaking her head in amusement. "That man can talk his way into anything, I swear."

I let out a huff. "Tell me about it. I hate that he always gets his way."

"Yeah, between that and his charming looks, it's almost like he should be a politician." I almost laugh because she's so right. "Sorry I knocked you out this morning, but you were so overwhelmed and exhausted. I got worried when you didn't respond to anyone, and I thought maybe your mind had just had too much."

I stare down at my arm and watch her start taking my IV out. She's probably right, but I still didn't like the fact that again, things were out of my control. That's all my life is made up of these days. The problem is, it doesn't seem like it's going to get better anytime soon.

She finishes up, and after giving a list of what to watch for, lets me go. I go to Luther's office but he's not there. I don't know where he would be this time of day. He's never in his cabin during the day. He must have left camp. I hope he didn't go to see Aerick without me.

I can smell dinner, but I don't really feel hungry, despite my lack of eating the last day or so. What I really want is to just sit and relax. I have an urge for tea, so I decide to head over to the cafeteria before everyone gets there.

The weather is clear and sunny, but it's so cold out that everyone is inside. Even though I have sweats on, I can still feel the sting of the frosty cold. A hot cup of tea while I'm swaddled in my blanket hopefully will make me feel a little better.

As I walk into the mess hall, it's still empty, but I hear Andi in the kitchen, probably doing last minute preparations. I make my way over to the hot water tank in the corner of the room and start filling up a cup for tea.

"This is so typical," I hear Andi say. I almost think she's talking to me until I hear Jake talking back to her. "It isn't like she could help it." *What in the world are they talking about?* I move closer to the door of the kitchen but make sure I stay out of sight.

"I swear, ever since she came here, everything is always about her."

"Andi, that is kind of messed up. I mean, she's been through a lot this last year."

"But still, I'm so sick of every time I turn around, it's always Nadi, Nadi, Nadi." *Holy crap, is she really saying this?*

"Andi, I'm sure she wishes none of this ever happened. Would you rather it happened to you?"

"Well no, not really. I mean, I feel bad and all for what she had to go through. I'm just tired of everything here always revolving around her." *Trust me, I would gladly give it up.*

"So, what you're really saying is that you're upset that you aren't the center of attention anymore... Hey, ouch! You didn't need to hit me, you know it's true. Besides, I thought you two were becoming besties these days. You two are always hanging out."

"Like I said, she's okay and all, I'm just tired of everything always focused on her. There are more people that work here besides her."

I can't listen anymore. I abandon my cup and quietly leave the mess hall. *Great, now everyone is mad at me.* I head back to my cabin before they find me here. I guess I finally saw Andi's true colors. Apparently, she was just using me too, now that she doesn't have Tia to follow her around all the time. This is why I don't hang out with women. They can be so two-faced and so full of drama. I thought Andi and I were becoming good friends, but it was all an illusion.

Is this how everyone feels about me? She is kind of right that all the bad things lately typically are attached to me, but it's not like I'm asking for trouble. Is it too much to ask to just live a happy and peaceful life?

I hurry to my cabin before I can run into anyone else. I can't handle dealing with anything or anybody for the rest of the evening. I curl up in my bed, hugging my pillow between my arms.

The unfortunate thing about Terrie giving me an IV is that now I'm hydrated, the tears have returned. So many things keep running through my head. How can so much stuff happen in such a short period of time? I even slept through a bunch of it. And where am I now? In my cabin with no one in sight.

Now I really do feel truly alone!

CHAPTER TWENTY-SEVEN

(Saturday, December 19th)

THIS WEEK HAS been exhausting. The end of the evening classes can't come fast enough. Tia is finishing her lesson on the advancement of technology, since the cadets have a paper due on Monday. It's kind of funny, I remember having to write that paper quite well. It was the day after our first bonfire, which also was my eighteenth birthday. The same bonfire that Aerick removed me from, taking me to his 'special spot,' and kissed me for the first time.

Tonight is our cadets' first bonfire. Unfortunately, I'm far from excited about this one. This week has been difficult on so many different levels. Despite everything, there are a few things lifting my spirits a fraction of an inch. One is that I finished the last of my finals yesterday, so with the quarter done, I now get a two-week break from schoolwork. Not only that, but winter quarter is over, which means my class load will decrease to four classes instead of six. It's amazing that I actually made it through this last quarter. I'm still in disbelief that I didn't drown under all of that work, especially with everything else that was going on.

As odd as it sounds, my schoolwork has actually been a welcome distraction this week. Ever since we picked up Aerick from jail, he's been distant.

Flashback to Monday

"Nadi, sit still," Luther scolds me. My leg is bouncing like a jackhammer and my hands alternate being shoved between my thighs or under them every two minutes. Too much energy has been building up inside of me and combining it with the anxiety, it's difficult even thinking about being still. We've been sitting here at the jail for over an hour.

It didn't take long after Luther made the call to Mr. Walker for them to release Aerick on bail. As much as I hate to admit it, I'm glad Sean is going to make it. I hate him with every fiber of my being but none of that even comes close to how it would feel losing Aerick if he got locked up permanently. Just knowing he's been in there for the last day is driving me crazy.

I spent all of yesterday evening in my room lying down. Unfortunately, sleep completely eluded me and I just lay there all night long. I was too afraid to see the darkness of the back of my eyelids and afraid of the dreams that would surely follow.

Standing up quickly, I start pacing, trying to pull my thoughts away from unwanted memories. *What is taking so long?* We got the call over two hours ago that he was being released. I need to see that he's okay. It's irrational of me to feel this way, he can clearly care for himself, but I need to see he's okay with my own eyes.

Luther is suddenly on his feet, drawing my eyes to him. Until now, Luther has been completely composed, but in this moment, the relief radiating off him is plastered on his face as well. I follow his stare to see Aerick behind a windowed door, where he's stopped at a counter and is signing something.

I close my eyes and let out my own sigh of relief. When I open my eyes, Aerick is standing in front of the door looking at me. He still seems so sad, but there doesn't appear to be any other damage to him other than the few bruises and minor cuts he left the camp with. The door is unlocked, and he finally steps through, but I'm frozen in place. My state of relief is overwhelming me so much, it's taking everything I have to even remain standing. I wait, rooted in place, knowing he'll come to me.

He only moves a few steps and then stops, unable to go any further, as Luther's arm shoots out to grab Aerick by his arm. "You okay?"

"I'm fine, Luther." He glances over to me once more, but his gaze only lasts a moment before he looks down.

We both seem to be taken aback when Luther suddenly engulfs Aerick in a hug. "Don't you ever do that to me again!" he says in a loud, scolding whisper.

I never realized how much this would affect him, but then again, with the history of his son, I can see how this probably weighed extremely heavy on him. On several occasions I have heard him call Aerick 'son' and it has always been clear that Luther and Aerick share a stronger bond than Luther and the other staff.

A second later, Luther remembers himself and he quickly stands up straight, composing himself once more. Stepping to the side, he points his hand to me, giving Aerick permission to continue over to see me. Aerick oddly hesitates, giving me an uneasy feeling. When he finally does move, he steps to my side, giving me an awkward side hug, and kisses me on my temple. *That's it?*

I stare up at him confused, but he isn't looking at me, he's glaring at Luther, who has the same baffled expression on his face. Aerick grabs my hand and pulls me along as we walk past Luther. It appears his actions are not up for discussion.

Once we get outside, he slows just a bit, so we are walking side by side instead of me trailing behind him. "Are you really okay?" I whisper to him, not wanting Luther to hear. Aerick is more likely to tell me the truth if no one else can hear his answer.

"Nadi, I'm fine. I can take care of myself." His tone is cold as ice, not something he normally does to me when it's just us.

"I know, I just... you seem..."

"Will you just drop it?!" he snaps at me, causing me to flinch. I gaze down, feeling almost ashamed, but for what I have no idea. He stops beside the camp's SUV. He draws in a deep breath and gives me another quick kiss on my temple before releasing my hand. He opens the rear door for me to get in, which I do quickly, keeping my eyes on my hands.

He stands there for a moment. When I don't move, he reaches in and pulls the seat buckle around me, clicking it into place. Pulling back a little, he runs his hand gently down the side of my face. "Sorry." I can hear the regret in his voice, and I know his rare apology is genuine. His actions are beyond confusing; it's like he has two people pulling him in two different directions. I nod my head in acceptance but keep my eyes down. His fingers linger on my neck for a moment before he pulls back and closes my door, getting into the front passenger seat.

"Let's get out of here, shall we?" Luther says as he turns on the car and quickly puts it into gear.

The ride back is silent. None of us says a word and with no music, the silence is extremely uncomfortable. This is not how I saw our reunion. There was a lot of tension between us since Saturday, but I was hoping things would at least have gotten a little better after he spent a day in jail. I suppose I'd hoped he felt the same unsettling feeling being away from me just like I've felt. It was stupid to think things would go right back to normal, but I hoped we could at least try and work for that. He is keeping me at arms-length and that worries me.

We pull back into camp and park the car. "Christian is waiting for you two in Nadi's cabin."

As we exit the car, Luther turns to Aerick.

"What for?" Aerick asks suspiciously.

"I want you to talk to him."

"I said I'm fine, Luther. I don't need..."

"It isn't a request!" he interrupts him and walks away quickly toward his office.

"Great," Aerick mumbles. "Come on, let's get this over with." He begins to walk toward the cabins, leaving me gawking at him. After a moment, I shake it off and quickly fall in behind him. We're back at camp, which means we're back into staff mode: no sensual touching.

End Flashback

As soon as we reached my cabin, Christian had me sit outside while he talked to Aerick. I waited on the porch for almost an hour while they talked. When he finally beckoned me inside, all he told us was to be patient with each other and not to place blame upon each other. He said we needed to lean on each other to get through it. That was it, that was his all-powerful advice. I was floored that was all he had to say, and it made me quite curious to know what he and Aerick had talked about.

Since then, Aerick hasn't really talk to me. He is often quiet and serious-looking. We've been working out every night after P.T. but he rarely touches me other than quick kisses to my temple. There's also the hesitation every time he goes to touch me, the conflict in his eyes when he glances at me, and on the rare occasion when he thinks no one is paying attention, there's a sadness that reaches deep in his eyes. It's creating so many conflicts of my own.

I'm beginning to long for his touch like I used to in the beginning. As much as anyone's touch scares me right now, I feel the need for him to touch me in the littlest ways. It makes no sense to me why he continues to be so distant, even after our talk with Christian.

"Alright, everyone. We're done for today. Don't forget that your paper is due Monday, and I expect it to meet all the standards listed on the handout you received." Aerick and Paulo's groups get up and leave the classroom. "Nadi, you can go if you want. I can finish up here." Tia gives me a knowing look. She really has a true heart.

"Thanks, Tia. I'll see you at dinner." I say gratefully and head toward the door.

Thank goodness today's weather is sunny, but there's a biting cold that still creeps through all my clothing. It snowed a few days this week, and it still blankets the ground.

"Everything okay?"

I turn to see Gavin standing behind me. I kind of spaced off there for a minute, looking at the snow-flocked trees. "Um, Yeah. I guess I got lost in the beauty of winter," I tell him, a little embarrassed to be caught daydreaming.

"It's fine. It is beautiful." He glances up to the trees. "I'm glad I caught up with you," he continues, appearing hesitant.

I raise an eyebrow at him. "And why is that exactly?"

He rubs his hand across the back of his neck and glances down momentarily. "Are you really okay?"

"Yes, I'm okay!" I snap and pin him with a glare.

"I'm sorry, I don't mean to intrude. It's just, I was out late last night, smoking on the porch. There were screams coming from your cabin. I thought you might seek out Aerick or even Jeff, but you didn't. You just stepped out onto your porch and sat there in the bitter cold."

I can't believe he saw me and didn't say anything. "You seemed so sad and lonely, yet you didn't seek out anyone. I figured you wanted to be alone, so I quietly went back inside." *Great.* I must have looked insane sitting out there in my pajamas in the freezing cold. I needed some air to shake off the nightmare that had woken me. The thought occurred to me to seek out Aerick, but I dismissed it when I thought about his distant and hesitant behavior. Going to Jeff just didn't feel right. His normal comforting touch hasn't been so comforting lately. It almost feels wrong, ever since I watched Aerick being driven away by the police. I did feel lonely, but I'm glad he didn't stay anything to me, because I probably would have broken down and embarrassed myself even more.

"Are you and Aerick having problems?"

I'm snapped out of my thoughts. "I really don't think that's any of your business," I say in disbelief. He really is just getting too personal now.

"I'm just wondering why he seems so distant around you lately. This is a time where he should be comforting you and being strong for you. Yet any time he's around you, he's lost in his own world." *He's right, he is.* I need Aerick right now, but he hasn't been there for me. I've waited all week for him to come around, to realize things would be okay, and to become the old Aerick again, but he just isn't there.

I've begun to think he may never be again. Christian had me so convinced that things would be okay between us, but just in the last day or so, my doubts have returned. "You know, I still don't see how this is any of your business."

"I made you an offer once, Nadi, and it still stands. If you need someone to just be there, to just be an ear to hear you, I'm here."

Honestly, it is tempting but the thought of talking to anyone else just doesn't sit right in my stomach. It's weird and I don't understand why I've felt so odd around Jeff. Maybe it has something to do with the fact that he was one of the people who found me, saw me in my weakest and most tattered state. Maybe it's the weight of all the embarrassment.

I'm on the edge of a cliff, hanging dangerously near the tipping point; I don't know what to do.

"We don't have to talk, if you don't want to." He nods his head toward his cabin. "Come on," he says, and starts walking toward it.

I cautiously follow. "Why are we going to your cabin?" I'm not sure why I'm actually following him.

"I have something for you."

"What would you have for me?"

"Just come on." Slightly curious, I continue.

We reach the front of the cabin and he unlocks it and opens the door, standing aside for me to enter first. "It's okay, I'll wait out here." I'm not sure going into his cabin is really a good idea. Not that I think he would hurt me or anything.

"Come on, I don't bite. You don't have to stay if you don't want to, but it's cold out and I have manners, so please step inside for a moment." I huff and go inside, it's kind of hard to deny a man that has manners. Ironically enough, it reminds me of how I used to think it was funny that Aerick is such a gentleman despite his tough man act.

I move to the corner as Gavin follows me in and begins going through stuff on his desk. It's become a little cluttered since the last time I saw it. He's obviously far from the neat and organized Aerick. He finally finds what he's searching for and comes back over to me.

He hands me a book. Not exactly what I was expecting; then again, I really didn't know what to expect. I stare up at him, confused. "I bought this and was going to send it to my cousin for her birthday. Jeff mentioned once that you loved to read. Maybe you could read it for me and tell me what you think of it first. It's really not the type of thing I would read."

I examine the colorful book cover.

"I was told it's actually one of three books in a series and the lady at the store said it was good." He shrugs at me. It's a sci-fi, which isn't the type of book I normally read either, but right now a Stephen King book probably isn't a good idea. I have enough nightmares about real life.

"I really appreciate it. Thank you." Maybe this is what I need.

"Please come by after dinner. We could just sit, relax, and read for a while. I usually come in here and read a little throughout the day. It's pretty calming."

I debate it for a moment. At least here, I'm less likely to be interrupted by everyone's constant worrying and checking up on me. It doesn't take long for me to make up my mind. "Okay. I'll be back in a little while." He nods his head and I hand him the book back. "Can I leave this here for now?" He gives me a crooked smirk.

"Sure." He walks over to the couch and sets it down. "It's waiting here for you, whenever you're ready."

With a nod, I leave to freshen up before dinner. Hopefully Gavin's intentions are pure. He give the impression to genuinely want to help me, but I've been fooled before, and the last thing I need right now is someone causing me any more problems.

I reach my cabin and after using the restroom and running the brush through my hair, I decide to check my grades. Bringing up my school site, I log-in and click on the tab for my classes. Joy begins to fill me as I begin to scroll through them. Only the powers above know how in the world I did it, but somehow I managed to come out of this quarter with an average of three point five. It isn't quite an 'A' but it's enough to make me happy, with everything that has gone on.

The blinking envelope in the top corner of the screen steals my attention, notifying me that there is an unread school email. It's probably saying that I have two weeks to pay for my classes that were not covered by the Pell Grants before I can sign up for next quarter. Since I took such a large class load, the grants weren't even close to enough pay for them all. I've been able to save up some money since there really isn't anything we need to buy at camp and we've been here for several weeks, but it still isn't enough.

Sometime in the next week I'm going to have to sit down with Luther and see if he would be willing to give me an advance or something so I can make up the several thousand that I probably owe. He told me we would be able to 'work something out' so hopefully it's something he had in mind. After all he's done, I don't want him to just pay for it, but I'm going to need just a little help until I can work it off.

I decide to open it and see exactly how deep I'm in. My stomach drops when the email opens, and my eyes scan the first few sentences.

'Thank you for your payment. The balance owed on your account is now $0.'

You've got to be kidding me? I scroll down, reading the rest, and my confusion turns into absolute frustration as I realize what's going on. I slam my laptop shut and head for the mess hall. Several people are already there, including my little group, minus Aerick, but that doesn't surprise me in the least. He usually makes sure all the cadets are here before he comes to meals.

I get in line and dish up my food before going to sit down in my normal spot. Jeff stares up as my tray hits the table a little harder than it should. He greets me, as do the few others sitting there already. I'm still getting those lingering looks from people, but it hasn't been so bad the last few days. I think people are finally putting last week behind us.

"You okay?"

"I'm fine Jeff, just a little annoyed."

"Anything you would care to talk about?" I glare at him. "Okay, okay, enough said. Just tell me one thing." I raise my eyebrow at him and wait for him to ask his question. "How did yesterday go? I didn't get a chance to ask you yet."

He's asking how it went when I met with my lawyer.

Flashback to Friday

"Good afternoon, Nadi," Mr. Leeks greets me as Luther, Aerick and I walk into his office.

"Luther, Aerick, good to see you as well," Mr. Walker says as he comes to stand next to Mr. Leeks and shakes our hands.

"Shall we all sit?" Mr. Leeks ushers us to the conference table in his office. We sit down and my stomach is in knots. We've been waiting to hear what's going on ever since there was a continuance of the case due to the kidnapping. Both of the lawyers are in high spirits, which eases my discomfort just a little.

"I would like to thank you guys for being so patient. This week has been quite long and drawn out with the new developments. I'm sorry to call you down so late in the afternoon but we wanted to wait until we knew the full scope of everything." Mr. Leeks says, glancing at us all one by one.

"I'm pleased to report some good news for all of you. After the events of last weekend, we retracted our agreement to let Liz plead down. After a lot of back and forth from her lawyer, she finally agreed to plead guilty to the original charge of first-degree assault with a deadly weapon, as well as kidnapping. The judge has yet to sentence her, but it will be a minimum of fifteen to twenty years, and she will be denied bail due to her recent actions. Pleading guilty was smart on her part, since she could have been facing an attempted murder charge."

I close my eyes as a tear trickles down my cheek. Rough fingers wipe it away and a comforting kiss presses to my temple. My joy is short-lived and my eyes fly open as I remember that's not the end of why we're here. "What about Sean, and what about Aerick?"

Mr. Walker sits up straighter as he begins talking. "Thankfully, part of Liz's plea deal was that she give a statement regarding your kidnapping. That included Sean's part in it. Of course, he denied it at first and went on about wanting to press charges against Aerick."

"What?!" I spit out, but he quickly holds up his hands, halting me before I can continue.

"I said at first, Nadalynn. Soon after first speaking with him, he received a visit from the camp's current psychologist, who was able to sweet talk the nurse into letting him talk to Sean. An hour later, I received a call from Sean, requesting another meeting with me. He has also agreed to plead guilty to second degree kidnapping and rape and will not be pressing charges against Aerick."

I peek over to Aerick, trying to hold in the dam that is waiting to burst from my eyes. He's staring at Mr. Walker in complete shock. It's obvious he had no idea. I stare back at Mr. Walker.

"You mean this is all over? No trial, no more meetings, it's done?"

"That is exactly what I'm saying," he says with a gleaming smile, and it's my undoing. I bury my face my hands as the dam bursts. Aerick's hands find their way to the side of my head, pulling me to him until he's able to rest his forehead against the other side of my head. A huge weight rolls off my shoulders as I try to get myself under control. I somehow manage to keep my sobs completely quiet and once the tears stop, I wipe them away from my face with the tissue Mr. Leeks offers me. *It's over, it's really over.*

End Flashback

They really don't need a play-by-play of what happened, so I give them the short version, explaining that they're both going to jail, and we won't be seeing them for a long time. The news seems to lift everyone's spirits, as I hear a chorus of compliments.

"Perfect reason to celebrate. We're all going to Brayden and Jake's to drink a little before the bonfire," Jeff informs me quietly. Wow, some things are obviously not going to change; not that it bothers me. "You're in, right?" he almost begs.

"I don't know, Jeff, last time didn't have a good outcome." Not that the entire night was bad, but the drinking may not have been the greatest idea.

"Nadi, don't be a downer. We won't get drunk, I promise."

"I think I'll pass this time around. I should keep a clear head right now." I give him a small grin because his sulking face is just adorable.

"Fine," he says, all whiny.

The bench shakes a little as Aerick sit down beside me. "Hey," he says softly. Again, he's treading like he's afraid I'm going to break.

"Hi." I say in a clipped voice, suddenly remembering my earlier irritation.

"What's wrong?" he asks, catching on to my quick mood change.

"Oh, I don't know. Maybe I just got my tuition statement and maybe I saw something unexpected on it?"

He glances down and begins biting the inside of his cheek. I notice Gavin giving him a curious look but I'm in no mood to delay this conversation for later. When he doesn't answer, I continue. "The weird thing is, it says I have a zero balance. You wouldn't happen to know who would go out of their way to pay a seven-thousand-dollar tuition bill after I specifically stated I wanted to pay for it on my own, would you?"

"I distinctly remember not agreeing to that. I just chose to drop it and not argue with you," he says quietly. "It was the least I could do. Please don't make this into a big deal." Here we go again. I swear this is going to be a never-ending argument between us. Although, this is the longest conversation we've had all week.

"Look, Aerick, you can't just come in and be the valiant Prince Charming anytime I have a problem," I say, lowering my voice and becoming more serious.

"I can try." *Ugh.*

"Aerick..."

"Please, Nadi, I don't want to argue," he says, cutting me off and closing his eyes. "Just consider it a gift." His pleading is enough to reel in my emotions. This week has been difficult for him too, but he needs to stop trying to fix everything.

"I will accept it for now, but I'm paying you back, no arguments about it." He finally looks at me, his lips pressed into a tight line. "I'm serious.".

"Fine," he finally says, looking back down at his food.

I finish my food quickly. I don't want to argue, and Gavin's offer is sounding better than ever right now. "I'll see you guys out at the bonfire."

"You're not coming to Brayden's?" Aerick asks.

"No, I just want to go relax. I'm fine – just want some quiet time."

"Alright." He sounds a little sad, but I'm doing this for me because it's the truth, I do just need some quiet time.

I get up and empty my tray before heading for Jeff and Gavin's cabin. I hope they don't mind me going in there when they're not there, but it's easier than waiting and having everyone's questioning stares. I let myself in and just like Gavin said earlier, the book is lying there on the couch waiting for me. I remove my shoes and curl up in the corner of the couch, pulling the throw blanket that was on the back around my shoulders before picking up the book.

I'm in the middle of the second chapter when Gavin walks in and seems a little shocked to discover me here.

"Sorry to intrude."

He shakes the shock off his face. "No, it's fine, I just didn't realize you were here. Please, don't let me bother you." He walks over to his desk and sits down, grabbing a book of his own, so I go back to reading my book.

After a few minutes of silence, I glance up. Gavin has his leg pulled up, resting on the edge of the chair, and is already engrossed in whatever he's reading. A tug threatens at my lip and I look back down to continue my story.

* * * *

"Hey, sorry to interrupt." I glance up, startled a bit by the noise.

"Huh?"

"Everyone is going to be heading over to the bonfire. Are you still interested in going?"

I peek down at my watch. I hadn't realized that an hour and a half had already flown by. "Oh, shoot. I didn't realize we'd been reading so long." I stand up and stretch. This little getaway has made me feel a lot better.

"I really should be going. I wanted to go to the bonfire."

"Okay, I was just going to say you could stay if you want. I have to head out. Luther is taking Ayla and I out for drinks tonight, but that doesn't mean you have to go. You can stay as long as you like." That's really nice of him.

"Thank you for the offer, but I want to go. And thank you for this. It's exactly what I needed. It's so nice to be able to sit and read and get lost in a whole other world. Even if it's only temporary. I feel a lot better."

"No problem. You're welcome to come by anytime. Of course, you're welcome to take the book back to your cabin too, but this one is pretty empty most of the time. Jeff's been busy hanging out everywhere else, so feel free to come and sit if you need some quiet time. Even if we aren't here." He gives me a sly smirk as he says the last bit.

"Thank you, and if it's alright, I'll leave this book here for now. It's really interesting and I would love to keep reading it, I just don't want to have to stop by my cabin to drop it off."

"Sure."

"Thanks again. I'll see you around." I finish tying my boots and head out to meet up with the others. I'm happier than I've been in a while, and I can only hope the rest of the night will go well.

I get to Brayden's and don't bother to knock as I hear everyone laughing and joking around. "Well, look who finally decided to join us," Jeff says moving his arm across my shoulder. I stare at him a little funny as a whiff of the strong alcohol emanating from him catches my nose.

"Hands off, Jeff," Aerick says, surprising me when he encases me with his arms around from behind me, successfully pushing Jeff away.

"Hey, Princess," he whispers in my ear and I melt. He reeks of alcohol too but if that's what it takes to loosen up this odd mood he's been in, then so be it.

"Hey to you too," I say, twisting in his arms slightly so my eyes can meet his.

He kisses my nose. "Glad you are here," he says, almost shyly.

"Me too."

Jeff hands me a soda. I give him a knowing look. "It isn't strong, I promise," he says, laughing at me. The light atmosphere is contagious.

"Fine, but only one." I don't want a hangover tomorrow, but loosening up a little won't be so bad.

"Let's go hang out by the fire," Trent says, and we all start toward the door.

Aerick and I fall behind everyone else as we begin to walk toward the fire pit. I hold onto his arm until we're almost there and then we part just enough so that we're not touching, but neither of us loses our ridiculous smiles.

The night flies by as we all sit around talking. Aerick sits next to me, keeping himself touching me at all times, whether it be our legs, arms or hips, without obviously holding each other. It reminds me a lot of how we were back when I was a cadet.

When it's finally time to head back, Aerick walks me back to my cabin while Brand and Jake clean up. I'm feeling warm and fuzzy inside. I had given in and took one more special soda from Jeff, but it was only enough to feel the alcohol a little. Tonight has been so amazingly carefree, I almost don't want it to end.

We reach my cabin and Aerick grasps my hand as he turns to face me. "You know I love you, right?" he says to me, slightly slurring his words. It's obvious he's had more to drink than me.

"Of course I know that, and I love you too." He's been so relaxed and content tonight, something I haven't seen in a while.

He leans down, connecting his lips to my own. My hands find their way to his hair and his kiss turns more passionate as he presses me up against my door. Whatever his reservations were this week, they've definitely dissolved. We finally break for air and he leans his forehead against mine. I really want to invite him in, but I'm not sure I'm ready yet for what would definitely follow.

He lifts his head and I gaze up to him. That goofy, happy grin I love is stretched across his lips. He leans down and places one more soft kiss on my lips. "Good night, my princess. Sweet dreams." He turns to leave without another word.

I stand smiling like an idiot as I watch him walk toward his dorm whistling some familiar tune.

EPILOGUE

(Sunday, December 20th)

I GROGGILY TURN my head slightly as I feel the bed dip down behind me. His familiar, comforting smell engulfs my nostrils as I feel fingers glide over my arm lightly. Electricity runs through my body as his fingers travel across my neck, moving my hair to the side so it can be replaced by his skillful lips. I let out a quiet hum of pleasure and I feel his up turned lips, a response he knowingly enjoys. His hands roam across my stomach and up to my tender breasts, caressing them softly. I turn my head until his lips find mine, his passionate lips kissing me until I'm dizzy.

This is what I've missed. His smell, his touch, his comfort, invading all of my senses. This is what I've been craving, to feel safe in his arms, to have him take away all my problems and all of my fears until it's only us.

I let myself get lost in him, not wanting for this moment to end. Something in the back of my mind says I should stop, but I won't let the fear in me take over. I'm strong; I will myself to be strong, not only for myself, but for him as well. I have put him through so much and I'm so grateful he has stuck with me through it all.

His lips move back down my neck to my shoulder as his hands glide across me, moving down toward my thighs. I'm not sure whether or not I'm ready for this but I want it, I want him. I want things to go back to the way they were before, when we were together and happy.

All of a sudden I feel him bite me. "Ouch, Aerick! What are you doing?" That wasn't a playful bite, that actually hurt. His hands become more forceful, more frantic. Something isn't right – this isn't like him. I feel another painful bite on my shoulder. "Aerick?" I say louder, hoping he'll come to his senses.

He doesn't answer, he just continues grabbing at my body in a feverish manner. "Aerick, please!" This isn't right, why isn't he answering me?

"Aerick?"

I glance toward Terrie's bed but there's no one there. Her bed isn't there either. A heavy feeling sinks into my stomach as I look around. This isn't our cabin, I'm not at camp. I'm in a cold, small room. A room that I know, a room from my past, that I hoped never to see again.

A cold breeze brings goose bumps to my arms. I'm naked. How am I naked? When did he undress me and how did I not know?

A hand grabs at my hip with bruising force but it feels different. It isn't the same. I try to turn around to look at who is behind me, but he doesn't allow me to, pushing my face back to the side. Tears begin to fall down my cheek as recognition comes to the forefront of my mind.

"Stop, please stop!"

"Hhhmmmm." That voice, I know that voice. It's not my Prince Charming, it's my worst nightmare. "I have missed you, my little whore!"

"NOOO!" I scream as I bolt upward.

"Hey, hey Nadi it's okay!" Terrie says as she crouches next to my bed. "It's okay, it's just us here."

I try to focus on her words and try to breathe through the heaviness in my chest. *Where did that nightmare come from?* "Do you want me to go get Aerick?" I shake my head no. I don't want to have to explain it to him. *How could I?* He's usually my protector in these dreams. But not this time; this time was different. It began with his comfort and it was torn away.

"Okay, what about Jeff?"

I shake my head again. "I'm fine. I just need something to drink." She nods her head and stands, heading for the bathroom. She returns quickly with a full glass of water and I drink it down quickly.

"Thank you, I'm fine. Let's just got back to bed."

She gives me a forced smile. "Alright, but if you need anything, just let me know." She goes and climbs back into bed. I lie down, focusing on shaking off the horrible feeling that still lingers in me. Something tells me that my stint of bad luck isn't over just yet.

Coming July 2020...

UNBROKEN
The fourth and final book in the Donnelly Bootcamp Series

About the Author

Danielle Leneah is a person with limitless aspirations. Whether she is working full time to help support her family, designing web sites for fun, or writing books to calm her mind, she always puts her heart and soul into her work.

Her reading and writing ambitions started at a young age. By sixth grade, she was reading full Stephen King novels and writing short stories. Her first publication came when she was in high school. Her work was accepted to be published in a well known poetry book. Even though her dreams of writing were temporarily halted as she began to build a family, it eventually drew her back.

As she began writing, she remembered the peace and joy it use to bring her. In astonishing 50 days, she had the rough draft of the first two books in a her new series completed.

In her mind, if she can make just one person happy with her stories, it would have been worth it.

Danielle was born and raised in the suburbs of Seattle, Washington where she still lives with her husband and children.

To get the latest news and stay up to date, visit her website at:
www.DanielleLeneah.com

Made in the USA
Coppell, TX
28 May 2021